TWO CLASSIC WESTERNS IN ONE VOLUME!
BY T.V. OLSEN

RUN TO THE MOUNTAIN

Bowie moved almost before the words were out, grabbing the barrel of Ekstrom's carbine and twisting upward. Ekstrom tightened his grasp too late. Bowie wrenched the weapon away and swung it in a tight arc, slamming the breech against Ekstrom's jaw.

"You son of a bitch. I kill you for that."

Bowie swung his arm and let go of the carbine, spinning it away into the brush. He settled his weight on the balls of his feet, waiting. Ekstrom did not move. Bowie reached inside his mackinaw now, pulled his knife from its sheath and gave it a hard flip that drove the blade into the loam at Ekstom's feet.

"Use it."

Ekstrom bent slowly and picked up the knife. Bowie watched him contemptuously, thinking it was no gamble at all. Though he wasn't altogether sure....

DAY OF THE BUZZARD

"You can leave us our guns," Jason said out of a dry throat. "You can do that anyways."

Heath's acid grin twitched wider.

"Listen, those 'Paches who hit Corazon was swinging west. We get caught on foot, two men alone, we wouldn't have no chance."

"Miserable prospect, isn't it? No chance. I know the feeling...."

— RUN TO — THE MOUNTAIN/ — DAY OF — THE BUZZARD

T. V. OLSEN

LEISURE BOOKS **NEW YORK CITY**

A LEISURE BOOK®

August 1996

Published by

Dorchester Publishing Co., Inc.
276 Fifth Avenue
New York, NY 10001

Printed in the United States of America.

— RUN TO —
THE MOUNTAIN

CHAPTER ONE

All morning long, blackening clouds had built like cobbled towers above the saw-edged peaks to the north. By noon they came driving down on the foothills and broke in a bleak wet fury across the parched timber and grasslands. The storm caught Bowie Candler on an open meadow, and he raised his face to it and cursed it with a tired tonelessness.

He was already chilled to the bone; he could hardly feel his fingers. Particularly the ones on the hand locked around the horn of his saddle, whose weight made a spreading ache across his shoulders. He had been toting it all morning and he was just about done up. His feet in their cowman's boots hurt like hell.

Jesus H. Christ. Bowie's disgust turned savage; his swearing voice husked into a snarl.

It wasn't enough that that goddam cat had spooked his jughead roan out of camp last night. He hadn't seen the cougar, hadn't had an inkling it was close by, till its high scream had set his horse lunging at its tether. Before he could reach it, the worn rope had parted and the horse was drumming away into the night. Nothing to do then but huddle by his fire and catch snatches of sleep till darkness had grayed to a sallow dawn and made enough light to track by. It was midmorning when Bowie had come on the horse's remains. The cat he'd heard, or another one, had gotten the animal; wolves had been at the carcass later on. Only raw bones and shreds of flesh and hide remained, along with enough tracks and other signs to tell the story.

7

So he had started tramping. He wasn't sure exactly where he was, but that didn't concern him too much. He could rough it off the country like an Indian if he had to, though he hated being reduced to such an extremity. There was plenty of game, besides edible roots, herbs, and barks if a man knew what to look for. The only real danger that the high country held for someone who knew it was its howling deep-snow winters, and this was still early September. What graveled hell out of Bowie was the whole stinking run of his luck.

The rains slashed in fierce gusts at his leaning body as he plodded on. He was quickly soaked to the skin, his whole body numb with cold and wet. Thunder pealed, caroming back and forth between the hills. Flickering tongues of lightning played below the clouds. Again Bowie raised his face to them and swore. Of all the Christ-bitten damned luck. He felt the bleak, despairing rage of a man whose load of bad fortune had been topped by a final breaking straw. And there was nothing to curse but the uncaring elements.

It had taken him three days to cross the mountains from K-town, the mining and ranching settlement at the north base of the great Elk range. Two months ago Bowie had sold his pack horse for tools and a stake to undertake a spell of lone gold-grubbing up on the high range. Five days ago, he'd returned to K-town with a few miserable ounces of color to show for his weeks of labor. After going on a well-earned drunk, he had awakened in an alley with a splitting head to find that his poke had been lifted.

All the local ranches had their full quota of hands for the fall roundup, he'd soon found, and his only choice was to drift out of the country and seek other prospects. Which meant southward, for the fall frosts were already gripping the high country and he wanted to winter warm. Bowie hated cold weather more than anything: legacy of a child-hood spent shivering in a sharecropper's shack for what had seemed endless months every year.

Ahead of him, the meadow sloped down toward a storm-whipped stand of aspen. Little shelter there, but at least the trees would break the rising wind. He reached the timber and plunged into it till he found a small glade. Here he crouched in sodden misery, flexing painful sensation back to his numbed right arm and shoulder as he waited for the storm to buck itself out. Wind and wetness hissed through the treetops; rain plunked on the drooping, wanly yellowing undergrowth. It dripped, glistening, from the greasy downcurl of his hatbrim; it runneled icily through every tatter in his old canvas mackinaw.

Bowie beat his unfeeling hands together till he could move his fingers, then rummaged through his worldly possessions: saddle, bridle, soogan roll, battered Winchester, saddlebags containing any range rider's odds and ends. He'd discarded his worn-out gloves and slicker a week ago, anticipating that he would buy new gear in K-town. At least he'd hung onto the ancient mackinaw, but it was so full of holes, its buttons long gone, that not even the greasy filth which coated it kept the wetness from working through.

His belly was growling with hunger pangs. And his grub was desperately low, as he'd had no money to buy supplies in K-town. Groping in the bottom of a saddlebag, Bowie found a few dirty strips of jerked deer meat. He mouthed one, slowly chewing its rancid hardness to a fibrous pulp that would slide down his throat. What the hell was he going to do now? Just keep dogging it south, he guessed, till he came out of the foothills. There were supposed to be roads and settlements below the southern Elks, and he was bound to hit one. But when? He knew this country only through what he'd been told. Several large outfits claimed most of the high and valley range hereabouts, for the tide of homestead migration had washed around these mountainous pockets. Hustled out by the big augurs or quickly broken by the brutal climate. . . .

Have to hunt up any sort of work he could get, Bowie bleakly decided, any short-term job that would tide him over. Swamp out saloons or stables if he had to. That was another old story with him. He peered at the sky. The storm was slackening to a timid drizzle and he might as well be humping along. Christ, he was tired. But a man might as well catch his death walking as squatting. Briefly he toyed with the notion of abandoning his dilapidated saddle, but figured he could wrestle it through the rest of today anyhow. Or did till he heaved to his feet, lifting the rimfire hull and slinging it across his back. Every ache in his body pulsed back to throbbing life. Pain shot into his calves, and his feet felt like dead blocks as he slogged stubbornly down the slope.

From somewhere below, a horse's thin whicker drifted.

Bowie halted, a faint excitement lifting in him. Horses? Well, by damn.

He trudged on till the trees began to thin away, then halted again. He was on the brink of a long valley of wild hay studded with scattered timber and oak thickets. Through the sweeping veils of windy rain, he made out the misted shapes of about twenty horses on the low ground to his right and well below. Bowie squatted down and dropped his saddle, scouring a palm over his stubbled jaw. He wet his thumb and tested the wind. Yeah—it would cut his scent at right angles away from them. But he'd have to work damned close before risking a cast, and it was a good hundred yards from the edge of timber to the herd.

Removing his catch rope from the saddle pommel, he went down the slope at a stiff-legged gait, clinging to the last trees. When he reached the open, he slowed and balled his body to a crouch as he moved carefully on, keeping the thickets between himself and the bunched horses. Patience. That was the watchword when you stalked horses. One thing, by God, he hadn't mustanged in the Mogollon country three years for nothing. But he'd have to shave his chances fine as froghair to get inside fair throwing range.

In a half hour Bowie reached the last thicket between him and the horses. They were still a hundred feet away. His throat tightened. Son of a bitch. Could he chance an approach across the open? He was close enough to make out a brand on the hips of several animals. Two linked circles. It meant nothing to him, except that this was owned stock, and the fact didn't deter him.

He'd begun easing to his feet, shaking out a loop of his

coiled rope, when the horses started to shift away. Had they picked him up? He couldn't be sure; he would have to wait. He couldn't afford to miss his cast, not when he lacked any idea how far he was from human habitation.

Waiting, he felt his muscles start to quiver with tension and exhaustion and a gut-knotting hunger. Finally the horses halted and resumed their placid grazing.

Bowie continued to huddle on his heels, teeth chattering, shoulders hunched against the slow rain. The mackinaw hung sacklike on his spare frame. Not a large man, he was stocky and hard. His callused, muscle-bunched hands, loosely closed around his coiled rope, made fists like knotty-oak dollops. His weathered features were blunt, not quite homely, with a truculent jaw sworled by thick black stubble and a craggy nose that had been broken a couple of times. His eyes were a darkish slate-gray and unpleasant; the rest of his face wasn't. His raven hair was streaked with gray at the temples and fantailed thickly over his ears and sheepskin collar. His appearance marked him as anywhere from forty to fifty; he was coming thirty-seven this winter. At least he reckoned so. Old Pap, a gaunt widower fighting all his days to wrest a living from red Georgia clay, had never kept clear track of his brood's ages or their doings: Bowie had been the youngest of seven.

Brooding in the rain, he had a brief set-to with his conscience. Not that he gave a hoot in hell about the letter of the law. Just that taking another man's horse violated a bedrock rule of his that was strictly personal. What the hell, though, it was just a borrow. He wouldn't keep his catch any longer than he had to.

The rain had nearly stopped, the thunder tapering to a sullen mutter, when the horses got restive again. They were pulling back this way. Bowie felt the heavy pound of his heart as he slowly rubbed his cold hands together. Close enough, he judged; it would have to be. He shucked off the bulky mackinaw and dropped it in the grass. Inching to his feet then, he shook out his rope and built a loop as he moved very slowly out to the open.

The horses gazed at him for a moment; men and ropes

weren't new to them. A big buckskin gelding on the near
flank of the bunch snorted and tossed his head. Bowie had
already singled him out and he continued his bold approach, taking his time, talking softly. Suddenly the whole
bunch wheeled and started to bolt.

Bowie lunged forward, at the same time whirling out his
loop and making the throw, all in a motion. The noose
spun smaller as it shot out; it was no wider than a barrel
rim as it snapped over the buckskin's neck. Bowie pulled
up short and set his heels as the animal's rush took up the
slack. He hung doggedly on for long moments, coolly
shifting to the horse's savage surgings as he bucked himself
out. Finally it came to a lathered, heaving standstill.

Talking low, soothingly, Bowie walked toward the animal, coiling his rope. The buckskin stood motionless except for a quivering of muscles in his shoulders. "You'll be
all right," Bowie told him. He laid his hand on the animal's neck, confident and friendly about it. "All right," he
said.

Back in the timber, he bridled and saddled his catch
while he gave the situation another gray study. Happen he
were to confront the horse's owner, he didn't figure any
explanation he might give would sound very damned con-
vincing. He had a vivid memory of once seeing a horse
thief kicking away his life from a cottonwood limb. Too
chancy, lifting another man's horse and then riding into
his place and explaining it was just a borrow. Best thing to
do was just ride the buckskin south till he caught sight of
the first habitation, then turn him loose and go in on foot.

The buckskin capered a little as he mounted, then
quieted down. Bowie reined him downslope and southward, and let him run off his raw edge. As they passed
through another belt of timber, the animal settled into a
steady ground-eating pace. It was good to have horseflesh
under him again, but Bowie's mood merely notched upward from sour to less sour. He was still wet to the skin,
his teeth rattling like castanets, and the wind cut his body
like icy blades. When he came to the far fringe of the
timber, he decided to make a stop and dry out as well as

he could. The rain had quit completely, but from the sky's dismal look it could start up again any time. About the time you get dried out, he told himself dourly.

He halted by the timber's edge where trees would serve as a windbreak, then dismounted and tied the buckskin to a tree, making sure the tether rope was secure. Scouring up dry wood wasn't easy, and he was fifteen minutes assembling a small pile of branches. Half his matches missed fire before he coaxed a pyre of twigs into flame. It smoked like hell as he fed it with larger pieces, then cut some green limbs and rammed them into the ground by the fire to drape his clothes on.

He had removed his mackinaw and was on his knees propping it on the limbs when a rifle slug whanged off a knotty root about six yards away and sang away into the scanty brush.

Jesus God! Bowie froze where he was, on his knees. Then he moved only his head till he made out four riders. They'd topped the brow of a hill off right and maybe two hundred yards away, their yellow slickers shining wetly. The man who'd fired held his rifle pointed up; he shot into the air as the four put their horses down the hill. A shot unnecessarily warning Bowie to hold still.

They pulled up a few yards away and the man with the rifle piled off and walked over to the buckskin. He gazed at the brand, then at Bowie, slowly shaking his head. "Jesus. You are one dumb son of a bitch, ain't you? You long-loop a Chainlink horse, then fire up a smoke a blind man could spot across the county line."

Bowie said nothing. He felt the man's green stare size him up, his worn gear and tattered much-patched clothing, and he gave back a stony stare of his own. The man tramped over to stand above him. "You cocky goddam drifter. Talk up or I'll feed this rifle down your throat butt first."

He was squat as an ape, his arms long and heavy, but didn't seem thick-bodied even in the bulky slicker. He moved with a trim rolling gait and his shoulders swelled with an oxlike power. His head fit the body: hair cropped close to a round brutish skull; features that were coarse and ruddy and underscored by a ruff of black beard. He was about thirty.

"Maybe that smoke says it, Brady."

Another rider had spoke up. Young and lean, he was dark-eyed, handsome in a Nordic way. But his straight black hair and coppery skin pointed to some blanket blood, and he sat his horse in a way that was definably Indian.

The apelike man's stare flicked to him. "How you mean?"

"Got a saddle, ain't he? Looks like he got set afoot and had to borrow a horse. If he didn't aim to keep him, why worry about making smoke?"

Brady gave a laugh and shake of his head. "I swear to Christ, Sully. Use them Injun eyes, why don't you? Look at this ugly-eyed bastard and his outfit. You can tell what he is plain as tits on a sow."

"Ho, then maybe he should say it," grinned another rider. He was a long and cat-flanked Mexican with a brown ax blade of a face. A knife scar hooked one corner of his yellow grin down to a gummy grimace. "What you say, Mester *chingado*? Will you tell us you don' steal the horse, hah?"

"Screw you, *chico*," Bowie said softly.

The fourth horseman gave a whickering laugh. He looked enough like Brady that they were brothers for sure. Only he was younger and slighter and his eyes were a milky blue; he didn't look or sound too bright. "I guess he don't like your face, Trinidad," he said.

"Ai-yi! But he has *cojones,* this ugly one."

"I don't think he likes nobody's face, Joe-Bob," Brady said.

Without warning he tipped his rifle stock down and drove the butt savagely into Bowie's face. Slammed over on his back, Bowie lay dazed and unmoving. Sky and trees pinwheeled in his vision. It cleared slowly. He saw Brady loom above him.

"I don't like his face neither," Brady said. "I think I'll change it."

Bowie rolled his body sideways as the rifle stock came down. It missed his head, thudding on the wet loam. Then he was rolling hard into Brady's legs, grabbing blindly and clamping him around the knees. A strong heave and Brady, already off balance, was thrown heavily to the ground. Bowie floundered on top of him, pinning Brady's rifle between their bodies. He wrapped one arm around Brady's bullet head and drove three sledging blows into his face.

Trinidad wheeled his horse in close, bending low as he whipped back the skirt of his slicker. His arm pumped up, then down, his pistol barrel rapping across Bowie's skull. In the haze of red pain Bowie felt his hold loosen, and then Brady's savage heave flung him on his back.

Brady got to his feet, swaying as he clenched both fists around his rifle. "Damn cocky drifter," he said in a shaky, raging whisper.

"Ai-yi," Trinidad laughed. "He has eggs, this ugly one."

"Maybe we can lay a few more on him," Brady whispered. "Drag him, Trinidad."

"Ah, *amigo*. I don' know. Your old man, what will he say?"

"He don't need to know about it. Jesus, what do you want? We caught the bastard lifting a branded horse. That's good for a Dutch ride anyways." Brady's lips peeled off his teeth. "Had my way, I'd string him up right here."

"We ain't sure of nothing, Brady." Sully's voice was flat with disapproval.

"You still think it looks like a borrow? All right, let him say it. Go on, you damn ridgerunner. I want to hear you say it."

Bowie had struggled to his hands and knees. He stayed that way a moment, hanging his head, watching blood drip from his cut cheek onto the leaf loam. Slowly he raised his head till his eyes focused on Brady. "You shove it, mister," he whispered.

Brady smiled. "That answers it fine." He stepped back. "All right, Trinidad. Put a rope on him."

"I don't want no part of it," said Sully. He started to turn his mount.

"Sully." Brady's head tipped toward him. "You don't spill off about this, understand?"

The half-breed didn't answer. He loped his horse back toward the hilltop.

"I bet he tells Faye," grunted Trinidad. "That breed, he's in your old man's pocket."

"The hell with Faye." Brady's face was darkly flushed with anger. "Get to it."

"I don' know, *amigo*."

"Goddammit, don't worry about Faye or the old man. Do as I say. I'll back you up."

Trinidad shrugged, then gigged his sorrel toward Bowie, shaking out a coil of his rope. Joe-Bob gave a high-pitched giggle. Trinidad was half smiling.

"Make him get up."

Brady took a long step and drove his boot into Bowie's side. He grunted and pulled away from the blow and Brady said savagely, "Stand up or you'll get another."

Bowie climbed to his feet, half paralyzed by the hurt of three blows. He hardly heard Brady's words; he only wanted to get his hands on him. He lurched painfully onto his feet and stumbled forward. Trinidad's noose shot out and brought him up short, pinning him around the chest and upper arms. The Mexican took a swift dally while his cow pony sidled against the slack. "She is a green rope," he grinned, "so you break in together, hey?"

He spurred away, yanking Bowie into a floundering run. He grabbed the rope in both hands and tried to brace, and was instantly jerked off his feet and scraped across the uneven ground for fifty bouncing, bruising yards. Then Trinidad reined up. Bowie lay face down in the wet grass, gagging. The raw pressure on his chest slacked a little. He looked up, his eyes swimming with pain.

Trinidad was chewing idly on a dead *cigarillo*; his gaze was sleepily amused. "Get up, tough one. That was only the little tickle."

Bowie got up on on knee, pausing to muster himself. He looked at the Mexican and at Brady and Joe-Bob watching from the grove's edge. His whole body twitched with raw hurt now, and he felt like retching. Instead he suddenly lifted his hands and whipped the rope off. He scrambled up and lurched in a blind stumbling run toward the Mexican, grabbing upward. Trinidad kneed his horse away, then planted a boot against Bowie's chest and shoved, knocking him backward in the grass.

Trinidad was no longer grinning. "*Jésus*," he murmured. "You are like a mad dog. Don' you got no sense?"

Doggedly Bowie maneuvered onto his knees again, then to his feet. As Trinidad whirled out another deft loop, he flung up his arms. But the rope snared him once more; Trinidad sank his spurs. This time he dragged Bowie in a long circle, but before it was half completed, Bowie felt his consciousness ribboning off. He was aware of the jolting friction of earth under his body, but there was no more pain, no other sensation.

Suddenly he had stopped again. He knew that much. And then he knew a spreading circle of red-hot searing pain; it was eating into his chest. He tried to make a sound, but none came out. Splintered echoes of laughter rocked his ears. And that was all he knew.

CHAPTER TWO

"Nice work," Faye Nevers said. He glanced at Trinidad. "Nice rope work."

The Mexican shrugged, lazily grinning around his *cigarillo*. He sat his saddle with slack ease and locked Nevers's eyes with an insolent stare. "Brady say drag him."

"That's fine. Cyrus just might can your ass for it all the same."

Nevers swung off his short-coupled grullo and walked stiffly over to where the drifter lay sprawled by his dead fire. He gazed down at the unconscious man. The drifter's clothes were in dirty shreds; his face looked like raw meat. The front of his shirt had been burned away and red angry flesh showed through its blackened shreds.

"Dragged him over the fire, huh?"

Trinidad shrugged again. "I drag him off it too."

Nevers raised his sultry stare to Brady, who stood by grinning a little, his rifle hanging from one fist. "You did a job on him, didn't you?"

"After he stole a Chainlink horse."

"You know that, do you?" Nevers nodded at Sully, who was sitting his horse a few yards off. "He figures you're wrong. He's going to tell it to Cyrus that way."

"Sure. The old man's pet breed." Brady looked at Sully and spat. "Pa's gone soft, Faye, and you know it. Leave it to him, all the long-looping trash in the country'll be cutting into our stock every time they take a mind. Somebody's got to show 'em the what-for of things."

"You can tell it to Cyrus." Nevers looked hard at Trinidad. "Cut a couple of poles and make a drag. We'll take him home."

Trinidad's grin faded and his gaze shifted to Brady.

"Don't look at him. I give you an order. Do it."

Brady tipped back his hat with his fist. "That's right, ain't it? Everyone takes your orders."

"That's what your pa says. You and Joe-Bob take 'em too. Any objections?"

"Why no," Brady said softly. "You're foreman, ain't you? But all my old man got to do is whisper cricket and you chirp."

Joe-Bob giggled foolishly.

Gazing at the two of them, Brady Trapp and his kid brother, Nevers felt a cold and savage disgust. The sons of Cyrus Trapp. But old Cyrus's blood had run thin as water in this pair: a thick-headed bully and a half-addled weakling.

Nevers said deliberately: "You know what, Brady? You wouldn't need to take my orders if you wasn't Cyrus's kin. Reason you wouldn't, I'd of kicked both your worthless asses off Chainlink long time ago. As it is, I'm supposed to keep you and the kid out of jackpots. That's an order too. I don't need to like it. It's just another job, even if it stinks."

Trinidad swung to the ground, pulled his Bowie knife from its sheath, walked to a straight sapling, and began hacking it down. Brady stood with his feet braced, the heavy blood crawling to his face. "The old man ain't going to be around forever, Faye," he said thickly. "You think about that."

"Now I'm scared," Nevers grunted. "Sully, give Trinidad a hand with that drag. You two," he added to Brady and Joe-Bob, "get over to Rock Spring and help Barney and Hilo comb the brush."

Brady climbed into his saddle and flung his mount around with a savage jerk of the reins. Joe-Bob stood where he was a slack-faced moment and then followed his brother as Brady kicked his animal into a run. Nevers knelt by the drifter and went over his body with deft hands, feeling for broken bones. Didn't seem to be any, though he looked more dead than alive. Just banged up all to hell. Great bruises were forming on his torso and the burn on his chest looked pretty bad.

Nevers stood up, gazing bleakly down at the man. Christ, what a scrubby-looking bastard. Brady was likely right about him. Not that it really mattered.

Faye Nevers looked bigger on his feet than on horseback. Tall, blond, roughhewn, he had the whittled hips of a horseman and the meaty, spreading shoulders of a smithy. His movements were easy, leonine, long-muscled. His face had once been handsome; it was heavy and crooked-nosed and dimpled with scars, the face of a prizering pugilist or an inveterate barroom brawler. Nevers had been both. His eyes were the palest blue, remote and noncommittal.

Be a damned good thing to just leave this drifter where he was and say nothing. But Sully, who was intensely loyal to the old man, was bound to tell him what had happened, and Cyrus would be up in arms. He'd rant and roar anyway when he saw what had been done to the man, but this way Brady and Joe-Bob would catch the worst of it.

Hell of it was, Brady was right. How else could you protect all the drifting stock on a range this size? Hang 'em or drag 'em. Only way to put the fear of God into other sons of bitches with the same idea. Let the word get out they'd mollycoddled one horse thief, all the cross-dog scum in the country would regard Chainlink as easy pickings. Outfit like this one, built by a man who knew the uses of power, the man Cyrus Trapp had been, couldn't afford to soften its old freewheeling ways as Cyrus seemed bound to do. Not and hold itself intact it couldn't.

Trinidad and Sully cut down three tall saplings and trimmed off the branches. Two saplings formed the parallel poles of the drag; the third was cut into three-foot lengths that were lashed between them. The ends were fastened to Sully's saddle. The men raised the limp, battered drifter onto the drag and tied him down with a few turns of rope.

They mounted up, and Nevers said: "Sully, I'll be riding in with you." He added to Trinidad: "You get over to Rock Spring and do what you're paid for."

"Sure, Faye. Uh, listen. You tell Old Man Trapp I just do what Brady say, huh?"

"All right. But you better read my sign straight from now on. You take orders from me, me alone. I hire and fire for this outfit and don't you forget it."

"Sure, sure—"

Damn that greaseball, Nevers thought, gazing after Trinidad as he rode gracefully away. He was a top hand, but you had to keep an iron rein on him. He'd been a *pistolero* in his younger days, and still had a taste for trouble that the cautions of middle age had only partly flagged down. Not that he was hard to handle except when he fell into company with the Trapp brothers.

Nevers's thoughts stayed sourly with that fact as he and Sully Calder rode southward, the burdened drag jouncing slowly behind them. If it wasn't one thing with that pair, it was something else. Brady had been raising hell of one sort or another since he was a kid; Cyrus had been bailing him out of one jam or another for years. Finally Cyrus had stuck both his sons on his cattle crew as punishment, and in hopes that working for wages would make them brace up. Did he really think that if Brady, at thirty-two, hadn't finished sowing his wild oats, he was likely to change? Joe-Bob, an addled twenty, merely followed his older brother's lead.

You couldn't blame the old man for being fed up, but it wasn't fair of him to expect his foreman to handle the affairs of a great ranch and assume responsibility for keeping his ne'er-do-well sons in line too. In his three years of ramrodding Chainlink, Nevers bitterly reflected, he'd welded its sprawling activities into a smooth-running operation. But how in hell could you keep the respect of crewmen who knew they'd be sent packing for pulling a fraction of the bullshit the boss's sons got away with?

Sully dryly broke the bleak run of his thoughts: "Going to cover yourself with Cyrus right away, eh? I'd say that's why you're helping me bring this fellow in."

"That's right," Nevers said bluntly. "You tell Cyrus how it happened and I'll be there to back you up. We'll scratch each other's backs."

Sully's eyes were darkly amused. "But you don't really reckon he was just borrowing that horse, do you?"

"Why, no." Nevers glanced at him with an open, contemptuous irony. "I'll leave it to you to help Cyrus uphold the goodness of man. Me, I just don't run against the boss's notions, no matter how damn fool they are."

Sully grinned. "Didn't figure you would. That's why I fetched you. Brady's right about one thing, though. He'll be heir to Chainlink someday—and it might not be far off. Kind of cutting your own throat, hard-mouthing him like you done."

Nevers's straight mouth tightened. "Maybe. Other hand, Cyrus could be around a long time yet. And I've taken all of Brady's smart-ass ways I can swallow."

"Too bad. When Brady takes over, you'll be out a place you was a long time working up to."

"What about you?" Nevers countered flatly. "You never really run afoul Brady before that I know of. Today you bucked flat against him, fetching me. Brady rides a grudge till kingdom come. Once he's in, where'll you and your sister be?"

Sully smiled wryly. "Out, I reckon. Not easy to think about that. Chainlink's the only place Tula and me can call home."

Nevers grunted. He remembered when Cyrus had taken in the two orphaned half-breeds many years ago. Their father, a hardscrabble rancher named Jim Calder who'd wed a Ute woman, had been a close friend of Cyrus Trapp's youth.

"Guess I'm like you," Sully said. "It came to where I had to stand up to Brady Trapp."

Sure, Nevers thought cynically, only for different reasons. Sully Calder was loyal to the man who had raised him and he shared Cyrus's new-found principles as well. Whereas Faye Nevers's star was to hold on with both fists to what he'd rightfully earned. He had climbed to the foremanship of Chainlink the hard way. His slum boyhood and years of oyster pirating in San Francisco Bay were long behind him. Fourteen years ago he'd started at Chainlink as a runny-nosed roustabout on one of Cyrus's chuck wagons. Eleven years later, when Cyrus's foreman had been killed in a town brawl, the man who was self-groomed to fill his boots had been Faye Nevers. He'd won every crumb, by God, that had fallen to his lot.

But Nevers had a gut-deep pride too; he wasn't taking any more of Brady Trapp's bullshit. Not even if it meant jeopardizing the only thing he cared for: the foremanship of Chainlink and the solid, hard-won respect that went with it. A bitter thing to think that he might have to start over one day. Hard too to think of ever leaving Chainlink. The place had become like a part of him, blood and bone.

And there was another reason, one he confided only to himself. There was Adah. The beautiful second wife whom Cyrus Trapp had brought to Chainlink six months ago, the wife less than half his age.

Adah Trapp. As beautiful and unapproachable as an iceberg. A Lady Priss-pants if he'd ever seen one: a fitting mate for an old man. But there was bitter self-mockery in Nevers's thought. He couldn't explain why; he only knew that no woman he'd ever known, and he'd known many, had affected him the way Adah Trapp did. He'd spent endless hours puzzling on why the sight of her made him go hollow-bellied and pulse-heavy.

And wondering what the hell he could do about it.

Bowie nearly came to four or five times in the next few hours, but each time the pain swept him away and he mercifully blanked out. He was aware of faces, of voices, of the inside of a room, but none of it made any sense. Finally he slept.

When he came to again, he was clear-headed. The room held steady in his vision as he lay still and let his gaze touch everything in it. Mortar-chinked log walls darkened with age and brightened by a few old calendars featuring Currier & Ives lithographs. A battered commode with a lamp on it. The flame was turned low, the room shadow-filled; the single window was a dark square. It was night.

And he was on his back in a big brass-framed bedstead with a bright-checked quilt pulled to his neck.

He moved òne arm. Jesus God! The movement showered echoes of pain through his body. Most of it felt like the blunt throbbing of heavy bruises. Except where pain centered like a live coal on his chest. And his head, which felt as if an ax had been sunk into it.

He grimaced, trying to remember.

Those men. Being dragged. His mind tightened around the memory with a raw, humiliated hatred. Those sons of bitches. Had they brought him to . . . wherever he was? Didn't make much sense, considering what they'd done.

Well, by God. Maybe he could find a few answers. Shudderingly he eased to a sitting position; every hurt blazed to agonizing life. He felt like vomiting; he sat quietly till the feeling passed. Christ. Ignoring the savage slugging in his skull, he threw off the blankets and slowly swung his legs to the floor. He was wearing a clean suit of baggy flannel underwear, not his own. He saw his saddle and other gear on the floor by a wall. Moving with infinite care, he got to his feet, stood swaying a moment as he crowded back the surging waves of dizziness, then moved to the commode and the scroll-framed mirror on the wall behind it.

The bastards had done a real job on him, all right. His face was scabbed with cuts and purpled with bruises; his jaw was swollen lopsidedly, one eye nearly shut. He didn't reckon the rest of him looked any better. But his chest. Christ, what had happened there? He undid the underwear buttons and saw a bandage with a flat bulge of poultice underneath. He touched it and shuddered at the raw swell of pain. A burn? The Mexican must have dragged him across his own fire.

A heavy pulse began to beat in Bowie's neck as he stared at his battered reflection. His swollen jaw knotted so tight that he winced. The rage he felt was hot, feral, unreasoning. Somebody was going to pay for this. Hobbling on bare feet to the window, he peered out. Faint outlines of ranch buildings in the darkness. Couldn't tell much except that this was a second-story window. So he'd go out another way.

First thing was to find his goddam clothes. Take them at gunpoint if he had to. He scanned his saddle plunder; everything was here but his rifle. Smart bastards. The blind fury curdling in him colored his thoughts to an unheeding violence. All right—all right. Find a gun. Then, by God.

He padded over to the door, palmed it softly open, and stepped out onto a wide landing. He saw a railed stairwell with lamplight shafting from downstairs. Faint voices drifted from below. Doors along the wall, probably bedchambers, and it must be early in the evening yet. He'd search for a gun. Matches. He'd need matches. A search of his saddlebags turned some up. Silently he tried the first door to his left, grimaced as he got a whiff of female cologne, and closed it. The next room was tenanted by somebody who worked cattle; he struck a match and saw a Spencer rifle mounted on wall pegs. He found a box of .54 cartridges in a drawer of the commode. He slid a shell in the breech and filled the Spencer's loading tube, then eased out to the stairway.

There he paused, listening to the voices from below, trying to single them out. A woman's. Several men's. And one throaty, surly voice that made hair prickle at the back of his neck. *Brady.* His hand clenched in savage reflex around the rifle.

Bowie went down the steep rises in silence. He was sweating profusely, his teeth set against pain, as he reached the bottom of the stairs. He stood in a short shadowy corridor that ended in a doorway on either end. He promptly guessed that the closed door on his right led to the kitchen. The ajar one on his left opened on the dining room. He could only see one end of it from here, but the voices coming from it, along with a tinkle of china and utensils, indicated that the people were at supper.

". . . time you'd have hung that sort of long-looping trash from a tree," Brady was saying sullenly.

"Times change," another voice rumbled. An older

man's voice, deep and commanding. "In my time there wasn't no law but what a man made for himself. I burned plenty powder making it stick. But them days is over. We're in a county now, we got elected officials. Man's got a complaint, he takes it to a sheriff. That's as it should be."

"Hell!" Brady said hotly. "That's the half of it—you changed too, don't tell me you ain't, you talk like——"

"You shut your mouth. Hear me out. I won't say this again. I'm the man I always been. But I made all the mistakes I mean to. There's a couple of my prime ones sitting at this table." A flat pause broken by Joe-Bob's quiet titter. The old man's voice went on, softly hard and unrelenting. "You ain't the man I was, Brady. You never will be. You couldn't build in a hundred years what I built in twenty. You'll never need to; I seen to that. But try to play the game like I played it, you'll lose it all."

Bowie edged noiselessly forward till he could see into the room. Brady was starting up from his chair; he crumpled his napkin and threw it on his plate. "All right, by God!" he shouted. "All right, you can——"

His lifting glance froze on the doorway where Bowie stood, lank and wiry in the loose underwear. He let out a whoop. "I'll be goddamned! Look at——"

He broke off, for Bowie was bringing the rifle up from his side. He thumbed back the hammer and pulled the trigger. A shard of brittle wood exploded from a wall log at Brady's back and less than a foot from his right arm. The roar of the shot was deafening in the room.

The woman screamed.

"Funny, wasn't it?" Bowie said.

He cocked the Spencer again.

Joe-Bob leaped to his feet, his chair crashing over. He gaped stupidly and made no other move. Brady hung against the table, both hands on it, his black-bearded jaw sagging. Bowie's glance moved across the damask-covered table. He barely looked at the woman; her face was wide-eyed and colorless. The fourth person at the table climbed slowly to his feet.

He was as big as his voice, a huge-boned, brown-faced man of about sixty. The years had been kind to him; his close-cropped chestnut hair and beard held only a few strands of gray. He moved as easily and powerfully as a man twenty years younger. His eyes were still eagle fierce, though a pair of spectacles rested on his beak of a nose. They didn't dim his solid presence; his face held neither surprise nor anger.

"All right, son," he said quietly. "You done your little bit of play-acting. I'm Cyrus Trapp. You got some'at to say, you say it to me."

Bowie grinned mirthlessly. "Cyrus Trapp don't mean a goddam thing to me, mister."

The woman gave a little whispered cry.

"Don't be alarmed, Adah honey," Trapp said. He patted her shoulder. "He is just shooting at walls."

"So far," Bowie said.

Cyrus Trapp shook his head. "They said you was feisty as hell. But you got a mote of sense too or you'd of bored Brady straight off. You ain't here for that."

Bowie nodded. "So far you ain't wrong. I want my clothes first. Then I'll tell you what next."

"Maybe you better say it now."

"All right. I'm going to wrap this gun around Brady's skull. Then I'm—"

A movement of the woman's eyes, then Joe-Bob's, warned him. He started to wheel around, but too late. Somebody had come silently up behind him and now he threw his arms around Bowie's torso, pinning his arms. Bowie heaved and struggled. Pointed up in his fists, the Spencer bellowed again; the bullet crashed into the ceiling.

Adah screeched again. Bowie ducked his head, then slammed it backward in the unseen man's face. He gave a pained yell and his hold loosened. Bowie drove a savage elbow into his ribs and knocked him away.

Brady was already coming fast around the table, was almost on him, and Bowie whipped the rifle up. The butt of the stock crunched against Brady's face and sent him slamming back against the wall. Bowie swung on Cyrus, who was coming at him from the other side. In the same instant the man behind him, recovering, wrapped an arm around Bowie's neck and rammed a knee in his back, arching him off balance.

Cyrus wrested the Spencer from Bowie's grasp and moved back, saying, "All right, Sully. Leave go of him."

Freed, Bowie stumbled against the table and grabbed at it for support. He glared at the old man, but the soreness of his body and the rifle in Cyrus's hands banked the unrelieved anger in him. He swung a glance on Brady, who was still sagging dazedly against the wall, fingering his split mouth. Blood funneled off the tip of his beard and splashed on his white shirt.

"How's your lip?" Bowie asked.

With a snarl Brady pushed away from the wall and started for him, but Cyrus roared, "That's enough, Brady!" He gave Bowie a prod with the rifle muzzle. "You sit down. Sit, I said!"

Bowie dropped into a chair, leaning his elbows on the table and cupping a hand to his aching head. He looked at Sully, who was holding a bandanna to his bleeding nose and, surprisingly, chuckling a little. "I told you he was a real hardnose, Cyrus. You should of put a guard on him."

Cyrus grunted. "What brought you from the bunkhouse so providentially?"

"Oh, I'd just come into the kitchen to have a few words with Tula. Overheard the talk in here." Sully grinned. "Glad I did, even if it saved Brady a busted head. Or did it?"

"That's funny, breed, funny as hell," Brady husked. His green eyes blinked hatred at Bowie. "Told you it was a mistake, Pa. Taking him into the house. I told you."

"Could be," Cyrus said dryly, "that you made the first mistake, having him dragged."

"Then I'll make it right." Brady's voice seethed with rage. "Turn the son of a bitch over to me now. I'll run his ass clear across the county line."

"Boy, you been warned to curb your immoderate language under this roof. Do I got to tell you again?"

"But *cripes*, Pa! You keep him here, he could murder us all in our sleep!"

"Not you, Junior," Bowie said, his voice soft and jeering. "I'll just pull down your drawers and spank your pink bottom for saying bad words."

There was raw murder in Brady's face. He stood flexing and unflexing his fists, then suddenly turned and tramped through an archway that opened on the adjoining parlor. He went out the front door, slamming it behind him. Sully was shaking with noiseless laughter. A girl had come from the kitchen, and as she moved up beside Sully, he dropped an arm around her shoulders. She was a lot smaller than he, but it was plain they were brother and sister.

Adah said faintly, "Tula. Will you bring my smelling salts, please?"

"Yes, ma'am." The girl went out, her steps going briskly up the stairs.

The front door opened; a big blond man stepped into the parlor. He paused, briefly taking in the scene. His eyes were as impersonal as a snake's. "Anything wrong? Heard a couple of shots and just saw Brady come stomping out—"

"All's under control, Faye," Cyrus said. "But you might dispatch one of the boys over here. Tell him to bring his hogleg. I think we'll put a guard by our drifter man's door tonight."

Faye nodded. "I'll send Barney." He went out.

Bowie rubbed his head. It was pounding unmercifully; his eyes were starting to blur. His muscles felt rubbery with aching exhaustion. "Jus' gimme my clothes," he muttered. "Don' wanta stay here."

"Why, son," Cyrus said dryly, "I make it you are feverish and not thinking straight. You better lay over tonight. Anyway you got no horse."

"I figure I earned the buckskin."

Sully laughed. "No end to his vinegar, is there? Maybe he's right, Cyrus."

Cyrus twitched a brief smile. "That's as may be. Sheriff might reason otherwise."

Bowie dropped the hand from his forehead and glowered at him. "That's why you're holding me, ain't it?"

"You sleep on the thought. We'll talk when you got that fever damped some. That sandy temper of yours too. You are starting to rub mine just a mite thin, son."

CHAPTER THREE

He was stiff and still sore as hell when he woke next morning, but his headache had subsided to a tolerable throb and he was ravenously hungry. A glance through the window told him the sun was midmorning high. The sky was a new-scrubbed blue; the day looked crisp and pleasant. Easing himself gingerly upright in bed, he saw fresh clothes, not his own, hung on the back of a chair. His own runover boots stood beside it. Bowie hobbled over to the door and opened it a crack. That damn guard was gone. Maybe he could clear out of here now. Then he uneasily remembered that his next move depended on Cyrus Trapp's whim. Even could he sneak out, Trapp could set the law on his trail. Hell!

Bowie pulled on the well-worn but clean shirt and pants and socks. The clothes hung sacklike on his gaunt frame, so oversize that he judged they were Cyrus Trapp's own. A pitcher, wash basin, and shaving gear had been set out on the commode. Damn considerate, he thought dourly. He didn't know if he could pare the wiry scrub off his raw face, but he felt mean enough to try. He whipped up a lather in the shaving mug and slapped it on his beard.

Waiting for the soap to soften his whiskers, Bowie tramped to the window and stared out. Chainlink headquarters was quite a layout, he had to admit. The intricate but well-ordered complex of sheds, wagon sheds, stables, horse troughs, bunkhouse, cookshack, smithy, smokehouse, storage cribs, corrals, and cattle pens was spread across a deep valley flat between timber hills. A hell of a

31

lot for one man to lay claim to, along with a parcel of range that must extend far into the foothills he'd covered yesterday. Studying the shape of the country from this north window, Bowie knew the headquarters was considerably south of where he'd been dragged yesterday.

Finished stropping the razor, he carefully attacked his beard, wincing and swearing. He hadn't noticed before that the worst of his facial cuts had been sewed up with small neat stitches. Not that it mattered a hell of a lot; his hide already bore worse scars than any Trinidad's dragging was like to leave. The poultices had nicely relieved the excruciating burn on his chest.

Stiff-legged, he descended to the dining room. Cyrus Trapp sat alone at the head of the table, eating his eggs while he peered through his spectacles at a frayed newspaper. "Morning, son. You don't look half as ugly without the fur. Sit yourself and eat. My boys are already up and out, and my wife sleeps late. Won't nobody bother us."

Bowie remained standing in the doorway. "You wanted to talk."

"That can wait. Fill your belly first. See a night's sleep didn't wear off none of your bark."

"Too damn bad, ain't it?"

Bowie seated himself at the foot of the table, turned over his face-down plate, and began loading it from the platter of ham and eggs. He attacked the food with a famished concentration and in silence. Cyrus said nothing until he'd finished and had washed the meal down with black coffee. Standing up then and chucking his napkin on the table, Cyrus said: "Come along. We'll palaver in the parlor."

As they entered the big sitting room, Bowie gave it an indifferent glance, but he was impressed. This was a man's room for sure. The west wall was graced by the biggest fireplace he'd ever seen, solidly built of soot-seasoned field stones. The oaken ceiling beams were polished by smoke and age to a rich darkness. The furniture was old and heavy, horsehair sofas and hand-carved armchairs scattered casually around the room, as were the thick-weave Indian blankets that served as rugs. The walls were hung with trophy heads of elk, antelope, and bighorn, along with flintlock rifles and muskets, old pistols and cutlasses, and a collection of Indian weapons. As he seated himself on the edge of the least comfortable-looking chair, Bowie fleetingly reflected that the haughty-looking woman called Adah wasn't Trapp's daughter after all. His wife. Huh. Pretty recent union, seemed like. She sure-hell hadn't yet dented the solid masculinity of this place.

Cyrus settled into an armchair with a grunt. "Now. You want to find me a reason I shouldn't turn you over to Sheriff Beamis?"

"Might be more interesting to let your cub kick my ass across the county line like he wants. Let him try."

Cyrus took a cigar from his pocket and eyed it almost with distaste. "All right, play it hardnosed. I can ride it out a little longer. Just for the hell of it, son, why don't you tell me the truth? Sully said he figured you just borrowed the buckskin. But you wouldn't answer up when Brady put the question."

"I didn't like how he asked it."

"Make a difference if he'd asked polite?"

"I'll tell you this," Bowie said flatly. "It would of made no goddam difference to Junior how I answered."

Cyrus sighed and nodded. "Well, I can't fault the truth in that—mind saying your name? You got mine."

"Bowie Candler."

"All right, Candler. You seem to understand tit for tat. You square with me, I'll square with you. Fair enough?"

Bowie shrugged.

"Goddamit, yes or no?"

"All right."

The chair creaked as Cyrus canted his weight forward. "Here's my side. I'd of heard you out and decided whether I believed you. Happen I didn't, I'd never drag a man on a rope or roast him on a fire. Time was I might of hanged you. But that's long past. Now I'd turn you over to Beamis. Still might if your story don't ring true. You want to tell it?"

"Ain't much to tell. Lion run my horse off night before last. I was afoot, wet, half-froze, and that saddle was damn heavy." Bowie paused. "I never lifted horseflesh before, but I didn't feel like drawing no distinctions. Meant to turn him loose soon as I raised a road or a ranch. That's all."

Cyrus rose and walked to a window, chewing his cigar. He faced out across his valley and said without turning: "Takes a lot to build up a place like this, Candler. Lot of years, lot of sweat, some blood. Takes a tough son of a bitch to do it, which I was. Still am. Brady don't think so. He's never understood there's different kinds of strength. Takes the biggest kind of guts to take a chance on people. He's never understood that either."

Cyrus half turned from the window, rubbing a slablike hand over his face. Then he pressed the hand tight against his temple. His eyes were squinted shut; his gritted jaw bulged against his beard.

"What's wrong?"

"Nothing," Cyrus said curtly. "Not a goddam thing." He dropped the hand and strode back to his chair. "I'll take your word, Candler. You still lifted that buckskin, borrow or not."

"So it's the sheriff."

"Christ, you're thick-headed," Cyrus said irritably. "I could hand you to Beamis without pumping you first. What I propose is to let you work out the buckskin's price if you're willing. If you ain't, you can walk out of here and straight to hell, for all I care. We're about to begin fall roundup and I need another hand. What about it?"

"I get to keep the buckskin?"

"Jesus." Cyrus shook his head, slowly and wonderingly. "I just said as much, didn't I? Maybe cow work's too complicated for you."

"I handled plenty before." Bowie met his wickedly measuring stare with one in kind. "You got a damn salty tongue yourself, mister."

"I can afford one." Cyrus was pressing his temple again, but the squinch of pain in his eyes didn't soften. "I can back it. Back it one helluva lot handier than any out-at-the-heels pilgrim can."

Bowie rubbed a hand over his mouth to hide the grin suddenly jerking at one corner of it. "Hope your grub's easier to swallow than you are."

"You'll find out. How you like them clothes?"

"Since you ask, they don't suit me worth a goddam."

"That's all right. You'll appreciate 'em better when you've worked out their price too."

"Like hell I will," Bowie said promptly, flatly. "I paid for the borrow of that horse by getting dragged. That squares it. But Junior ruined my duds too, and god-damned if I'll pay a plugged penny for your cast-offs."

Cyrus merely nodded, mild again. "All right. Just one more thing, Candler. You got any sand left in your craw concerning my son, get it spit out."

Bowie thought it over, then nodded. "That's fair. But I won't take no goddam rawhiding off him. You tell him."

"He'll get the word. Faye Nevers, he's my foreman, has got orders to put his heel on Brady any way need be." As if the admission shamed him, Cyrus got abruptly to his feet. "Fetch your plunder to the bunkhouse. Rest up all you can today. Last chance you'll get to while you're eating Chainlink grub."

"Honest to God, Pa," Brady said savagely. "I don't understand you at all! First you let that mangy drifter con you with a goddam lie, then you hire him on the crew. It's like patting a thief on the back because he lifted your poke."

"That'll do," Cyrus said curtly. "I don't want to hear no more on it. And you don't raise any more ruction with Candler, hear me? He's on, and that's an end of it."

Faye Nevers sat with elbows braced on the table, revolving his coffee cup between his palms. A faint frown creased his heavy face. Cyrus had invited him for supper so they could discuss plans for the roundup, but the whole meal had been another session of bickering between Cyrus and his older son. Adah sat picking at her food, mouth pursed with disapproval. Joe-Bob just listened and grinned. Cyrus slanted a dry glance at Nevers.

"What's sitting in your craw, Faye? Speak up."

Nevers set his cup down. "You kind of closed the subject."

"Never mind. Say it."

"We got a full crew for roundup. We don't need this Candler, even if he wasn't a horse thief. All right, you believe his story. But he's a hardnose, you seen it for yourself. Man like that on the crew'll make trouble."

Brady thumped his fist on the table. "There, your foreman said it——"

"Shut up," Cyrus said, not looking at him. "Go on, Faye."

"It's been my understanding that I do the hiring and firing for Chainlink. If that's changed, I'd like to hear it said."

"You'll hear it said when I change it. I been dealing with men all my life, Faye. If I'd made many wrong guesses, I'd not be alive to tell you. All right, I'm taking Candler on faith. If I stretched our understanding, call it an old man's whim. Give him a chance. If he's troublesome, let him go. It's still up to you."

Nevers gave a noncommittal nod. "Fair, I reckon."

Brady scraped back his chair and stood up, muttering, "Jesus. Come on, kid."

"Just a minute. Where you off to?"

"The bunkhouse." Brady gave his father a hostile grin. "For a turn of cards. *That* all right?"

"You mind what I said about Candler."

Brady and Joe-Bob went out; the door slammed. Cyrus sighed, took out his daily cigar, now chewed almost to a stub, and set it in a corner of his mastiff jaws. "I hope them poker games are kept low stake."

Nevers smiled. "Only kind the boys can afford. You know how it gets after payday. Everyone's wages is pretty much common property, way it changes hands. One good night in town and it's all blowed anyway."

Cyrus grunted. "Just so long as Brady blows his share on redeye and crib girls."

"Cyrus, please." Adah's face had pinkened; her eyes were lowered.

"Sorry, honey. I forgot. You don't know about that."

"About what?"

"Couple years ago, Brady run up some heavy debts at the gaming tables over in Saltville. I paid up his score under the strict condition that his big-gambler days were over. He has got to confine his bellystripping to the bunkhouse. So far's I know, he has."

Nevers sipped his cold coffee to hide his ironic twist of mouth. He knew that three months ago, Brady had again begun frequenting Lucky Jack's casino in Saltville. Seemed a fair bet that by now the owner held a bundle of Brady's IOU's. In his gambling, as in most things, Brady was plunging and incautious, too stubborn to learn better, too hot-headed to give a rip about the consequences. Nevers's lips curled wryly. Cyrus knew men, but that trusting nature of his was a blind spot. Bred by the code of his generation of cattlemen, the iron code that a man's handshake was his bond, he expected to be dealt with in kind. Damned if I'm sticking my neck out, Nevers thought. Leave him find out in his own time.

When Tula had finished clearing the table and Adah had retired to the parlor to pore over the latest *Century Magazine,* Cyrus brought paper and pencil to the table. He and Nevers spent the next hour going over details for the big roundup. It would involve roughly fifty square miles of valley and foothill country and all the cattle outfits within that range. The meeting place for its northern division would be the valley of the Oro River along Chainlink's east boundary. Some two hundred men and fifteen hundred horses would be divided between a half-dozen captains and their wagons, and they would work the country in the pattern of previous roundups. As foreman for one of the biggest outfits, Nevers would be a wagon captain, with the job of representing and cutting for all brands in the division.

"That's about it," Cyrus said finally. "Gonzales has laid in plenty of supplies and his wagons are loaded and ready to roll. You'll start out at daybreak tomorrow."

"That sounds like you won't be coming along."

Cyrus pursed his mouth. "I'll be along in a couple days.

You'll have letters of authorization from me and our ten-cow neighbors that ain't sending reps. That ought to satis-fy the inspectors from the stock associations. I—have got a few things to take care of here. Then I'll be along."

Nevers's eyes narrowed; his attention sharpened. It wasn't like Cyrus to pass up the neighborly hurly-burly of a roundup. Not like him to be vague about reasons either. Nevers was debating whether to put the question to him when he noted a jerking, painful squint in Cyrus's eyes. A condition he'd noticed before, more frequently in the last week or so. One moment Cyrus seemed clear-eyed and healthy as a bull; the next, he was blinking and wincing as if against some pain that was intolerable. His big hand came up to his temple and began to slowly massage it.

Nevers decided to state it flat out. "Look, if it's none of my business, say so. I been wondering what the trouble is."

Cyrus let the hand fall. "No damn trouble at all."

"Sorry."

"Hell, it's nothing. Get these headaches now and again. Come and go. Need new spectacles is all." Cyrus leaned suddenly hard against the table, his elbow slamming down. His broad face twitched and twisted against an invisible agony. "Christ," he whispered. "Christ!"

"Listen—" Nevers started to his feet. "What's ailing you?"

"Nothing," Cyrus said hoarsely. His shaggy head was bent, both hands cradling it. "Leave it be—"

Nevers skirted the table and went to the archway. "Mrs. Trapp, you better come in here."

Adah rose from the settee and came quickly into the dining room. "Cyrus—Cyrus, not again."

He gave a jerky nod, not raising his head. "Lea' me be. All right in a minute."

She laid her hands on his shoulders. "Please, dear, come to bed. You don't want to fall down as you did . . . once before. Let me help you."

Cyrus lowered his hands, slowly and heavily nodding. "All right." His face was a sweaty gray; his gaze shifting to

Nevers was dull with pain. "Faye, you don't tell a soul about this. Not a soul."

"I won't," Nevers said. "Here, I'll lend a hand."

Between them, Adah and Nevers helped Cyrus to his feet. He was as unsteady as a year-old baby, his eyes blind and unfocused. Nevers took the bulk of Cyrus's weight against his own shoulder as they maneuvered the big man up the stairs to his room. They lowered him onto the bed. Nevers tasted the strangeness of seeing a man he had always thought of as a monument, invincible to wear and time, helpless as a kitten.

"Maybe we better send to Saltville for Doc Rawls. If——"

"No!" Cyrus snarled the word, hands pressed over his eyes. "No doctor. Goddamit, Faye, mind what I told you."

"All right. Take it easy. Couple blasts of home-grown painkiller might help——"

"You know I can't take any booze."

"Right," Nevers said softly. "I forgot."

Adah touched his arm. He nodded and followed her out the door, gently closing it as a muffled groan exploded from Cyrus. They went down the stairs; Adah halted by the archway. Her face was pale and unreadable. Almost. She's scared, he thought.

"It's happened before, eh?"

"Twice—this badly, I mean. Once last week. Again two nights ago. But the headaches—he's been having them off and on for nearly two months. I've urged him to see Dr. Rawls, but—" Her shoulders lifted and settled.

"Uh-uh. He wouldn't, not Cyrus."

She shook her head; a stain of worry darkened her eyes. "I don't know . . . what I can do. Several times—in the night—I've lain awake in the next room listening to him toss and groan. Sometimes for hours. But he refuses even to discuss it. I fear the worst, Mr. Nevers."

So Cyrus and his bride didn't share the same bed. Nevers had suspected as much from his sight of Cyrus's room. He remembered the same rickety old bedstead and spartan furnishings from years back. It might have been consideration for Adah, as his affliction had grown worse, that had caused Cyrus to move back into his former room. All the same, Nevers felt a burning curiosity.

It made him more sharply aware of the woman's nearness. The familiar surge of rampant feeling boiled into his guts; he had difficulty holding his expression still and just faintly concerned. The problem had begun when Cyrus had brought his bride to Chainlink six months ago.

Cyrus Trapp's remarriage after nineteen years as a widower had come as a complete surprise to everyone, even his sons. As it turned out, he'd been a frequent visitor at Adah Landry's home in Denver for many years. Adah's father, also a widower, had been one of Cyrus's oldest friends. After an accident had left him crippled and half paralyzed, Adah had devoted her youth to caring for him. Apparently they'd lived pretty much from hand to mouth; though Cyrus had never said so, Nevers had gathered that he'd helped the Landrys out more than once, and very likely he'd footed the bill for Adah's education at an excellent boarding school. Cyrus's forceful generosity was legend; he'd practically belabor a friend in need to accept his bounty. Adah had been a spinsterish twenty-six when her father had died two years ago—and Cyrus had continued his regular calls.

The affection between them was genuine enough. But romantic? Nevers couldn't see it. For all the difference in their ages, of course, Cyrus was still a vital, far-from-doddering man; Adah was a thoroughly mature woman. There had to be that much. Cyrus had been lonely too, hungry for a familial warmth he'd never found with his sons. Nevers summed up Adah's position with a sardonic judgment. She'd been grateful. Also destitute. And she'd wanted another father.

But Jesus, what a waste. A woman like this thrown away on an old man. When Cyrus was seventy, she'd still have it all. The chiseled beauty of a face with tantalizing planes and tilts that reminded Nevers of the Oriental girls he'd known in his West Coast youth. Eyes of a lovely sharp-colored turquoise under delicately winged brows. Skin like pale satin and black hair that glistened like fresh tar in its prim chignon. The proper high-necked dresses she always wore couldn't do justice to her erect slim full-breasted figure. Gentle, genteel, quiet: that was Adah. The Adah everyone saw. But a woman couldn't look like her and not have a fierce womanliness waiting to blossom just under the surface. . . .

She was gazing at a wall, and now her eyes moved back to his face. "What did Cyrus mean—that remark about booze? I know he never drinks, but——"

"Thought you knew. Reckon he'd of told you if the matter ever came up. He can't take the stuff. Never could."

"I don't understand."

"All I know is what he told me once. Little bit of liquor, enough to warm another man's innards, does something to Cyrus—sends him off his head, he told me. He never takes a drink because he don't dare to."

"Oh," she said softly. "I had no idea."

Momentarily Nevers debated whether to add what else Cyrus had told him. That only after he'd once beaten a man to death with his fists while drunk had he taken a vow never to touch liquor again. No—that wasn't for him to say.

"Is there anything else I can do?"

"I'm afraid not." She bit her lip gently. "If you could persuade him to see a doctor—but if he won't listen to me, will he to you?"

Nevers shook his head soberly.

Again he held a cool mask over the quick sensuous turn of his thoughts. What would she do if he touched her? Scream? Slap him? He felt a reckless amusement, toying with the possibility.

Her eyes seemed to dilate darkly as they met his now. But that was all. Maybe he'd imagined it.

"Good night, Mrs. Trapp."

"Good night."

Nevers felt a gnawing uneasiness as he tramped through the darkness toward the bunkhouse. Just how serious was Cyrus's condition? What did it mean for Chainlink—for his own future here? But these speculations ebbed behind the excitement still thrumming in his veins.

Adah. Prissy Adah. He tried to mock her in his thoughts. But damn it, damn it to hell, he was only mocking himself. . . .

CHAPTER FOUR

The work was hard and the hours long. Starting in the foothill country below the Elks, the northern division of the roundup pushed southward along the great Oro valley. Ahead of the wagons, outriders fanned out in wide circles, pushing all the cattle they picked up down toward the valley flats where the roundup crews would take them over. On the morning following each day's drive, all the local cattle were cut from the gather and turned loose. The strays were headed into a separate herd, which was driven along at a distance from the wagons. Actually six different roundups were carried on at the same time across the valley, with six different crews each assigned to a wagon and a captain. Every night the separate details met up with their wagons at a rendezvous point down river.

It was familiar work to Bowie, assigned as an outrider to Faye Nevers's wagon. Work he didn't mind as much as he did the miserable weather that had plagued the roundup from the first day. Every time it seemed to be letting up some, mare's tails of storm would curve out of the dismal stewing sky above the northern Elks. In an hour or so the prairie hills would be enveloped in a powdery murk of drizzle that was halfway between fog and rain. It wasn't as bad as a good honest storm; it was worse. Gray and depressing, the damp eating more into a man's disposition than into his slicker-clad body.

Bowie's mood wasn't improved by having young Sully Calder in his vicinity most of the time. He had the idea that Sully was deliberately hanging close, and the half-breed's undented cheerfulness fed his irritation. He remembered what Trinidad had said to Brady about Sully being "in your old man's pocket."

Finally he said bluntly to Sully: "Trapp figure I need a wet nurse?"

"Nope," said Sully, unfazed. "A watchdog. Cyrus dropped a word to Nevers, and the word is I am to stick close to you."

"They figure I can run off this whole damn herd?"

"You sound mean enough to try," Sully chuckled. "Hell, they're only curious how you'll work out. I'll be asked about you. Nothing to get sweated over." He added thoughtfully, "Cyrus seems to of taken a personal interest in you."

"What the hell for?"

"You'd have to ask him."

"I wouldn't ask that crusty old fart the time of day."

They were trailing in the drag of the day's gather, and now Sully reined over close to his stirrup and said: "Listen, Candler." He didn't sound angry, only positive. "You're about as sour a pilgrim as I ever butted against. Maybe you got reason to be, I wouldn't know. But don't make no mistake about Cyrus Trapp. All right, times he's like a Dutch uncle, other times he gets under your saddle like a gallsore. But rain or shine, he's the best man I ever knew. Best you're ever like to meet."

"Yeah? What's he done for you?"

"Everything," Sully said flatly. They jogged along in silence for a minute, and then he said: "I was fifteen year old, Tula just twelve, when our folks died. Our ma was one of a big band of Utes that used to summer in the high country. Pa had a one-loop spread west of here and my ma's relatives used to camp in our back yard half the year round. Pa was practically the only white man we ever seen. Tula and me grew up with our Ute cousins, learning their ways, talking their tongue. I used to hunt and fish with my full-blood kin." His lips smiled with memory. "It was a great life."

"Sounds like it," Bowie said, and meant it.

"Yeah. What ended it, the pox hit that summer and just about wiped out the band. Our ma was one of the first to go. Tula and me only come down with light attacks. Our white blood, I reckon. Anyway Ma's death hit Pa pretty hard. He got drunk in Saltville and was killed in a shooting scrape. We never did get the way of it straight. Cyrus took us kids in. Raised us like his own. Sent Tula away to school; she just returned a few months back. Me, I had a choice as to the same, but was satisfied with things way they was."

"You might's well be." Bowie swiveled a glance at him. "You two ain't aught but servants for the Trapps. Pretty damn beholden, ain't you?"

Sully smiled, shaking his head. "You just naturally like to prod a man, don't you? I'm doing what I choose, Candler. As for Tula, what better you think a half-blood girl will find any other place?"

Bowie shrugged. "I ain't spent a lot of time this far north. A breed don't amount to much down by the border."

"He don't amount to much up here either. Anyway Chainlink is our home, Tula's and mine. Reckon you wouldn't understand that."

Bowie didn't consider that worth affirming.

It was late in the afternoon, though you could hardly measure the fact by the neutral gray of this bleak day. Bowie could gauge a day's length by his slow accumulation of saddle aches; a man acquired a built-in timepiece as he began to lose the green resilience of youth. The chill dampness reaching to his joints aggravated the usual twinges.

The six-man detail pushed their gather across the last rises and into the river valley. The big roundup bivouac sprawled across the lush-grassed bottoms. Six campfires were strung along the banks of the Oro, chuck wagons pulled up beside them. Both horsebackers and men on foot made moving shadows in the dull light. The freight and calf wagons were set off toward the big herd, which made a bawling, discordant mass south of the camp. The

detail pressed their bunch into the herd, exchanged greet-
ings with the guards, then turned their horses into the *re-
muda* tended by three wranglers.

Bowie and Sully separated from their companions, all
men from another crew, and tramped tiredly toward their
own wagon. Third from the north end of the line, it was
drawn up in a motte of cottonwoods that slightly sheltered
it from the weather. Gonzales, the Chainlink cook, was a
gaunt Mexican so dourly cadaverous and hollow-eyed that
an undertaker wouldn't believe it. He already had a big
cow-camp coffeepot bubbling on a tripod over the fire, for
the incoming riders were cold and wet tonight as well as
tired. Bowie and Sully were among the first ones to arrive.
They filled their tin cups and squatted by the fire, soaking
up the heat.

Brady Trapp came tramping in with Joe-Bob and Trinidad. His green glance touched Bowie; his jaw hardened
truculently against his beard. He rode a grudge like an Indian, Bowie thought. They'd seen plenty of each other
these first two days of roundup, and each time they met,
Bowie was aware of Brady's silent bridling.

"You pa, he is come to roundup a little while ago," said
Gonzales.

"Yeah." Brady's tone was surly. "I seen him."

Presently Cyrus Trapp came up to the fire, resembling a
bulky yellow grizzly in his slicker. His face seemed drawn
and tired, as if he'd perceptibly aged in the few days since
they'd seen him. He spoke a greeting that included everyone.

"How's it going?" The question was directed to Sully.

"Fine," Sully said. "Everything's fine."

Which, Bowie knew, was Cyrus's quiet way of confirm-
ing that he'd been a good boy. That was all right. Man's
privilege to learn how his gamble was paying off.

The mizzle was letting up. Dusk had started to thicken
the gray murk. More men coming off work were drifting
toward their fires, their forms blurry in the clotting dusk.
Gonzales set a Dutch oven loaded with pans of freshly
made bread in the fire and shoveled glowing coals on top
of it. He hooked another Dutch oven out of the coals and

knocked off the lid. The oven contained three inches of sizzling lard. Working swiftly, he cut many thin steaks the size of his palm from a beef quarter, rolled them in flour left over from his breadmaking, and dropped them into the hot fat. The savory smells began to melt the men's weary taciturnity. They guzzled steaming coffee and exchanged small talk.

Men continued to drift into camp. While they waited for supper, Brady Trapp cajoled three of them into a turn of cards. Bowie studied his avid face in the firelight as he dealt the pasteboards onto a dry square of canvas. Cyrus was drinking coffee and watching. Abruptly he dropped his empty cup in the wreck pan and walked off into the trees. It was presently clear why he couldn't abide watching. Brady became exultant as a kid each time the cards ran his way, then turned sullen and cursing when he lost each hand. It was an old story to the men looking on; they exchanged amused glances.

"He ever win a game?" Bowie asked dryly.

"Sure, when they let him. Call it politics." Sully shook his head. "Something to watch, ain't it? There's a man with a fever that won't burn out and no bottom to back it."

"Ain't half his pa's man, that's sure."

"He ain't. But he's strong as a bull and hard as rocks. Would bear that in mind if I was you."

"You trying to worry me?"

"I am telling you a fact you best stay on top of. Brady has got one mean burr up his ass where you're concerned. No mind what his pa told him, he ain't through with you."

"Hell, I know that."

Sully gave him a speculative, faintly baffled glance. Bowie walked out on the flats a few yards to stretch his legs. He halted, listening to the cattle and the camp noises, old and familiar sounds. Damned if it wasn't true, as old-timers always claimed, that the whole business got into a man's blood after a fair round of years. Gazing across the faintly lit flat where firelight carried, Bowie made out a spectral blot of white moving his way. A canvas-topped wagon, and it wasn't one that belonged to this roundup.

Someone came tramping up beside him. It was Faye Nevers, coffee cup in hand. Does he ever miss a damn thing? Bowie wondered.

"Looks like a Conestoga," Bowie said. "Emigrants?"

"Another damn sodbuster." Disgust thickened Nevers's voice. "Batting around in the dark miles from anywhere. One gets you ten he don't know where he is."

The wagon jolted toward them across the bunch grass, rolling and pitching. The driver pulled up abreast of them, his rough voice halting the team. He stared down at them, a stocky man with a pale ragged mustache and pale tufted brows above deep-set eyes. He was about forty. His broad face was sullenly pugnacious and there wasn't a jot of apology in his manner.

"What is this place?" He had a heavy accent that sounded German or Scandinavian.

"A roundup camp," Nevers said curtly. "You've come a way off your trail."

"Eh." The man squinted at a shimmer of water. "This is the Oro River?"

"That's right."

"Then I am not lost."

"Depends what the hell you're looking for."

"Bottomland. Good bottomland and water. I am told this is the best in the country."

"They tell you it's Chainlink range too?"

"They say it's public domain that is used by some cattle outfits. It can be filed for a homestead." The man's tone was surlily matter of fact. "This I am going to do."

Nevers was already shaking his head. "It's like I told you. You're way off your trail, fella. Now you turn that ratty rig of yours around and get the hell off this land."

The man hunched forward, thick shoulders bunching against his frayed blanket coat. "You are the owner of this —Chainlink?"

"No. I am." Cyrus had joined them; he spoke calmly, flatly. "I'm Cyrus Trapp. What's your name?"

"It is Jan Ekstrom."

"You can file a claim anywhere up and down this river you're a mind to, Ekstrom. The law says so. See you leave my beef and horses alone while you're around. That won't be for long."

Cyrus was already turning away. Ekstrom said, "Wait!" He was scowling, his square blunt-fingered hands flexing around his reins. "You are saying you'll let me get started —then run me off?"

Cyrus moved his head in negation. "I won't need to lift a finger. You can't crop this country and make it pay. Growing season's way too short. You'll be wiped out in a year. Less."

"Why let him plow up good grass?" Nevers said angrily. "Man, I can——"

Cyrus raised a peremptory hand. From inside the wagon came a weak, fretful wailing, broken by little coughing noises. A baby. And a woman's soft voice soothing it in a foreign tongue: *"Sov nu, sov min pojke. . . ."*

"It's my wife and kid," Ekstrom said sullenly. He turned and spoke sharply into the open canvas pucker at his back. Swedes, Bowie thought. He had spent one bitter-cold winter he'd as soon forget working in a Montana logging camp with Swedish and Norwegian lumberjacks. Ekstrom was telling her to quiet the kid.

But she gave back a spirited answer. Now the pale oval of her face showed in the pucker hole by her husband's shoulder. "Please—sir. My baby is sick." Her English was halting and broken. "Can you help us?"

Cyrus pulled off his hat. "I surely can, ma'am. Why didn't you say about the baby, Mister?"

"We ask for nothing," Ekstrom snapped.

"Doesn't matter what you ask or don't. Nobody in need ever got turned from my door. You'll lay over here tonight. We'll see what's to be done. Get your wagon under those trees. Faye, have someone take care of the team."

Ekstrom peered at him from under shaggy brows. Opened his mouth truculently, then closed it. Cyrus's manner was unmistakably that of a man accustomed to giving commands. A man ready to back up his word. Ekstrom put his team in motion and pulled up under the cottonwoods. After he had passed the baby down to Cyrus,

Ekstrom gave his wife a hand down. Did it kind of roughly, Bowie thought.

Cyrus gently poked aside the blanket that hooded the baby's face. Laid a callused forefinger on the small forehead. "How old is he?"

"Eight months," the woman said. "Please, can you do anything? All the time he coughs—for a week now."

"No wonder. Out in this weather, bumping along in a wagon. Running a fever too. Don't you people know better'n to go kiting off in the middle of nowhere with a sick infant?"

Mrs. Ekstrom nodded, fixing a level gaze on her husband as she spoke. "Already the baby was sick when we stop at Saltville. The doctor, he said what you say, Mister. Didn't he, Jan, eh?"

Ekstrom turned away, muttering to himself. It left little doubt where the responsibility lay. The crew looked on in curious silence as Cyrus handed the baby back to his mother, then tramped over to the chuck wagon.

"Mr. Gonzales, I want a piece of beef boiled up for broth. Nothing like it when a baby's ailing with croup." The cook nodded and dug a copper pot out of his wagon. Charlie the roustabout hauled the Dutch ovens from the fire; the crew got plates and lined up to receive their grub.

"Tomorrow I'll take you to my place," Bowie heard Cyrus tell the Ekstroms. "Only sensible thing to do. Baby wants proper caring for. I'll have Doc Rawls brought from Saltville."

Ekstrom glowered at him. "Why you do this for us? Eh?"

"Not for you." Cyrus's tone was dust-dry.

"It ain't your kid. Charity we don't need."

"Charity you don't get. You look husky enough to haul your own freight. Ever work cows?"

"Nah. Just the *milch* kind."

"You'll learn."

"*Helvete*! I did not come all the way from Minnesota——"

"Listen, Mister," Cyrus cut him off flatly. "This baby of yours is ailing bad. I know the signs. I lost a daughter to

the croup when she was three years old. There's things we
can do for your child at headquarters—keep him warm
and dry, burn sulphur under a blanket tent. You tried
that?"

"No," Mrs. Ekstrom murmured, rocking the feebly crying baby in her arms. "Oh, Jan. We must take this man's
help, we must let him do what he can."

"Not much a man can do, but my womenfolk can lend a
hand. Got a young Indian housekeeper knows medicine
ways you wouldn't believe." Cyrus looked hard at Ekstrom. "Mister, you can go ahead and start your homestead like you want. You'll be lucky to get a cabin up before first snow. Meantime there'll be bitter frosts of a night
and plenty of fall weather. Rain, sleet, weeks of it. And a
bad-sick baby to worry about. You got any sense at all,
you'll figure on wintering at Chainlink. You want some
food, ma'am, I'll fetch you a plate."

"*Tack*—thank you."

Cyrus tramped over to the chuck wagon. Ekstrom
walked stiffly away to the edge of firelight and stood with
his back to the camp, hands rammed in his pockets, his
shoulders hunched with pride and anger and resentment.
Cyrus fetched a crate for Mrs. Ekstrom to sit on, then
brought her a plate of food and cup of coffee. He held the
baby while she ate; he paced a slow circle, a bear-big man
who cradled the tiny bundle as gently as a woman might.

"What's his name, Missus?"

"Eric."

"Fine name for a boy. You know, Missus, my girl 'ud
be about your age if she'd lived. Could of been the proud
grandpappy of a boy like Eric around now."

As the crew finished eating, they began clattering tin
plates and cups into the wreck pan. Gonzales growled at
them to keep the noise down; *Santa Maria,* with a sick
bebé here, did they have no better sense? Cyrus handed
the baby back to Mrs. Ekstrom, took her empty plate and
cup to the wreck pan, then went over to the Dutch ovens
to load a plate for himself. Gonzales had lifted the pot of
broth from the fire; he carried it to his wagon tailgate and
filled a cup with the steaming liquid.

"She's plent' hot, boss. I let her steep and cool before we give to *bebé*, eh?"

Cyrus grunted assent, leaning against a wagon wheel as he ate. Brady came tramping up to him and halted, feet apart. His stocky body was braced with a tense truculence. "Pa, I want to talk."

"All right. Talk."

"We better step off a ways."

Cyrus gave him a dour look, then laid his plate aside. The two walked around back of the wagon; Brady began talking in a low, heated voice. Bowie had been taking in the scene as he ate, overhearing most of what had been said. He dumped his utensils in the wreck pan and then, never a man to shy off from an impulse, walked over to Mrs. Ekstrom and her baby.

He touched his hatbrim. "Ma'am."

She raised her eyes with a small curious nod. Deep-lashed eyes that were finely gray, like night mist. She wasn't over twenty-five; her face was oddly tranquil in a resigned sort of way. She looked as if she might smile easily whenever she wasn't so worried and fine-worn.

Bowie peered at the baby's reddened face. Even between coughing spasms, it seemed to screw up as if from jabs of pain, the small body half-doubling. "Seems to me that is more'n the old croup, ma'am."

She nodded. "His little belly, it's very sore."

"Could be cramps from the coughing. Or maybe his innards got bruised some way. There's a tonic my ma used to make when one of us kids had a cold or a sore gut. Sort of a soothing syrup."

Gonzales came up with the cup of warm broth. "Now she's cool enough, you give him some of this, Señora."

"Oh, thank you. I do not know if he will take it. He does not take much to eat and maybe it will not stay down."

"Might be able to fix that with a dose of the old syrup," Bowie said. "Cook's got the makings in his wagon. I can fix some right away. Have to go into your kitchen, cook."

Gonzales nodded reluctantly. "Sure, if it help the little

one. Here, Señora, hold the *bebé* so, and we give him some of this."

Bowie moved over to the wagon and set out the ingredients he needed. Tallow lard, blackjack sorghum, powdered alum from the medicine chest. He dropped some tallow in a cup and set it by the fire to melt. Poured another cup a third full of sorghum and, after a moment's hesitation, added a dash of alum. Stuff could fetch the baby some more belly pains if he had an open sore there, but it would also heal; just a dash would do. He'd added the melted fat to the sorghum and was waiting for the mixture to cool when an angry, heedless lift of voices carried from the motte of trees off behind the wagon. Cyrus and Brady had been talking quietly up till now.

". . . damn quick have every son-of-a-bitching rawhider in the country scrounging off us," Brady was saying bitterly. "Time was when we hustled trash like that off our open range straightway."

"All right," Cyrus rumbled with thinning patience. "We hustle him off. Then he goes to the federal marshal and we got real trouble. I told you times have changed. Biggest of us can't make the kind of tracks we used to in this country. There's law here now and it's come to stay."

"But Christ, Pa! Let one get away with it and you'll have a whole flood of his sort pouring in."

"No help for it. Law says that this man or anyone like him can file one hundred and sixty acres with the land office and make his improvements, and it's his. But none of 'em'll last. Nature'll see to it."

"What goddam difference will that make when they're done plowing it all to hell?" Brady said savagely. "You say you built up Chainlink for us, Joe-Bob and me. What'll there be left?"

"We got plenty patented land that's ours free and clear," Cyrus snapped. "Anyways it'll never go that far. The sodders'll give up before long. Now you simmer down."

"Goddammit, law's got nothing to do with way you started coddling rawhider trash! That damn drifter, this snorky and his family. Don't give me no more crap about old-time hospitality, you gone soft, that's the whole thing, plain goddam soft!"

"Not so soft I can't still bust you ass over teakettle." Cyrus's voice was notching upward with a quiet fury. 'You—*uh*!"

"Pa—Christ, what is it? What's the matter?"

"Nothing that's concern of yours," Cyrus snarled. "Get the hell away——"

He came plodding out of the trees, head sunk between his shoulders like a ringy bull's. His face was ashen with pain; his eyes wore an unfocused glaze. He lurched across to his bedroll and collapsed on his back, throwing an arm over his eyes. An uneasy murmur ran through the crew. The incident had confirmed a possibility they'd begun to suspect and discuss in hushed mutters some time ago: that Cyrus, for all his giant's strength, was a desperately ill man.

Brady tramped into view now. His eyes, glassy with rage, fell on Bowie standing by the wagon only yards away. He came over to him, long arms swinging. "You get a good earful, bum?"

"Yeah."

"I ought to unscrew your goddam head right here!"

"I gave your pa my word. Maybe you didn't get it."

"I got it," Brady said hotly. "You handed him a string of taffy and he swallowed it. I don't!"

"I'll tell you, Junior. I'm tired of getting high-heeled by you. You want to settle things so damn bad, we can do it back of them trees."

Slowly and wickedly, Brady shook his head. "Not yet, bummer. There'll be a time. A place. I'll pick it. You wait."

CHAPTER FIVE

Sofie Ekstrom hummed contentedly as she sliced up onions and potatoes for the stew. Plenty of *sill och potatis* there must be, the way Jan liked it. How good to once more be able to dip into a root cellar for whatever she needed in the way of vegetables. It was like home again. Home in Sweden, or in Minnesota? Both, in a way. Coming to America at seventeen had meant tearing up one set of memories. But she had come to think of the Ekstrom farm in Douglas County, Minnesota, as home too, and there were so many Swedish settlers in the region that in most ways life had differed little from what it had been in *gamla hemlandet*, the old country.

Sofie had a need of roots and permanence. When Jan had announced his decision to sell the farm and move to a Western place, her reaction had been a panicked wish to hang on to all that was, the fixed comforts she'd come to know and be comfortable with. It was harder to tear up roots a second time; you were older, jelling in your ways, and making a change came harder.

Of course she should have supposed that something of the sort was brewing in Jan's head. The loss of his wheat crop two years in a row: first to drought, then to flattening hail. His restless mutterings of discontent. It couldn't be said that he'd ever shared his thoughts with her, being glum and close-mouthed at his best, surly and black-tempered at his worst, but rarely did his moods leave her in any doubt of his feelings. *Ja*, no doubt Jan's decision to leave Minnesota had been ripening for a long time and she merely hadn't wanted to believe it.

Eric let out an earsplitting yell and flailed his arms. Sofie went over to the long-unused crib that Mr. Trapp had dug out of the harness shed loft; she pulled up to Eric's chin the comforter that he'd kicked off. "We do not play now," she said. *"Var en snall pojke. Sov nu."* Eric wasn't interested in being a good boy or in going to sleep. He wanted attention and proclaimed it by giving a lusty good-natured squawl.

Sofie didn't mind in the least; she was smiling as she returned to cutting up vegetables. How fine it was to see him carry on like any normal baby. Eric had been rather sickly from birth; weeks in a jolting wagon, then the raw cold and wet, had slowly worsened his condition. In those last despairing days before Cyrus Trapp had taken them in, Sofie had felt a deepening dread for her child. And something else, as Jan Ekstrom had blindly, stubbornly refused to stop somewhere, anywhere, for the baby's sake. Something like the beginning of hatred for a man she had married out of an ill-defined sense of duty.

Yet Eric hadn't taken a real turn for the worst till just before they'd encountered the roundup outfit. By then, at last, Jan was feeling a flush of guilty alarm. She'd known this by how he had yielded, though with poor grace, to Cyrus Trapp's insistence on helping them.

Sofie glanced out one of the two small windows that fronted the single-room cabin. Dusk was a blue mist deepening toward purple, so the crew would be in soon. She quickly finished up the potatoes and dropped them in the stewpot. Jan would be home directly and be very ugly if he had to wait long on supper. *Home!* It was really coming to seem like that after only two weeks, and it surprised her that this should be, everything was so different from what she'd known. Yet not altogether, thanks to the kindness of these Chainlink people.

Mr. Trapp had insisted that the Ekstroms stay in the big house, where Eric might be properly looked after. A room had been prepared for them; everyone had outdone themselves fussing over the baby. Dr. Rawls was summoned

from Saltville; Tula Calder had fixed many mysterious
brews and poultices from plants she'd gathered. But Sofie
wasn't sure that Eric's dramatic improvement wasn't due
as much to the constant attentions of three women to his
every need and comfort. Especially to the ministrations of
childless Mrs. Trapp; her husband had confided to Sofie
that Adah hadn't seemed so satisfied since he'd brought
her to Chainlink. And what of Mr. Candler's wonderful
syrup? For the first time in months, Eric's belly had ceased
to hurt him. The remedy must have healed something in it,
for after a few doses he had complained no more. The
high thin air of this mountain valley and some nice fall
weather of late had also helped, Dr. Rawls had told her.
In any case, Eric's general health had not been so good
since his birth.

Once the baby's improvement was certain, Cyrus Trapp
had moved the Ekstroms to permanent quarters. This was
the original cabin which he'd built on the headquarters site
more than thirty years ago, the home to which he'd
brought his first bride. It was furnished with such spare
furniture, utensils, and so on as could be found, along with
what the Ekstroms had brought in their wagon. A few repairs here and there, the logs freshly chinked and new
shakes nailed on the roof, and it made as snug and
weather-tight a home as one might wish.

From out by the corrals came the faint noises that indicated the crew was coming in. Sofie glanced out a window
and made out the shadowy forms of men and horses. She
hung the pot of stew on the fireplace lug and stoked up the
fire, then began to set the table. Soon Jan came roughly
through the door, yanking off his hat and coat. He stared
grouchily at the table.

"Where's supper?"

"It will not be ready for awhile. Mrs. Trapp was here.
She——"

"*Gud bevara*," he growled, flinging his coat and hat on
a wall peg. "That damn woman, she's got nothing to do
but gad about all day, eh?"

"She is lonesome, Jan, and she likes the baby. She
comes calling and I can't just tell her not to."

"She has got a housekeeper to do her work. That Injun *flicka*." He walked to the crib and stared bleakly down at the cooing Eric. Then went to a shelf, took down a bottle, and drew the cork with his teeth. "Let her talk to the Injun. You got work to do. Tell her that."

"*Vaska dig*," she said tartly. "Wash yourself before you start drinking."

Her day's contentment was already dampened. It was the same as always, as it had been through the four years of their marriage. She was glad of the long hard hours that kept him away from daybreak till dusk, here as back in Minnesota. But Jan hated this job of working beef cattle. "Maybe it will seem better in time," she had told him. "Now it's so new." But no; this work was hateful, it was beneath his pride, and he loathed working for anyone else. If not for Cyrus Trapp's generosity, she'd felt impelled to remind him, they'd have been in sorry straits; yet he hadn't voiced a word that might indicate gratitude. That, from Jan, was only to be expected.

What Sofie had not expected was that he'd take to whiskey to dull the edge of his resentment and frustration. Jan had never been much of a drinker except on holidays, and these occasions were really welcome; at such times he would be halfway pleasant, even boisterous sometimes. The kind of drinking he'd done of late, and he indulged every night, only emphasized the surly, taciturn ways that had grown on him year by year. Sometimes, too, he would yell and curse at her, which he'd never done before.

Grumbling, Jan washed up and toweled his head and hands, then got a cup and filled it from the bottle. Sofie noted, not for the first time, the avid tremble in his hand as it brought the cup to his mouth: she knew only too well what it meant. Drink was becoming the same disease in him that it had been in her father. She couldn't count the times in her girlhood that she'd put that luckless, foolish, gentle man to bed with his load of *schnapps* and self-pity. One problem, at least, that hadn't plagued her marriage. Till now.

Jan continued to drink, slumped in a chair. By the time she had supper on the table, he was blearily, morosely

drunk as she couldn't remember seeing him. He stamped
to the table and slid onto the bench, almost knocking it
over. Sofie felt a stab of self-reproach: if she'd had the
meal ready earlier, his nightly intake wouldn't have fallen
on an empty stomach. He sluggishly spooned up the hot
stew, spilling half of each mouthful. Sofie kept her eyes
lowered and ate without appetite.

Someone rapped gently at the puncheon door. Almost
with relief, she hurried to open it. Bowie Candler stood
there; he touched his hat.

"Evening, ma'am. How is the boy?"

He had a swift laconic way of going to the point that dis-
concerted and amused her. "Oh—he is fine now, *fint som
snus*. Won't you come in, Mr. Candler?"

"No'm, thanks. Just dropped by to inquire after the
boy. That sorghum-tallow mix still settling his belly all
right?"

"Oh, yes. But I have not had to give it to him lately. His
belly is all well now."

"That's good." Candler touched his hat again. "Night,
ma'am."

He turned and was gone. Thoughtfully Sofie closed the
door.

What a strange man! She had mentioned his kindness to
Mrs. Trapp, who had given a slight shudder and called
Candler a tough, a tramp, below a decent person's notice,
and said she couldn't understand why Cyrus had hired
him. To Sofie he'd merely seemed abrupt, not a man to
waste words. One who showed his streak of kindness in
perfunctory flashes, as if he shunned the notion of anyone
getting too close to him. Yes, a strange man . . .

As she came back to the table, Jan said heavily:
"What's that fellow want?"

"Didn't you hear?" She sat down and picked up her
spoon. "He asked about the baby. Eric's belly is all better
for that syrup he show me how to make."

"How often does he come around?"

She looked up, startled by the open hostility in his face.
"Why, he has called twice in two weeks. He only ask
about the baby. *Himmel*, what is wrong——"

"I don't want that fellow around here!" His fist banged on the table. "You hear me? Tell him to stay away!"

"You are a *dumskalle*!" She bit her lip in anger. "I tell him nothing. You tell him what you want."

"Maybe you like bums coming around, eh?" His voice slurred drunkenly; he changed to Swedish, spitting out the words. "I will not tolerate a *gris* like that around my wife. Even if she has taken a fancy to pigs."

Sofie got to her feet, feeling the choke of all her stored-up fury and disgust. "You are the pig. Not only a pig but the biggest fool God has made. I will not talk to you."

"No, you will not talk *that way* to me—"

He was on his feet, clumping unsteadily around the table toward her. Beyond his raised hand she saw the mad glitter of his eyes. He hit her hard, flat-handed. The blow swiveled her head; tears jetted from her eyes.

"Clear the table. Then ready yourself for bed. It's time you remembered who your husband is."

He stamped back to the bench, gave his plate a bearlike swipe that sent it clattering to the floor, and went to his chair and collapsed into it. He picked up the bottle. Sofie stood with her head down, hand pressed to her cheek. He could have hit her much harder. But he'd never hit her at all before. Numbly she began to gather the dishes from the table and carry them to the battered wreck pan.

Afterward she went to the crib and gazed down at the sleeping Eric. She felt suddenly forsaken and alone, as she hadn't felt since her father had died. *Min lille gosse.* My little boy. He is all there is.

Jan cleared his throat: it held a warning note.

She went over to the bed that was built into one corner of the room, undressed slowly, and lay down. He came across the room, fumbling along the table for support. He said something hoarse and inarticulate; it ended in a labored belch. As he loomed above her, she turned her mind to a stony nothing. To a blank unfeeling wall. Then shut her eyes as his weight came down on her.

CHAPTER SIX

Brady Trapp threw down his hand of cards with a curse, scraped back his chair, and stood up. He glared at the three crewmen still seated at the table in the smoky, ill-lighted bunkroom. "Deal me out. Had enough of you bastards and your bellystripping for one night."

"You get any more small change burning through your pocket, drop around," one of them drawled. The others laughed.

Brady wished that one of them had taken offense. He was in the mood to hit somebody. But none took offense; they never did. They enjoyed pampering his gaming fever, cracking jokes at his expense, taking the few coins he could dredge up for these penny-ante turns of poker. Momentarily he toyed with a notion of provoking one or a couple of them, he wasn't particular, to a free-for-all. But Faye Nevers's chill stare damped the idea. The foreman lay in his bunk, dragging on a cigarette as he watched. Damn Faye; a man never knew what he was thinking.

Swinging toward the door, Brady halted as it was pushed open and Bowie Candler came in. He had stepped out a while ago. Brady stood flat-footed in Candler's path, not budging. But Candler only crossed his livid stare with an indifferent one, skirted around him, and went to his bunk. Brady tramped out, slamming the door, and headed for the big house. Each time he saw that goddam drifter, the urge to bust his jaw ate deeper.

He shivered at the deepening hint of fall in the chilly night; a familiar worry prodded his mind. Maybe the best solution, he thought glumly, was to throw himself on the old man's mercy. Lucky Jack Hackett in Saltville was getting impatient for his money. Brady's new run of IOUs with him ran over a thousand dollars. If he didn't cough up soon, Hackett would drop the fat in the fire himself by going directly to Cyrus.

Brady dreaded the thought. Better if Cyrus got it straight from him. Not much better, though. Cyrus had coupled his paying off of Brady's debts two years ago with a hard promise. If Brady didn't straighten up and stay straightened, he'd burn his old will and have new instructions drawn up: Chainlink to be sold at public auction after his death and the money split among a half-dozen shirttail relatives. A limited sum to be set aside for Joe-Bob; for Brady, nothing. It was no bluff; Cyrus didn't bluff.

Christ, Christ! There had to be some way out of this goddam pickle. Some way . . .

He tramped onto the back porch and into the kitchen. Tula was washing dishes in the big copper sink; for once Brady forgot to ogle her lustfully. He went to the cookie jar, dipped out a fistful of cookies, seated himself at the kitchen table, and scowled at the floor.

Two voices were raised in the parlor.

Sounded like Cyrus was het up about something and Adah was trying to placate him. He'd been getting proddy as hell lately as those head pains had worsened. Old fool hadn't the sense to see a doctor; too damn proud even to admit anything was wrong. Well, that was his lookout. Just that it was a damn nuisance being wakened every couple nights by his damn groaning.

Brady considered the implications with a sudden calculation. Just how serious *was* whatever the hell was ailing him?

Then he thought bleakly: forget it. Couldn't count on anything for sure regarding Cyrus's illness. One thing certain was that Lucky Jack could pull the roof down on him, Brady, any time. He crammed another cookie in his mouth, all his bitter frustration swelling back now. Again he considered making a clean breast to the old man. Decided once and for all against it. But there had to be *something*—!

Brady's moving jaws stopped. Maybe. He thought of Red Antrim and his crowd of tough nuts. They were a shiftless gang of ne'er-do-wells who spent most of their time hanging around Hackett's and other Saltville dives, gambling, drinking, picking quarrels. They always had a few dollars to carouse with, and rumor had it they engaged in whiskey-selling to the Utes and a few other shady sidelines. Complaints had been lodged from time to time, but nothing was ever found to firmly implicate Antrim's blue-ribbon outfit.

Yet—Brady puckered his brow, remembering how Antrim had bought him a drink last time he'd been in town and then let fall a sly suggestion. Brady, having dropped another bundle at the tables that night, had been in a particularly vile mood. Proceeding to get monumentally drunk, he'd been swimming in a boozy fog when Antrim had made his proposal. Matter of fact, he'd flared up and almost swung on Antrim. Now, trying to recall what Antrim had said, he could only summon up a few dim and disjointed bits. But that little was enough to warm him with a slow excitement.

Brady pondered it carefully. The idea carried a high risk. But it could be the way out if Antrim had meant what he'd said. And he'd be a damn fool to broach such a suggestion if he hadn't.

Adah came briskly into the kitchen, her face paler than usual. "Tula, is there any coffee left from supper?"

"Yes, ma'am. I'll heat it."

"If it's still warm, that won't be necessary."

Adah crossed to the cupboard and took down a tin cup; she went to the stove and felt the coffeepot. Brady watched her with a mild curiosity. His youthful stepmother was easy to look at, but she was too proper and lah-de-dah to stir up in him what Tula, bronze-skinned and free-moving, could. Or that Ekstrom's wife. Man, there was a lush piece. Damned shame she had to be wasted on a miserable hoegrubber.

"You change your brand?" Brady asked idly. "Thought tea was your poison."

Adah filled the cup and turned from the stove; worry glided shadowlike behind her eyes. "It's for your father. I think you should know—he has been drinking."

"Yeah?" Brady began to grin. "You whip him up a jigger of lemonade, Miz Adah?"

"It's no laughing matter. He is drinking whiskey."

Brady stared at her. He swung his weight forward on the chair, clapping his hands on his knees. "You serious?" He saw that she was. "Why, holy hell, he's never taken a drink in his life!"

"You mean in *your* life."

"Never that I seen him, I mean." Brady chuckled. "Never been bluenosed about it; we always had booze around for anyone fancies it. Hell, I never really thought about it."

"You'd better think about it now. Mr. Nevers told me that Cyrus can't take strong drink—not as other men can."

"What's that mean?"

"I think I am finding out." The cup was trembling in Adah's hand; she clasped both hands tight around it. "One of his headaches began a while ago—the pains were particularly severe. He took a drink—then another—to blunt them. It seemed to work. But his whole manner changed —almost violently. His language became—coarse and abusive. And now he is drinking more. Excuse me."

She brushed out of the kitchen. Frowning with curiosity, Brady rose and slowly followed her to the parlor. As he entered, Adah was saying: "Please, Cyrus, take the coffee. It will—"

Cyrus was standing by the walnut sideboard, leaning one spread hand on it. The other hand was fisted around a half-filled tumbler. An open bottle of J.H. Cutter stood at his elbow. His head was bent and now he slowly raised it and heeled around. Brady felt a thin shock. Cyrus's face had a red thickened look; his mouth was half open.

"Cyrus?" Adah said anxiously. "Please—"

His arm swept up and knocked the cup from her hands, spraying coffee across the carpet. Adah gave a small cry and retreated from him. Cyrus stood with legs planted apart, squeezing the tumbler in his fist. He stared at Brady, wagging his head blindly; his words came slow and labored.

"Don't—you sons a bitches—tell me what t' do."

Brady licked his lips. "Listen—Pa. You better slack off before, uh, before you hurt yourself."

"Slack off—y'self—you bastard. Smash y' goddam teeth—clean down y' throat."

Jesus, Brady thought, he don't know me. What the hell? He advanced slowly toward Cyrus, putting out his hand. "You just ease off, Pa. Hand me that glass."

Cyrus swayed on his feet, hands clenching; his eyes glistened with a bloodshot fury. The tumbler cracked in his fist. He squinted and growled, opening his hand; bloody glass shards tinkled on the carpet.

Adah screamed.

Cyrus was already moving in on Brady; his red-dripping hand rose. Brady stumbled wildly away, but his father's powerful backswing caught him flush on the jaw. The blow spun Brady half around; as he fought to catch his balance, both of Cyrus's hands clamped on his neck.

"*Paaa—*"

The word choked off in his throat. Cyrus's great weight carried him backward and hammered him against the wall. Brady tugged at his father's wrists, but he was half stunned as it was, everything blurring away in his sight. The hands squeezed and tightened. His eyes popped; his tongue swelled from his mouth. His last sensibility faded on the sound of Adah screaming again and again. . . .

Adah had never felt such unnerving terror. In these first stunned moments as Cyrus began strangling his son, she could only stand numbly, unbelievingly, and scream. And then Tula came running into the room, a skillet in her hands.

The half-breed girl didn't hesitate. A quick turn and she

was behind Cyrus, rising the heavy skillet two-handed and crashing it down on his hunched back. He let go of Brady and swung around with a roar. Tula darted nimbly away, half-circling from him, holding the skillet ready. Cyrus lurched after her, crazy-eyed.

Adah didn't wait to see what happened next. She threw open the front door and ran across the porch. Fell going down the steps, landing on her hands and knees. She scrambled up and, heedless of shattered dignity for once, started running again, clenching her skirts, panicked sobs tearing in her throat. Cyrus . . . God, oh God, what had happened with him? What—

One blind thought filled her mind: to reach the bunk-house and Faye Nevers. But she'd only covered half the distance when a man loomed out of the dark yard ahead. A startled cry escaped her. And she saw it was Nevers, coming on the run.

He caught her by the arms. "What is it? What's all the——?"

"It's Cyrus—he's crazy, oh, God, he's drinking and he's crazy—"

Already he was brushing past her, heading for the house in great loping strides. He plunged across the porch and through the door. Adah, still holding her muddied skirts, started after him. As she came onto the porch, there was a crash of falling furniture and breaking glass.

Adah stopped in the doorway. Cyrus must have lunged at the retreating Tula, for she stood just beyond him and Cyrus lay sprawled on the upended taboret he'd fallen across, a scatter of broken gimcracks littering the floor. He was heaving laboriously to his feet as Nevers advanced slowly into the room, his voice gentle and placating.

"Easy, Cyrus. Just ease off there—"

Cyrus reared upright, shook himself like a ruffled bear, and glared around. There was no recognition in his eyes; they still wore an unheeding sheen of madness. He growled at Nevers; he started toward him, arms lifting. "Don't!" Adah heard herself cry. But the cry wasn't directed at Cyrus; it was for Nevers, warning him not to get in range of Cyrus's great crushing arms. She knew his strength too well, the strength she'd felt and silently feared even at his gentlest times.

Nevers, though, didn't try to close with him. He moved back and around, easy as a big cat, retreating while he kept quietly talking to Cyrus. He came to a stop by the sofa, and then Cyrus bulled straight for him. Nevers's arm dipped and snatched up an Indian blanket on the sofa; he stepped sideways and whipped the blanket at Cyrus's face as he charged past. It wrapped around Cyrus's head; he jerked to a bellowing halt and grabbed at its muffling folds.

Nevers took one long step, yanking out the pistol rammed in his belt. His arm lashed up and down; the gun-barrel thunked like an ax as it slammed Cyrus at the thick-muscled joining of neck and shoulder. His knees folded; he toppled. His fall shook the room, his forehead banging hard on the floor.

"Oh God," Adah said in an agonized whisper.

Brady was sprawled on his side by the wall, making feeble wheezing sounds. Nevers gave him an impersonal glance. "What happened to the son and heir?"

"Mr. Trapp was choking him," Tula said calmly. "I had to hit Mr. Trapp to stop him."

"That's too bad."

Nevers sounded ambiguous, almost indifferent. He knelt by Cyrus and eased him over on his back. He was out cold, his body heavy and loose. A redness of mashed skin stained his forehead. Nevers raised his head and stuffed a soft pillow under it. He felt of Cyrus's neck and shoulder where he'd struck him and then looked up at the women.

"Hit him pretty hard, but it had to be done. Fetch some cold water and cloths. We'll bring him around and get him to his room."

Tula went out to the kitchen. Her brother Sully appeared at the front door, two other crewmen crowding behind him. "What's happened?"

"It's over," Nevers said. "I had to put Cyrus out. Been drinking. We can handle him all right."

Sully gave a slow nod, as if he knew about Cyrus's problem. He turned to the others. "Let's clear out, boys." They tramped out the door, Sully closing it behind them.

Adah dropped on her knees by Cyrus's head, kneading her underlip between her teeth. It was an effort to hold her voice steady. "Will he be all right?"

"Nothing busted." Nevers gave her a quiet, speculative look. "You all right?"

Her answer was a tight bitter nod. "Oh, yes."

Tula returned with a pot of water and some clean dishtowels. Nevers wet one and laid it on Cyrus's forehead. Brady was sitting up now, his back against the wall. His eyes were still glazed with shock and pain, his neck mottled with darkening bruises; all he could get out were tortured huskings of sound. Tula handed him a wet towel and he shakily held it to his bruised throat.

"Crazy . . . old . . . bastard," he finally managed to whisper. "Near . . . killed me. You better . . . tie . . . him . . . up."

Nevers gave him a pointed look. "You better tie up your jaw. After you thank the girl. Seems she saved your —hide."

Tula glanced up from bandaging Cyrus's cut hand. "I did nothing for him," she said calmly. "I did it for Mr. Trapp."

"*You*——*!*"

Brady's voice failed him. He climbed unsteadily to his feet and stumbled out of the room. His footsteps slogged up the stairs. The bind of fear was unloosening in Adah's throat; her gaze briefly crossed Nevers's and then fell away. His intense yet expressionless eyes made her uneasy.

Cyrus moaned faintly; his bearded lips fluttered open. He began to stir. "Let's get him upstairs," Nevers said. "Girl, lend me a hand. Mrs. Trapp, you go on up and light a lamp."

Adah's legs felt shaky as she ascended the staircase. Coming onto the landing, she could hear Brady's soft groans from his room. Joe-Bob's door swung open; he stood shirtless in the lamplight, blinking and buttoning his trousers over his underwear. He ran a hand through his tousled hair, yawned, and gaped at her.

"Hey, what's goin' on?"

Unbelievable, Adah thought. Sleeping was Joe-Bob's foremost pastime and he had slumbered through most of the commotion downstairs. "Nothing," she said. "Go back to bed." She entered Cyrus's room and felt for the matches and lamp on the commode. As a sickly glow of light spread across the room and its almost ascetic furnishings, she felt a hard knot of revulsion form in her throat. *He* slept here. Except for those times, mercifully rare of late, when he visited her room. This one reflected its tenant: rough, direct, uncompromising in his strength.

Adah threw back the bedcovers on the narrow bed; Nevers and Tula came in, supporting Cyrus's drag-footed hulk. He was muttering incoherently, his eyes strange and opaque. They laid him on the cot; Nevers wrestled off his boots. Joe-Bob came to the doorway and peered anxiously at his father, but didn't say anything.

"Best leave him as is," Nevers said. "Can't be sure how he'll be as he comes around, but my guess is he'll just sleep it off." He glanced at Adah. "You want, I can send a couple men to sit guard."

"That won't be necessary. He should be all right now." The calmness of her own voice surprised her. "And Brady and Joe-Bob are nearby."

She pulled the covers over Cyrus and turned down the lamp. Joe-Bob had entered his brother's room; Adah heard his hushed question, Brady's whispery snarled reply, as she and Nevers and Tula descended to the parlor. Tula righted the overturned taboret and began picking up the bits of broken china. Adah felt like crying. Her treasured figurines, all in fragments. Maybe she would cry later.

As Tula exited from the parlor, Adah met Nevers's searching look. "I don't know," she murmured. "I just don't know."

"Get him to see a doctor."

"But he won't. I told you."

"Try again. You can see how out of hand the situation's got." He nodded at the liquor sideboard. "Get rid of all the hooch. Throw it out. That for a start. Then talk to him."

"I'll—try."

"You're the only one has a beggar's chance of making him listen." He moved closer, towering in front of her. "I know Cyrus. Whatever you say to him, even if he gets mad, no need to fear he'll be like that again. Not without booze in him."

"I know. That doesn't worry me. It's just— Can you guess how it's been? Half the night, every night, listening to him toss and moan? I don't think I can stand very much more."

"You know what I think? You're tougher than you know."

A smile turned up his lip corners; small lights kindled in his eyes. As if for this moment he'd let his careful guards slip to show her more than he ever had. But I knew all along, she thought, feeling the overpowering thrust of his masculinity as she had before. She felt her face go warm. Heat tendriled in her veins; her breasts tingled. If he hadn't glimpsed behind her prim composure as yet, God, how could he fail to now?

"You needn't worry. I will be all right."

He half-raised a hand. Didn't quite touch her arm. Turned wordlessly and went out the door, closing it gently behind him. Adah stood rubbing her wrists. A light shiver ran through her. Then she straightened, her mouth firming, and went upstairs again. As she entered Cyrus's room, he raised his head. His eyes were sick and groggy, but rational now.

"My good God." His lips hardly moved. "What—what happened down there?"

"It's all right now, dear. You had too much to drink."

Cyrus groaned. "Any at all's too much. My God." His hand reached and caught hold of hers. "Honey, I can't take a drink, never could, I———"

"Mr. Nevers has explained that."

"If I'd hurt you. If I'd hurt anybody . . ."

"Nobody's hurt. Dear, will you listen to me now? I want you to see a doctor. I can't take any more of what's been. Do you understand?"

He was silent a long while, staring at the beamed ceiling. Finally: "Know where I was first two days of round-up? Why I didn't go out with the crew?"

"You went to Saltville. On business, you said."

"Business. I seen Doc Rawls. Stayed over a night so's he could make all the tests he wanted."

"And what—?"

"Wasn't sure of anything. Said I'd need to see a specialist in Denver. I been putting it off."

"Then Cyrus, please . . ." Her voice turned softly vehement. "Don't put it off any longer! Not one more day."

"Don't mean to. I'll ride to Saltville tomorrow. Take the train from there."

Watching him, she felt an unexpected surge of affection. Not for the man she had tried to love and couldn't. For the guardian and benefactor whose kindly fortitude had borne her up through her father's final illness and afterward. What she felt for Cyrus Trapp the man was pity: the awful pity of a giant in pride and strength being steadily reduced to a helpless pain-wracked ruin.

"Cyrus—didn't he have *any* idea?"

"Doc? He just couldn't be sure."

It sounded evasive, Adah thought.

"Will find out in Denver what's what." Cyrus's lips twitched; his face looked grayish and old. "Doc wanted to give me laudanum for when the pains come. Wouldn't take it. But I will do whatever the Denver man so says. You got my word to that."

CHAPTER SEVEN

"They been pushing 'em through right here," said Sully.
"Through Yellow Pass and back into the Breaks. We
found some heavy sign there and nowhere else."

Standing by the big map of Chainlink range that was
tacked to the wall above Cyrus's desk, he traced a finger
across the northwest corner. Cyrus leaned forward and
peered through his glasses, then eased back in his chair.
"Well, that would figure right. There are damn few places
you could run beef through the Elks if you want to make a
northerly market. Then it would have to be fifty miles to
Craigie or over east to Sundog."

Sully nodded. "You drove your herds up to Craigie
years ago, didn't you?"

"Sure, before the railroad run a spur line over to Saltville. All the big outfits hereabouts did. But we swung way
west around the Elks. Long drive to a railhead, but you
couldn't push a sizable herd straight across all that mean
country in the Breaks. Bust your cows' legs all to hell, run
a hundred pounds off each one. But move 'em in small
bunches like these jacklegs been doing, and if a man ain't
in no hurry, no reason it couldn't be done."

"So now we start hunting the Breaks?" Sully asked.

Cyrus grunted. "You don't know that country like I do,
boy. Take us months to comb it all. Once they're through
Yellow Pass, the thieves can scatter their sign to hell and
gone. Must be holding the cattle in one place, but they
could reach it by a dozen different ways. There's rock

stretches they can drive across and cover their trail easy, long as they only take a few head at a time."

Heaving out of his chair, he paced slowly around his office, rolling a well-chewed cigar between his jaws. Sully gave Bowie, who was slacked in a chair by the door, a wry glance. Both men were dirty, unshaven, dog-tired. For three days they'd been scouring the wild and rugged country along Chainlink's north range in an effort to turn up something certain about the thieves' operation.

Chainlink line riders had begun to notice signs of strange horsemen a couple of weeks back, sign that was scattered but a lot of it. They had been pushing cattle. A ranch this size, whose north boundary lay along the Elk Breaks, a shallow, barren, broken terrain that slashed deep between mountains, was bound to be plagued with penny-ante thieving by backhill ne'er-do-wells. This was different. Only the next range tally would show the loss with any accuracy, but the sign which kept cropping up indicated steady strikes. No large single ones, just quick drive-offs of small bunches, furtively and by night, but they were adding up.

Cyrus paced heavily, scowling at the floor. "Gentlemen, somebody has put some thought behind this. They are hitting at irregular times and at wide-apart spots. Cutting chances of getting caught by breaking up the pattern. That is clear, but other things ain't."

"Like how they mean to peddle the stuff," Bowie said idly.

"Yeh. We got bummers hereabouts who'll steal a cow or so for the beef or for hides and tallow. But these bastards got to be stealing for profit. Suppose they vent the brands and try to sell the beeves at Sundog or Craigie. Even if the buyer himself is crooked as a dog's hind leg, he knows the yards'll demand a bill of sale from the original owner. They don't get it, they will hold the beeves, wire the owner, and credit him for the cattle."

"Ain't like you to wait till that happens," Sully observed dryly.

"Ain't likely it will, either," Cyrus said impatiently.

"These people know the Breaks country, which argues they are local. Maybe a clutch of them spindly-shanked hill trash who've thrown in together. Maybe some hard-case crew like Red Antrim's. Whoever, they got to know they can't peddle vented Chainlink stock in this part of the territory and not get caught. Argues they got something up their sleeves I can't rightly tell as yet."

Sully dropped into Cyrus's swivel chair, extended his legs, and crossed his boots. "Fine. So you tell the sheriff. But Sam Beamis can't do more'n we can."

"That's right. He'd have to pay a couple deputies to do the same and no telling how long it'll take."

"What you got in mind?"

"Catching 'em in the act," Cyrus said flatly. "We don't know where they'll hit next or where they been taking the cattle. But they been moving 'em through Yellow Pass till now. All right, when they try it again, we'll have a couple men up by the pass."

Sully raised his brows. "They could be up there a long time."

Cyrus nodded, rubbing a hand along his temple. It was a thoughtful gesture, not an anguished one. Sometimes, like now, his eyes were clear, his mind as keen as ever. Other times he seemed stuporous and dull, moving like a man drunk or drugged. The crew had done a lot of quiet speculating about it. Everyone was sure that Cyrus's abrupt trip to Denver had been for other than business reasons. Those times he was heavy-eyed and slow-moving, they figured, he was full of drugs he'd been given for the head pains. But nobody was sure what his real trouble was.

"It's no job for daisies," Cyrus went on. "The men'll have to watch day and night, spelling each other. They'll have to stay out of sight. No fire. They'll have to keep a cold camp, and there's been an ice scum on the water bucket every morning for a week now. They want to cook their grub, one'll have to move a mile or so away from the pass and lay a fire. Smoke seen hard by the pass could undo everything. One man's got to stay on guard all times. Hell, you wouldn't want the job."

Sully made a wry face. "Sounds like a bitch of a stand."

"It will be. That's why I'm asking, not ordering. I want these people trailed if they show up. Want to find where they're holding the cattle. I want the men too. But we can take 'em later if we know where they are. All the same, you could run into gunplay."

Sully nodded, modestly studying the toe of his boot. "Can't be no question who's the best tracker on your crew. And a mean shot to boot. Seems I'm volunteering."

"I figured you was too big-headed not to." Cyrus swiveled a glance at Bowie. "What about you?"

"What about me?"

Cyrus snorted softly. "Forget it, Candler. You don't want to go on a stand like this one. Man could get his toes frostbit. Even catch a bullet. Like I said, it's no job for a daisy."

Bowie felt a stirring of anger. The old bastard. He knew exactly how to lay it to each man who worked for him. How to touch a man's pride, if he had any. "I'll take it, and the hell with you."

"Good," Cyrus said blandly. "You boys get a night's sleep and head for the pass first thing tomorrow. Take enough grub for two weeks. I'll tell Gonzales to have it packed and ready in the morning." He paused. "One thing more. We'll keep what's been said here between us three. Anyone asks, I'm sending you up to our east line shack. That's a goodly ways from the Pass."

Leaving the office by an outside door at the house's southwest corner, Bowie and Sully headed for the bunkhouse. It was late in the day; a curdled-looking sunset was souring in the west and a hard wind was blowing off the peaks. Bowie shivered and rammed his hands deep in the pockets of his mackinaw, thinking bleakly of the October days and nights that lay ahead. An open fireless camp in the high country. Rain, freezing sleet, maybe snow, before the job was over. Or maybe he'd get lucky and catch a bullet. Christ!

"Damned old fart," he muttered. "Knows right where to grab a man when he's got a mean job wants doing."

"Well," Sully grinned, "you're learning."

"What I should of learned first of all was keep my goddam mouth shut. I dropped mention I'd trailed and hunted horses for a living, so I get sent out with you to round up sign on them rustlers. Shitkicker and me ain't warmed our heels in three days, now this."

Sully laughed and shook his head. "Leave it to you to give the buckskin a name like Shitkicker."

"Why not? Damn good name for a horse."

They cut past the weathered log house that the Ekstroms were occupying. Sofie Ekstrom was in the yard removing her day's wash from the clothesline, her skirt furling in the wind below a bulky coat. She waved and called, "Hello, Mr. Candler," the wind almost snatching her words away.

Bowie nodded and tugged his hatbrim. "How's the baby?"

"What? What did you say?"

"I said, *how's the baby*?"

"Oh, oh. *The baby is fine—fint som snus!*"

Bowie's mouth stretched in a grin he couldn't stop. "That's fine."

"What?"

"I said that's fine. *Fine as snuff!*"

"Oh, *ja!*"

Her bright laughter spilled out. And quickly stopped; she turned back to her task as the cabin door opened. Ekstrom stood in the doorway, legs braced wide. His face was red and angry; he yelled something at her in Swedish.

"That son of a bitch got born with a sour belly," Sully observed as they tramped on. "You notice that big bruise on her jaw?"

Bowie nodded and didn't say anything.

Yellow Pass was a funnel-shaped wedge in the deep foothills below the first peaks, broad at its mouth and tapering back to a narrow cleft hardly wide enough to drive single cows through. But it gave access to all sorts of possible trails in the wild Breaks beyond. Bowie and Sully bivouacked high on a timbered bluff to one side of the wide canyon mouth. Their camp was in a sheltered pocket back in the trees, but they kept a vigil from a granite shelf that gave a clean view of the pass and the rolling country that faced it, the edge of Chainlink's north range.

The days passed slowly. It was a damned boring stand to be stuck on, but at least they were favored by fairish weather. The early fall rains had passed; the wooded ridges were a vista of molten color, scarlets and russets and golds. The dawns were nippy with frost that yielded reluctantly to the pale sunlight of later morning. Afternoons were tolerably warm or cool, but soon gave way to the swift chilly twilights. Much of the time Bowie shivered on watch, hunkered on the shelf wrapped in three blankets, and he shivered off to restless sleep between watches. Could of been down in the border country by now, ran his frequent thought. God damn!

Still, it wasn't all cold and boredom. Only one man was needed on watch; the other could use his off hours to prowl for game, so long as he did it away from the pass. Cyrus had cautioned them not to fire a gun close by it. And Sully was a pretty good man to be stuck up here with, Bowie admitted to himself. They worked well as a team, a fact that he guessed Cyrus Trapp had given due consideration.

After five days, the thieves still hadn't tipped their hand.

"Don't see why in hell they don't make a move," Bowie grumbled. "They drove off some beeves in the pass not two days before we found the sign. And plenty of tracks that was made before then. They was using this way regular. Goddammit, I wonder if we got taken notice of some way."

"Not likely," said Sully. "No way them shorthorns could spot us before we see them. We ain't fired a shot or made a smoke inside a mile since we took up the stand. No way it could leak out neither, with just Cyrus knowing about us. Likely these jaspers are just playing it cagey. They was hitting fast and hard for maybe a couple weeks. Now they slacked off for a time."

"Maybe they got so cagey they quit. We're likely freezing our asses off up here for nothing."

"Ain't for nothing. Paleface soft. Teachem to count his blessings."

"Go to hell."

Sully shook his head sadly. "Sometimes I think paleface not appreciate good company."

"I do. That's the trouble."

They were squatting side by side on the shelf in the gray light of a late afternoon. Wet needles of sleet slapped against their clothing and stung their bent faces. Might have known the last week's weather had been too good to last, Bowie thought disgustedly.

"You don't fool me, white brother. I know that under your stony hide there beats a heart of solid flint." Sully yawned and peered at the sky. It was roiling with great lead-colored clouds driving ominously out of the north. "Hell might not be a bad place to winter, at that. Devil keeps a warm hearth. And from the look, I'd say we are going to get a whole lot of weather dumped on us before nightfall."

Sofie Ekstrom kept fighting sleep. Her eyes were heavy and redly throbbing. No matter how hard she tried to stay alert and stiffly upright on the hard straight-backed chair, her mind would start drifting in a saffron fog, her body would cant sideways. Then she would catch herself. God, don't let me sleep. Don't . . .

Aware of the door softly opening behind her, she lifted her head. Adah Trapp had entered the room. Tiptoeing over to the bed, she gazed down at Eric. Touched his forehead, which Sofie knew was dry and hot. Adah looked searchingly at her now.

"Mrs. Ekstrom."

"Uh?"

"Please—why don't you lie down a while? You haven't had a wink of sleep in two days and nights."

"No—I do not sleep."

Adah frowned with a kind of vexed compassion. "At least let me bring in a comfortable chair for you."

"No," Sofie said dully. "Then I go to sleep for sure. I must be ready if he need me."

From the first it had seemed very important that she stay awake. Eric might need her any moment, yet there was really nothing she could do. Nothing. Only a dim and dogged reflex held her stubbornly by her baby's side, listening to his weak, faint fits of coughing and the even more ominous silences between.

Adah said gently, insistently, "But you can't well tend him, don't you see, when you're so terribly exhausted. A few hours' sleep would do wonders for you. Tula and I can keep watch as well as you, and let you know at once if anything happens."

Adah had made the argument before. Sofie couldn't remember how many times before and didn't care. She moved her head in negation. "No. I must be here then."

"That is foolish," Adah said sharply. "Look at you, all but falling off that chair. Could you stay on if you weren't holding on?"

Sofie's hands were clenched on either side of her chair seat. She raised one hand and looked at it dull-eyed. It was swollen at the knuckles, welted red across the palm from the hard-cornered wood. She felt her body sway heavily and grabbed at the chair edge again.

"I guess I would fall." The matter-of-fact words made a trailing hum in her ears.

If only she had not left Eric alone. That single guilty refrain kept stabbing through her dead exhaustion. But the baby had seemed well, so well and healthy these three weeks past, that she'd failed to realize he couldn't throw off his frail sickliness since birth so quickly. But *himmel*, he had been on his way to getting better. And then suddenly, so suddenly, it was all undone.

Only two days and nights? The nightmare of waiting seemed endless. It had begun so thoughtlessly, so easily, her leaving Eric alone for the very first time. Mr. Trapp had given the crew a day off and all had gone to town except for Jan. But she and Jan had quarreled about something, *ja*, the drinking it was, and he had cuffed her several times and then, since there was no more liquor in the house, had followed the others to town. Though glad enough to have him gone, she'd become restless and worried as the day wore toward evening. She'd decided to visit the big house for a brief chat with Mrs. Trapp. For once she hadn't taken Eric along; as he was sound asleep, she would not disturb him, and she'd be back in a few minutes.

The storm had been brewing as she'd left the cabin. Not much of a storm then: some sleety drizzle and a little wind, and she'd thought nothing of it. Her chat with Mrs. Trapp had lasted a bit longer than she'd intended, but she'd excused herself in reasonable time and headed back for the cabin. Hurrying because the storm had suddenly picked up, sleet lashing in fierce spurts at her bare head. Quick alarm rose in her as, nearing the cabin, she saw the door hanging ajar and banging in the wind. *Gud bevara*, how could this happen? She'd made a point of securing the latch firmly.

Running inside, she'd almost stumbled over Jan. Face down on the floor, dead drunk and passed out. Returning before her, he'd either failed to close the door or had left the latch unfastened. Wind was caroming savagely around the room, drawn by hairline cracks in the old building, blasting sleety charges of cold and ice and wet over everything. But Sofie's eyes were all for the crib where Eric lay in his damp chill blankets and a whipping draft, coughing and crying. Crying for a mother who hadn't been there. That was all she could think as she'd stripped away damp bedding in a rush to make the child warm and dry. It was quickly done, and even in her weeping, angry dismay with herself and Jan, she hadn't felt fear. Not then, not yet.

Eric had quieted down, his coughing ebbed, he slept. Yet it was a twitching, restless sleep; his skin was touched by fever. So, worriedly, Sofie had stayed up by his crib all night. She'd left Jan where he was, snoring off his drunk on the floor, but a bitter resolve had burned in her mind. She would not live with such a man any longer. It had been bad enough with her father, a gentle-natured drunk. But this brute, this *gris*! He'd beaten her for the last time, but that was nothing to the endangering of his son's life. No. *Her* son. All hers now; she would take him away, anywhere that was far from Jan Ekstrom.

But Eric's fever had worsened during the night. By morning Sofie was in a near panic. As usual the Trapps had been helpful and solicitous, Cyrus sending a man to Saltville for the doctor, Adah insisting that the baby be moved to the big house again. And Sofie's long vigil had begun. Now she remembered the doctor's grim look and words. Croup. Grippe. Complications. The fever would build to a crisis; then they would know. But Sofie was sure she already knew. Her baby's life was slipping away, ebbing before her eyes as the hours wore on, and there was nothing she could do.

Again Adah was speaking with quiet insistence. "Sofie, listen to me. You must get some rest. If you're to be of any help to your baby . . ."

She turned the sense of these words sluggishly over in her mind. Yes. Mrs. Trapp was right. Only her twitching nerves were keeping her from sleep now. Sodden with exhaustion, she wasn't merely useless, she was a danger. Someone fresh and alert should keep the watch. She raised her eyes to Adah's.

"You call me if there is anything? You promise this?"

"Of course. You're being sensible now. My room is next to this one and you can rest there. Come along."

Unsteady, stumbling a little, she let Adah help her into the next room. The moment she hit the soft bed, her senses blacked away. She slept totally and dreamlessly.

Someone was shaking her by the shoulder. Sofie's mind fought stuporously against that imperative hand. She wanted only this warm fog of sleep. Then the shock of remembrance came; she sat up wildly.

"Eric—"

Adah stood there, her face stricken and helpless. She said nothing. There was no need. The look on her face said it. . . .

Sofie remembered little of afterward. She thought that she'd only been asleep for minutes, but Adah said no, she had slept for many hours, and during that time there had seemed no change in Eric's condition. She or Tula had stayed by him constantly. It was over very suddenly. One minute he still burned with fever. The next he was gone.

Sofie sat in the Ekstrom cabin by herself, not sure how she had gotten here, only that she'd insisted on being by herself. She shivered in the cold room. Thought of her shawl, but made no move to get it. Just sat and stared at the empty crib. She had not cried, she did not cry now. Her body and mind stayed strangely frozen.

The door creaked open. Cold air poured into the room and it roused her slightly. Then she saw Jan Ekstrom on the threshold. His face was ugly, furtive, bloated. He did not look at her. As he stumbled toward the bed, she smelled the heavy reek of whiskey.

She got slowly to her feet. Something broke in her like ice slivering to pieces. She began to tremble.

"Murderer!" She rushed suddenly at him, her hands up and fisted. "Murderer, murderer, *murderer!*"

She beat crazily at the flushed smear of his face. He gave a hoarse cry and stumbled back to the door. She followed him, beating on his head and shoulders, screaming the word over and over. Then he was out the door and weaving blindly away across the yard.

Sofie sank down against the door, her weight pressing it shut. She dropped her forehead against the rough wood. "Murderer," she whispered. Then the grief spilled out of her in deep, wrenching sobs.

CHAPTER EIGHT

Cyrus felt tired to his bones as he slumped into his old swivel chair. He took off his neatly blocked Stetson and dropped it on the desk top, and stared at it. What the hell, he wondered, was the use of it all? He let his weary glance rove around his office and touch its familiar objects, finding no comfort in them. Life. What did it mean, if it meant anything? Hell. He was full up with living.

He couldn't remember feeling so depressed. He hadn't been able to refuse Mrs. Ekstrom's request that he say the words over her baby. He'd suggested sending for the circuit preacher, who was due in Saltville around now, but she wouldn't hear of it. She'd wanted Cyrus to say the words for the departed. He knew them well. Had said them before. How many times over the long years? For a daughter. A wife. Crewmen who had died in Chainlink's service and whose faces he no longer remembered. Most of them dead before their time, victims of a country that took its toll quickly and savagely, slowly and savagely. Always unmercifully.

Maybe you'll be the next, Cyrus thought. Maybe that was the thing. God, what had happened to his old vitality these last few weeks? Even the slow walk to the little cemetery back of the east ridge, walking behind Sofie Ekstrom and the small pine box in her arms, standing while two crewmen dug the grave, and the dreary walk back here, had left him feeling drained and useless. He felt a dull pain stir in his temples and gripped his knees, waiting. But the pain subsided. Sometimes it still did. A seldom thing these days without recourse to the needle.

Cyrus roused himself with a self-chiding grunt. He still had strength, and duties to perform while he had it. There'd be a time—but cross that bridge when it came up. He stretched his arms, swore mildly at the unaccustomed constrictions of a broadcloth suit, then shucked off the coat and swept his hat aside. Flipping open an account book, he scanned the figures. But it was hard to concentrate over the blurry spotting of his eyes which he couldn't —any longer—lay to a need for new glasses. Restively he swung his chair to face a window, clamping his jaws against his aches. A ride. Good long ride. Goddammit, why not? Hell with taking it easy. Hell with medical warnings that likely wouldn't stretch his time by a single day. Take that ride while he could. Might be his last.

He reached for his hat and was pushing out of his chair when someone knocked lightly at the outside door. Cyrus slacked back. "Come in," he growled.

Sofie Ekstrom entered. She closed the door and stood with her back to it. She had on the black dress she'd worn to the funeral. Her face was haggard, pale, numbly calm, as it had been ever since he'd first seen it after her baby's death night before last. But there was something else in it too. Something hard as glass that Cyrus sensed might shatter like glass. He glanced at the worn carpetbag she held before her, both hands clenched around the handle.

"What's this, now?"

"I am leaving. I want to thank you for your kindness, Mister Trapp, and I ask one more thing if it's not too much."

Cyrus stroked a finger along his jaw. "Leaving, eh? Kind of sudden, that."

"No. I think so before, even before—" She checked herself. "Don't, I ask you, try to stop me."

"Nobody'll stop you."

"Maybe you will have a man hitch a wagon and take me to Saltville. It is trouble, but I will give you no more."

"There's no trouble here you brought," Cyrus said dryly, quietly. "You just hold off a minute, Missus, and hear me out. You want to leave then, I will drive you in myself." Heaving himself from his chair, he paced a half-circle. He felt her eyes waiting; they wore a bright glaze that made him think of blue china scrubbed to a shine. Go easy now, he told himself.

"He still sleeping it off? Your husband?"

She didn't reply, which was answer enough. Ekstrom had stayed drunk all yesterday. She'd refused to remain in the shack with him and had spent the night in the big house.

"Where you plan to go? Back to Minnesota?"

"There is a railroad out of Saltville, eh?"

"Yeah, a spur line. Train comes there maybe twice a week. You'll have to lay over at the hotel. You got money?"

She was silent a moment. "I can find work in Saltville for a couple weeks maybe."

Cyrus's grunt expressed doubt. "You got people in Minnesota?"

"In Douglas County, neighbors—that were."

"No kin? A brother maybe? Sister?"

"No. There is nobody. I make my way. I have always."

"Maybe," Cyrus said gently, "you had better give it a little more time."

Sofie's clenched hands whitened at the knuckles. "Maybe you think I ever forgive what that man did?"

"All I'm thinking, it's not a thing to decide now."

"I will not live with him any more. Never."

"Nobody's all to blame for any one thing that happens. You lived long enough to know that, Sofie."

"It is not only this, there are other things." A nerve twitched in her cheek. "These you know nothing of."

Cyrus gave a weary nod. He hadn't failed to notice the bruises on her face from time to time. "All right. But take it slow. You can't go kiting off with no plans. There's a spare room upstairs. You go up and rest yourself. You can stay there or move back into the other place when he's gone."

"Gone?" Her eyes flickered. "You will make him go?"

"Up in the hills, sure. He can work a line job for awhile.

Be out of your hair that long. Then we'll see. How long's he been this way? I mean the booze."

"It started when we came here," she said dully. "Never before."

"All right, give him a spell. There'll be no booze where he's going. Time and roughing it some'll take it out of his system."

"That will not change the man."

"You know that, eh? What's happened might."

"I don't know. I don't want to. . . ." Her voice trailed off. The bright edge of masked hysteria had faded; her face was dull and indifferent now. But docile.

"Thing is, you are going to wait. You're in no shape for thinking on what's to be done. How long since you had a good sleep? Go on up to the room and lay down." Cyrus tugged his beard, nodding a little. "Go on. You don't think about things any more for a spell, Missus. Then we'll talk again."

Bowie and Sully were on the lookout ledge above Yellow Pass when two riders came jogging across the humpy plains below the foothills. Bowie spotted them first and directed Sully's attention, pointing an arm as the half-breed trained his field glasses.

"Paleface got Injun eye," said Sully. "One's Cyrus. The other—damned if it ain't the Swenska."

"Ekstrom?"

They exchanged puzzled glances, then moved back off the ledge. They were waiting in the clearing where they'd located their dry cold camp as the horsemen, having ascended the ridge along the old game trail that led to its summit, gigged their mounts into view out of the trees.

Cyrus dismounted, growling, "Seems I caught you just sojering around in camp."

"Do tell," Sully said dryly. "We only spotted you about a half mile off. You come to take over the watch, you're welcome to it."

"You wouldn't be that lucky. I only brought you some company." Cyrus came over to them, rubbing his big hands briskly together. "*Is* cold up here, ain't it?"

"I'm surprised you noticed," Sully said sardonically.

Standing in front of them now, Cyrus lowered his voice. "The Swede's in a bad way. His baby is dead."

Both men just looked at him, then Sully said quietly, "Christ." They watched Ekstrom drop heavily out of his saddle and stand with his head sunk between his hunched shoulders. His face was blotched and puffy and sick-looking.

"It's a bad thing," Cyrus said grimly. He told them briefly what had happened. "Don't know if it's the best thing to bring him up here, but couldn't think of no better. Either of you got any booze in your possibles, I want you to get rid of it."

"We had any redeye on hand," Sully said dourly, "it would of disappeared a good while back."

Cyrus grunted. "Want you men to keep an eye on the Swede. Keep him busy if you can." He motioned at the pack horse. "Brought you some more grub. I take it nothing's happened."

"Nary sign of a long-looper," Sully said. "We been wondering if they got wind of us some way. Don't see how, though. We been following your orders. No fire, no shooting. So there's no word on vented cattle being put up for sale."

Cyrus shook his head. "Maybe those jacklegs quit the raids, but they got to be holding the cattle somewhere. Maybe back in the brush till spring comes. In that case, no use leaving you boys sitting up here till your asses freeze."

"We been wondering if that might occur to you."

"Well, I did allow how tender your sensibilities are. Keep the watch a few more days, then we'll see. Unload the pack horse, Sully, and tell Ekstrom to help you." Sully looked dubious, and Cyrus said: "He'll take your orders right enough. He is acting kind of strange, but that should wear off. Just don't let him sit around and don't pamper him."

Sully walked over to Ekstrom and spoke to him. Without a word the Swede turned to the pack horse, bracing the tarp-wrapped supplies on its back while Sully loosened the diamond hitch. Cyrus watched a moment, then turned to Bowie. "Come along, Candler. Want to see your lookout."

Bowie tramped ahead, leading the way through some scrub trees. They stepped out on the flat spur of rock jutting above the pass. Wind cut icily at their faces: sunlight touching the peaks belied the chill of this late fall day. Cyrus stood with hands rammed in his mackinaw pockets, gazing into the pass.

"Nice view from here. Ain't been up on this rim in years."

"You ought to squat on it for a week some time," Bowie told him.

Cyrus grinned. Bowie thought that he looked definitely older, strangely tired, as if some part of him had burned out. And Cyrus's next words, quiet and abrupt, surprised him.

"How old are you, Candler?"

"Crowding thirty-seven."

"Hell, you're just touching the prime years. You a native Texan?"

"You mean was I born there, no. Georgia."

"Huh. How you come by a good Texican name like Bowie?"

"Same reason my two older brothers got named Houston and Crockett. Pap got to Texas just once, in the Mexican War."

Cyrus seemed to be in a talkative way. Bowie felt a difference in him that went deeper than surface. His manner was reflective, sort of; his gaze seemed weary and far away. In answer to his questions, Bowie said that his Pap had always wanted to return to Texas one day, but had never made it. There'd been a farm, a wife and kids, a life of hardscrabble drudgery just to make ends meet.

"Sounds like your pa kept that one dream alive," Cyrus said musingly. "Man does that. He needs a dream."

"Pap died at forty-five," Bowie said tonelessly. "Milk sickness took Ma when I was two. Dreams didn't do old Pap a lick of good."

"You're wrong, Candler. Just one good dream is what

keeps a man going. Me, I made mine a reality right enough, but I still say the struggle was the best of it."

"Easy to say when a man's made his."

"Easy, hell," Cyrus growled. "I was damn near thirty before I got started on mine. Had made good money selling broncs I caught and rough-busted till my bones lost their green. Man gets his fill of cracked ribs and busted fingers. Maybe I had one edge, but it sure-hell didn't seem like one at the time. I'd a been a spending fool except that I couldn't go see the elephant like the other boys done. So I saved up."

Bowie eyed him. "What edge?"

"I couldn't take spirits."

"Come again?"

"Few swigs of tanglefoot'd turn me into a wild man. That was my edge. I'd become a damn lunatic, a holy terror. Time was mothers kept their kids offen the streets when they heard Cyrus Trapp was in town. Well—" Cyrus took his hands from his pockets and held them open. "Happen I finally killed a man with these. That's when I swore off for good. Turned out best for me, all right, but that never helped the poor bastard I beat to death. Whatever you get in this life, boy, you pay for. One way or the other, you pay."

"So it don't hardly seem worth it."

"That's bullshit," Cyrus said flatly. "Near got thinking that way myself, and it's bullshit. Just as long as a man can keep the candle going is worth it. Only—" He shoved his hands back in his pockets and squinted across the valley. "A man wants to leave something behind him too."

"I'd say you're leaving a hell of a lot."

Cyrus jerked out a dry chuckle. "Sure. Land, maybe? The land was here before I set eyes on it. All I got is paper to show tenancy, you might say. Buildings, cattle, money? Couple sons to leave it all to? A wife? Adah can't run Chainlink. All I can leave her is enough money to see she'll be comfortably off. And I can tell you right now that when I'm gone, Adah will go back to the city. Joe-Bob can't take hold. And Brady, it'll run through his fingers like sand."

"You're talking like you—"

Cyrus's gaze sharpened on him, and Bowie broke off.

"Like I might be gone tomorrow?" Cyrus grinned mirthlessly. "The boys in the bunkhouse been speculating, have they? Well, that's the fact of it, Candler. You're a close-mouthed sort; you won't be needing to pass any of this on." He hunched his shoulders as if against a deeper chill than the biting wind. "There's a thing growing on my brain. Have got the pain checked for now. Laudanum, opiate hypodermics. But I look to go hard when the time comes. Maybe I won't wait for it. No telling what a man will do, come to that."

Bowie didn't know what to say, and after a moment Cyrus went on: "Maybe it all evens out somewhere. A man likes to think so. There's a lot to think on when his time comes. My boys, now. Maybe I was too hard on 'em when they was tads. Expected more'n they could give and whipped their asses raw when they couldn't match up. Now—maybe I gone way too soft, like Brady says. Happens when a man comes to look for peace with himself." He turned his glance full on Bowie. "It don't shine much when a man's alone, Candler."

Bowie shrugged. "You got to choose for yourself, I reckon."

"You think you do. Always figured a man makes his chances. Always lived by that thought. But a man alone don't stand a chance. Remember what I say." He looked away. "Woman to share with is a pleasant thing. But not one with different ways. Not one half your age either. It don't work worth a damn."

Cyrus fell silent, staring across the valley as if drinking it in for the last time. Then he turned and tramped back to the clearing, and Bowie followed. Cyrus took Sully aside now; they conversed for some minutes, and then Cyrus motioned Bowie over.

"If anything breaks," he told them, "you boys send Ekstrom back with word. You two take care of any rough doings. I'm thinking of his wife."

Sully glanced at Bowie, then said casually, "How's she bearing up?"

"She wanted to leave him. Leave Chainlink. I made her see that idea wasn't for the best on her own account, but rest of it's up to Ekstrom. If we can fetch him back dry and straightened up some'at, it'll be worth it."

"Sure," Sully said.

They watched Cyrus mount and ride away into the trees. Thinking back on their talk, Bowie felt only a little puzzled. Cyrus had some private words for Sully too, but Bowie had already concluded that Sully was more of a son to him that his own sons. Speaking frankly with a pilgrim he hardly knew was something else. Yet thinking it over, Bowie realized it wasn't so strange after all. For this had been a lonely man telling his feelings to a man who could take something kindred from his words. *Remember what I say*, Cyrus had said. And Bowie knew he would.

Before the day was out, Ekstrom was completely sobered. The high chill air was a crisp bracer to his whiskeyshot system. But it didn't improve his disposition by a jot. Earlier he had dulled the savage edge of his remorse with drinking. As he began rousing from his lethargy, he was a man brooding and balky and trigger-tempered.

Bowie got the first hint of trouble to come when he took Ekstrom with him to the place where he and Sully had been cooking their grub, a sheltered back canyon some distance from Yellow Pass. Bowie began laying out the grub by the ashes of an old fire while the Swede stood by making no move to help, a sulky blond bear of a man who glowered in silence.

"We need wood," Bowie told him. "Make yourself useful. There's some dead brush down the canyon a ways."

"You think I'm your goddam servant?" Ekstrom growled. It was the first thing he'd said all day.

Bowie straightened up, watching him. "We're up here to do a job," he said quietly. "You do your part, that's all."

He thought for a moment that Ekstrom was going to crowd it here and now. He'd seen the same hair-trigger look in other boozeheads suddenly cut off from the means to feed their craving. Compound that with a naturally surly man freighted by guilt and you might have a wildcat by the tail. Bowie could make allowances for Ekstrom's state of mind, but he was ready for anything that might happen.

Maybe Ekstrom saw it. After a moment he turned to his horse. Bowie said, "You can fetch it better on foot," but Ekstrom ignored him, swinging into his saddle. He flung the animal around on a brutal rein and kicked him into motion up the rocky floor of the canyon. Bowie shook his head, then bent back to his task. Laying a slab of bacon on a flat rock, he hacked off strips and laid them in a skillet. He half-filled a Dutch oven at a spring that bubbled up through rocks nearby. As he was opening a sack of pinto beans, he heard the shot. Its echoes clapped wildly up and down the wooded slopes of the canyon.

Bowie muttered, "Jesus," and loped over to Shitkicker. Mounting, he heeled the buckskin into a hard trot up the gorge. Angling around a bend, he came on Ekstrom's mount with the reins trailing. No sign of the Swede.

"Ekstrom!"

A rustling in the dense oak scrub that cloaked the south slope. The Swede came tramping into sight, his saddle gun swinging from his fist.

"What the hell was that shooting?"

"I got a deer."

Bowie stared at him a moment, then swung to the ground. "Where'd you drop it?"

Ekstrom wore a look of sullen vindication. He pointed. Bowie went past him and rammed through the thickets going upslope. Easy to pick up the trail of broken twigs and blood-splashed leaves where the mortally hit animal had bounded away. Bowie followed it a few yards to where the deer, a small doe, had dropped in the graceless sprawl of death. Ekstrom came tramping up beside him.

"We didn't need the meat," Bowie said thinly.

Ekstrom shrugged. "All Trapp said, no shooting close to the Pass."

"There was no damn need."

Ekstrom eyed him with a sultry arrogance. "Shit. It is

just a deer. There's plenty deer around here, tracks all over. If there's trouble to come, maybe I need the practice, eh?"

"God damn a man that kills game and then leaves it to rot." Bowie spoke with deceptive softness, but couldn't keep the shaking from his voice. "You're going to skin this carcass and cut it up. Then you're going to pack the meat back to camp."

"Like hell I——"

Bowie moved almost before the words were out, grabbing the barrel of Ekstrom's carbine and twisting upward. Ekstrom tightened his grasp too late. Bowie wrenched the weapon away and swung it in a tight arc, slamming the breech against Ekstrom's jaw. The teeth-rattling clout knocked him backward, stumbling. He caught his balance and stood rubbing his jaw.

"You son of a bitch. I kill you for that."

Bowie swung his arm and let go of the carbine, spinning it away into the brush. He settled his weight on the balls of his feet, waiting. Ekstrom did not move. Bowie reached inside his mackinaw now, pulled his knife from its sheath and gave it a hard flip that drove the blade into the loam at Ekstrom's feet.

"Use it. The deer or me. It's your choice."

Ekstrom bent slowly and picked up the knife. Bowie watched him contemptuously, thinking it was no gamble at all. Though he wasn't altogether sure. Not until Ekstrom shook himself and let his yellow-eyed glance slip away. Wordlessly, then, he knelt by the deer and began skinning it out.

CHAPTER NINE

Leaving Ekstrom to butcher the doe, Bowie gathered an armload of wood and returned down canyon. He took the Swede's carbine with him. He had finished cooking up the grub when Ekstrom came trudging into sight leading his horse, the deer's hide slung from its back and bulging with the saddle and quarters of venison. His clothes were stained with blood and slimy fluids. Bowie didn't have to check the meat to know that he'd botched the job of butchering. There was raw hatred in Ekstrom's look, and now Bowie wondered if he'd crowded too hard. This was a man already crowded to a savage edge by grief and guilt and a cold-turkey cut-off of his habit. Salted by a streak of plain damn meanness. A good thing he'd taken the gun away, Bowie decided.

They packed the grub and meat back to camp. Bowie told Ekstrom to hang the venison from a tree limb for a night's cooling. While the Swede was occupied with that, he quietly told Sully what had happened. Sully shook his head. "Verily, I believe you grabbed the bull by the balls there, paleface."

"What would you of done?"

"Hell. Somewhat the same, I reckon. But I don't like his look a damn bit. He was riding grudge on you before. Makes it worse."

Bowie said flatly: "You want to enlarge on that?"

"You want me to?"

"Don't hedge with me, boy."

"Well, when you was looking to that baby's well-being,

94

talking with Miz Ekstrom now and again, some of the boys taken it you was shining to her. Ekstrom got wind of what somebody said and blew up over it."

"That kind of talk could get somebody killed," Bowie said thinly.

"That's what I figured. You wasn't about when it happened and I didn't see a need you should know."

"Thanks."

"Look, you can get pretty damn redheaded yourself. Seemed best to let it lay. Hell, I knew they was cutting wrong sign on you, but Ekstrom didn't. I caught him looking knives at you a couple times after. So watch yourself."

Next morning they peered out of their pine-bough shelter to find the weather a little warmer than usual and a wet fog blanketing everything. It had turned the bottom of Yellow Pass to a misty void, but that didn't matter a lot; sounds of riders or cattle going between its stony walls would be easily picked up. Ekstrom was the big problem. He seemed to have worsened overnight. He went mechanically about the tasks he was assigned muttering continually to himself, his bloodshot eyes glassy and glaring. As if he were squeezing every atom of his desperate rage into a bombshell that might go off any time. Bowie took Sully aside; they talked.

"I dunno," Sully said soberly. "Am beginning to think he ain't altogether right in the head. But we got orders."

"Orders be damned," Bowie said. "One of us is got to take him back to headquarters. This job is a bitch as it is. Having a man who's sick or crazy dragging about waiting a chance to put a bullet or a knife in me is cutting it too damn fine."

"Well, I do appreciate it's your hide, white brother. All right, you keep the watch. I'll ride back with him today. Tell Cyrus how it is."

Their supply of water was low and the nearest place to get more was from a spring at the base of this same ridge a few hundred yards east. It was Bowie's turn to fetch it. With two wooden buckets swinging from his fists, he set off down the old trail and, coming to the ridge base, headed eastward parallel to it. Great rocks that had fallen from the steeper faces of the ridge littered the ground, half-seen shapes in the milky shroud of fog.

Bowie reached the spring, which pooled in a deep trough below where it cascaded from the lower slope. He was kneeling to dip the buckets when the shot came. It followed the whine and snap of a slug that spattered rock particles head-level from a boulder to his right.

Jesus!

Bowie dived sideways and flattened out on his belly, twisting his head around for a look. He saw a man's figure dodge from one rock to the next, clutching a saddle gun. Just a gray silhouette briefly seen, but its heavy shape was easy to identify. Ekstrom had followed him here. Bowie hugged the earth, heart pounding. He hadn't packed his pistol along, but Ekstrom wasn't sure of that or he'd be coming on straight and fast to cinch his kill.

What had happened to Sully? Bowie hadn't heard a shot; Ekstrom might have put Sully out of action some other way. So here he was, unarmed, within a minute or so of having bought it unless he could get away from Ekstrom. It was all open flats down here, the ridge too steep to scale at this point. The rocks and fog offered the only hope of covering an escape.

Lunging to his feet, Bowie piled into a crouching run toward a belt of tall boulders. Another shot sent flinty echoes caroming across the rock field and now Ekstrom lifted his voice in a bawl of rage. A fragment of rock turned under Bowie's right foot; in his driving run he skidded sideways, then plowed on his shoulder into the stony ground.

He tried to get his feet under him. Pain stabbed his ankle and he fell to his hands and knees. Ekstrom's boots crunched over the flints as he came on at a run, his fog-grayed form looming darker and larger by the moment. Suddenly he was close, pulling to a stop.

He laughed as he levered his carbine and threw it to his shoulder.

Bowie had lurched to his feet, but he was helpless to do anything except brace for the slug's impact. His body shrank with the slam and grunt, the echo of gun blast. But it was Ekstrom who was hammered forward by the shot, falling, his arms flung wide. He struck the ground in a broken sprawl and didn't move.

Bowie had often seen game go down hard-hit; he knew Ekstrom wouldn't move again. His stomach pitching hollowly, he stumbled over to the dead man. His eyes moved to Sully as he came tramping through the rocks, rifle in hand. He and Bowie reached the body at the same time. Sully knelt and turned it over and said bleakly: "Well, he had to buy it all. The sorry goddam fool."

"Thought he might of got you some ways."

Sully shook his head tightly. "He sneaked off. Told him to throw his stuff together while I fetched the horses. Didn't take much to figure I meant to fetch him back—directly I was gone, he found his carbine and skinned out after you. I found him gone, all I could do was follow fast as I could. But Christ. Who'd a thought he'd go off a-sudden like this, like a goddam string of Chinese firecrackers?"

"Nobody," Bowie said. "You done what had to be."

A shudder ran through Sully. "Jesus. I guess I did. I'll pack him to headquarters and tell what happened. My job."

"Wonder if we couldn't cover what happened. Bury him here, give out a different story. Say he got killed in an accident. Be a sight easier on his wife."

"Yeah." Sully rubbed his chin. "Only any story we give out'll look goddam funny. Cyrus might go along with us, but then he'd have to explain unusual circumstances of death to the sheriff. Coroner'll have to see the body, hold an inquest. Let's take a day and night to think on it. He'll keep."

"All right."

"How's that foot?"

Bowie tested part of his weight on it. "Hurts like hell. Pulled something, but I can hobble. You better pack him up to camp."

The fog got thicker as the day wore on; its wetness sheened like dull pearl on rocks and trees. The chill mois-

ture worked under Bowie's slicker and into his flesh as he
crouched on the lookout ledge. He and Sully had reached
no conclusions on how to handle the telling of Ekstrom's
death. It made no difference except on Sofie Ekstrom's account, and Bowie drowsily wondered if she'd care all that
much. Even allowing that Ekstrom might once have been a
good husband in his way, it seemed unlikely that feeling
had ever run deep between them. Too many differences.
Ekstrom had been older that Sofie by perhaps fifteen
years, but that wouldn't mean so much; it wasn't too great
an age gap. Bowie sleepily reflected that he was a good
dozen years older than her himself. . . .

He was half-dozing when the faint noises first reached
him. Then he snapped to alertness. Muffled sounds of cattle on the move. A good-sized bunch. And very faintly,
men's voices hoorawing from hoarse throats. Bowie
strained his eyes against the pale broth of mist. The pass
below was a foggy gulf; only a growing nearness in the
sounds indicated that the cattle were being funneled into
its mouth. The voices grew louder and sharper.

At last. And about time, by God.

Bowie got stiffly to his feet and returned to the camp at
a limping trot. Shaking Sully by the shoulder roused him
out of his damp blankets. They hustled to fetch their
horses. "Christ, they picked a night for it," Sully grumbled
as he threw on his saddle, but a rising excitement tinged
his voice. Bowie allowed that more likely the night had
picked them; it would be no picnic to haze off stock in this
murk. The fog would also make good cover for anyone
trailing them.

The two Chainlink men picked their way down the
ridge trail and, once they achieved the bottom, swung in a
short arc to enter the V-shaped cleft of Yellow Pass. The
rustlers would have a slow time of it, chousing their beeves
through this tight defile. Bowie and Sully were careful to
hold well to their rear, keeping the distance by ear.
Though the floor of the pass stayed at a generally uniform
breadth, in some places the walls above cramped almost
together in sheer drops of a hundred and more feet from

bulging crags of rimrock. Men's voices, gravelly from
shouting, drifted a surprising distance down the gorge.

The canyon flanks began to taper low. Finally they
dwindled away altogether. The trail continued to follow
the dry bed of the ancient stream that had carved out Yellow Pass centuries before. Dense gouts of fog made it hard
to tell much else about the country they were crossing. It
was strewn with huge boulders that materialized from the
mist and receded into it; occasional crooked leafless trees
thrust up like crabbed skeletons. You had the eerie feeling
of crossing the face of a dead world. Good place for a
drive-off, all right; you'd be hard put to pick up cold track
on this sort of terrain. At the same time, sounds of cattle
on the move carried sharply here and were easy to follow.

Soon the trail left the old stream bed and bent roughly
northeast, threading circuitously around rugged heights of
land. The raiders kept up a steady pace, completely sure
of their route despite the fog. Twice Bowie caught a purl-
ing of water ahead and each time the trail crossed wide
shallow streams or, what seemed more likely, different
crooks of the same stream. And each time the cattle were
driven a distance upstream through foot-deep water before
they were pushed up the opposite bank. Cyrus had been
right, Bowie thought; the best trackers trying to pick up
this trail later might be confused any number of places.

The night hours crawled by; the fog began to lift. But as
it cleared, its wetness dissolved into a mizzling rain. The
damp cold increased. Rocking at this held-in pace, Bowie
felt familiar cramps ease into his joints. He had to contin-
uously flex his legs and arms, toes and fingers, to keep
them from going numb. What miserable goddam weather
to dog out a slow trail.

The land was starting to climb perceptibly; the rocky
scape gave way to patches of turf and occasional mottes of
the lodgepole pine that forested much of this high country.
The trees were stunted and gnurled at first, growing taller
and straighter as the trail climbed. The loam underfoot
was spongy pine detritus which, like rocks and water, left
practically no sign. Except for the old or fresh cattle drop-

pings here and there. A flare of gray light rimmed along a forested swell of ridge to their right. Real dawn was still hours away, but the night was starting to heel off. With the visibility improving, Bowie and Sully began to catch occasional glimpses of the raiders and the bunched cattle. Accordingly they dropped farther behind.

The land continued to climb, but just ahead it seemed to fall sharply away. Cattle and men showed on the paling skyline and then they dropped out of sight.' When Bowie and Sully reached the same spot, they found themselves at the head of a long slide of collapsed shale down which the cattle had been driven. It had crumbled long ago from the rimrock of a short sheer cliff, forming a kind of uneven ramp to the floor of a rich-grassed valley.

The bowl-shaped depression was several hundred feet across, irregularly oval in shape, and hedged around by natural barriers of crumbling shale walls and thick stands of lodgepole. The meadow of wild hay was dotted by giant isolated pines and rambling clots of brush, giving the valley a parklike appearance. A growing band of light showed bunches of cattle dark against the sun-cured grass.

"You feel heroic, any?" Sully murmured.

"I feel like a froze jackass," Bowie growled, watching the men haze the Chainlink cattle deep into the valley. "I count six riders. More than we figured on. I vote we take word back to headquarters."

"Yours is the speech of gray hairs, brother. Take us a whole day to reach headquarters and fetch men back here."

"Christ, boy. You think these cows are going to stray some'eres?"

"Men might. They likely be gone when we get back. Paleface, we waited many suns to catch these jacklegs in the act. Getting the cattle back won't satisfy Cyrus if we lose the men."

"So we just take on all six."

A reckless glint touched Sully's glance. "No harm in waiting to see what they do next, is there? Might show us a way to handle 'em. You can't tell."

Bowie thought it was a piece of damn foolishness, but he conceded there was no harm in watching a while. Just that he had no intention of sticking his neck out against odds. The misting rain held a bite of sleet now; he shivered and dug his chin deep in his collar. The raiders were showing no disposition to leave yet. After dispersing the cattle, they rode to a sheltering motte of pines and dropped out of their saddles. Soon a spot of fiery orange showed at the edge of timber. They were going to warm themselves anyway.

"Listen," Sully said now, "why'n't we sneak down there? Go in on foot. If we can't take 'em, we might get close enough to identify 'em. The law likes a couple witnesses, doesn't it?"

"Yeah."

Bowie's growl held a resigned note. But feeling the taste of high excitement himself, he knew that he was of Sully's mind. They had waited out a long hard stand for this time; that should give a man some rights. Maybe, just maybe, they could bring it off.

Leaving their horses back in some trees, carrying their saddle guns, the two descended the slide and worked cautiously toward the fire. Fading darkness still offered some cover; it was easy to conceal their approach by holding behind the fingers of brush that laced the valley floor. In a short time they were hunkered down in a patch of chokecherry scrub a couple hundred feet from the fire. Its glow picked the gang out clearly. They were passing around a bottle. Bowie couldn't identify any of them until one, a bulky figure of a man, turned against the throw of flamelight. It caught on his face.

Brady Trapp. A moment later Bowie recognized a slighter figure that was Joe-Bob.

Sully said in a shocked whisper: "You make out what I do?"

"I make out the Trapps are helping steal their old man's beef. I don't make sense of it."

Neither did Sully. He quickly named two of the others. The tall brick-haired man was Red Antrim; one sallow puffy-faced weed of a fellow was called Blue Searls. "Don't know that other pair, but Searls is one of Red's cross-dog outfit."

"Seems they're the rest of it."

"Uh-huh."

They continued to watch. Needles of sleet rattled on their hatbrims; wind curled fiercely off the heights. It blew the fire to yellow tatters and carried snatches of talk. Apparently Brady and Antrim were debating whether or not to head the cattle toward market now or wait out the bad weather. Brady was impatient, chafing against delay, arguing that the sleet might be followed by heavy snow, stranding the cattle here till spring and risking their loss. Antrim acknowledged the danger, but he was more concerned about the cattle getting bogged down by a snowstorm in the rugged country between here and Craigie, at least the cattle were sheltered here. The talk grew heated. Meantime the bottle had been emptied. Another was broken out and passed from man to man.

Antrim appeared to have won the point. Brady retreated into surly silence, settling on his heels by the fire and gazing into it. Antrim's men were getting louder as their innards warmed. One of them threw the empty bottle high in the air and all three blazed away at it with pistols, whooping. Nobody hit it. Antrim grouchily told them to lay off the goddam racket.

"Brother," Sully whispered, "if we gonna to make the move, best we do it before it gets any lighter. Three of 'em are hooched up and that Joe-Bob, he'll be no trouble."

"All right. We better split apart, take 'em from two sides."

"Yeah. You stay here, I'll circle onto the other flank. Will sing out when I am set. Too bad we can't run off the horses, but they're too close to 'em." Sully's teeth flashed. "Injun always go after horse first."

"So I heard. When you sing out, see you give 'em a chance to give up."

"Why, yes. Honest to Great Spirit, o white brother, Sully is not one of your murdering savages."

Bowie grunted. "Sure, sure. Get moving."

Sully slipped away through the straggling thickets, vanishing among them in utter silence. Bowie crouched with his rifle across his knees, putting all his attention on the camp. His tendon-pulled ankle ached steadily. Antrim kept pacing up and down, as nervous in his way as Brady. Sometimes he hauled up and peered out at the valley, sometimes in Bowie's direction. That's a tough old lobo, Bowie thought. Did he really suspect something amiss? Hard to say. He wasn't one easily caught off balance, that was sure.

The seconds grew into long aching minutes. Or maybe he only imagined they did. What the hell was taking Sully so long?

Bowie was almost startled when the half-breed's order rang out: "Hold it like you are. This camp is surrounded!"

In an instant every man was on his feet, facing around toward the voice. Bowie rose swiftly to his feet and levered his rifle, stepping out to the open. "Shuck your guns," he called. "Any man of you bats a winker, he is done——"

Antrim wheeled like a catamount, palming up his side gun. Bowie's shot merged with Sully's. Antrim spun like a lanky dervish and then crashed across the fire, his body whipping up a shower of sparks. Another man had already dived for his rifle where it leaned against a deadfall. Bowie, levering fast, squeezed off a second shot. It took the man between the shoulder blades and slammed him against the deadfall like a broken doll.

Searls, his pistol out, had snapped two shots at Bowie. Mindful of the range then, he lunged for a horse and the rifle scabbarded on its saddle. Just then Sully stepped out to view, pistol leveled, and shot him in the leg. As Searls fell with a scream, Sully was turning the drop on Brady, who stood uncertainly, his gun half drawn.

"Try it," Sully invited.

Brady raised his hands. Antrim's third man hadn't moved a muscle after Sully's first order. He stood exactly as he'd been, holding his arms away from his body. Bowie came tramping up. "Take their hardware, Sully," he said. Sully moved from one man to the next, collecting guns and knives. Bowie glanced at the smoking fire half-smothered by Antrim's body; his clothes were smoldering.

"Pull him off," Bowie told the man who hadn't moved.

The fellow's eyes were like muddy ice, cold and wise. Wordlessly he walked to Antrim, grabbed him by the boots, and dragged him away from the fire. Joe-Bob hadn't moved either. Just stood looking on, round-eyed. Now he made an inarticulate sound, shaking his head.

"Oh, it's happening, all right," Sully said gently. "You got done to death by two men, boys."

Searls heaved himself from his belly onto his back with a screech of pain. His face was bloodless. "Jesus God—" He clutched at his leg. "Arch, Christ, I'm bleeding to death!"

Sully said: "Bleed, you cow-lifting bastard."

"You." Bowie tipped his rifle at the cold-eyed man. "Fix him up."

Sully raised his brows, then shrugged. The one called Arch said meagerly, "Need a knife." Bowie nodded at Sully, who handed Arch back his hunting knife. He kneeled by Searls and ripped open his pants leg.

Sully's dark glance shuttled to Brady. "You got some tall medicine to make, big brother."

"What you going to do?" Brady said huskily.

"Depends how good you talk." Bowie kicked up the fire. "I'm tracking some sign on you, Junior. You tell me if it's right. If Antrim's bunch vented the brands and then tried peddling the cows, they'd be ass-deep in trouble. So you got hand-picked to do the mischief. No need to vent brands."

Brady's face looked fishgut gray. He nodded. "My part was to sign the bill of lading at railhead."

"As a Trapp representing his pa's outfit, eh? You're a real bucko lad, Junior. Your pa's cattle. You must need money damn bad."

"For that big new gambling debt he run up," Sully put in. "I know about it, Brady. Reckon everyone does but Cyrus."

"I was supposed to get a third," Brady muttered. "It would of cleared my debt."

"That's too bad," Bowie said. "That debt ain't half your problem."

"Goddammit, if you gonna take me in, go ahead. If you gonna shoot, do it! You got the chance." Brady added with a guttural ugliness, "That would suit you, ridgerunner."

"Sure," Bowie said. "Suppose you tell us all about it, Junior. Then I'll tell you what suits me."

Brady talked in a weary, strangled voice. Antrim had a contact at Craigie, a buyer who would take on wet cattle and ask no questions. The legitimacy of the transaction would be checked out by stockyard officials; with a bill of lading signed by Brady, the buyer would have no difficulty passing Chainlink cattle off at the yards. Antrim had slacked off some after that first quick flurry of raids and waited on word from Brady, surmising that Cyrus would take some counteraction. When Brady had reported that apparently Cyrus had no such plans under way, Antrim had gone ahead with a last big raid, tonight's. They'd throw these cattle in with their previous pickings, then trail the whole herd north to Craigie. Antrim had already meticulously scouted a good trail north through the Breaks. One hard push, trailing the herd day and night, and the stolen beeves would be off their hands.

"How come you and Joe-Bob was with Antrim's crowd tonight?" asked Sully.

Brady said that Antrim had needed a couple extra men for this last big strike and the drive to Craigie; Brady had offered his services and had taken Joe-Bob into his confidence to fill out the crew. They'd be gone from Chainlink a few days, but a ready-sounding story that they'd gone on a drunk in Saltville would cover their absence. Cyrus would rant about it later, but wouldn't have cause to doubt the story.

"All right, Junior," said Bowie. "Now I'll tell you what suits me." Bowie glanced at Sully. "It's got to suit you too."

Sully cocked a brow. "I don't make out your sign, pale-face. What's to suit? We take the lot in."

"Listen," Brady argued, "no reason you can't let the kid

go and not tell Cyrus, is there? Hell, he ain't done nothing. He come with me tonight, but he ain't really in it, he didn't know about it before."

Bowie didn't even look at him. "Stop and think a minute, Sully. How's old man Trapp going to take this?"

"Hell—" Sully shook his head. "It'll break the old man's heart, I suppose. He'll never bat an eye to show it, but I know him. Don't make a whit of difference what manner of pups he sired. They're his own. Ain't nothing changes a blood feeling and Cyrus has got the feeling deep in his guts."

"That's what I figured."

Sully looked slightly incredulous. "You saying we should let these Trapps go scot-free—say nothing to Cyrus?"

"That's about it. Ain't a case of liking to. Lesser of two evils, I reckon."

"Forgetting something, ain't you?" Sully gestured at Searls and Arch. "They got no reason not to tell the sheriff everything."

"And no good reason to, if they're turned loose. Every reason not to."

Sully was silent a moment, scowling as he digested the thought. Mizzle hissed on the coals. "Might be a better way," he said then. "Way to make sure. They're scum. Nobody'd question it much if it happened they got killed in the shoot-out."

"No," Bowie said flatly, promptly. "It's my way or no way." His eyes narrowed on Sully's. "Could you do that?"

Sully sighed and shook his head. "Come down to it, I reckon not. Just pitching pennies."

Bowie's glance slid back to Searls and Arch. "You hear what I'm saying?"

"Sure," Arch said softly.

"Searls?"

Searls raised his face. It was contorted and glistening; he kept fighting back squeaks of pain. He managed a nod.

"You cauterize his leg," Bowie told Arch. "We'll hold him for you. Then you'll help us bury your partners. Then you both get clear away from here. Our story will be you made a clean escape—in case the sheriff checks on who-all got buried here. You can make camp somewhere till Searls is fit to ride. When he is, you both clear the hell out of this country. Way out. Don't show your faces hereabouts again. You got that?"

"Sure," Arch murmured. "I got it, mister."

"There's just one thing." Sully moved over to Brady and wrapped a fist around the front folds of his slicker. "I want you to cinch onto something, big noise. It's on your pa's account you're walking away from the biggest jackpot of your life. But get this. From here on you are going to tread the straight and narrow. Cyrus ain't got a lot of time, but for what he's got, you are going to be a son of sorts. I'll be watching."

He dropped his fist and stepped back, his flat-lidded eyes fixing Brady's face. "You slip just once for that old man to see, and I'll make you the sorriest snake on two legs."

CHAPTER TEN

The yard was a chocolate-colored mire as Bowie slogged across it, his head bent against the gusts of sleety rain. Every step balled his boot soles with more gumbo, throwing him off balance, but he couldn't even dredge up the will to curse. He was dog-tired right to his guts, his ankle still hurt; he wanted nothing more than to collapse in his bunk and sleep the clock around, as Cyrus had ordered. But utterly spent as he was, he didn't think he could catch a wink till he'd gotten this errand over. It wasn't a welcome one; it just had to be done. And he grimly reckoned that it was his to do.

The windows of the Ekström cabin showed lamplight against the gray darkness of this late afternoon. He reached the door and paused to scrape his boots awkwardly on the sill, knocking off the mud. The noise brought Sofie Ekstrom to the door; she opened it.

"What is—oh, Mr. Candler."

"Yes'm. Could I come in?"

"*Ja*, of course. Here, let me take the coat and hat. *Himmel*, what weather it is."

Bowie moved into the room, shucking out of his slicker. "Yes'm. Can't stay but a minute."

"Come by the fire. I fix coffee."

He crossed to the fireplace, where a cheery blaze was going and held his hands to its warmth. He didn't quite know how to approach something of this sort. He'd never had to do the like. He glanced at Sofie as she poured water in a blackened coffeepot, ladled in Arbuckle's, and came over to slip the pot bail onto a fireplace lug. Her face was calm and pleasant; if she was grieving, it didn't show.

"Um, Miz Ekstrom, we took up a collection at the bunkhouse." He dug in the pocket of his duck jacket and pulled out a wad of greenbacks and held it out. "This is for you."

Sofie straightened, gazed at the money, then raised her eyes to his. "What is this for?"

"Well, it's something we do when a man dies on the job. If he leaves kin, wife or kids or maybe old folks, we get up some money for 'em."

She shook her head once, stiffly. "I cannot take money, Mr. Candler."

"Well, sure, but it's a custom, like. It's the right thing to do." He thrust the bills at her half awkwardly, half roughly. "You take it. It's from all of us. All the boys want you to have it."

Still she made no move to accept it. Bowie laid the money on the table. Slowly then, she picked it up. "It is so much." She began to blink and bite her underlip. "*Gad va-lingne def*," she whispered. "God bless you—all of you."

Bowie nodded uncomfortably. "I better be going."

"No, please, you have coffee first. It is ready soon." She pressed the bills between her hands; tears began spilling from her eyes. "*Tack*—thank you." She was crying, but she was smiling too, trying to fight the tears. "Thank you. Sit down, please, don't mind me."

Bowie slacked into a heavy carved chair. He looked at the fire. A few snifflings and she seemed to perk right up, hurrying back and forth from cupboard to table, setting out cups and spoons. It wasn't unpleasant to sit like this and soak up the warmth and listen to her movements, and he felt faintly guilty. He hadn't a notion what she might be feeling. No grief, like enough, or damned little. No blame to her for that. Earlier, when he and Sully had brought in Ekstrom's body and reported to Cyrus, telling him all—almost all—that had happened, Cyrus had said he would take care of telling Mrs. Ekstrom. So she'd been told; that was all he knew.

Sofie served the coffee and pulled up another chair by

the fire. Her eyes were a bit reddened, but her face was steady again, her voice matter of fact. "Does Mr. Trapp move his cattle back now?"

"Soon as the weather breaks a little, I reckon. He'll want to pull 'em out of the Breaks before snow flies, and that'll be soon enough." Bowie sipped his coffee, watching the fire. "How much he tell about what happened?"

"Only that Jan was killed in the fight with the men who stole the cattle."

That was the version he and Sully had cooked up; they had confided the truth to Cyrus, who'd agreed that no good would be served by giving out the real story. The man was dead and the best he could leave his widow was one good memory. "I want to tell you he went out like a brave man." The words soured Bowie's mouth; he didn't look at her. "I guess there's no more to say."

"No," she said soberly. "There is no more. If it's the truth, Mr. Candler."

The devil! What made her say that? "Yes'm. It's the truth."

He met her eyes with the lie, and she nodded slowly. "That is something then, eh? I don't mean to say bad of him, now he's gone, but there is so much——" Her face was troubled; she looked away. "It was not good with us, this you know. But it was not all his fault."

"Well, that is strictly your affair."

As if she hadn't heard, she went on musingly: "I don't blame Jan. Not now, thinking how it all was. He was a hard man, but his life made him so. My pa and me, we were very poor. He—my father drank a lot. So we did not have much money. Jan was our neighbor. He offered to help us because—because he liked me. I did not want his help, but when Pa took sick toward the end, there was the doctor to pay, no food in the house . . . I took his help then. And Pa left debts which must be paid. If I married Jan, he would pay them all. And he did. It seemed the right thing—then."

"I reckon it was."

"Do you think so? I do not know. Jan was not so hard a

man then—gruff, you would say?—but not mean. This
came when he lost the crops two years in a row. It was a
good farm and he worked many years to make it so—and
then, nothing there was but to sell out."

Bowie settled his head back, narrowing his eyes against
the ribboning firelight. You never knew all of what was in
anyone, he thought tiredly, till something happened to
bring it out. Even then you were never sure. You kept
stumbling on unexpected pockets in people you thought
you knew. Take Sully. He wouldn't have suspected the
streak of pure hardness Sully had shown after they'd taken
Antrim's gang. Or take himself. Been years since he'd
given a damn about much of anything. These weeks at
Chainlink had shown him he could still care, by God, and
that was something to know. Sofie. Her baby. Cyrus
Trapp. Sully. They were all part of it, one way or another.

It felt good to pay off a debt too. Like Sully, he felt
deep gratitude to Cyrus for taking him in, then for some
kindred assurance that Cyrus had conveyed to him when
they'd spoken together. Bigger things than they'd seemed.
Odd that they'd both squared their debts to Cyrus with a
lie: telling him that two of the cow thieves had escaped
and omitting mention of Brady's and Joe-Bob's part.
Would it be for the best? They could only hope.

He was half dozing. Sofie's voice pulled him gently
awake. "You are pretty tired, eh?"

"Been that kind of a job. Better get to my bunk before I
get carried there." He stood up and so did Sofie; they
looked at each other. He felt tentative and unsure. "You
still plan on leaving here?"

"I cannot decide yet what I do, but I know I must work
and earn my way. Mr. Trapp says I should stay the winter
anyway."

"Maybe you should."

"I think so. I will help Mrs. Trapp with the household,
whatever I can do. They are kind people here. You are
kind."

Bowie's glance moved to the empty crib. "I was sorry to
hear about your—about Eric."

"It is hard to think about yet. But this will pass. I think it was God's will—I do not know, but it's easier to think so. You tried to help, Mr. Candler. This I never forget."

"Well, you don't need to think about that."

"I never forget."

Bowie picked up his slicker and shrugged into it, feeling her eyes all the while. As he moved toward the door, she said: "Maybe you come again to talk? I like this if you would."

"Sure." He cleared his throat. "That would be fine."

It was a miserable Sunday afternoon and the crew didn't mind spending the day loafing around the bunkhouse, playing cards, mending clothes and gear, or dozing in their bunks. Faye Nevers stood by the single small window that fronted on the yard, staring moodily out at the desolate weather. He felt restless—the sound of Barney's tinny harmonica irritated him; so did the mutters of the cardplayers and the deep snoring of Candler and Sully Calder in their bunks, sleeping off a sleepless night and the ordeal of their long stand at Yellow Pass.

Always alert to the politics of his position and Chainlink matters in general, the foreman had lately found more than enough to think about. Mostly he worried about Cyrus's deteriorating condition. Two days ago, after Cyrus had taken Ekstrom out to Yellow Pass to join Candler and Sully on watch (telling Nevers that he was taking Ekstrom to a line camp duty), he'd suffered an attack of head pains so severe that only a double dose of opiates had numbed it. Yesterday he'd been lurching about acting cockeyed and drunk, bumping into furniture, his speech slurring, giving contradictory orders and forgetting things he'd said only seconds before.

Cyrus was on his last legs; his days were running fewer. When they'd run out, what would Faye Nevers's prospects be? He hadn't an inkling of the contents of the will that was filed with Cyrus's attorney in Saltville. More than likely Cyrus, aware that he couldn't safely entrust his affairs to Brady's improvident hands, had made other provisions. By, say, leaving a controlling interest in Chainlink to

Adah, with a stipulation that Nevers be retained as foreman. That would be the sensible thing to do. But Jesus, how could he be sure? He couldn't go to Cyrus with a flat-out query; he'd learned long ago that Cyrus tolerated no prying in his personal business.

Looking out the window, Nevers stiffened to attention. That was Adah leaving the main house, wearing a riding habit. She hadn't gone for a ride more than twice since coming to Chainlink. Why choose a day like this for it? She was coming toward the bunkhouse. Guessing her purpose, Nevers made a quick decision.

When her knock came at the door, he lounged over to open it.

"Hello," she said. "Would you please have a man saddle a horse for me?"

"Sure thing. But it's a sorry day even for ducks."

"I am riding, nevertheless."

"All right," he said carelessly. "I'll saddle the horse myself." Ignoring the curious glances of the crew, he went to his bunk and pulled on his own slicker, then asked Hilo, smallest man on the crew, for the borrow of his. Hilo said sure. Nevers carried it to the doorway, saying, "You better wear this, Mrs. Trapp. You'll get pretty wet otherwise."

"Very well."

He held the bulky wrap while she slipped into it, then walked beside her as they crossed to the stable. Cold moisture had already stung her clear-cream skin with fresh color, and he had never seen a woman look so damned beautiful. "I'll ride with you if you've no objection," he said idly. "I mean if you plan on going far. Looks like the weather might get worse."

"If you like, Mr. Nevers."

He didn't ask questions; he could feel the tightness in her, reflected in her set lips and stiff tilt of head. A clash with her husband? Wouldn't be any wonder. This morning, the drugs worn off, Cyrus had been cranky and sharp, proddy as an old bull. Might be a fair day for a ride after all, Nevers thought speculatively.

They rode east from headquarters.

She held the sidesaddle well, but there was a hint of tension in her hard use of the bit. Nevers sensed that her usual placid temper was ruffled and any criticism would bring a sharp retort. The wind blew colder; sleet began to varnish the grass and earth with a tinselly jacket of ice. Grass blades crackled under the horses' hooves.

When Adah said, "We'll stop a minute. Please help me down," he merely nodded. Dismounting, he moved to her side and swung her to the ground. They were cut off from headquarters by a low hillock. Adah stepped away from him and stood gazing across the misty swells of dun-colored range eastward. Sleet slanted against the sides of their slickers; it prickled her face to a richer color.

"You want to go back now?" he asked.

"Not yet."

"What do you want, Mrs. Trapp?"

His dry and sardonic question, half amused, half impatient, brought her around facing him. Her eyes looked dark and driven; he felt a twist of heat rise in his belly. He couldn't read anything in her expression except a trace of fear. But fear of him or of herself? he wondered. Knowing that the growing, feverish attraction between them would never come to a head unless he forced it.

"I suggest that you mind your place. If I told my husband that you used such a tone to me, he'd horsewhip you off the ranch."

Nevers's patience thinned away. "But you won't tell him. That's the whole thing. Here—"

He took a step and enclosed her waist with one arm, his other hand roughly clamping her chin and twisting her face up. He kissed her for a long time and felt no fight in the heated bow of her body. Then he let go; she stepped backward, fisting both hands around the crop, but didn't raise it.

"You don't leave a person anything, do you?" she whispered.

"Not my fault if you lie to yourself about yourself."

"I didn't lie—" Her face was agonized, not angry; it resembled a crumpled petal. "But oh, God, it's wrong, so wrong. We're such different people. Why—tell me why!"

She was trembling all over as he took her in his arms, holding her tightly.

"I don't know why," he said gently. "But it's not wrong. You don't believe that either."

"I don't know—it's all strange. Once, a long time ago it seems, my world was ordered and sensible. All of it was. Now—"

"No need to think on it." Nevers tightened his arms, smiling above her head. "I'll do all of that for both of us."

There was plenty to think about, by God. He felt a heady sense of power that made him want to laugh aloud.

CHAPTER ELEVEN

Two weeks went by before the season's first big snow hit the high country. Cyrus stood on the little stoop outside the entrance to his office and watched it come. The sky over the northern Elks was boiling with big smoky clouds roiled and driven by sliding, battering currents of wind. Some weather for sure. Real snow this time. There had been a few dismal flurries last week before the land had settled down to a silent frozen waiting. Now true winter was rushing in.

His last winter. The thought was a mere dull reflex, about all he could summon up these days. Cyrus wondered if he would live out this winter's end; he hoped not. Not if the steady failing of his strength and senses continued to the last. Even leaving his desk to come outside was a slow, labored ordeal.

He leaned a weary hand on the door frame, feeling sick and drained in every fiber of his being. His appetite had gone twelve days ago; his weight was melting away day by day; he could take a fistful of slack flesh on any part of his torso. In an incredibly compressed time his massive frame had withered to that of a huge-boned scarecrow, all the ravages of an advanced age he'd never see crushing down on him, blurring his eyes to horny film for long periods, riddling his memory with blank spots that would have broken another man to weeping frustration.

The pains were no more intense. They'd already ripped his brain and body with their exquisite worst; they merely came and went more frequently. Lately pain had come to seem like a perverse comrade. He now awaited the coming of each onslaught with a kind of fierce resigned pride; he could sit in stony endurance through interludes of agony that a month before would have reduced him to groaning fits. Always now he met it face on, grinding his will against it with an insensate fury until, gasping with a sense of bloodied triumph, he could let himself surrender to the double hypodermic that would bring a sodden twilight of unfeeling half-death where a man slid strangely back and forth on oblivion's edge. . . .

Christ, what a way to go.

Unless nature balanced its merciless toll with the final mercy before too damned long, he knew what he would do. God damned if he'd spend his last months as a helpless, bedridden wreck, unable to manage his simplest functions, babied by gruels and warming pans to a slobbering, mindless exit out of life. No, by God. A man deserved the dignity of final choice: his own way out.

Cyrus tipped his tired gaze down past the foothills to the old wagon road that crooked up from the terraced plains southwest, the road to Saltville. Man on horseback coming. A man alone, pushing a brisk pace on the ice-rutted road. Not a grubline bum, Cyrus thought; this fellow rode like a man with a mission. Whoever it was, he had good reason to complete it and be on his way with that hellsmear of a storm threatening to break before the day was out.

While he was slowly forming these thoughts, the rider reached the haysheds at the east edge of the corrals and swung his mount up toward the house yard. Damned if it wasn't Beamis. Old Sam himself. He hadn't seen the old rawhide bastard in six months. Something warmed and thawed in Cyrus's chest; his mouth jerked in a grin. He always felt good on seeing Sam again, and never more than now. Not very many men in this country went back as far as he and Sam did, to its raw pioneer roots.

Sheriff Beamis raised a thick arm in greeting as he halted at the rail that sided the veranda. Swinging heavily to the ground, he tied his horse and tramped over to the side entrance. Cyrus noted the veiled shock in Beamis's eyes under the tufted brows as he extended a burly hand; Sam was finding it hard to believe this was the same Cyrus Trapp he'd known for three and a half decades.

"Hello, you goddam old catamount."

"How you doing, Cyrus?"

Beamis's lips twisted faintly as if with instant regret at the inference in a casual greeting. He was a squat buffalo of a man in his late fifties, with a face like a sleepy bulldog's and a full head of stiff gray-shot black hair.

"Pretty obvious, ain't it?" Cyrus said dryly. "Well, let's don't stand out here cooling our butts. Come inside." They stepped into the small cluttered office; Cyrus motioned his visitor to a chair. "What brings you over this way on such a day?"

Beamis unbuttoned his mackinaw and settled into the chair. "Oh, some business. Nothing important. While I was here, thought I'd drop by for a chat."

Cyrus backed to his swivel chair and, gripping its arms and clenching his teeth, carefully lowered himself into it. He studied Beamis's impassive face and smiled sardonically. "Sure as hell you did. With a sight of mean weather ready to hit every foot of road between here and Saltville. You'll be riding out a blizzard before you reach home, Sam."

Beamis grunted, crossing his thick legs. "Well, there's just no easy way to say it. Heard talk you was doing poorly of late, so debated some whether you should be told right away. Don't seem no odds in putting it off."

"Christ, Sam, will you kindly not bandy words with me? We known each other too long."

"Yeah," Beamis said bleakly. "To cut it brief, then. Few days ago a couple hardcases named Blue Searls and Arch Quade tried for the bank up at Craigie. Heard about a big safe full of cattle-sale money and decided they wanted it. They didn't make it, but killed young Seth Winters, the cashier, after he went for a hideout gun. They panicked and run, but Searls had this bum leg that slowed 'em down. My deputy at Craigie, Jim Wetherall, captured 'em both."

"Good for him." Cyrus's brows lifted. "Searls and Quade, huh? I know the names. Both of 'em were side-kicks of Red Antrim's. They'd be the two that got away when a pair of my crew busted Antrim's gang back in the Breaks two weeks ago. Hell, I sent you word about it."

"I got your word. Thing is, this blue-ribbon pair claim they didn't get away from your men. Claimed, in fact, that they got turned loose by 'em."

Cyrus's eyes slitted down; he heaved painfully forward in the chair. "That sounds fine. Suppose you tell me just what the hell it means."

"I'm coming to it. Quade'll hang for killing Winters and he knows it. Likely on account he's got nothing to lose, he opened up about all the little sidelines Antrim had cooking, from whiskey-peddling to the Utes to high-grading your cows. Out of pure spite, I'd say, he implicated half a dozen gentlemen, solid citizens all, who'd been secretly involved in various shady deals with Antrim one time or another. Then Searls got talking; he backed up everything Quade said. I been checking back on all they told us. So far they ain't lied."

"What the hell's that got to do with what you said about my men?"

"Easy there. You don't need to fret about your men. Seems they covered up purely on your account."

"Sam, make sense, Goddammit!"

Beamis shifted uncomfortably. "Quade and Searls both claim there was two others in with Antrim on high-grading that stuff of yours. Your sons. Brady and Joe-Bob."

Cyrus said nothing. Just looked at him unblinkingly.

Beamis talked on quietly. A gambling debt, Quade had said. Lucky Jack Hackett held Brady's notes for over a thousand dollars. Brady had agreed to sign a rigged bill of lading for Antrim's buyer; his share would redeem his IOUs from Hackett. Beamis had gone to Lucky Jack and asked him about the notes.

"And?" Cyrus said hoarsely.

"Had to lean on him some before he showed me the

IOUs. Said he'd threatened Brady with going to you unless
he paid up. Those two men of yours wouldn't be around,
would they?"

Cyrus stared at the floor, slowly rubbing his temple. His
arm felt numb and heavy; a ragged pulse beat in each
fingertip. Patiently Beamis repeated the question.

"What? Oh, Candler and Sully?" Cyrus shook his head
heavily. "They—they're out riding line. They should be in
before long."

"They'll know what the truth is. You can get it out of
'em; I likely couldn't." The sheriff rose and walked to the
window, peering out. "Gonna be a helldimmer, that storm.
I better be getting back home." He walked to the door and
paused, hand on the latch. "Cyrus, we been friends a long
time. It's your sons, your cattle, we been talking about. I'll
leave it to you what's to be done. You can prefer charges
or not. Take your time; think on it. Send me word what
you decide." Another pause. "One thing. The story can't
be hushed up. Quade will talk at his trial. Then it'll be
public record."

Cyrus scrubbed a hand over his face. He nodded once,
up and down.

Beamis said gently then, "I'm sorry to see you like this,
Cyrus."

"I'm sorry you had to." Cyrus lifted his head with an effort. "Sam. Much obliged."

"Sure," Beamis said glumly. "Take care. I'll see you
again."

"Wouldn't count on that this side of hell."

When the sheriff had gone, Cyrus sat unmoving for a
long time. A red slow fury began to sizzle at the back of
his brain. Twitches of raw and violent impulse shook him;
he damped each one down. But the effort to stay calm
started him shaking uncontrollably. Calm—Christ. How
could he be calm!

Brady—Brady, God damn you.

He didn't have to question Candler or Sully. He knew
the answer already, knew it as surely as he did the core of
Brady's miserable-pup soul. His sons. God. The only flesh
and blood of his own he could leave in this world. His

sons. The words had a naked echoing mockery. Like cold laughter, savage and shattering. Blood thickening in his head brought the relentless knife of his pain, that familiar comrade of fierce agony and heavy sweats, pressing in. *Come on, you bastard, come on.* He needed something to fight. Something to contain the waiting edge of his rage until Brady and Joe-Bob returned from Saltville, where they had gone to throw a spree.

We're gonna get drunk, Brady had arrogantly told him before slamming out of the house, he letting them go because, weakened and dull, he no longer gave a damn.

Had thought he didn't.

It was graying toward dusk, the snow beating down thick and fast, as Brady and Joe-Bob came off the Saltville road into Chainlink headquarters. The storm had caught them halfway home and by now both were reasonably sobered. They angled past the cookshack. Lights squared the windows; the crew was at supper. They rode on to the stable and dismounted unsteadily.

The cookshack door scraping open pulled Brady's watery glance; someone came out. Brady couldn't identify his dark figure through the torrent of swirling flakes, but he was heading diagonally across the yard toward the old house Cyrus had turned over to the Ekstroms. That would be Bowie Candler—a frequent caller these days on the widow Ekstrom. Brady tasted hatred like a vicious bile; just thinking of Candler could do it for him.

He dragged open the stable doors. Joe-Bob could hardly stand; he was gulping wretchedly as they led the horses inside. Brady lighted a bull's-eye lantern and hung it on a post. His head was pounding; his savage mood deepened. He was in no damn mood to face Cyrus, though he hadn't caught hell from the old man in some time. When he'd unsaddled the horses and turned them into the stalls, he pawed through the hay in a vacant stall till he located a half-empty bottle he'd cached there several days ago. Uncorking it, he took a long swig and held the bottle out to Joe-Bob, who was crouching in the clay runway, head between his knees.

"Better have one, kid. It'll put some hair in your gullet."

Joe-Bob shook his head without raising it. "I—I'm gonna be sick, Brady."

"Go ahead. Fighting nature ain't no odds."

Joe-Bob threw up, dry-retching afterward for a half minute. When he got to his feet, he was pale and shaking. "Gonna go up to the house—go to bed."

"You do that. I got some thinkin' and drinkin' to do first. I'll be along. Go on."

Joe-Bob stumbled out; Brady hauled the doors shut. Tramping over to the empty stall, he settled himself in the hay and took another long pull from the bottle. Getting slowly drunk again put an edge on his blackly bitter thoughts. He'd dreaded facing Lucky Jack Hackett today, but had known he couldn't put it off much longer. Mustering cold courage, he'd told Hackett that he'd be unable to pay what he owed him now or very soon. Had all but gone on his knees to the son of a bitch. Lucky Jack had been unsympathetic. You got one more week, he'd said, and then I pay a call on your old man.

Well, that tore it sure. Cyrus's wrath would be monumental, but even that might not be the worst of it. Overshadowing everything was the threat that Candler and Sully could divulge his collaboration with Antrim any time they had a mind to. Brady remembered Sully's warning: *You slip just once for that old man to see. . . .*

If he got the old man upset and they learned of it, what then?

There was still the bleak option he'd discarded before. Throw himself on Cyrus's mercy and hope. Brady hadn't seriously considered that it would do any good, but he'd come close to it a couple times. Trouble was, anything he started to tell his father always came out as sass. He couldn't help it; something in the old man's manner scraped him raw every time he tried talking to him. Far back as he could remember, his father had loomed across his world like a frowning, bearded titan. Prodding him always to measure up, savagely castigating him when he couldn't. How in hell could anyone measure up to Cyrus Trapp's standards?

True, the old man had softened in recent years. Enough to dumfound Brady, who'd modeled all his precepts on the harsh and roughshod Cyrus of his boyhood. And lately, watching the titan of memory wasting away before his eyes, he'd realized that the old Cyrus was no more; only a failing, indifferent husk remained. Was there a shred of hope in that fact? Sinking toward his end, Cyrus might be willing to call quits to every old score—and forgive. Yeah —he might just be approachable as hell now. If, Brady thought, he could screw down his temper and blunt ancient resentments with a few more drinks, he'd be mellow enough to beard the old bastard in a reasonable tone.

His fast fiery pulls at the bottle had nearly drained it, warming his confidence and giving a slushy twist to his thoughts. He wondered how Candler was doing with the widow Ekstrom. God damn! Imagine that scruffy pilgrim stepping in and taking over slick as pie. Lucky bastard. A lush piece like her could warm up a lot of winter nights. That smooth leggy walk put you in mind of wind curving a young pine. And man, what a set of jugs on her.

He struggled unsteadily to his feet. He felt sickish, his head swimming, and had to grab at the stall partition for support.

In the same instant one of the double doors burst open and cold air lashed him. A moment later Joe-Bob, propelled by a powerful shove, plunged through the open doors and fell in a headlong sprawl on the runway. After him came Cyrus; he jammed the door shut behind them.

Brady gaped at him. Cyrus's face looked swollen with rage; he loomed in the lantern light, his shadow flung huge and formless on the wall. His fists were closing and unclosing.

"Pa—?"

Cyrus came tramping up to Brady. Without a word, he swung his big palm. The blow smacked Brady's jaw like a club, tearing loose his hold on the partition. He landed in the runway on his hip and shoulder, rolled over once, and stopped on his back. He simply lay as he'd fallen, paralyzed with whiskey and shock. Reaching down, Cyrus fisted a handful of Brady's mackinaw, dragged him to his feet, and slammed him against the support post.

"We'll hear some truth from you for a change," Cyrus said hoarsely. "I heard plenty already. First from Beamis, then your simple pup of a brother. But it's really you, boy. You're the one."

His knotted fist was doubled up into Brady's throat, almost crushing off his wind. Brady clamped his hand around his father's wrist, but he couldn't summon the strength to break the savage grip. Blind fury was feeding Cyrus's ravaged body with a strength beyond itself.

"Your partners got caught. Searls and Quade—" Cyrus jerked Brady forward and back, crashing his head on the post. "They told Beamis everything. Now—" Again Brady's head slammed against the post. "You tell your old pa all about it!"

"Leggo, Pa," Brady choked. *"Jeezus——"*

"Just as soon as you talk. Then I let go. Then I mean to kick the living shit out of you, you thieving bastard!"

Joe-Bob was on his hands and knees, stupefied with terror, lank hair falling in his eyes. Scrambling to his feet now, he lunged at his father, seizing his arm. "Don't, Pa. Don't go hurting Brady—"

He nearly succeeded in wrestling Cyrus away, and then Cyrus roared "God damn!" and half-pivoted, lashing back with his free hand. It caught Joe-Bob flush on the temple and sent him stumbling backward. Momentarily free of Cyrus's pressing weight, Brady flung himself sideways, breaking Cyrus's hold. Stumbling wildly away, he was groggy but cold-headed now, tasting brassy fear.

Cyrus started after him, a great vein pulsing in his neck.

"Don't, don't do it, Pa," Brady wheezed. "Don't you lay a hand on me again, by God!"

"You gonna do nothing," Cyrus whispered, "except get booted clear off Chainlink. You won't be able to walk away when I'm done with you—"

A mad light quivered in his eyes. God, he's gone out of his head, he's going to kill me! The single thought flashed through Brady's mind with chill clarity before Cyrus's fist caught him full in the face.

Brady backpedaled, tripped, and fell into a stall. He shook his head, blood drops spraying from his pulped nose, then surged to his feet, fingers clawing for support. They closed on a pitchfork rammed in some loose hay; he yanked it free.

He tried to lunge out of the stall, but Cyrus, coming on bear-big and red-eyed, had blocked him off. Cornered, Brady screeched, *"Pa, don't!"* And swung the pitchfork up and forward in a desperate unthinking reflex. The tines flashed wickedly, momentarily, before Cyrus's deep-flung shadow dulled them as he came bulling straight on. Unthinkingly Brady braced his weight to meet the charge—

Cyrus's body ran onto the twin prongs with the full force of his rush. He staggered back, clutching at his belly. Red wetness crawled over his clenched fingers. He sighed, a soft explosive "Ah!" and turned slowly on his heel and walked out of the stall.

Brady dropped the pitchfork. Watched in sick dreading fascination as Cyrus halted in the runway. Then Cyrus's legs caved; he fell to his knees, his wet hands lifting to his head. He pressed them against his temples as if trying to squeeze out the intolerable agony that twisted his face.

His hands dropped; his body canted forward. He pitched on his face and was motionless.

Brady's legs moved; twists of hay crackled under his feet. Feeling nothing at all, he knelt by Cyrus. His arms felt weak as water. It took all his strength to heave his father's body over on its back.

Joe-Bob was whimpering, "Pa, Pa, Pa. . ."

"Shut up," Brady muttered.

"You killed him. You killed Pa."

"He killed himself. Shut your goddam mouth. I got to think."

Brady rasped a palm over his face, trying to scour feeling back into his numb flesh. God, you done it now, haven't you? You really done it. Goddam those two oozing wounds. They weren't deep enough to kill. That thing eating in Cyrus's head had really killed him; he might have gone any time. But no question that the shock of being double-stabbed in the guts had triggered his premature end. And not a way under the sun you could cover up the fact.

No. That somebody had stabbed Cyrus was unarguable. You couldn't cover that. But why did it have to be him? Brady's mind began racing with hot calculation. Tula, he knew, had left Chainlink yesterday in order to visit some Indian friends halfway across the valley; she hadn't returned yet.

"Kid. Listen to me. When Pa collared you in the house, was there anyone else about?"

Joe-Bob's face glittered with tears; he gazed dumbly at his brother.

"Snap to, Goddammit! Did anyone else see it? Was Adah there?"

"Uh—I didn't see 'er. She mighta been in bed with one of them headaches. You know how she gets."

Yeah. Dead to the world when she had to sleep off a headache. If so, it was unlikely she'd heard anything either.

"Brady, what we gonna do? What we gonna do now?"

"Well," Brady said softly, "we ain't gonna bawl over it."

Standing now, he tramped over to his brother. Roughly cupped his hand around Joe-Bob's chin, squeezing it between thumb and fingers. Joe-Bob winced; Brady shook him gently. "You're in this with me. Don't you forget it. No matter what anyone asks, you say what I'll tell you to say. Just that. We're gonna come out of this smelling like spring flowers."

Clean as a whistle, Brady thought. If it worked—his mind sprinted exultantly ahead to all that might be. If it worked.

CHAPTER TWELVE

"Then I mustanged in the Mogollon country," Bowie said. "That's catching wild horses. I caught and rough-broke plenty till my bones began to brittle up. Happens way before a man turns thirty."

"Long ago Mr. Trapp did so too," Sofie observed. "He told me."

Bowie smiled. "Yeah, only he worked for himself and saved his money. I worked for an outfit for wages and generally blowed what I earned in a few days. You know, drinking and things. Course a man learns. I finally laid by a good stake and throwed in with another fellow, Danny Spike, on a little freight line. Only there was a bigger outfit freighting the same route between Silver City and Redrock. When we cut rates, they didn't like it. Shot our mules and burned us out."

"*Himmel*, was there no law?"

"Law don't always shine for the little man. This top dog owned a lot more than we did, including a bought sheriff and judge. Danny and I busted up and drifted our own ways. What I heard of Dan later on, he got killed in a gambling scrape in Redrock."

Bowie fell silent in his chair, gazing at the crackling fire. Friends. He had buried a few. Others he hardly remembered. The faces came and went over the years, jostling and merging in memory, and after a while most of them seemed the same. It was no different with the jobs. Bunkhouses you called home while you sweated or froze your ass for the fatcats who owned the ranches, the mines, the

127

lumbering operations. Sometimes you tried striking on
your own; he'd dredged up a few of those memories for
Sofie tonight. Memories that seemed even bleaker in the
telling than in the way they totaled to beat a man down
over the years. But talking about them smacked of self-
pity, which his fierce pride rejected. Hell, most men he'd
worked with lived with their lot and bitched as a matter of
course, rarely feeling sorry for themselves. The ones who
did cracked apart without fanfare. Hanging themselves
maybe, or whipping razors across their throats. It was too
bad, but life had to go on. Like old Cyrus had said, long as
you could keep the candle going was worth it.

Sofie gently broke the silence. "What do you think of
now?"

"Nothing much."

"Oh *ja*, Bowie. You think a lot." She laughed. "You
hardly talk at all, you think sad things so much. Your face,
I can tell. I like to sit and wonder what does he think of."

"Man like that can be pretty tiresome."

"No. No, not to talk is all right when that is a man's
way. But you talk a lot tonight, more than you have before. This I like too, but I don't like to think you're sad."

Bowie felt a faint embarrassment. He could tell her that
sadness as she meant it wasn't a part of it any longer. But
how to say such a thing? To say it all, he'd have to laboriously explain how it seemed that every time a man got
something going for him, it would sour out. That after a
time he sickened of even trying. That he blamed nothing
and nobody for it, but that didn't change how the bill always totted up. That these two weeks of evenings by her
fireplace had left him with something altogether different.
That watching Sofie and listening to her quick lilt of words
and laughter tickled up a good warmth that made him
lighthearted (or lightheaded, he wasn't sure which) in a
way he'd never known.

Hell, he couldn't tell her all that; he wouldn't know how
to begin. Or how to get out a lot more that kept crowding
to his mind and became harder to crowd out. Sofie had
married a failure of a man; she deserved better next time
around. This was the sadness, sharp and regretful, that

coupled with the goodness of these times in her company. He couldn't take more from her than a string of gentle firelit evenings allowed when all he could give in return was a mass of failings. What else could he lay claim to?

"I better be turning in," he said, getting to his feet. "Have to look to my horse too."

"*Ja*, the horse. You always look to him."

"Well, I worry he'll take the green heaves from grain-feeding sometime. You never know about a high-plains mustang."

"No wonder you worry, an animal so fine to look at. Has he a name?"

"Uh—Kicker. I call him Kicker."

Pulling on his mackinaw, he looked at her standing in the firelight. Straight and firm-bodied and very young-looking in an old calico dress. Her hair was done in a single thick braid twisted in a coronet atop her head; it caught the light like pale flame. It was getting harder to push away what he couldn't say and feared he might. Damn. Maybe he shouldn't have started these visits. But he knew he wasn't sorry. That he wouldn't stop them, either, unless or until she said the word.

"Good night, my good friend. Maybe I will pray you don't be sad any more."

Bowie colored a little. That was her straight-faced way of laughing at him, with a gentle warmth that made it stingless.

As he tramped across to the stables, the warmth stayed with him; it reached to his insides like a soft hand. The snow was pelting down so thickly that it veiled the ranch buildings to dark blurs; it had a fresh squeaky crunch under his boots. Coming to the stable doors, he reached for the swingbar and found it off the brackets; somebody must be inside.

He dragged one door open, stepped inside, and came to a dead halt. The dim light of a bull's-eye showed him a scene he couldn't believe.

Brady waved his pistol slightly, motioning with it. "All the way in, pilgrim. Then shut the door."

Bowie slowly obeyed. Then he took the scene in wholly, feeling chilled to his guts. Brady facing him spraddle-legged, gun pointed. Joe-Bob crouching on his heels, looking furtive and miserable. Cyrus stretched on his back in the runway, his face waxen and still.

"What's happened here?"

"See for yourself."

Brady moved aside and Bowie tramped past him and bent down by Cyrus. His mouth was partly open, his eyes sightless. Touching his face, Bowie found the flesh already cold. He saw sticky darkness on Cyrus's coat and started his hand toward it.

"That's enough," Brady said softly. "You got the idea."

Tight-throated, Bowie shook his head. "No. I don't get it. You—*you*?"

"It was an accident. Kind of your doing too, ridgerunner. How you like that?"

Bowie stood up now, watching Brady's face. It held a heavy mockery, the jaws grooved with tension. Blood crusted his nose.

"You should of shot them two yahoos you turned loose, boy," Brady said. "Seems they got caught and spilled everything to Beamis. All about me and Joe-Bob. So the old man came r'aring after me. Way it happened, he just r'ared hisself to death. Might of happened different if you'd been honest with him first place."

"You son of a bitch."

"Yeah, but I'm gonna be the live one." Brady shifted his feet, grinning. "Like I say, it was an accident. We won't pretend it was nothing else. Only you gonna be the one that pushed the old bastard over the edge." He slapped a bottle that bulged the pocket of his coat, its neck protruding. "You asked what happened here. All right, I tell you, pilgrim. The old man run out of that stuff he's been injecting in him to kill his goddam pains. He had to fall back on booze. You want to know what booze did to my old man? Turned him crazy. As much like to attack friend as foe." Brady jerked out a flat chuckle. "Well sir, he went clean out of his head, that's what. Cornered you down here and they wasn't much you could do but defend yourself. With that."

He pointed at a pitchfork on the floor. Its tines, Bowie saw, were stained at the tips as though something wetly dark had frozen on them.

"Too goddam bad about that," Brady went on. "I mean, hell, Adah knows how Cyrus got when he had some redeye in him. So does Nevers. Likewise Tula. Too bad you didn't know, pilgrim, 'cause see, you'd have a good self-defense plea. Only you didn't know. After you killed him, you panicked and went kiting off in the storm, nobody knows where. When the storm lets up, your tracks'll be long gone. Longer than anybody's gonna realize, boy. That is, till they turn up your body come spring."

Bowie was getting the picture. Not all of it. But enough to turn a man's guts. "Who you think's going to believe all that?"

Brady laughed. "It don't make such bad sense, pilgrim. Why you figure we been waiting here for you near an hour? Hell, everyone knows you been cozying your ass over at the widow Ekstrom's ever' night around this time. Ain't no secret either you always have a last look at that buckskin before you turn in."

"That's what brought me here," Bowie said softly. "What you suppose brought your pa?"

"Why, horseshit, man, who knows why somebody who goes off his head from a lick of booze does anything he does when he's got some in him?"

Bowie shook his head. "It won't work. It's got too big a smell about it."

"Brady," Joe-Bob said shakily, coming up off his haunches, "you know, he's right. I mean, we run into Sam Beamis on the road and he give us a godawful funny look. He knows about us and Antrim, he———"

"He told the old man, sure. But he didn't arrest us directly he clapped eyes on us, why not? I'll tell you why, lunkhead. 'Cause the old man told Beamis he wasn't pressing charges. If that was the old man's last word to him, Beamis ain't gonna stir up the kettle on't now, not the kind of friends they was."

"But Jeez, Brady, he's gonna figure we musta tangled with the old man soon's we got home———"

"It don't make no goddam difference what he thinks," Brady snapped. "He's gotta have proof. Told you, we're gonna set it up to look like pilgrim here done it, and we're gonna tell it that way. Unless Beamis can prove otherwise, he's gotta accept our story."

"But Jeez, he'll *know*———!"

"Shut up!" Brady half shouted, tense muscles ridging his face. Sweat glistened on his cheekbones. "It'll work like I said if you just keep your goddam head!" His voice quieted. "I'll do the talking when the time comes, but you got to back me all the way. One wrong word and you'll kick over the bucket. Keep the story straight and we'll have everything. Every damn thing. . . ."

As he talked, Brady tramped over to his father's body, pulled the bottle from his pocket, drew the cork with his teeth, and poured a little of the remaining liquor into Cyrus's mouth. The rest he spilled on Cyrus's shirt where his coat fell open. He straightened with a grunt, ramming the bottle back in his pocket.

"All right, pilgrim. Fling your hull on that buckskin. Then saddle that bay of mine."

"You go to hell," Bowie said quietly.

Brady tipped his gun up. "You want it right here?"

"That won't do your story a lot of good, will it?"

With a savage curse, Brady took two long steps and swung his pistol, slashing the barrel across Bowie's temple. He grabbed at his head as he fell to his hands and knees, pinwheels of pain rocking his skull. Dimly he heard Brady say, "Get his saddle on, kid. Hurry it up."

When the two horses were readied, Brady bent and grabbed Bowie roughly by the shoulder. "On your feet, damn you. Get up on that nag unless you want more of the same."

Bowie staggered against the buckskin's flank as Joe-Bob held the animal steady. For a moment he held to the pommel, sickly mustering his strength, and then he swung up. Brady stepped into his saddle, saying, "It's gonna

work for us, kid. You do like I said. Get up to the house
and clean the old man's supply of drugs out of his desk.
Don't miss nothing. Here, take this bottle—leave it in his
office. Then get back here and wait for me. Got that?"

Joe-Bob nodded dumbly.

"Open them doors for us. Pilgrim, you ride out ahead
of me. I'll tell you where to go."

They skirted wide of the bunkhouse, dark and silent
now in the skirling snow which almost hid it from view.
The crew was all abed, Bowie thought, setting his teeth
against the battering ache of his head. But they wouldn't
be abed too long; he could picture how it would go. Brady
excitedly arousing them with the news: Cyrus dead in the
stable and he'd seen Bowie taking flight. Or would Brady
handle it another way? The details didn't matter. Soon the
increasing wind would sweep all the tracks smooth, making Brady's story unshakable. As he'd said, it might smell
to high heaven some ways; but who could disprove it?

At Brady's order, Bowie pointed the buckskin toward
the north peaks. He couldn't make out much in the shroud
of blowing snow, but Brady had an unerring eye for the
few dimly seen landmarks; he knew where he was going
and his cursing commands kept Bowie headed on what
seemed like a straight course.

Snowflakes whipped Bowie's face in deepening gusts;
his eyes stung and watered. He clamped his hat low and
hunched his head into his turned-up collar. The snow still
mantled the frozen ground thinly, letting the horses move
at a steady pace. But in a few hours, Bowie knew, it would
be drifted a foot or more deep. The full cold certainty of
his predicament was settling into his marrow. Wherever
Brady chose to dispose of him, his snow-covered corpse
wouldn't be found till spring.

Chainlink's rolling north range extended far into the
foothills country. Northwest were the Breaks; northeaster-
ly, the land climbed toward the high passes through which
Bowie had come south weeks ago. He guessed they were
moving in that general direction, which made sense
enough if he were clearing out in panic, as Brady's version

would have it. But how far did Brady intend taking him? Probably not too far, with the storm threatening to develop into a lot worse.

About the time he could feel the ground tending to rise, Bowie made out a black broken spine of ridges against the lighter sky ahead of them. Almost before he realized it they were moving sharply upward through stunted pines; they were on an age-old trail that the Indians had probably used. Wind whistled through the pine tops, which somewhat broke the storm's force. Occasionally he glanced back at Brady's dark muffled form. He couldn't see the pistol, but Brady would have it close to hand.

His only chance lay in making a break for it, but so far there'd been no possibility of bringing it off. Brady kept close on his heels, never falling more than three yards behind. Nor was he likely to find an opportunity unless the storm increased in fury, enough to cover his break beyond the distance he'd gain on the steep gamble that he could catch Brady briefly off guard.

Suddenly they came out of the trees, and then they were climbing straight upward across black spurs of shale outcrop; the horses' hooves skidded slickly here and there. Here in the high open the wind shrieked down off the heights, buffeting men and mounts with icy fists. Bowie felt his horse shudder and snort as they came unexpectedly against a sheer rock wall, or what felt like one.

"To your right!" Brady yelled. "Push on right—there's a trail."

Not very goddam much of a trail. It was treacherously narrow, bending out of sight where the wall curved away. Bowie's spine crawled as he edged the buckskin along it, feeling out every step on the snow-frosted rock. On one side the wall soared almost straight upward; on the other, so far as he could tell, the trail lipped off in a snow-swirling gulf. A gorge that was deep but pretty narrow, he could make out the opposite rim.

Jesus! He felt a chill certainty before Brady spoke.

"Stop where you are, pilgrim."

Bowie halted, looking back over his shoulder. He didn't dare to make any other move on this slender ribbon of ledge. Brady hadn't advanced a step onto the ledge trail. He sat his horse waiting, and now he cocked his gun. The metal *snack-snack* was crisp and specific.

"You run your last ridge, boy. End of the trail."

"You think I'll just hop off here for your convenience, that it?"

They were half-shouting; the wind tore their words away.

"That or get shot off. Your choice!"

"Horse and me'll get found come spring, Brady. Think about it!"

"You was pushing hard when you lit out. You don't know the country good, you took a bad trail, you slipped here and went over. Both of you. That's how it'll look."

"With a bullet in me?" Bowie jeered. "There might be enough left of me to show a bullet hole. How'll you explain that? Because you'll sure-hell have to put one in me, Junior. Go ahead."

Deliberately he heeled the buckskin forward along the ledge trail. A few more yards and he would pass out of Brady's sight, and now he braced for the worst.

Brady fired, but not at him. The shot creased the buckskin. He squealed and surged crazily against the wall; rock gouged Bowie's leg. Brady shot again as Bowie kicked out of his stirrups and scrambled sideways, trying to leave the saddle. The buckskin was fiddlefooting in pain and terror, and then he bolted. Instantly his hooves skidded; his sloughing weight went out of control and over the edge of the rimrock.

Bowie dropped free of the falling horse, hitting the ledge in a loose horsebreaker's roll. Landing on his back, he felt one leg slip over the rim; he tried to twist onto his belly and claw for a hold, but too late. His hand closed on wet snow and slick rock, and then his whole body went over.

He was plunging down a rough slant, body straight and head up, but there was nothing to hold onto. Only loose snow and rotted shale that broke and clattered downward under his scrambling hands. In the same instant that his feet slid off into nothing, his fingers closed on a projecting nub of rock. For a moment it stopped his fall, but it was too slick and shallow for him to gain purchase. Abruptly his hands slipped off.

He dropped several yards in a free fall, then struck a lower slant of the gorge wall with a force that battered him numb, body and senses. Afterward he bounced and scraped downward on a steepening pitch, flinty points ripping at his clothing and flesh. Suddenly this slant too ended. A moment of cold space and rushing darkness. Then he hit bottom with an impact he hardly felt. Lit on his feet, but his buckling legs flailed away his footing and his body slammed on frozen earth. A smashing blow on the head. Then the world spun away from his last flicker of sensibility.

CHAPTER THIRTEEN

Sully Calder lay awake in his bunk, watching the dim square of window on the south wall. When it began to turn light, he would make his move. Not before. Around him the vague snores and grunts of sleeping men made a rude blending above the seething whisper of snow against the outer walls. Funny how men slept. Some as silent as death; others grumping and tossing; some with sodden snorings like buzzsaws cutting wet wood. He'd never particularly noticed such differences before; but tonight, his nerves alert and waiting, Sully had catalogued the sleeping habits of every man in the bunkhouse.

Just a manner of whiling away the time. That and thinking. But he'd pretty well worried every thought in his head to extinction. Only false dawn might offer some of the answers. All he'd need was sufficient dull light to track by. Luckily the wind appeared to be holding low so that, God willing, there'd be undrifted sign enough for him to follow.

Sully forced himself to relax and go over the whole thing again. Brady's account of what had happened hinged on coincidence that wasn't so wildly improbable in itself. It just might have occurred that way. What gave his story such a patently false ring to Sully's mind was knowing the people involved as he did.

Way Brady had told it, he and Joe-Bob had returned from Saltville and were approaching the stable, thinking it funny the doors were hanging open, when a rider had come lunging out of the building, spurring his horse wildly. Nothing but a dark shape in the storm, he was quickly swallowed by it. The brothers, hurrying into the stable, had found their father's body. The rest, if you wanted to believe Brady, was clear as spring water. Hell, a blind man could figure how it had gone. Cyrus had found Candler in the stable looking to his horse. Christ, who knew what reason the old man had for going down there? Likely no reason. He smelled hog-high of booze and it was no secret what effect liquor had on him. He must have attacked Candler, who'd defended himself with the pitchfork. Lightly stabbed in the guts, Cyrus had died then and there: the final shock to his system. Candler? He'd simply panicked and run out. He'd already followed Candler's tracks a short way, Brady added, but he was too far ahead to overtake in the night and storm. Natural enough to cut out like he did, figuring odds wouldn't favor anyone believing it had been an accident.

Natural for some men, Sully thought. But Bowie Candler getting that badly rattled? Sully's instant reaction had been one of flat disbelief, though he'd said nothing. Only after Brady had roused the crew and they were all in the stable, gazing at the body and listening to Brady's reconstruction of what must have happened, had Sully put a casual question to Brady.

"You touch the body at all?"

"No," Brady growled. "Why should I?"

Sully pointed at an isolated patch of blood which had soaked into the clay two feet from Cyrus's body. "That looks like he fell on his belly. No other wound on him, is there?"

"Well, he must of turned over before he died. Or maybe Candler turned him over."

Sully nodded soberly. "Yeah. That'd be it, I guess."

But the unexpected question had caught Brady off balance. Something in the tight, defensive way he'd responded suggested a man who hadn't adjusted all sides of his story. If Faye Nevers thought anything was fishy, he'd masked his thoughts, merely listening to Brady and saying little. But that was like Faye. It was he who'd gone up to the house to break the news to Adah Trapp.

Anyway, Brady had gone on pointedly, it had to be Candler, didn't it? He was gone; so was his buckskin horse. And Nevers, returning from the house, had confirmed that the drugs Cyrus had kept in his desk were gone too—and he'd found an empty whiskey bottle. But a number of factors, as Sully sized them up, didn't jog into place at all.

If Cyrus had run low on pain killers, why hadn't he renewed his supply before now? And where had he gotten the booze? Tula had said that after Cyrus's drunken fit some weeks ago, Mrs. Trapp had ordered her to throw out every drop of liquor in the house; Tula had done so. It was unbelievable that Cyrus, hardly a man to compound one near-tragic mistake, would conceal a bottle somewhere. Something else too: Sully had taken the opportunity to touch Cyrus's face, its flesh cold in death. If he'd been killed only minutes before Brady had rousted out the crew, how had the heat run out of his body so quickly?

He wouldn't be the only one puzzling over those questions, Sully reflected grimly. Trouble was, even if they did riddle the situation with suspicious overtones, mere unanswered questions couldn't discredit Brady's story. Only Bowie Candler could do that.

And where was Bowie?

That he'd ridden away on the buckskin seemed unarguable. Sully had checked the tracks leading to and from the stable—and that was something else. The prints left by the returning Trapp brothers were deeply blurred by the fast-falling snow, yet to a considerably lesser extent than the horse tracks leading out in the storm. But these, too, had already been blown into as if a far longer time had elapsed since they were made than Brady's telling would bear out.

The whole damn business had more holes in it than a wormy apple.

Most of all, Sully wondered what had really happened to Bowie. His concern for his friend was as keen as his shock of grief at Cyrus's death. That had been expected; yet a man like Cyrus Trapp deserved at least the dignity of a decent end. Not an interpretation which said he'd been

stabbed with a pitchfork while in the throes of a drunken
rage. Thinking about it all, Sully felt a clean and feral
anger that honed his determination sharper.

All right. Carry it a step farther. Had Brady arranged a
deliberate frame-up against Bowie? Even considering Brady's hatred of him, that didn't seem likely. The situation as
it stood smelled of a hasty improvising. Brady, give him
credit, had brains enough to concoct a frame far more
cunningly rigged than this leaky piece of business. The
real circumstances of Cyrus's death remained unclear; all
Sully could dredge up were uncertain guesses.

Well, maybe he could resolve them one way or the
other. It was time——a vagueness of gray light had begun to
stain the window. That was all he needed. If enough still
remained of the tracks.

Moving in total silence, Sully lifted his blankets off and
swung his sock feet to the floor. Fully dressed except for
his boots, he felt for them by his bunk and pulled them on.
His mackinaw and hat and a couple of wool scarves were
ready to hand; he donned them, picked up his rifle, and
slipped noiselessly as a cat across the bunkroom to the
door. Opening and shutting it without arousing anyone
would be the ticklish part. The latch creaked softly as he
lifted it; he eased the door open just a foot. A soft gust of
cold swept the room as he slid outside and swiftly closed
the door.

So far, so good. Sully scanned the ground as he hurried
to the stable, noting that the tracks trampled out a few
hours before were still plain. But they'd blown over to
shallow depressions and were filling fast; the wind was
picking up. No time to lose. Glancing toward Mrs. Ekstrom's house, he saw a light in the window. She too had
been roused by the excitement when Cyrus's body was discovered; she knew that Bowie Candler was missing. Sully
wasn't sure what-all had developed between Bowie and
her, but he guessed it ran deep enough that she too would
be getting little sleep this night.

Entering the stable, Sully located and lighted the bull's-
eye lantern. By its sickly light he quickly saddled and bridled his favorite horse, a sturdy short-coupled pinto. In a

few minutes he was on the open flats north of headquarters, riding briskly. The snow hadn't deepened
enough during the night hours to seriously impede him,
but here on the flats wind and snow had conspired to all
but erase the horse tracks. Two horsemen had ridden this
way; one had returned. Sully was soon convinced that
Brady had lied about following Candler's tracks a short
distance. The tracks of both horses continued far onto the
flats. Brady hadn't followed Bowie this far in the storm
unless he was right with him, Sully knew.

Though still held to guesswork, he was beginning to
fear the worst.

In places the tracks had drifted completely over. Time
and again Sully was forced to go slowly, keeping on a
straight line and hoping; each time he did, his calculations
were rewarded. Here and there, where a bank or swale
had broken the drive of wind and snow, tracks still showed
faintly. Before long he was climbing an old trail into a belt
of pines which had sheltered the light prints so well that
sign of two horses, one following the other, told a plain
story. *Only one rider had returned.*

More and more Sully felt chilled by the implications:
Bowie didn't know the landscape well enough to cut
string-straight for this ridge trail in a storm. But Brady
did. Brady had been in control; he'd deliberately herded
Bowie in this direction.

The light was steadily growing, the storm still holding
low. As he advanced into the timber and it closed behind
him, Sully hipped around in his saddle without drawing
rein. Scanning his backtrail was an instinctive precaution;
he didn't expect to see anything.

His heart gave a sickening jolt. A rider was following
him. Scarcely more than a faint shadow on the murky
scape, he was holding a good distance. But unmistakably
he was on Sully's trail.

Brady hadn't been sleeping either, Sully guessed bleakly. Had he kept a watch from the house on the chance that
somebody would try to pick up the fading trail that would
prove him a liar? No matter. He saw me ride out, Sully
thought with conviction, and he knew why.

Deep in the trees now, Sully pulled up behind some clustering pines and dragged his Springfield from the saddle boot. All he need do was sit his horse offside the trail and wait. Snow flurried down through the branches in wicked gusts; he had the bone-deep feeling that this slow building storm would be smashing down with blizzard force before very long.

He heard the rider coming up through the trees; then he swung abruptly into view. Sully lifted his rifle and crossed the rider's chest with his sights. "You—stop there!"

Even as he spoke, he saw with surprise that this wasn't Brady. It was Sofie Ekstrom, firmly astride a man's saddle with her skirt bunched tight around her legs against the cold. She looked lost inside a bulky mackinaw; tendrils of her hair blew free of the scarf knotted over it.

"Mr. Calder? You do not shoot, please."

Sully clucked his tongue in disgust and rode down to her, reining up by her stirrup to stirrup. "God almighty, Miz Ekstrom, what you think you're about?"

"The same you are, I think." She blinked against the snow gusts; her face was pink with cold. "I watch from my window when you ride out. You do not believe Mr. Brady Trapp, eh?"

"Miz Ekstrom, you better turn that nag around and get back fast as you can. This weather'll be turning a sight worse directly."

"*Ja*. Maybe I know winters better than you, eh? That's why I come after you. If Mr. Candler's somewhere hurt, he will need good care. I have brought some stuff will help. Did you think of this?"

"We don't know anything for sure yet," Sully snapped. "I can't have you dragging along and time's growing short. Don't argue with me."

"I do not argue." Her tone was quiet, her jaw stubborn; worry overlay her face like an angry shadow. "I am going with you. Do not waste time, go on now. I follow you."

Swearing softly, Sully gigged his horse onward, through the last trees and onto a steep ridgeside where black bulges of rock thrust up through patchy veins of snow. He could only hope to God that Brady had taken Bowie this way and that the trail would end soon. For on this high open slope, the wind had swept every vestige of their tracks clean away.

Bowie dragged his eyes open. He couldn't see much of anything and he felt nothing at all. He moved a hand; it felt like a chunk of ice. So did his whole arm as he raised it and brought the hand to his face. Like ice touching ice. Jesus! He lifted his head and forced his arms and legs to move; he sat up. Shattering pain in his head. The whole right side of his face was numb where it had rested on the snow. He gazed stupidly at the bloody claws of his hands. Then he began to remember.

He climbed to his feet; snow sifted from his clothing. He took a tottering step and nearly fell. Stood dizzy and swaying, trying to collect his senses. Feeling started to flood back to most of his battered body. A multitude of bruises quivered to life; agony tore midway at his legs. Clothes ripped all to hell, pants and underwear shredded to bloodied tatters at the knees. Bowie batted clumsily at the numb side of his face, feeling a thrust of panic now as he realized that he could hardly feel his hands or feet. He braced his trembling legs and forced himself to take one slow step, then another, setting his teeth. He could walk; could he move his fingers? He forced them to curl against his palms. He could hardly tell that he had toes, but they wiggled. Nothing was broken, nothing frozen.

He strode up and down stamping his feet, beating his arms against his sides. Gathered up a handful of snow and rubbed it vigorously over his face; it helped clear his head. Burning sensation prickled sharply into ears and toes. Bowie felt a mighty surge of relief. Touch of frostbite, nothing worse. His palms and knees had been savaged raw in his descent of the rugged gorge flank, but the stabbing pain was actually welcome. His head seemed to balloon with a crushing pulse of pain, but running a hand over it, he found only a swollen knot behind his ear. The skin hadn't even been broken.

He halted by the crumpled body of the buckskin. The sloping wall and thin cushion of snow that had saved

Bowie's life hadn't benefited the horse. He'd plunged down in a straight battering fall that was unbroken till he'd hit the flint-edged fragments of fallaway rock that littered the gorge floor. Bowie crouched down, brushed away some mounding snow, and laid a hand on the still warm flank. Neck broken. Spine probably severed clean and instantly. One break for you, old Shitkicker. You were a good one. Bowie's eyes stung; he felt a rise of seething rage.

God damn Brady Trapp. God damn his meeching dirty soul to hell.

Had to see to getting out of this place. He hadn't a notion of how long he'd been unconscious, but it was still dark. The weather hadn't appreciably worsened in the interval; he was pretty well sheltered from the wind here. But the storm could pick up fiercely any time, the relatively light cold plunging much lower. He'd be all right while he kept moving about, but the main thing was to find a way out of here.

Bowie scanned the walls of the gorge up and down, squinting against the darkness and eddying flakes. Both the flanking slants were so steep that he doubted he could climb either side. No rugged projections that he could make out, only rounded nubs of rock that his raw palms would be unable to grip.

Maybe he could follow the gorge to its end. Or at least to an easier point of ascent. He tramped about a hundred yards northward till he came to a dead end: the gorge boxed off in a sheer wall. Retracing his steps down canyon, he found that the cleft narrowed steadily. Finally the walls pinched down to a crack he couldn't wedge his body through.

Jesus God. He was in a goddam trap.

A first real fear began to nettle Bowie's guts. No way out except up one treacherous wall or the other. And he was like to break his neck trying. What were the chances of someone being suspicious enough of Brady's explanations to backtrack him? Sully might do so, good chance that he would, but suppose the goddam tracks were covered up by morning? No—no odds in just waiting. Particularly when Brady himself might return by daylight to make sure of him.

Soon as there was light enough, he'd make the try. He whiled away the time tramping up and down, studying the walls. He could barely make out the rimrock, but he reckoned it to be some sixty feet above his head. He sized up a spot where he might be able to climb part way with the aid of a rope, at the same time taking note of a sizable bulge about halfway up. It just might block his further ascent, but he couldn't locate a likelier place to make the climb. Bowie got the lariat from his saddle and worked the cold-stiff coils in his hands as he walked, gritting his teeth against the agony of his palms.

The rimrock grew sharper against a slowly graying sky. Long minutes more passed before enough light reached into the gorge to pick out the separate heels of projecting rock. Bowie's rope was thirty feet long; he couldn't snag anything higher than halfway up. After considerable study, he settled on a fairly rough-edged spur just above the bulge. Be a tight cast even if his rope could reach it.

After a half-dozen throws, he looped his noose over the spur. Gathering the shreds of his will, he gripped the rope tight in both raw hands and swung his full weight on it. The effort was excruciating, but the noose was securely fixed; the spur itself held firm.

Agonizingly, slowly, he began going hand over hand up the precarious slant, using his feet all he could to take some of the savage pressure off his hands. Pebbly fragments rattled away from under his rasping boots. Sweat crawled down his forehead and half blinded him. Holding on briefly one-handed, Bowie brushed it away with his sleeve. Climbed on. He felt a sharpening alarm when pain began to subside because his hands were going numb. Worms of blood crawled warmly down his wrists, slicking his tortured grips on the jerking line. He could feel the creeping weakness in his fingers.

A little farther—just a little. Then he could rest a minute.

Several feet below the obstructing bulge was a rugged

knob broad enough to offer footholds. At last, unable to
see for the reddening haze on his vision, Bowie halted and
groped with his feet. Felt the knob solidly beneath them.
Cautiously relaxed his straining holds as he let the projection his full weight. It held. Rubbery and trembling in
every muscle, he leaned hard against the wall, supporting
himself with a light grip on the rope.

Almost halfway. But Jesus. Did he have enough left to
pull himself to the spur where his noose was anchored? If
he did, how would he get the leverage to cast it over a
higher projection—if he could locate one? Bowie settled
his chin wearily on his chest. Nothing to do but rest a
while, and then try calling on a reserve of strength he
wasn't sure he possessed. His teeth began to chatter as the
chill of immobility ate into his flesh.

Something off key touched his dulled nerve ends.
Sounds that weren't a part of the gaunt dawn or the whispering snow.

At first he thought he'd imagined them. Shook his head
to clear it and listened. Faint voices carrying on the low
wind—one a woman's. At least two people. Bowie called,
"Here," his voice a husky croak.

A moment later they edged into view on the rim above.
For a moment he couldn't quite believe it, yet who else
might he have expected? Nobody, of course. Nobody but
Sully and Sofie.

"How you doing, paleface?" Sully called.

"I could use another rope if you got one."

"That's what we got. One."

Sully pulled back from sight. Reappeared with his
coiled catch rope. Dropping its noose end over the rim, he
paid out line till it dangled a couple feet above Bowie's
head. "That's all she'll run," Sully said. "Wait a minute."
He stretched out on his belly and extended his arm downward, gripping the rope end. The noose brushed Bowie's
shoulder. Slowly and awkwardly, hardly able to work his
finger, he crudely tied it to his own rope.

"You pull 'em both up and make a good hitch knot,
we'll have more'n enough."

"You can hold on?" Sofie said anxiously.

Bowie hugged the cliff, his bloody palms flat against the icy rock. Now supporting his whole weight, the knob under his feet felt abruptly slick and precarious. "Sure. Haul away."

Sully swiftly drew both ropes up to the ledge, jerking Bowie's noose free of the spur. He tied the rope ends together with a series of hitches which he knotted in at several places. Again he dropped a noose to Bowie, this time with plenty of slack to spare. "Fasten that under your arms and hold on tight as you can. My horse'll pull you up."

The rest was comparatively easy. Sully hooked the rope over a rounded jog on the rimrock's lip, then backed his horse far enough onto the ledge trail to secure its end to the pommel. Mounting, he heeled the animal gently into motion. Bowie let his weight swing out, hanging briefly free over the long drop till he was dragged past the overhead bulge. From there on his body bumped gradually up the rough slant to the rim. Sofie was waiting, her strong hands reaching down to grasp his wrists. A moment later he was heaved up bodily onto the rim.

Utterly spent, Bowie stayed on his knees as Sofie lifted the rope off. His muscles felt like cold jelly. Sully came hurrying up. With the two of them supporting Bowie between them, they edged back single file along the narrow trail to safe ground.

CHAPTER FOURTEEN

Bowie should have shelter and warmth; he needed tending to. And the sooner he got them, the better. Brady was in-control at Chainlink now, and the other nearest ranch out-fit was miles away. That was how Sully summed it up. Best place to go, he said, was a line camp on Chainlink's high summer range north of here. It was deserted for the winter and it wasn't too far. But the storm was worsening as dawn advanced, so they'd best waste no time.

With Bowie on Sully's paint horse, Sully tramping ahead and Sofie bringing up the rear, they circled off the jag of ridges and swung north into a gentle rise of foothills. Sully led the paint, for it was all Bowie could do to hang on with his knees clamping the horse's barrel and his torn hands gripping the pommel. Sofie had ripped up some flannel rags to tie around his hands and Sully had pulled his own thick-fleeced gloves over them. They felt as if the nerves had been flayed bare; a fiery pulse quivered in every finger. Bowie knew if he relaxed his hold for a moment, he'd fall off.

The terrain had a feel of getting higher and more rugged. Despite the light of new day, the snow was blow-ing harder and thicker; you couldn't make out objects beyond a few yards away. Sully tramped steadily and sure-ly against a wind that cut like blades off the heights. Most of Bowie's face was muffled in a scarf that Sully had pro-vided; spikes of cold drove against every inch of his ex-posed skin. Cold seeped through his clothes and ate deeper into his already chilled flesh. His ears echoed with the wind's howl. His thoughts kept raveling away except for one: hang on and ride it out.

He didn't know how long the journey lasted. Minutes or an hour—maybe longer. He knew that Sully angled onto a high twisting trail; dark stands of pine marched by in the pelting whiteness. Here and there the trail would level out and then climb some more. Several times Bowie felt his hands slipping. Somehow dredged up the reserves of will to make his fingers tighten again. But he couldn't keep it up forever, before much longer he would weaken, he would fall. . . .

Suddenly the wind was cut off. He knew that first of all. Then Sully was saying words that jumbled senselessly in his ears. He raised his head blindly. A dimness of shed walls enclosed him; the paint horse had halted. Sully's hands tugged at him and Sofie was there too, helping ease him down to a stable floor. His legs gave way; they had to hold him upright, Sully saying: "Just a few yards, boy, you'll be all right, move your legs, that's it—"

Being able to move again, tramping upslope through deepening snow, wind fierce on his face, revived Bowie's sluggish senses. But he felt exhausted, bone tired, weary to the marrow. A long low building of peeled logs took form ahead and then they were in the lee of it, out of the wind, and Sully was unlatching a warped door, heaving his weight against it till the stiffened rawhide hinges bent and it scraped open. They pushed into a dark drafty room.

Bowie sagged gratefully onto a straw-tick bunk. Sofie found blankets and heaped them over him. Sully went back to tend the horses and fetch an armload of wood. He laid a fire in the field-stone fireplace and built it to a roaring blaze. It washed the time-darkened walls with a mellow glow and picked out the rough comforts of a puncheon table and benches, two bunks built into the cabin corners, and pantry shelves lined with crocks and utensils.

Sully made several more trips for wood till a sizable pile of oak lengths was stacked by the fireplace. Meantime Sofie rummaged among the shelves; she found a shallow pan and a coffeepot, filled both with snow, set the pan by the fire and hung the coffeepot on the fireplace lug. When the pan water had melted and warmed, she washed Bowie's lacerated hands and knees, treated them with bluestone and sweet oil she'd brought, and carefully tied them up with more rag bandages.

Sully dumped a final load of wood, unbuttoned his coat, and held his palms to the fire. "You thawed out yet, paleface?"

"Just about."

The fire's spreading warmth was nesting nicely around Bowie's body. When the coffee was ready, he sat up in the bunk and cradled a steaming cup between his bandaged hands, sipping it slowly. They exchanged stories and offered each other speculations. Came to a few cautious conclusions, though some things still weren't clear.

"Up to you what you want to do now," Sully said. "You can cut across the peaks to K-town. That's if the storm lets up soon. Another day of it and the high passes'll be closed for the winter. But you been across that country and know the way. Barring a heavy snow, you can make it."

"But better he should go back and tell his story," Sofie objected. "Otherwise Brady Trapp gets away with all he did, eh?"

Sully filled a cup for himself. "Yes, ma'am, I reckon. Bowie's the only one who can tell the right of what happened. You and me, we can back up part of his story. We all go to Sheriff Beamis and tell him all, including how Brady stole his pa's cattle, I'd say we can stop Brady square in his tracks."

"Depends what sort of man the sheriff is," Bowie said.

"His own. I know him pretty well. He and Cyrus was life-long friends; Beamis knows what a cross-dog pup Brady is, too. You'll get more'n a fair hearing. Anyway you'll want to clear up it wasn't you stuck that pitchfork in Cyrus. Even allowing self-defense, it could mean a manslaughter charge."

Bowie nodded and yawned. He was snug as toast in a cocoon of blankets, but every ache and bruise twitched to his slightest movement. "Sounds all right," he said drowsily. "Should be fit enough to head for Saltville in a day or so. You two best get back to headquarters. But listen, you watch out for Brady. He'll guess what's up."

Sully flicked an unpleasant grin. "Let him guess. His tail's in a nice tight crack. Let him sweat it. He won't dare a damn thing. And I'll open his gizzard for him if he tries."

"Just be careful. You better tell Faye Nevers what's happened."

Sully scowled into his coffee cup. "I don't know as it's smart to tell Nevers anything."

"Why not?"

"Just a feeling. He's an off ox—you never know what's ticking in his head. Now Brady's in, he could just be out."

"What's bad about that? Puts him on our side."

"Might not be that simple. I suspicion Faye has got a stew of his own in the cooking. My sister told me that Faye and Miz Trapp have been carrying on a private thing for a good while now."

Bowie raised his brows. "She sure of that?"

"Tula don't miss much that goes on around the place. Yeah, she's sure."

"I think this is right," Sofie said quietly. "I have seen them together. It goes on a long time now. I do not think Mr. Trapp knew."

Sully laughed sardonically. "You can lay bottom dollar he didn't. Did he, ol' Faye would have got decked out for a shotgun funeral."

He inspected the pantry shelves and shook his head. "Coffee's about all that's laid in here saving some jerky strips that'll be tougher'n old whangs. I better fetch up some grub. You got everything else you need." As he spoke, Sully buttoned his coat and pulled on his gloves. "Listen to that wind. Tearing up a blue streak. We better get going, Miz Ekstrom, or we'll be riding out a real blizzard."

Sofie shook her head. "I stay here," she said firmly, her eyes on Bowie. "He needs looking after."

Sully smiled. "Well, maybe so. You suit yourself." He tramped to the door, saying over his shoulder, "Will be back shortly with that grub unless the weather turns a sight worse."

Faye Nevers had no concern about being seen as he crossed to the big haybarn. The snowy gusts had turned to a full-fledged blizzard that cut off visibility beyond a few yards. His mental map of the whole headquarters guided Nevers unerringly to the barn. His outstretched hand slapped against its wall now, and he felt along it to the small side door. Lifting the latch, he pushed inside and then jammed the door shut against the deafening howl of wind.

Blinking in the hay-musty dimness, he said, "Adah?"

A quick dark movement and she was in his arms, pressing close, her mouth hot and eager. Then she drew back, smiling ruefully. She was muffled in a black hooded traveling cloak; cold stung her face with fresh color. "Seems I've waited hours—not really, but it seemed so. Then the blizzard picked up and I was frightened—till just now. I don't believe I could find my way back to the house."

"Couldn't help being late." He took off the scarf that tied down his hat, then the hat itself, and batted both free of snow. "We had to move some weak stock back to shelter in the east draws before the big storm broke. It's a stemwinder, all right."

Adah pressed herself to him again, burying her face against his coat. Nevers moved his hands down the sleek curve of her back, but his thoughts were barely on the woman in his arms, a woman who ordinarily enflamed him with a look or touch.

Cyrus's death, though he'd been braced for it, had come as a stunning blow to Nevers. He felt nagging and angry doubts about how Cyrus had met his end; the flaws in Brady's telling had been only too apparent. Sully Calder must have thought so too, for he'd been gone this morning, evidently to strike out on his friend Candler's trail. All Nevers had done was dispatch a crewman to bear the news to Sheriff Beamis in Saltville; what else could he do?

Actually he felt little interest in the *how* of Cyrus's death. All that really mattered was that he was gone. That

Faye Nevers's whole future suddenly rested on a precarious footing. Whatever happened next might depend on a lot of things. But one thing was certain: nothing would be the same as it had been.

"I shouldn't be happy," came Adah's muffled murmur. "How can it be right at such a time? But I am happy! Now there's nothing to keep us apart. Nothing—"

"Sure." Stroking her back almost absently. "Sure. . ."

Adah tipped up her face, slipping back the hood. "And you're not a bit happy, are you? But I don't think it's Cyrus—what is it, Faye?"

He smiled crookedly. "Oh, just wondering if I'll have a job shortly. Any old thing to support a wife on."

She half smiled. "You've told me there's bad blood between Brady and you. But it's the same between Brady and almost anyone, isn't it? He'll still need a foreman, and he's not likely to find a better."

"You don't know Brady." Nevers glumly shut his jaws. He eased himself into a pile of crackling hay and pulled her down beside him. "The final word'll come from Cyrus's will. I'd give a pretty penny to know what it is."

She gave him a surprised look. "Why, I can tell you that."

In his tormented last days, Adah said, Cyrus had been moved to share some of his thoughts with her. He'd wrestled long and hard with this particular dilemma, but once made, his decision had been firm. No matter what else they might be, Brady and Joe-Bob were his sons. His will as it was already filed would stand: full control of Chainlink would go to Brady. Cyrus's one hope had been that Brady's impulsive vigor would refocus and steady under the pressure of responsibility. If that hope didn't materialize, the fate of Chainlink was of no consequence; he'd built up this place for his sons and their sons to come. Brady would see after Joe-Bob; Cyrus had no concern on that score. As for Adah, she would be handsomely provided for, well enough to permit her to return to Denver and make a comfortable life, which was all that she really cared about.

"It's what I *did* want, Faye," she murmured. "All I

want now is to be with you—wherever or however it pleases you."

Nevers had listened to her recital with mounting impatience. "That's fine, honey. But answer me something if you can. Didn't he have a word for me in all this?"

Adah showed an uncertain little smile. "Well—the will does advise Brady to retain you as foreman."

He stared into her face. *"Advises*—that's all?"

"Cyrus said that he didn't want to leave any hard and fast restrictions on Brady's behavior. He'll have to make all his own decisions, wise or foolish. No other way to bring out whatever mettle he might have. And—" Adah paused, worrying her underlip between her teeth.

"All right, what?"

"He—Cyrus didn't trust you, Faye. He told me it was nothing personal. That he couldn't ask for a better foreman. But he was afraid of—well, the ambition he saw in you. Said he feared what might happen if you ever got the littlest toehold on Chainlink."

"He did, did he?"

"Oh, darling, I told him it was nonsense. But he only gave me that dreadfully sardonic look of his. It was useless to argue."

Nevers stared blindly at a wall.

So this was it. His reward. For years of ramrodding Chainlink better than any damn outfit in the territory was ramrodded. Cyrus had admitted that no small part of Chainlink's prosperity was owing to Faye Nevers. Not that he'd ever had illusions that Cyrus might think of him as a son, any crap of that sort. But he'd given the outfit the best years of his life and every drop of his loyalty.

And now. Jesus. A legacy of zero. With Brady in the saddle, it would come to that. The knowing congealed around his guts like ice.

"Faye," Adah whispered.

Nevers's eyes moved to her face. Saw a shadow in it edging on fear. He cleared his expression with a smile and a shrug. "Seems that's how it is then, honey. Let's forget about it. Like you say, we got each other. . . ."

Bowie slept for several hours. When he woke, it was plain that Sully wouldn't be returning to the line camp today. The blizzard was hammering at the house in full fury. The building trembled; the wind knifed between wall logs where the clay chinking had fallen out. Sofie plugged such gaps as she could locate with wads of cloth and paper, but the wind leaked through unseen cracks, making the place miserably drafty, wildly guttering the fire. She had to constantly replenish it to keep the room just above freezing.

Bowie broke a long silence. "Don't reckon you'll be welcome at Chainlink after this."

"No, I don't think so." She sat on the other bunk with her coat and a couple of blankets wrapped around her. "When you leave here, I go with you to Saltville. Later I send to Chainlink for my stuff, eh?"

"Sure. What then?"

"I must find work—work of some kind." Shadow and firelight played on Sofie's face; it looked indrawn and sad. "What kind of man is he, Brady Trapp? Did he kill his pa?"

"Maybe by accident. Like how he claimed I done it. No saying for sure what led up to it."

"Cyrus Trapp was very good to me. Why does a good man die like this?"

"Don't have to be a reason. No reason to much of anything else in life."

"Does it seem so?" She moved her head slowly. "I can't believe that. I hope there is something."

"God, maybe?"

"For some people there is God, Bowie. For some there is very much God. . . ."

The hours passed. Bowie drifted in and out of sleep, running a slight fever. Gradually he became aware that the blizzard was bucking itself out, the wind no longer shrieking and yammering like dying horses. That it was growing dark outside, the room filling with deep shadow as the fire ebbed to cherry glimmers. And vaguely, that Sofie went out and came back many times with armloads of wood from the kindling pile under the eaves, clattering them on the floor by the hearth.

Bowie woke with a jerk. It was uncomfortably warm; sweat dewed his face and damped his whole body under the blankets. Sofie had stoked up the fire; the room was bright with steady firelight and heavily warm now that the drafts had died down. His confused, half-shuttered gaze found Sofie. She had thrown off her snow-caked coat; she sat on a bench peeling off her long black stockings, which had gotten wet in the wood-fetching. She worked her cotton drawers off from under the skirt and then, moving over to the hearth, hung the damp garments on the mantel to dry.

Stepping back, she gazed at the fire a moment. Then she bunched her skirt and camisole in one hand, holding them high as she slowly turned against the heat, warming her bare legs. After a moment, still turning, she went up on tiptoe, murmuring with pleasure. Beating firelight made a tawny shimmer on the smoothly beautiful legs, golden-fleshing her round and sturdy thighs, the flexing curves of her calves. Shadow undercupped her big breasts; it limned her young full body with an incredible witchery.

He tried to shut his eyes. Couldn't. Kept them clear open and watching till her gaze crossed his. She became motionless, looking at him; she let the skirts fall from her hand.

"Bowie—oh, Bowie." Whispering it.

He dimly felt that he should be surprised. He had never dared hope for anything like this. Not so that he'd consciously realized it. Yet he must have admitted something to a hidden half of himself. For now, as she came over and slipped into his arms, it seemed as easy and natural a thing as he'd known. . . .

CHAPTER FIFTEEN

Brady and Faye Nevers come to his father's office because this was where Cyrus and the foreman had often discussed matters of ranch routine. Arrogantly slacked in Cyrus's swivel chair, his crossed boots cocked on Cyrus's desk, Brady gave Nevers orders for the usual rounds of winter work: on riding line, on keeping the waterholes open, on feeding the bulls and weaker stock. Faye knew better than anyone exactly when and how all such work should be carried out; that fact was the source of the wicked pleasure Brady felt in seizing a position from which he could needle Faye with superfluous commands. Faye had made him sweat when the old man had set him under the foreman's thumb; now Faye would sweat. But as always, it was hard to be sure what Faye was thinking. He leaned his big-shouldered frame against the wall with arms crossed, listening, making no comment. Melting snow puddled around his boots.

"That's about it," Brady said, folding his hands behind his head. "Any questions?"

"Just one. I always figured the day you come in, I'd be out."

Brady chuckled. "We don't know who's in or out yet, now do we? Not till the old man's will is read—and the only copy we know of is filed with his attorney in Saltville. Safest thing for you to assume is that *I'll* get the whole outfit, lock, stock, and barrel. But hell, you know that."

"Not what I asked."

"I tell you, fella——" Brady leaned forward, thumping his boots to the floor. "You're likely to be guessing about it for a long spell to come."

Nevers's veiled stare narrowed slightly. He said nothing, just waited.

"Yessir," Brady said cheerfully, "if the old man's will don't get thrown into probate, I will be the big cheese around here damn shortly. Then I'll have you right by the balls, won't I, friend?"

"You waited for it long enough," Nevers observed dryly. "But what's it going to mean?"

"Why, just that I can keep you on as foreman if I want. Or fire you if it suits me. Any goddam time it suits me. Y'know, Faye? I can see where wondering on something like that could drive a fellow right up a tree."

A wicked glint of anger flicked out of Nevers's pale eyes. It made Brady sharply aware of what he didn't intend to forget: that Faye Nevers could be a dangerous man. "Don't crowd me too hard," Nevers said gently. "You'll find that has its limits."

Brady grinned lazily. "Why, hell, Faye, I got more sense'n to do that. But you gonna be walking soft from now on too. You sweated your ass too long and hard working up to what you got here at Chainlink to just turn on your heel and walk away from it all."

"That's right. Just don't make a mistake how much I'll take off you or any man."

"Sure." Brady smiled. "Don't worry."

Wordlessly Nevers clamped on his hat and went out. Brady rose and walked to the window, watching Faye head for the cookshack where the crew was at breakfast. The point was made, Brady thought, the knife slipped in with a deft twist: an unvarnished threat that without warning, at any time of his choosing, he could yank everything from under Faye. No need for a reminder, ever. From now on Nevers would live with that bitter knowledge; it would eat at his guts like corrosion. The thought filled Brady with a wicked pleasure. For the present he needed Faye; he had no illusions about stepping cold turkey into his father's boots. He had a lot to learn, all he'd neglected to absorb through a profligate youth. But all that was going to change. And the time would come.

If. One continuing worry nagged Brady as he gazed out at the snow-smoothed rollaway of the valley floor. Had Cyrus ever carried out his occasional threat to have a new will drawn up? Brady mused narrow-eyed on the ominous possibilities of such a development. Swore in a vicious undertone at his own lack of diplomacy in dealing with the old man those last weeks. But he felt a steely resolution too, which kind of surprised him. Seemed like the old man's death had freed him of an oppressive presence that had always cowed and weakened him.

That was done with, by God. He could do any damn thing he wanted now. Any damn thing necessary to cinch his control of Chainlink.

Beamis. The sheriff might be a problem. Yet what could he finally prove? Nothing. Candler's mouth was shut for good; only he and Joe-Bob knew the truth. Yesterday's blizzard had erased any last trace of sign left by his and Candler's horses. It would have buried the bodies of Candler and the buckskin under inches of snow, not to be discovered till spring and maybe not then. If the remains were ever found, it would be assumed that Candler had blundered over the rimrock in his flight.

Suspicions, sure. Be a barrelful of suspicions. But let anyone prove a goddam one of 'em.

Brady watched the crew ride out to their duties, then opened a drawer of his desk and took out a bottle and water glass. He filled the glass to the brim and drank off a third of it. Ahhh—good by God to be able to drink when and where he pleased in his own home. He toasted his new freedom with another deep swig.

"Excuse me—"

Brady lowered his glass and glowered at Adah standing in the open office doorway. She was pointedly eying the glass, disapproval cold in her voice and her composed face, which contrasted palely with the mourning black she wore.

A vicious irritation welled up in him. "Goddammit, can't you knock?"

"The door was open——"

"All right, all right! What the hell is it?"

"I want to discuss arrangements for the burial. You can spare a minute or two for that."

" 'Arrangements for the burial,' " he said in savage mimicry. "Nothing to it. Tell one of the boys to chop a hole in the ground and drop the old bastard in it. Or leave him in a barn till spring. He'll keep."

Adah's face had delicately colored; now all the color ran out of it. She moved her head slowly back and forth. "I—I can't believe that even you could be so, so utterly bestial, so callous——"

"Ah, Christ. Get out of here." He flung out his hand with the glass, sloshing liquor on his wrist. "G'wan," he roared, "get t'hell out!"

Adah wheeled and was gone. He heard her quick steps on the stairs. Muttering, he refilled the glass and drained it in a couple of swallows. Walking over to the window again, he stared out at the widow Ekstrom's cabin some hundred yards distant.

A new thought flicked at his hotly savage mood; more than whiskey began to stoke his innards. Abruptly he lifted his mackinaw off a wall peg, shrugged it on, and left by the outside door.

Tramping toward the cabin, he wasn't quite sure what approach he might take to back up the hot impulse boiling in him. Only that one way or another, he meant to have Sofie Ekstrom. Be diplomatic about it, sure, but make her understand who was running this outfit now. She'd either come to taw or get that nice round ass of hers booted off Chainlink.

Even before he reached the cabin, Brady's whiskey-fuddled mind cooled to attention on something that seemed damn funny. Not a trace of smoke coming from the chimney. The widow, usually an early riser, should have laid her breakfast fire a good hour ago, particularly on so cold a morning. No tracks showed outside the door; snow had drifted up against it.

Frowning, Brady rapped his knuckles on the door. No answer. He lifted the latch and stepped inside. The cabin was deserted. And cold. He went to the fireplace and touched the ashes. Dead for hours. But how long had she been gone? Before the blizzard had ended, that was sure. Bedclothes mussed, but everything else neat as a pin. Which indicated that she'd likely left at night and, for some reason, in haste. Also her disappearance could explain the horse that had been discovered missing after the storm.

But last night or the night before? Come to think of it, she hadn't been out and around all yesterday. Damn strange, that, unless she'd left Chainlink the same night that Cyrus had died—the night he had taken care of Candler. She and Candler'd been thick, all right. *Suppose she'd followed those tracks come morning?* Before the real blizzard had hit. Yeah . . .

Sudden fear made a phlegmy knot in Brady's throat. Might be a handy idea to ride up to the gorge where he'd left Candler and make sure. That was all he had to worry about. That Candler might be alive. In the darkness and storm night before last, unable to see to the gorge bottom, he'd reckoned it a safe assumption that even if Candler had survived the plunge into the gorge or escaped being too busted up to move, there was no way he could climb out. He was sure to be froze to death by now.

Unless someone had helped him out. Christ!

Five minutes later Brady was throwing his saddle on his big grullo, having returned to the house just long enough to get his rifle. He rode north from headquarters, goaded by a feverish haste as he bucked the grullo savagely against a foot of drifted snow, breaking trail.

From a kitchen window of the big house, Sully and Tula watched Brady head northward. Turning her dark quick glance on her brother, Tula said, "He'll go to that gorge. What will he do when he doesn't find Candler in it?"

Sully smiled thinly. "Think on it a spell. Then figure what I did. Nearest shelter outside of headquarters 'ud be that old line camp. Get that grub together, sis. I got to hustle up there before Brady does."

"But he'll be ahead of you."

"Huh-uh. He'll go to the gorge first. There's a shorter way from here to the line camp. I'll lay up on the trail for him."

Concern shadowed her gaze. "Take care, Sully."

"Don't worry. Verily, sis, no Trapp is gonna deadfall this Injun. Get the grub ready."

Sully, who had the winter wrangler's job of breaking in ranch horses, keeping them fed and gentled through the winter months, hadn't ridden out with the crew. As soon as they had gone, he'd slipped quietly up to the house and told Tula to pack some grub which he'd fetch to the line camp for Bowie and Miz Ekstrom. Seeing Brady head for the Ekstrom cabin, they hadn't been hard put to guess his intent, or the furious conclusions he'd have reached on finding Miz Ekstrom gone.

When Tula had loaded a flour sack with bacon, beans, cold biscuits, and coffee, Sully said a hasty good-by and hurried to the stable. After saddling his paint and tying the grubsack to his pommel, he checked the action of his Winchester. Smooth as baby skin. Brady's mood would be downright savage; even if a man got the drop on him, he might be inclined to push a showdown.

Standing in the stable doorway, Sully peered across the snow flats in the direction Brady had gone. He was still in sight, a diminishing dot on the plain's sweeping whiteness. Sully waited minutes longer for a roll of high ground to cut him off. Not until Brady had dropped out of sight did he start away from headquarters, cutting toward the northeast at an acute angle away from the trail Brady had broken. By the time each of them reached the timbered foothills, their trails would have diverged widely.

The sun poked out of the overcast now and then, sheeting the flats in glittering white that made Sully's eyes ache. He was glad to leave them for the first rise of scrub-timbered ridges. The route he'd chosen to the line camp was the quickest way he knew to get there; it was also the roughest. After passing the first mild ridges, he came to the base of a giant hogback that towered below the first peaks. It was treacherously steep; its long rugged flank extended several hundred yards from bottom to crest. Thrusts of broken shale studded its glaring mantle of snow. But it was the quickest way up, and the trail to the line camp followed its crest. Brady, when he came this way, would take the easy switchback trails leading up from the east.

Sully rested his horse a minute, then put the animal into a lunging ascent of the slope. Powder snow and loose stones flurried away from the paint's driving hooves. When he'd covered two-thirds of the distance, Sully dismounted and rested his animal again. Wiping sweat from his face with his sleeve, he peered up the final stretch of deep-tilted slope. He'd have to tackle it on foot. Leading the paint, he resumed his steady climb. Soon his leg muscles ached and trembled with each slogging step. Sweat puddled his skin under his heavy clothes; a raw band of pain grew around his rib cage. His face felt brittle with cold as sporadic gusts of high wind raked the open slope.

At last, his heart pounding, Sully achieved the stand of lodgepole pine that marked a rounding off to the ridge's flat crown. A few more yards and he would hit the line camp trail. In saddle again, he pushed swiftly through the timber. It was easy going here, the snow only inches deep, the bulk of it caked thickly atop the interlacing pine branches overhead, shrouding the forest aisle in a pale gloom.

Sully pulled up suddenly. A prickling feel of something not quite right rippled up gooseflesh on his back. What the hell was it? Something his senses couldn't quite catalogue. Listening, he heard only a low moan of wind. Scanning the trees and the snow barred by their pale blue shadows, he couldn't detect anything.

Nothing—of course. Hell, how could Brady get ahead of him?

Yet he eased his Winchester from its boot before he nudged the horse cautiously forward. Ahead now, he saw the half-drifted trail between the tree boles.

The only other thing he saw, and the last thing of all, was a flicker of dark movement among the pines just off the trail. He didn't even have time to draw rein before something slammed him in the chest with piledriver force. The first thunder of the shot touched his senses, but that single edge of awareness was already dimming as he fell.

Then there was darkness. And there was nothing.

CHAPTER SIXTEEN

Bowie paced the cabin floor in a slow circle, gingerly working his muscles while he chewed an extremely tough piece of jerked deermeat to bits of fibrous pulp that would slide down his throat. His hands and knees still hurt like hell; some of the worst bruises on his carcass would be a long time fading. Yet he figured he was in shape to hold a saddle. Anyway he was impatient to get to Saltville and have his powwow with the sheriff. If he had to eke out a couple more days on flinty jerky and weak coffee, he thought dourly, his belly would be playing tag wrassle with his backbone.

He walked to the bunk where Sofie was still sleeping, curled on her side. One deep hip mounded the covers; her pale hair fanned out on the rough tick. He slapped her hip gently. "Wake up. Daylight on the mountain."

Stirring, she twisted onto her back like a big lazy cat, stretching her bare arms. "Come here," she murmured. "Come down here. *Ja ar kall.*"

"Better get up if you're cold. It's halfway to noon. Got to be getting a move on if we're going to raise Saltville before dark."

She lifted on her elbows, her eyes sultry. "So late? It cannot be. I am yet so sleepy. . . ."

He grinned. "Well, you didn't get a lot of sleep. Come on, up. I'll get the horses ready, you put the fire out, all right?"

"Mmm. *Tack sa mycket.*" She stretched again, yawning. "But are you fit to ride?" Then laughed at her own

165

question. "*Ja*, I think so. But we should wait for Sully, eh? Today he should come."

"No point waiting. We'll leave him a note."

She tossed the covers aside and rose. Began unself-consciously to dress, so that he delayed putting on his coat for the pure pleasure of watching her. Her long hair, a shining shawl on which firelight twinkled, covered her almost demurely to the waist. It swung to her slightest movement, showing flashes of pearly flesh, the firm rises of half-melon breasts, the pale pink of softened nipples that hours ago had flowered to fierce firepoints in the surging, timeless clasp of passion. It was still hard to believe. All of it was. *I never knew any man but Jan before,* she had told him, and he knew it was true and did not know how he knew. Nor why the wonder of it would stay with him always, for he knew that too. There might yet be a lifetime of times, but this shining first would isolate itself in some corner of memory that kept inviolate, strangely young.

She gave a peal of laughter. "Is that how you get the horses ready, you *dumskalle*!"

Grinning, he shrugged on his mackinaw and tramped outside, closing the door behind him. For a moment he stood gazing across the broad fallaway of land on all sides. Damn strange place for a line camp, perched on a high bulge of ridge off from much of anything, including good graze or water. Still, it commanded a hell of a view. Northward, great peaks grew into the low-banked clouds like squat wedges; their snow-veined heights greened with timber along the lower slopes, shading to dull buff and slaty grays above. To the south lay pine ridges and snow flats across which Bowie could see for miles, making out trickles of smoke from the house and cookshack at Chainlink headquarters. The sky was rapidly clearing; belts of sunlight raced below the wind-chased clouds.

Cold nipped at his ears as he trudged down the slope toward the horse shed with the little corral strung out behind it. Then he came to a dead stop. A man's booted tracks were freshly trampled in the snow fronting the shed. But he saw them too late.

The unlatched shed door creaked as a hand nudged it open.

Brady Trapp stood just inside the doorway, a Remington-Keene rifle nested in the crook of his arm. Gripping both hands around the weapon now, he stepped out of the shed and began tramping upslope to where Bowie stood. Dull light raced along the tipped-up gunbarrel, which never wavered off Bowie's belly.

And Brady never stopped grinning.

He halted square in front of Bowie. "Hell, pilgrim. You didn't need to come down here. I was coming to you—"

The rifle swept up in one streaking vicious motion. Its barrel crashed against Bowie's neck. Dark lights shattered in his eyes. Then he fell on his hands and knees, retching. And his head rocked and pounded to the endless roar of Brady's laughter.

Trying to feign being hurt worse than he was, Bowie sat hunched on the end of a bunk, elbows on his knees, gently rubbing the swollen side of his neck. He was sideways to Brady, but could see his reflection in the cracked bowl of a hurricane lamp. Brady's image swam grotesquely in and out of it as he stalked up and down the room, restlessly bouncing his rifle in the circle of his fist. He kept talking a blue streak, punctuated with bursts of savage laughter.

Now he was telling them how he'd concealed his horse back in the timber before stealing up to the line camp. Not seeing tracks outside the cabin, he'd looked in the horse shed to be sure. They'd have horses. And the horses were there; but just then the cabin door had opened as Bowie started coming out. Brady had swiftly pulled the shed door shut after him and then simply waited. Seemed he wanted to brag on and on. That was all right; it would hold off whatever he had planned for them. Which didn't take much figuring.

They had already absorbed the ugly shock of Brady's first brutal revelation: he had killed Sully. He'd also filled in the picture of how Cyrus had died.

Swallowing against sickness, Bowie watched the warped

leer of Brady's reflection, thinking with a kind of vague wonderment that he'd never seen this sullen man so feverishly jubilant. Not even at those times when he was riding a tight gamble in a poker game: the only thing that Bowie had seen lift his surly spirits to a similar boisterousness. And Bowie wondered: was this the same with him somehow?

Moving his head now, Bowie let the edge of his gaze touch Sofie's. She was seated on the bench by the table where Brady had ordered her to sit; her eyes followed him up and down the room. Scared, but not showing it much. The cold timbers creaked to Brady's heavy tramp; his glance flicked against their faces whenever he swung past one of them. He was enjoying hell out of this.

". . . sonofabitching breed wasn't as smart as he figured." Watching quick-eyed for their reactions as he talked. "Hell, it come to me halfway to that gorge where you'd be unless the widow got you out of it. Say she had—" Wheeling to a halt by the bunk, he gave Bowie a wicked prod with the rifle. "Only goddam place up here you was likely to go is here, right?"

"I never knew about this place," Bowie said in a dull voice. "Sully brought us here."

"I bet he did. Shit, I figured that out myself, after." Brady chuckled, resuming his clumping stride. "After I got the son of a bitch, that is. I never went to the gorge, switched northeast and cut straightway up here. Had got on the trail yonder along the hogsback when I hear this noise like someone's scrambling along up the side of it. Left my horse and got by the edge of timber, and yessir, it was old Sully, climbing up pert as you please. So I faded back a ways in the trees and laid myself up. When the bastard come in sight, I busted him clean."

The savage callousness touched a cold nerve of fury in Bowie. He forgot his injured pose. Raised his head and stared straight at Brady with a chill, voiceless hatred.

"He'd a done the same for me," Brady went on cheerily. "That's why he short-cut across country to get up here ahead of me. He'd a made it, too, if I hadn't thought me to cut straightway over to this old camp. Put me up here just a hair ahead of him. . . ."

He was like a gramophone that refused to run down. Rambling on about plans he had, dwelling on each detail. He didn't figure that getting rid of them with nobody the wiser would pose too much of a problem. All he had to do was dump their bodies into a convenient ravine, along with the breed. The three of 'em would keep well enough till spring, when he'd return and cover them more permanently. This first snow would melt down quickly in a day or two of sun; that would take care of tracks. Of course a lot of questions would be asked, but he'd have his trail covered all right; take more than three people dropping out of sight to get anything pinned on him.

Bowie was hardly listening. His head was pretty clear by now; keeping it lowered while he slowly massaged his neck, he focused everything on trying to think of a way out. He could make a dive for Brady any time Brady's pivoting stride carried him close, but there seemed little chance of completing it. Brady never swung closer to him than six or seven feet. Moreover, Brady was faster than his stocky-bull build might suggest, Bowie knew; he was in top condition and Bowie was still feeling the heavy punishment of two nights before. Also Brady had the rifle.

I need an edge, ran Bowie's tight thinking, any sort of edge. Whenever Brady's glance swiveled off from him, Bowie let his eyes move quickly over the room. Trying to discover anything that might help tip the balance. A hand ax which Sofie had used to split some of the larger chunks of firewood she'd carried in was sunk in a sizable piece she'd used for a chopping block. But the hatchet was a good fifteen feet away. Brady would easily cut him down before he reached it.

"How can you do so?" Sofie's voice cut passionately across Brady's ramblings: "Your pa first! Sully Calder then. Us now. You cannot just go on killing. What kind of poison is in you to think so?"

Brady looked surprised. He came to a halt and stared at her. "For a bitch who's been living on Trapp bounty all these weeks, you take on a Christawful lot of airs. What you got to be so goddam sniffy about anyway? Cozying your ass up here with this pilgrim—" A red smoldering flicked his gaze. "Maybe we should see what you got that's so great. Take it off."

"What?"

"Take your clothes off. Right now. Every goddam stitch!" Brady's voice was climbing; he leaned forward hard and then settled back on his heels. "Every stitch," he said gently.

Sofie shot a glance at Bowie. Then moistened her lips, gripping the edge of the bench with both white-knuckled hands. "I will not. You go ahead, you shoot. You cannot make me do this."

"Sure, I shoot," Brady said softly. He moved the rifle in a semi-arc till it covered Bowie. "I shoot that son of a bitch sitting over there first of all. Then I'll take your goddam clothes off myself. You like that idea better, just say so."

"No, no—" Her unbraided hair stirred to her quick shake of head. "I do what you want. Please—"

"That's better. I like you better scared." He motioned sharply with the rifle. "Get to it."

Sofie rose slowly to her feet. Her chin was up, her face white. She unbuttoned her coat and slipped it off, dropping it to the bench.

"Take your time." Brady's beard cracked in a goatish grin. "Just see you don't miss nothing."

She dropped to one knee to unfasten a shoe, her hair falling over to curtain her bent face. Brady watched avidly, his jaw hanging a little. Bowie felt the thinnest lift of hope now. Let Brady be distracted just enough. . . . But he was standing side-on to the bunk and could easily detect and stop any move Bowie made.

So he didn't go for the hatchet. Taking a long chance, he climbed shakily to his feet. Stumbled slowly toward Brady, saying hoarsely, "You bastard. Stinking bastard—"

Brady swung the rifle to cover him. "Now that's being purely stupid, pilgrim. I can drop you straightway any time it suits. Might's well relax and get your enjoyments out o' this. Gonna be your last."

Bowie lurched sideways in a loose stagger as if he'd gone off balance; it brought him close to one end of the fireplace. Grabbing at the mantel for support, he sagged there, watching Brady balefully.

Sofie straightened up, shaking back the white-flame veil of her hair. Slowly she flexed one leg, reaching down to one loosened shoe; it thudded on the floor. The other shoe followed. Her stockinged feet whispered on the rough boards. Then she reached for the neck of the rough hickory shirt she wore. Doing it all deliberately and without haste, never taking her eyes off Brady.

Bowie understood. Sofie was striving to give an extra edge to his chances. As he'd intended, his move to the fireplace had brought him inside four feet of the hatchet.

One quick reach, a twist to free the blade, a hard fast throw. Hell, he'd played throw-the-ax many times as a kid. Only throwing at a target painted on a broad stump. If you'd missed, the only forfeit had been a hooting by your opponent.

Be a sight steeper penalty here.

Sofie's fingers moved slowly down her shirt front, unbuttoning it to the waistband of her skirt. She pulled out the shirttail, unfastened two more buttons, slid out of the shirt, and let it fall from her hands. Lampglow washing through the gloomy room turned the creamy flesh of her shoulders and arms softly golden. The lace-edged camisole partly showed the pale mounds of her large firm breasts; lamplight filled the deep cleft between them with satiny shadow. Brady was leaning forward in his intensity, his underjaw slack; sweat sheened his cheekbones. The corners of Sofie's lips tilted softly upward as she watched him. Now she raised both hands to her shoulders and slipped the straps of her camisole downward. . . .

Bowie took just two swift steps sideways; his outwhipping hand closed on the ax and wrenched it from the block. Brady snapped partly around just as he swung the hatchet back and overhanded it in one savage motion.

Too low. The thought flashed across Bowie's mind even as the ax left his hand. Aimed at Brady's head, turning over once in flight, it was coming in shoulder level. And Brady desperately twisted his body at the last moment. The arcing blade sheared through his coat and shirt and then, deflected at an angle, glanced away and clattered to the floor.

As Brady still hung off balance, rifle pointed down, Bowie was already diving at him. Brady had just caught his balance and was turning on his heel, bringing his rifle up and around, when Bowie's head and shoulder slammed into his ribs under his right arm. Brady gave an explosive grunt, and then Bowie's impetus carried both men against the wall with an impact that shook the cabin.

Bowie clinched, trying to pin Brady to the wall while he grappled him for the rifle. But Brady held the weapon high, shifting his hold on it, then hammered the barrel down on Bowie's hunched back. Bowie's body arched in a spasm of pain; he let go and staggered backward. Brady pushed away from the wall, swinging the rifle up for a full-arm blow at Bowie's head. Beyond the red haze of his vision, Bowie saw Brady's crazed swollen face.

And in that instant, with Brady wide open, legs braced apart, Bowie put all his remaining strength into a quick, savage kick. Its power rippled out of the big muscles of his thigh and spurted the length of his leg into his straightened foot.

The toe of his boot drove square into Brady's crotch.

"Aaahh—"

A wounded roar burst from Brady's throat; his fingers splayed open in a reflex of pure agony. The rifle fell to the floor. Bowie took a stumbling step and then bent to snatch it up. But even half paralyzed with pain, Brady wasn't out of it. Before Bowie's hand could close on the rifle, Brady's heavy palm clapped against his neck, swung him in a powerful sideways heave, and flung him away. Bowie kited into a bench and overturned it, then tripped and fell across it. His ears ringing, he scrambled up on his knees and stayed that way a moment, gathering his strength.

Brady was half bent over, holding his groin, face twisted and bloodless. His whole right sleeve was wet red from the deep cut that the ax had opened in his shoulder. But even wounded, his eyes glazed with sick pain, he was still a formidable bull of a man: ape-squat and brutishly muscled, his body packed with the power of coiled spring-steel. To close with him again could be suicidal, a realization that cleared Bowie's head completely.

For this moment all that Brady could manage was to bend over, wheezing and holding himself. But in another moment he'd be able to pick up the rifle at his feet. Sofie stood by the bench as if gripped in a trance. Bowie's glance found the hatchet, which had skittered almost against her skirt hem. But there was no time to go after it, for abruptly Brady was bending deeper, reaching down for the rifle.

Bowie yelled *"Sofie—the ax!"* as he lunged at Brady again.

Already Brady was coming up with the Remington-Keene, snapping its finger lever down. In the last straining instant Bowie batted wildly at the barrel, cuffing it aside as Brady pulled the trigger. The shot was thunderous in the room; crockery crashed and tinkled as the bullet whanged into the pantry shelves.

The two men struggled for the rifle, Brady still half hunched with pain. Bowie surged his weight backward, trying to wrest the weapon away. The effort yanked Brady forward off balance, but he kept his hold. Then Brady's plunging weight caused them to fall together, Bowie on the bottom. As his back hit the splintery floor, he tried to bring his knee up into Trapp's injured groin. But it only caught his hard-muscled thigh, and then Brady's bulk crushed him flat.

Bowie heaved upward, but Brady had him solidly pinned, and now Brady's hands were forcing the rifle down on his throat. Bowie put his last strength into holding it back, but the rifle began pressing into his throat with a crushing power. He felt his hold slipping.

A hard *tunk* like a mallet hitting a melon: Brady's

snarling face went blank and he slumped across Bowie. Sofie stood over them, the hatchet poised in her fist. She'd brought the blunt heel of it down on Brady's head.

Bowie rolled Brady aside and then, with Sofie's help, climbed shakily to his feet.

"I could not kill him," she said simply.

He wanted to smile at that, but only managed to bare his teeth in a painful grimace. The short brutal encounter had wakened every bruise on his body to pulsing life. But he couldn't rest now. Not with the end of this in sight.

"We'll take him down to Saltville," he told Sofie. "We'll tell the sheriff all that's happened."

"I hope he will believe us. He must."

"Well"— Bowie did smile then—"when Brady got running off like molasses in July, he told quite a lot. Put it all together, I think we got a story the law will listen to."

CHAPTER SEVENTEEN

The sun was lifting fiercely past noon, making an eye-stabbing glare on the rapidly melting snow. It lay warm against Faye Nevers's right side and back as he swung the ax in hard measured strokes. He'd peeled off his mackinaw some time ago, but still his flannel shirt clung sweatily to his broad back.

Nevers liked the solid rhythm of this work, into which a man could throw his full muscle. Pausing, he wiped sweat from his forehead and glanced around the oak clearing to which he'd brought four of the crew on a wood-cutting detail. Barney too was swinging an ax, felling the scrub oaks and limbing them off; Hilo and Sam were bucking the logs into ten-foot lengths with a cross-cut saw; Trinidad was loading them onto the bed of a post wagon. The ring of axes and rasp of saw and clean resinous smell of fresh-cut wood all seemed to blend into one.

Trinidad topped the loaded wagon with an oak length, jammed it tightly into place, and glanced at Nevers. "She's pret' big load, Faye. You want me to drive her to headquarters now?"

"Yeah. Sully's there; tell him to help you unload. Then get back here double time. I want to get in three-four more loads today."

Trinidad was about to swing up the wagon seat. He paused and tipped his hat down, shading his eyes as he peered past the trees. "Someone comes. Looks like the kid. Joe-Bob."

It was. He came into the clearing on a lathered, hard-driven mount and dropped to the ground. Half stumbling, he went to Trinidad and grabbed him by the arm. "Trin, you gotta come with me!"

Trinidad stared at him and said: "What's 'at?" Then gave Nevers an uncertain grin.

Nevers set his ax down and tramped over to them. "I boss these men, kid, remember? You want Trinidad. What for?"

Joe-Bob swallowed, his eyes furtive and miserable. "I can't tell you nothing 'bout that, Faye."

"Sounds like something Brady don't want talked about. Is that right?"

Joe-Bob stubbornly shook his head. "I want Trinidad to come with me. You don't need to know any more."

Nevers glanced at Trinidad, who stood by hipshot, arms folded. "You know what he's talking about?"

The rawboned Mexican shrugged, his dark eyes veiled and amused. *"Quien sabe?"*

"Sorry, kid. I need him here."

Joe-Bob's milky eyes flared slightly. "Listen, Chainlink ranch will be part mine, Faye. You better not forget that."

"Let's wait till the will is read." Nevers smiled. He seated himself on a stump and cuffed back his hat. "Seeing you're the big augur here, they ought to listen to you. How about you, Trinidad? You listening?"

"Shee-yit, Faye." Trinidad showed a small cautious grin. "It's you gives the orders, ain' it? I ain' been told otherwise." He laid a hand on Joe-Bob's shoulder and said apologetically, "That's how she is, old *amigo*. Maybe you tell Faye what she is that is itching you, he leave me go with you, hah?"

"It ain't none of his mix, Trin!" Joe-Bob looked on the edge of tears. "I thought you was my friend."

"Why, shee-yit, boy, I ain' nothing else. But Faye here's my boss, tha's different. Anyway he only want to help you, ain' that right, Faye?"

Nevers half-lidded his eyes, nodding. "That's right, Joe-Bob. But I won't oblige a man who don't trust me."

"Brady don't like you," Joe-Bob said sulkily. "He don't like you any, Faye. He said so."

"Listen, Brady is wrong," Trinidad said sternly. "I am Brady's big *amigo*, but I say in this he is wrong. Faye Nevers done plenty for you Trapps, he helped make this Chainlink big and rich. Now you pa is gone, he is stick by you. And still Brady, he say he don' like Faye." The Mexican clucked his tongue sadly. "That is ver' bad way to pay a man who don' ask nothing but you be honest with him."

A kind of quizzical doubt crept into Joe-Bob's look. "I dunno," he muttered. "Might be all right. Brady didn't say about nothing like this—I gotta have some help."

"Look—" Nevers slid off the stump. "Nobody but the three of us needs to hear it. We can walk off a ways. How's that?"

"Yeah—I guess so."

Nevers waved the other men back to work. He led Joe-Bob and Trinidad deeper into the oak grove; they halted by a half-frozen creek. Joe-Bob's words spilled out almost frantically. From what Nevers could gather, Joe-Bob (not unusual for him) had overslept this morning and had gotten up to find Brady gone. He'd queried Adah, who'd told him that Brady had been acting peculiar; Brady had gone to Mrs. Ekstrom's cabin, afterward returning to the house to get his rifle, then hurriedly saddling a horse and riding off north. In a little while, what had seemed more peculiar, Sully Calder had left the house with what appeared to be a sack of food, had likewise gotten a horse and, after apparently waiting till Brady was out of sight, had ridden north too, but not the same way. Adah had seen it all from her upstairs window. Out of curiosity, then, she'd gone to the Ekstrom cabin and had been astonished to find Mrs. Ekstrom gone; she'd also questioned Tula, who wouldn't say a word. Adah had made no sense of it.

Neither did Nevers, but he was avidly alert now. "All right, kid," he said impatiently. "What's it all mean? Why'd you need Trinidad?"

"Brady could be in trouble, bad trouble. That breed is got it in for him, but Jeez, I'm no shakes with a gun, I can't do nothing. That's why Trin's gotta help, but we gotta get going."

"Not so fast," Nevers said softly. "There's still no sense to it, Joe-Bob. You better tell me everything, the whole story. What the hell's going on? Why would Sully have it in for Brady?"

Joe-Bob hesitated.

"Come on, boy. You trust me or you don't. Time's wasting."

Joe-Bob's talk came halting and uncertainly now. Nevers's guess that Brady had sworn his weak-witted brother to silence was quickly confirmed as Joe-Bob unfolded the truth about how Cyrus had died. And about the recent cattle-stealing which Candler and Sully had broken up, followed by Sully's grim pledge to Brady. Nevers cut in frequently with questions, extracting the facts behind recent developments which had left him puzzled. So Brady had framed Bowie Candler for Cyrus's killing and then disposed of Candler—or thought he had.

It was easy to start drawing speculations as to why Brady, then Sully, had suddenly departed Chainlink this morning. Mere speculations. But meaty enough to make Nevers's deepening excitement balloon into a savage exulting. Jesus, yes. This could be exactly the situation he'd been waiting for.

"From what you say," he told Joe-Bob, "I'd hazard that breed means trouble for your brother. We best hustle and hope we're in time."

Joe-Bob blinked in surprise. "You coming?"

"For sure. Always told your pappy I'd watch out for you boys. You, me, Trinidad, that's three guns, enough to handle anything needs doing."

They tramped back to the cutting site.

Nevers mounted his own horse and borrowed Barney's for Trinidad, merely telling the crew that something had come up and they'd be gone a while; Barney was left in charge of the detail. Afterward the three of them set a quick jogging pace toward the northeast. No point returning to headquarters, Nevers said; they'd shave off an hour by cutting Brady's trail where it entered the foothills.

Riding a tight anxiety, Joe-Bob pressed ahead of his

companions. Nevers reined over close to Trinidad, saying quietly: "I figure there'll never be a better chance."

"Bueno. That is what I think. Now?"

"Not yet. I want 'em both. And it's got to look like someone else done it."

Trinidad raised his brows. "Ah. Sully?"

"Maybe. But I got a better notion." Nevers paused. "Mrs. Trapp told the kid it looked like Sully left with a sack of grub. What's that mean to you?"

"Maybe you better say it, Faye."

Nevers ticked off the points of what Joe-Bob had said: it added up, he thought, to possibilities that Bowie Candler was still alive, that Sofie Ekstrom might be with him, that Sully was fetching them food. Say Brady had figured out the same and had ridden up in the hills to confirm or refute the idea. Say Sully had figured out what Brady was up to and had gone to get ahead of him and deadfall him. All this was guessing, but Nevers thought the pieces fitted together.

Even if his guesses weren't wholly right, this looked like a prime opportunity.

How many people knew that Brady had left Bowie Candler for dead the other night? Only the Trapp brothers and the two of them. Brady had told everybody that Candler had fled into the mountains after killing Cyrus. All right now. Suppose it could be made to appear that today Brady had gone up there looking for his father's killer. If everyone knew there'd been no love lost between Brady and Cyrus, they also knew there was bad blood between Brady and Candler: reason enough for Brady to go hunting Candler alone.

Only suppose when he found him and they traded shots, it was Brady who was killed. And suppose that moments later Joe-Bob and Nevers and Trinidad had come on the scene and shot it out with Candler—and both he and Joe-Bob were killed.

Trinidad pursed his lips, nodding. "We follow Brady's tracks, we find Brady. Then we fix both brothers dead, huh?"

"Simple as that. Simpler, if Sully's fixed Brady for us."

"But Candler, we don' know we'll find him. You just guessing he's alive."

"All right, say he ain't, say Brady did finish him two nights ago. But say he's alive, whether he drops out of sight or shows up later, it'll be the same. Our story's that Bowie Candler killed both the Trapp boys, maybe with his friend Sully's help. Be a hot day in January before anyone can prove different."

Trinidad began to show his teeth. Then the grin faded. "But the woman. Suppose Candler *is* alive and they're together?"

"Why," Nevers said gently, "in that case they'll be dead together. Maybe I had you wrong. Figured you'd do about anything to become foreman of Chainlink."

Trinidad showed all his teeth then. "You were not wrong, *amigo*. I am with you. Is just I want to get her all straight. And Sully, we run into him too, it's all the same, hah?"

"That's the picture. No witnesses."

No witnesses.

Part of Nevers's mind could coldly wonder at the insensate savagery of his own determination to carry the whole business exactly as far as need be. Yet he knew himself well enough to admit that if such an opportunity had been presented him any other time in his life, it would have been no different. Just a matter of recognizing the main chance and having the guts to seize it.

His moment had come when Adah had revealed the contents of Cyrus's will. And with it had come decision, cold and instant. Both Trapp sons must die. Their deaths might get the will thrown into probate, but the outcome seemed certain. Cyrus had no other close relatives. Adah would have Chainlink. And he would have Adah.

Getting Trinidad aside for a private discussion last evening, Nevers had put it to him just that way. Nevers had watched the man for years. He was as amoral as an alley cat; his friendship for the Trapp boys was only skin deep. With his reckless *pistolero* years behind him, Trinidad had an eye to the modest ambitions that a man of his race might realize in a gríngo world; what better might he hope for than the foremanship of Chainlink? It was simple. All he had to do was help ensure that the next owner of Chainlink would be Cyrus Trapp's widow. Nevers couldn't say how or when; Trinidad would have to keep alert and be ready to follow any cue at a moment's notice.

Trinidad had done well so far.

Joe-Bob dropped back beside them, his face twitching nervously. "Snow's going fast, Faye—we gotta pick it up before them tracks is melted away."

"All right, kid. Let's pick it up."

They quickened pace. In a half-hour they angled across Sully's horse tracks and, a little farther east, onto Brady's. These they followed north into terrain that climbed steadily, and then the trail bent sharply west. Nevers was puzzled for some minutes till he realized that Brady had turned toward the old line camp. Which might have been a shrewd guess on Brady's part.

Suddenly Trinidad drew rein and pointed. "Faye—look there!"

Nevers followed his pointing hand. On the slopes above them, the long trail up to the line camp wound in and out of sight among pine groves and across bare shale promontories. You could see parts of the trail from a long way off. And coming distantly into sight now was a party of three riders descending the trail, slowly and single file. Nevers dug his field glasses out of a saddlebag and trained them.

That was Brady in the lead. Were his hands tied in front of him? Bowie Candler rode close behind him, and then came Sofie Ekstrom. Nevers noted that Candler was riding Sully Calder's paint horse.

As he scanned, Nevers told his companions what he saw.

"Jeez," Joe-Bob said bewilderedly, "what's happened, anyways?"

Nevers shrugged. "Anyone's guess. Come on, let's get higher up. I know a good place to wait for 'em."

The place Nevers had in mind was a dense stand of pine at the base of a long snow-mantled slope where the trail snaked upward. Here he ordered a dismount, and the three of them concealed their horses back in the timber and took up a watch at its edge. Perhaps ten minutes later, Brady and Candler and Mrs. Ekstrom rode into view from the woods that crowned the rugged slant, picking their way slowly. Brady's head was sullenly lowered. Yes, his wrists were lashed together; he was a prisoner.

Suddenly Joe-Bob's horse released a loud blubbery snuffling.

The sound caused Candler to pull up sharply, peering at the trees below. They were still a hundred yards away, Nevers thought, but no help for it. Cupping his hands to his mouth now, he yelled: "All right, Candler, come on down here! We want to talk to you."

Brady lifted his head. If he didn't realize what was happening, he was quick to seize the opportunity it afforded. Giving a wild yell, he clapped his heels against his bay's flanks and lunged it downslope in a heedless run. Halfway to the bottom the animal's hooves skidded on melting snow; it pitched head foremost, flinging Brady ahead of him. The horse's cartwheeling fall narrowly missed Brady, who kept rolling head over heels, finally jarring to a stop. He lay where he was, stunned.

Candler was already hauling his horse around, yelling something at Mrs. Ekstrom. In a moment the two of them had vanished in the trees.

A faint smile hovered on Nevers's mouth as he tramped upslope to where Brady lay, Joe-Bob stumbling ahead of him. They pulled Brady to his feet, wet snow dripping from his clothes. Nevers took out a clasp knife and cut his bound wrists free. Brady's face had a pallid, shaken look; blood trickled from a gash on his forehead. Otherwise he wasn't hurt.

"Lemme be." He batted their hands away; his gaze focused on Nevers. *"You?"*

"Uh-huh. Me. Joe-Bob told me the whole story. Everything. Thought you might need some help."

Brady swung his head, looking a raging question at his brother. Joe-Bob gave a small wretched nod.

"Don't be blaming him," Nevers said mildly. "I kind of

wrassled it out of him. To repeat, we figured you might need help. Didn't you?"

Brady rasped a palm over his jaw, scowling. "Yeah—I sure as hell did. But Jesus. You?"

"Why not? My job's my life, Brady, you know that. It's pretty clear that if I want to keep it, I got to get on your right side. You're a Trapp, you'll try to hold Chainlink together. Am I right?"

"Yeah—sure."

"You got the feeling for it I got. Somebody else might split the outfit up and sell it off in chunks. I want to keep my place, I got to keep your ass out of prison. Does that make sense?"

Brady tugged his beard; his eyes narrowed. "Maybe. But just how far you willing to go?"

"Far as need be," Nevers said calmly. "We'll have to tend to Candler and the woman, you know."

"Yeah—track 'em down." Brady's gaze turned indrawn and vicious. "Candler for sure."

"Both of 'em. The Ekstrom lady can carry tales same as a man. You can trust Trinidad here. He's with us."

"I can see that," Brady snarled. His glance swiveled upslope to where his bay stood, reins trailing, trembling but unhurt. "Let's quit jawing and get going. I get first shot at that pilgrim bastard—don't forget it."

CHAPTER EIGHTEEN

As he and Sofie rode back up the twisting rocky trail with reckless haste, Bowie was cursing in a quiet, monotonous, bitter tone. It was pure luck that a horse's snuffling had stopped them from riding into the jaws of a deadfall. But he had nobody but himself to blame for letting Brady break away. If he hadn't been startled totally off guard by Faye Nevers's shout, Brady wouldn't have made it. They could have used him as a hostage to get by Nevers and anyone with him.

Nevers might have come up here alone. Or he might have had others with him in the trees. Unable to tell which, Bowie hadn't hesitated to turn tail. And the only way to retreat was up the trail they'd just descended. Of course he couldn't be sure of Nevers's intent, but summing up what he knew of the man, it seemed logical to suspect the worst. Considerations of justice or loyalty wouldn't mean a damn to Nevers; whatever had brought him up here had to involve some private ax he was grinding.

So it made plain sense to get clear of the man. If he'd misjudged Nevers, he'd be made aware of it soon enough. For unquestionably Brady would want to hunt Bowie Candler down. What would Nevers want?

He halted; Sofie pulled up beside him.

"They'll want me if they want anyone," he told her. "You stay here."

"I go with you, Bowie. Wherever you go. Don't you know this now?"

"They won't hurt a woman," he said harshly. "Not un-

184

less they catch up with me and you're along. Then they
might not give a damn if you're in line. You understand?"

"I understand. But it doesn't matter. I go where you
go."

To her it was that simple. Bowie gave a soft angry
groan. He growled: "All right, come on. We are going to
make time, and if you can't hold up, I'll have to leave
you."

"*Gud bevara*—how tough you talk." Her lips curved up
at the corners. "I can hold up. But if I could not, you
wouldn't leave me. Go on—go on now."

They moved at a brisk pace up the trail until the buildings of the line camp came into sight again. Here the trail
ended, and Bowie had the bleak thought that if they went
on, they'd be heading into terrain unknown to him, country where pursuers would have all the advantage. But did
they have a choice?

Motioning Sofie to halt, he sat his saddle and pondered
their situation. The afternoon was deepening, long sun
rays gilding across the snow-sided peaks with a pale lemon
glow. Striking across the unknown range to the north at
this time of year would be foolhardy, he thought. Just the
notion of getting caught by a blizzard on those rugged
peaks made him queasy. Over west a ways, they could
have cut across through the passes he had followed from
K-town, but from their present vantage they'd have to set
out blindly. Best chance, it seemed, was to circle into the
ridges and then down to the Oro River valley and on to
Saltville. He didn't have Brady, but he did have the truth,
and the sheriff would listen. No chance of reaching Saltville before tomorrow; that meant a night of camping out.

Dismounting, Bowie went into the cabin and stripped
the bunks of blankets. He rolled them together and lashed
them to the cantle of his saddle. A lot of the thin snow
cover had melted off today, but what remained was
enough to permit easy tracking. *Would there be a pursuit?*
That was something he wanted to be sure of before he and
Sofie went much farther. He led the way down an easy
graded slope back of the line camp, and dipped into a long
timbered vale.

Ten minutes later they emerged from the timber as the land climbed to another barren-looking ridge. At its summit Bowie halted and got out his old army binoculars, which had served him well in his horse-hunting days. He trained them on the line camp at the crown of the ridge they'd quitted.

Yeah—there they were. Four of them. He identified them easily. Brady, Joe-Bob, Nevers, Trinidad. That pretty well answered it, he thought. It didn't matter what their individual motives might be. No party made up of those four boded any good for him.

Already they were following the tracks into the timbered dip, and there was no time to lose. So far Sofie had followed Bowie's lead unquestioningly. Now, as they picked their way across the ridge to its other side, he told her how he had the situation sized up. Best hope was to keep ahead of the Chainlink men till nightfall. With any luck they could keep on going for a time after the failing light forced the pursuit to halt.

For the next few hours, Bowie continued a gradual swing toward the west, climbing steadily higher but not wanting to penetrate far into the mountain range. As it was, they were swinging around the northernmost foothills, brushing the base of a great top-squashed peak. Sunset was bleeding horizontally along the rim of earth, its pink rays flaming across the south slopes of the range. Dusk and darkness soon. And the last chance for escape. Bowie headed into a wedge-shaped cleft between shouldering ridges, pressing for speed in his worry that the men behind might be making better time.

Minutes later, he knew that he'd blundered Sofie and himself into a trap. The cleft angled out of sight ahead of them, but even before they'd made the turn and followed the passage to its end, Bowie had the sinking conviction that he'd boxed himself in. The premonition was right: the cleft ended in a blank granite cliff where the two ridges folded together. The sides were too steep and high to climb.

"Get out of here—fast!" he told Sofie.

Wheeling their animals around, they clattered back down the cul-de-sac. Even as they broke into the open once more, four men were riding out of a scattering of pines a few hundred yards distant. Coming on slowly and spreading apart as they came. Of course—they'd known. Had known of the false pass and that Bowie was bound to head into it once he was fixed in this direction.

Now he and Sofie were in a real bind. Boxed at their backs by a dead-end trail. At their right by tall bluff-faced ridges. Ahead, four men were advancing, rifles up. To his left lay the slow-rising base of the squashed peak. Bowie hesitated, and then one rider raised his rifle and sent off a shot. Powder snow geysered yards ahead of their mounts.

"Come on!" Bowie yelled. Clapped his heels against the paint's flanks and whirled the animal up the mountain slope.

As if on signal, the four riders broke into a concerted run. They were opening up with rifle fire, but Bowie knew that the chance of hitting anything at this range on running horses was practically nil. Up ahead of him mottes of young spruce made zigzags of dark green along the slope. At this height the day's sun had hardly affected the fresh snowfall; it spun in flaky swirls from under the horses' hooves as they lunged into the ascent of a steepening escarpment.

Then Bowie reached the first of the low, thick, close-growing spruce; he reined the paint into them and piled off. Yanking Sully's .45-.70 Winchester from its scabbard, he dropped onto one knee, facing downslope. Sofie slipped to the ground and came running over to crouch down beside him.

"Down flat," Bowie snapped. "Can't fight off four men and worry about you too."

Obediently she stretched out on her stomach under the spruces. Bowie brought the Winchester to his shoulder and settled his sights on the first rider, Joe-Bob, as he poured recklessly up the slope. Then Bowie quickly lowered his aim and pulled trigger. He had nothing against Joe-Bob, but he might be as gun-handy as any other.

The horse shuddered and fell to its knees with a piercing whicker. Then crashed on its side, pinning Joe-Bob's right leg. He let out a chagrined wail of surprise and pain.

Brady, Nevers, and Trinidad scrambled off their animals and scattered for the shelter of granite thrusts which studded the slope. Bowie, firing as fast as he could lever the Winchester, sprayed up snow around Trinidad's legs as he ran for cover. Just as he reached a towering boulder, a bullet smacked into his leg. Trinidad went down into cover with a howling curse: *"Válange Dios!"*

Both Brady and Nevers had dropped down behind sizable outcrops, and Bowie held his fire now, waiting. On this open slope he could easily pick off either man if he showed himself. As they'd taken cover many yards apart, they would have to communicate by shouting; he'd be forewarned of any joint move against him. By now the whole mountainside was sheeted in a last fiery flush of sunset.

"Brady!" Nevers called.

"Yeah?"

"The light's going. Get dark enough he can't pick us out good, we can break cover and swing around to either side of him. Take him on two sides. What about it?"

Brady grated an assent that was almost unintelligible, as if grinding his teeth in a raging impatience.

They'd left Brady's Remington-Keene at the line cabin, but he seemed to have another rifle: Joe-Bob's, Bowie guessed. He and Sofie had one rifle. If Brady and Nevers reached the thin skirmish line of spruce, they could face him on equal terms.

Except there were two of them. Bowie felt Sofie's hand close tight on his arm, but she said nothing.

The minutes dragged by in aching silence, except for an occasional cursing groan from the Mexican. Even Joe-Bob, helplessly pinned by his dead horse, was quiet. The red light faded to dusky rose and then to beige-gray; dusk thickened.

Suddenly Brady's bear-thick form bounded out of cover and off to the right with surprising speed. Running low and fast from rock to rock, hummock to hummock, so that Bowie had only fleeting glimpses of him in the blurry dusk. He tried to fix a bead; he shot twice and heard the bullets scream off rocks. In a moment Brady would be out of sight and circling up toward the spruces.

Bowie bore down on a tight bead as Brady flickered into sight again, this time leading Brady's faint shape with a careful precision. He fired. Brady staggered and went down on his hands and knees. Bowie held his fire now as Brady floundered to his feet, yelling "Faye!" with a note of pure panic.

Nevers hadn't even moved, Bowie realized. Just as the thought touched the edge of his mind, a rifle spewed orange flame in the gray seep of dusk. It was Nevers's. And he wasn't firing toward Bowie's position. Brady whirled as the slug caught him in the shoulder. Then Trinidad fired. Brady was catapulted backward by the slug's force as it caught him full in the chest. His body sprawled darkly against the pale slope.

"O God," Sofie whispered.

Joe-Bob found his voice. "Trin!" he screamed. "You, Faye, you killed Brady! My God, you killed him——"

"Candler!" Nevers's voice sawed coldly across the slope. "You hear me?"

Bowie was silent for a stunned moment, trying to digest this. Nevers and Trinidad together in a play to get rid of Brady? "Yeah—yeah, I hear you."

"We don't want you. We want the kid. Joe-Bob. That's all. You and the woman can ride away from this. Get clear away. All right?"

"You sure you want a couple live witnesses walking around, Nevers?"

"You shoot too damn well," Nevers yelled back. "I might be next. I never counted on a stand-off like this. Let's both sides back off. You both get clear out of the country and keep your mouths shut about what happened here. I'll take your word."

Like hell you will, Bowie thought. For a moment he was puzzled by Nevers's willingness to let Sofie and him ride free. Abruptly the answer came to him. Nevers and Trinidad would give out a story that *he* had killed both the

Trapps in this fight. Since Brady himself had already given out that he'd killed Cyrus, who wouldn't believe it?

"Sounds fine," Bowie called. "Only I got a better idea."

"Yeah? What's that?"

"Suppose you and Trinidad ride away from here instead. Leave the kid be. What about that?"

A long silence followed. Then Nevers gave a mirthless laugh. "Look, let's talk it over, all right?"

"You're talking."

"Well, it's damn hard talking this way. How about coming down to meet me halfway?"

Bowie's throat felt cold and parched. "Sure. Step out and start walking."

"All right, sure, you do the same. Eh?"

"Just as soon as we even things out. You tell Trinidad to throw out his rifle. Handgun too."

Another humorless laugh. "All right. You hear that, Trin? Do it."

"Yeah, I hear." The Mexican's voice was husky with suppressed pain; Bowie guessed his bullet had smashed a bone. Disarmed, Trinidad would be out of it. "You really want this, Faye?"

"Do it. Throw 'em out, both guns."

Trinidad's arm holding his rifle lifted above the boulder. "Way out!" Bowie called. The rifle spun away from the shelter and slapped into the snow. Trinidad's pistol followed.

"Start walking, Candler—"

Nevers's voice was like a steel rowel grating on flint. Slowly he rose to his feet. Bowie sized the bad light and the distance between them. Too far for a good shot. And Nevers would start firing the instant he was sure of the range. Well, it was an even chance.

"Bowie? No!"

Sofie clutched at his arm as he got up. He pulled her hand away and tramped out of the spruces and started downslope. The last daylight was gone, but Nevers's dark form stood out vaguely against the white slope as he slogged upward.

Stumbling and slipping on the rough snow-whipped

slant, the two men closed the distance between them. Wind sliding off the peaks burned coldly on Bowie's sweating face. His rifle was clamped in his right hand; his whole arm ached with tension.

When he saw Nevers's arms start to lift, he didn't hesitate. Coming to a dead stop, he took quick aim. The two shots merged. Powder smoke bloomed and frayed away on the wind. Nevers's curse echoed thinly across the rock field as he fell to his knees. But he was barely hit, or had only slipped. Instantly he was up and plodding onward, levering his rifle and bringing it up to fire again. Bowie stayed where he was, waiting.

Yes, Nevers was hit. Staggering slightly as he came on now, firing as fast as he could jack fresh shells into the chamber.

Close enough, Bowie thought, and settled his eye along his sights, firing and working the lever and firing again, again, again, steadily and carefully. Shooting downhill in the near dark was a hard challenge, but he didn't surrender to the wild dogged fury that had seized Nevers as though more than his life were at stake.

A bullet drove Nevers off balance. He seemed to roll with its impact as a boxer would roll with a punch, somehow keeping his feet. But he was hard hit. He stood swaying, his rifle sinking downward. With a dragging effort he raised it again.

Bowie was already settling a bead. The moment his sights hung steady, he shot.

Nevers was smashed off his feet, tumbling and rolling down the slope. Almost as soon as he stopped, he was floundering back to his feet. Bowie couldn't believe it. His sense of two serious hits on Nevers was positive. Yet he was rallying for another try.

Very carefully Bowie aimed and pulled trigger.

Nothing. The Winchester's chamber and magazine were empty. And Nevers was lurching on and upward while Trinidad was crawling away from his rock toward the guns he'd discarded.

Then Nevers's legs began to fold in midstride. He took a final straining step and pitched forward in the snow.

Trinidad stopped his laborious crawl. "Faye," he yelled. When no answer came, he resumed crawling.

"I can see you," Bowie shouted. "Stop there or I'll blow your head off."

He was pointing an empty rifle, but he didn't think Trinidad knew it. He was right. Trinidad let out one clear despairing curse. Then he came to a stop on his belly.

Bowie called up to Sofie, then trudged slowly down the long slope, a vast weariness dragging at his heels. He paused to collect Trinidad's guns and tramped on to where Joe-Bob lay pinned. Joe-Bob was weeping in broken husky sobs.

"Brady, oh Jeez, Brady—"

"He's dead," Bowie said harshly. "Like you ought to be. Like you meant me to be."

Joe-Bob wagged his head back and forth, gulping miserably. "I didn't mean nothing. Brady worked it out and I done what he said. Trin and Faye, why they want us dead?"

Bowie glanced at Sofie as she moved up beside him, then looked back at Joe-Bob. "You can ask Trinidad. You'd be as dead as Brady if I hadn't been here. Be the easiest thing I know to just leave you like you are."

"Aw, Jeez, no—" Joe-Bob gave a hysterical whickering laugh. "You wouldn't do that."

"Depends on you. You can tell the sheriff just what Brady was up to. Or you can stay where you are."

"Jeez no, I'll tell him whatever you say, all right? All right?"

"The truth," Bowie said wearily. "Just tell him the truth."

He looked at Sofie beside him. Where she belonged, he thought, and wondered that he'd ever thought otherwise. Wind sliced at their faces. Icy wind and growing darkness and the side of a lonely mountain. He felt tired as hell and it seemed as though they were a long, long way from much of anywhere.

But it didn't really matter. It didn't matter at all.

—DAY OF—
THE BUZZARD

I

THE TWO RIDERS came into Corazon at mid-afternoon. Both of them were exhausted, sweated and punished by hours and miles of heat that shimmered in distorting waves off the desert floor. They rode warily, eyes squinted against the slant of sun, their rifles held ready to hand across their pommels, Corazon wasn't much. Squatting like a neutral-colored cur against a red-tan rollaway of scorched flats, it consisted of one rambling 'dobe building, built in three sections: dwelling, general store, swing station for the Largo and Lansing Stage Company.

The two men had seen the spiral of oily black smoke an hour back; minutes ago they'd marked the static-winged dots that were buzzards circling above the smoking ruin. When they were still yards from the station, the men hauled rein and took in the scene carefully. The sun-baked walls were standing, but the roof had burned and collapsed, a tangle of blackened timbers and charred rubble that continued to smolder fitfully. Off behind the station stood a mud-walled stable with a corral of ocotillo poles. Both were empty, the stable doors gaping open, one side of the corral broken down. Trampled earth showed that the livestock had been driven off in a body.

Dismounting stiffly and cautiously, the pair approached the main building. Angry clouds of flies swirled up. The older man's flint-cold gaze appraised everything. His young companion had eyes for nothing but the three dead bodies. The flies settled again; their dim droning ebbed into a brassy wash of silence.

The older man broke it. "Our men been here sure. Track says so. But they didn't do this."

"Apaches?"

"Sure, 'Paches. Cherry-cow work, Cayetano's bunch. Wouldn't be no others."

Jason's throat muscles worked. Staring at the bodies, he fought to keep from being sick then and there. One of the men, an old Mexican, lay in the dust by the corral, his calico shirt and trousers clotted with dark stains. A hayfork stood upright in his chest, the tines driven clean through his body. He must have been shot several times, dead before the fork was thrust in; little bleeding showed around the tines. The hot wind stirred his gray hair. The woman's body lay half in, half out of the station door, her clothes and hair burned away. A Mexican too, probably in her middle years. Few of the details of sex or race or age had survived the terrible butchery, and they no longer mattered.

The worst of it had been inflicted on the third Mexican. A rope had been slung around his ankles and flung over the limb of a lone cottonwood, his body yanked upside down a couple feet off the ground, and the rope lashed down. Then a fire had been built under his head. The buzzards had been at all three bodies.

The older man followed the direction of Jason's gaze and said in that flat, chill, stolid voice that the youth was learning to hate, "You boil a man's brains in his skull a spell, they just naturally bust out. One thing, 'Paches don't lift hair. You got to say that for 'em." He spat into the dust. "Leave that to the Mexes. Greaser governors

down in Chihuahua and Sonora got a bounty on 'Pache
scalps."

"God, Mr. Penmark." Jason's jaws were clamped; he
gritted out the words.

"God ain't got a whit to do with it, boy."

Penmark turned away, a tall, gaunt and weather-worn
man whose wide shoulders strained his hickory shirt. He
was in his mid-fifties, but it hardly showed except in the
piebald streaking of his hair and the deep grooves in his
saddle-brown face. Nearly three decades of coping with
this land on its own terms had made Val Penmark tough
as rawhide, beating every shred of softness out of him.
His nose curved like a hawk's beak. The eyes, socketed
deep below his dust-powdered brows, glimmered like
pond ice, dead and cold.

Tucking his Winchester under his arm, the muzzle
slacked downward, Penmark studied the ground.

"Been a time. Happened, I'd say, before noon." He
flicked a glance at the carrion birds wheeling on the tar-
nished sky. "Time enough for them to get in some work.
Not too much. Our men coming here would of interrup-
ted 'em. That'd be 'bout an hour ago."

Jason, unable to tear his eyes from the bodies, hardly
heard him. Stories heard in his Missouri boyhood, tales of
bloodletting and massacre told by a grandfather who had
fought the Creeks and Seminoles with Andy Jackson,
flashed across his memory with a raw force; and suddenly,
in the blistering heat of mid-afternoon, he shuddered with
a sweepback of childhood fears. Abruptly the roiling in
his guts surged bitter-hot to his throat. Stumbling a distance away, he bent over and threw up every particle in
his stomach.

While Jason was still feebly retching, Penmark said in
his flat and indifferent voice, "Time we got moving. Our
men been here and gone. We are closing distance. Good
chance we can come up on 'em before sundown."

"Mr. Penmark—" Jason swallowed a couple times and
looked up, blinking. "We got to bury these people. Take
time for that anyways."

Val Penmark's mouth was a tight slash in his granite

jaw; it gave a dry twitch that was no smile. "You can't
even bear the looking, Drum. You got the belly for burying?"

"Yes. It's the Christian thing, sir."

"Jesus Christ, boy. It's your time then. I ain't wasting
mine putting a passel of Papist greasers 'neath the
ground. Not when we're this close_I ain't. You do what
you want."

Penmark raked him with a contemptuous stare, then
turned and walked to his horse. Getting the canteen from
his saddle, he carried it to the rock-edged well and cranked
up a bucket of water to fill it. Jason stared at him a bitter
moment, then got his own canteen and followed suit. . . .

They had come a goodly way in forty-eight hours,
counting two breaks for sleep, and of course they hadn't
dared press the horses too hard. Even so, Jason was tired
to the marrow, drained by the searing heat. Hardened by
years of tramping behind a plow and more recently by
working cattle, he was hard put to match the tireless drive
of this man nearly forty years his elder. Penmark had
more than an iron constitution. He was a man totally obsessed. Jason had a strong reason of his own, but even the
stamina of a tough eighteen-year-old had its limits.

Tall and big-boned himself, Jason Drum hadn't yet
filled out with a solid maturity to match his size. His
sweat-patched shirt hung like a rag on his cord-muscled
trunk; his arms and legs gangled awkwardly. Though he
usually carried himself with a neat wiry grace that made
up for his awkwardness, he was drag footed with exhaustion now, queasy and shaken by what he'd just witnessed;
his step was stiff and plodding. The tan of his thin face, a
face that seemed too sober for its years, had yielded to a
ruddy burn below the brim of his old slouch hat. His
sandy hair was sun streaked, his big-knuckled hands
stiffly swollen, and they shook enough to spill water as he
filled his canteen.

The two men drank their fill, watered their animals at
the trough, then mounted and rode away on a trail that
now bent somewhat southeasterly out of Corazon. Neither
looked back at the smoking carnage of the station. The

Santa Rita mountains rose in dim purple serrations to the south; more dimly yet, ranging south and west into Mexico, rolled the San Ignacios. Except for a slight change of shape, the peaks seemed no nearer than they'd been a day ago.

Jason and Penmark had been part of a posse that had ridden out of New Hope two days ago, but the others of their party had given up the chase in less than a day. You couldn't blame them. High June had turned the land to a baking desolation; even those possemen who weren't storekeepers or other counter-jumpers of the same ilk had little taste for tackling it. The posse had been ill prepared to start with, while the seven men who'd robbed the New Hope Bank had laid the groundwork for their escape only too well. Having extra saddle mounts and packhorses, they could hold well ahead of any pursuit with no danger of riding their animals into the ground.

At first it had been almost touch and go. The hastily organized posse had ridden out of town minutes behind the escaping robbers. The latter hadn't gone far before they'd split into two pairs and one trio, afterward forking off on three widely separated routes—another move that appeared to have been nicely calculated in advance. Since they'd had no time to divide the loot, they obviously intended to rendezvous somewhere to the south. Maybe in Mexico. Coming to where the trail had broken three ways, the posse had separated too, splitting up four men to a group. Jason and Penmark had joined two others on the main trail, that of the bandit trio.

Their companions—Manly Jones, who owned the livery stable, and a rancher named Trautmann—had given up yesterday morning and turned back toward New Hope. They'd had good reasons for abandoning the chase. Both were family men; neither had a compelling motive for continuing a pursuit where all advantage lay with the pursued. As Trautmann, the stolid Teuton, had pointed out, their own supply of water and provisions, thrown quickly together in the need for haste, wasn't sufficient to stretch much further. With their horses tiring beneath them, they were losing ground by the hour.

Damned risky to proceed farther into a barren country
none of them knew well enough to be sure of finding
water. Something the robbers had surely packed in abundance. *Ja,* and besides, there was Cayetano. . . .

The Chiricahua war chief was up from his stronghold
in the Sierra Madres again, cutting a zigzag of lightning
raids across a wide swath of southern Arizona. Cayetano
made a deadly game of it, hitting where the army and the
loosely scattered civil population least expected. Both
Miles and Crook had failed to run him down in other
years, and the wily Apache had never pressed his guerilla
activities too heavily. Making casual strikes into both
American and Mexican territory where and when it suited
him, he could always fall back to his mountain retreat. A
periodic nuisance, he was rarely a severe one. Yet he had
an uncanny talent for organizing the chronic malcontents
of the Apache tribes; he was a flawless tactician and even
a strategist of sorts. Lazily exercising what seemed to be a
purely racial vendetta, never taking his own game too
seriously, he was a capricious and unpredictable enemy.
Just now he had the whole territory jittery as hell.

The towns were safe, but travel between them had died
to a trickle. East-west stage runs had ceased a couple
weeks back. Men making journeys of any length traveled
in groups, armed to the teeth. Mine operators hired gangs
of tough nuts to guard their ore wagons from mines to
milling plants. Troops of cavalry had been dispatched
from New Mexico to strengthen the garrisons at Forts
Bowie and Stambaugh. Nervous ranchers didn't range far
from their headquarters and slept with rifles by their beds.
Since Apaches doted on slim odds, a posse of twelve
heavily armed men might tackle a trek across hostile territory with some confidence, provided the trail didn't
stretch too far. But broken into fours, each party was a
sitting duck. Sure, Cayetano might be a hundred miles
away. But there was no telling. The fear of never knowing
was fed by the furnacelike heat that pressed on a man's
senses like a deadening hand; by the deadly oppressive-
ness of this scarred and sun-blasted land, whose mesas and
playas were threaded by a few lonely roads that linked its

ranches, mining hamlets, and roadhouses. No, you couldn't blame Jones and Trautmann for turning back. . . .

Jason Drum wasn't reckless or foolish. Working with his muscles on a daylight-to-dark grind since he was ten had burned all the ordinary restless bravura of youth out of his system. He didn't smile much; there was little in his young life to smile about. He had his share of Missouri mulishness, but it wasn't unthinking stubbornness, either, that kept him at the relentless Penmark's side long after good sense had told him that the whole business had turned into a long-odds gamble just about any way you looked at it.

Old Man Penmark simply didn't give a damn. Nothing, not even his own life, mattered next to accomplishing what he'd set out to do. He'd accomplish it or die in the attempt. You couldn't help wondering if Penmark was looking for death. The thought gave Jason a ripple of gooseflesh. But the older man's granite mask was never cracked by even a self-revealing twitch. . . . You couldn't be sure.

Jason's own driving desperation to overhaul the robbers might not have carried him this far if it hadn't been for coming on a place yesterday, around high noon, where the three men had rested before going on. Strips of blood-crusted cloth they'd discarded had told the story. One man had been wounded in the shooting fracas with townsmen before the escape. Still losing blood, he must be in serious condition by now. A fact, Penmark had grimly observed, that was bound to start slowing them.

Penmark, reading the sign, had announced at nightfall that they'd begun overtaking the trio of fugitives. By mid-morning today it was apparent that the trail was bending southwest toward Corazon. Whatever the wounded man's companions had meant to do at the swing station, get care for him or perhaps just leave him there, they hadn't lingered. Nothing that was left in the wake of an Apache raid would be of any use to a seriously injured, perhaps dying man. So the three had pushed on, quartering back toward their original route and an unknown rendezvous. . . .

The trail was straightening into a southward line again. Penmark rode slowly in the lead, holding the track with a hard-bitten patience. He followed it easily and intently, sometimes bending from his saddle to study it out better. Jason rode loose and slumped; the burn of raw sunlight darkened his eyes. He thought of the cool cottonwoods at the home place. His mother and sisters would be relaxing under them right now, taking a break in the day's work and sipping lemonade or buttermilk.

"Mr. Penmark," he said.

"Yeah."

"What happens when we come up on 'em?"

Penmark didn't take his eyes off the ground. "Got another bug in your belly, Drum?"

"No sir, I just wondered—"

"I tell you what don't happen. These men are killers. What we don't do, we take no damnfool chances with 'em."

"I just wondered how we will do it."

"It'll go how it goes." Penmark swung his head up, locking stares. "You want to back out, say so now."

"I ain't backing out."

"These men got nothing to lose, boy. When the shooting starts, it's them or us. You ever hit anything with that squirrel iron of yours?"

"Sir, I make myself a middling good shot."

Penmark's lips pursed up in a wait-and-see twist. "Man ain't a squirrel. I don't look for a whole hell of a lot from you, Drum. Just don't get in my way."

He bent back to his tracking. Jason rode in a resentful silence, rolling spit with his tongue. He was scared right enough, but no call for Penmark to set him down. He was here, wasn't he?

Yet he had to ask how logical his reason was now. Penmark figured the gang had split up without dividing the loot; these three they were trailing might not be packing a cent of it. Could turn out a pretty fruitless chase from his standpoint. But he'd had to take that chance; he couldn't just do nothing. Wondering if the possemen who'd followed the other bandits had given up as Jones and Trautmann had, he decided it was likely. None but he and Penmark had deep reasons. . . .

They were pressing into rougher country. Sand-colored cliffs and spurs broke up the flats; the two men struck gravelly stretches where nothing grew but bear grass and prickly pear. White sparks of light danced off the mica-laced ground. Penmark was frequently dismounting now to look for sign. Checked to a slower pace, he was getting restless and angry, muttering to himself.

"You sure we're heading right, Mr. Penmark?"

"Use your goddam eyes," Penmark said savagely. "I am tracking most by blood drops you can see yourself. That hurt one is throwing blood. He's in a bad way. They got to stop soon. Goddamit, they got to!"

The sun slanted lower, painting the rocky scape with a pink-orange glare. Sunset wasn't far off. The dead quilt of heat lifted a little, and it was comparatively cool in the lee of cliffs where the long shadows grew. Passing through a lacy green fog of mesquite, they came to the edge of a shallow valley. Penmark raised his hand for a halt and pulled back off the skyline, studying the scene below. The slopes were littered with splintered blocks of sandstone and cut by several deep notches. The long and narrow valley floor was partly masked by thickets of mesquite and catclaw and some scrubby oaks.

There was a lot of cover down there, Jason thought, but he couldn't see anything out of the ordinary. You'd make them out if they were on the move, horseback. If they had stopped, it would be harder. No trace of smoke. But even figuring they'd shed pursuit, they might not risk a fire in country where the Apaches were out.

"They're down there," Penmark said abruptly.

"I don't see nothing."

That green-slate stare. Penmark spat. "Boy, I wouldn't expect you to kick up a frozen turd in a muleyard on a cold morning. They're down there. I'm going to take them. You hark close and do what I tell you."

II

PENMARK LAID OUT the plan in a precise, intent, steel-hard voice, as if he were daring Jason to misunderstand a word. It was simple enough. Jason would merely bait the trap; he, Penmark, would close it. He pointed out where the men were encamped, a dense clot of brush near the valley's center. Studying it through the field glasses Penmark passed him, Jason managed to pick out one of the robbers' tethered horses through the screening brush: a dun animal that was almost the color of the ground. Penmark had spotted it without the glasses; he'd also noted movement in the brush thereabouts. He figured they could get onto the valley floor without being seen by slipping down through one of the wedge-shaped notches in the slope, and Jason was to try for Christ's sake not to make too much noise.

"All you got to worry about is your end of it," Penmark told him with the same controlled, stony care, as though addressing an idiot. "You got hardly anything to do. Just stay down. They can't see you and you can't get hit. Any of 'em comes poking your way, you got all the advantage. You're on the ground and you can hear him and see him first."

Leaving their horses ground-hitched back in the mesquite, the two quarter-skirted around the valley's rim to its east flank. For the descent, Penmark chose the second deep cleft they came to. It was a brush-filled ravine that scored deep into the earth and rock, following the downslope clear to its bottom. Jason tried not to make noise as he followed Penmark, but the brush ripped at his clothes; every snapped twig sounded like a gunshot. It was hard going down the steep jumble of broken rock, which kept turning under his boots; his rifle and the coiled rope he carried over one shoulder didn't help his balance. Luckily the rubble was too large to make much sound as it grated and stirred beneath his driving feet.

Stealth was hard to manage when you were big built, over six feet tall, and made clumsy by pure exhaustion. Jason couldn't remember feeling so bone tired in his life, and he wondered if it was partly fear. But his mind was razor tense. It must all be the deadly heat and the long hours in saddle. Nor had they gotten much sleep on the night stops. Val Penmark would keep pushing right up till dark and have them rolling out in the gray light before dawn, soon as track showed.

Penmark was iron. Pure iron. He moved with a stiff grace and contained his exhaustion as he did his rage—as if it were a trained tiger.

Once they were on the bottom, it was easier to move quietly. The masses of brush grew enough apart for the two men to slide between them, their bodies balled in awkward crouches, as most of the foliage wasn't chest-high to a man. Jason, totally unsure of the camp's position now, blindly followed Penmark's lead.

Suddenly the older man motioned for a halt and raised his head, listening intently. Straining his ears, Jason picked out the faint mutter of men's voices.

They moved on, Penmark picking the way with slow care. Sweat glided down Jason's ribs, made a stinging wash in his eyes; he sleeved it away without pausing. When the voices seemed uncomfortably loud, Penmark stopped again and studied the terrain around them. He pointed wordlessly at a cluster of scrub oak that reared taller than the green clouds of mesquite around it. Jason nodded, slipping the coiled rope off his shoulder as Penmark glided away to his right, the brush swallowing him.

Working quickly, Jason fastened the rope's end around one stem of the oak clump, then moved away through the mesquite thickets, paying out line. When the lariat was gently taut, its full length uncoiled, he stretched out on his belly beneath a screen of mesquite and gave the rope a sharp tug that rattled the oak leaves. Twice more he jerked it before a break in the drift of voices told him they'd caught the sound.

A long trailing silence. Again Jason yanked the rope.

He heard one man speak quietly, as if giving an order. Jason lay motionless then, his heart thudding against the earth. Brush crackled; slow steps crunched the flinty soil. Penmark had hoped the trick might pull the wounded robber's companions into the open, but they were being cagey. Only one of them was coming this way. Jason heard the sharp click of a pistol being cocked; the man was close, but there was no sign of him. Must be prowling through the brush in a deep crouch so he wouldn't expose his head and shoulders.

The steps paused. Jason jerked the line once more.

Suddenly the stalker fired into the oak thicket three times. Leaves and twigs showered down, and Jason promptly hauled the rope taut. Part of the oak scrub sprang sideways as if a man concealed there had limply toppled and bent it. That was what the rifleman was supposed to think. But would he? Would it draw him into the open? . . .

Jason could hear him moving again. Following the sound with his eyes, Jason saw the man's blocky head and shoulders lift to view, and then he was tramping warily out of the brush—a chunky fellow whose Sonora hat cut a hard slant of shadow across his swarthy face. Coming straight on toward the oak thicket, he'd discover the ruse in another moment.

Jason tightly fisted his rifle. Would he have to shoot? Buck fever grabbed him; he began to shake. Where was Penmark? He was supposed to . . .

A rifle's clear, splitting report came. The chunky man spun like a top and went down.

"Miguel!" his companion yelled.

Getting no answer, he came plowing through the brush on the run. The crash of sound broke Jason's paralysis. Coming up on his knees, he levered his Winchester and, as the second man came bursting into the open, shot quickly.

He made a clean miss.

Not pausing in his run, the tall robber veered sideways, loping in a bent-over run into more brush that abruptly cut off Jason's view.

Jason fired blindly at the sound. The man was cutting around him in a wide arc, seeking a better vantage point. And then Penmark's rifle spoke again. The robber pulled to a halt—or was he hit?

Another hot drowsing silence. If he wasn't hit, Jason thought, at least he realized he was facing two rifles, not one. Through a break in the brush, Jason could see the chunky Mexican sprawled on his face fifty feet away. He had made no movement.

Jason strained his ears for the hint of a sound. Finally he raised his voice in a shout, "Mr. Penmark!"

No reply.

Jason crawled to his feet and moved forward in a slow crouch, threading between the thickets. Penmark was either unsure he'd hit the tall man or else knew he hadn't. Either way, Jason reasoned, Penmark was likely to be working silently nearer the man's position. Might be they could catch him between them. . . .

A shot clipped through the mesquite two feet from Jason. He dived to the ground, slamming heavily on his chest, hugging the gravel in a burst of gritty sweat. No other shot came. The robber must have fired at some tell-

tale sound. Cautiously Jason pushed himself up on his
hands, peering through the tangle of mesquite and broken
rock ahead of him.

Then he caught a flicker of motion. In the same moment Penmark's rifle opened up again. The tall man was
falling back the way he'd come. Toward the camp. And
the horses. Jason tried to bring his rifle to bear, but in-
tervening brush gave him only fleeting glimpses of the
running man. Then he was cut off.

On the heels of the tall robber's retreat, Jason heard
another scramble of sound off to his left. The Mexican!
Apparently not hard hit, he'd been playing possum; he
too was making for the horses.

Too late to cut him off. Jason headed after him in a
heedless run; Penmark was breaking brush in the same
direction. Momentarily all four of them were converging
on the brush-hidden camp from different angles.

But the two robbers reached it first. Suddenly both
were shooting from its concealment, using rifles now.
Jason hit the ground again; he had a glimpse of Penmark,
only yards away now, lunging for the shelter of a sandstone spur. Gunfire hammered against Jason's ears, as
Penmark, partly exposing himself, returned the robbers'
fire, pumping shots into the brush as fast as he could.

Sudden hoofbeats then, followed by a crash of thickets.
The two were making a break from the other side of the
packed brush. From here it cut them off completely.
Cursing, Penmark sprang up and skirted the heaviest
brush at a run, Jason following.

The valley was scantily brushed toward its south end;
the two men, flattened to their horses' necks, were streaking across it at an all-out run. Penmark braced to a halt,
raised his rifle, and sighted carefully. His shot sent the tall
man's horse crashing to the ground. Twisting free of his
falling animal, the robber landed heavily, rolling over and
over.

He staggered to his feet almost at once. Penmark drew
bead again; his firing pin fell on an empty chamber. He
dropped the gun and wheeled on Jason, his face livid.

"Your rifle, boy!"

Jason didn't have time to relinquish his grip on the Winchester; it was wrenched from his hands. The Mexican twisted in his saddle, then yanked his fiddlefooting black to a stop. He whipped around and headed back for his companion. The tall man put his head down and ran, straining for speed. Penmark began to fire with a steady, dogged fury, swearing as he tried to sight in the unfamiliar weapon. Shots kicked up powdery fans near the running man's legs.

Suddenly he went down, somersaulting in his run, staggered up again, and almost fell on his first step. He was hit, his right leg dragging. The Mexican careened his animal up beside him and tried to help him swing up behind. But the Mexican's own wounded arm was flapping and useless. Reaching out his good arm, he lost control of his horse. It shuffled away from the tall man's effort to mount; he couldn't brace his bad leg, and it gave way when he tried to swing up the other leg.

One of Penmark's bullets must have seared the black. It lunged into a panicky run, as the tall man, limping alongside, made another wild grab for the Mexican's arm. He stumbled, his hold slipped, and he plunged down in a moil of dust.

Unable to control his horse, the Mexican lost his nerve. He sank his spurs with a hoarse yell, and then the black was racing away toward the valley's end. The tall man rolled dazedly to a sitting position and watched them go.

Penmark was already running stiffly forward, rifle half-pointed, and Jason was on his heels. They were yards away from the downed man as the Mexican drove his mount recklessly up a broad notch in the far slope. Moments later the escaping robber had topped the rim and was gone.

Penmark's face was wolfish, the lips peeled back from his teeth, as he tramped up to the man on the ground and halted. His lifted rifle was pointed at the robber's head. Jason thought for a moment of wild disbelief that Penmark meant to kill him.

The man raised his sweaty face; it was square and heavy-boned, divided by deep looping mustaches. His hat lay yards away; his curly black hair was matted to his head. He was brown as an Indian, but his eyes were steely blue. He reached a hand to his hip.

"You touch that hogleg," Penmark said tonelessly, "and I'll blow your head off."

The man's broad mouth grinned. A couple tiny scars grooved one corner of it, touching the grin with a wry irony. "From your look, sir, you wouldn't need that much reason."

"I got just one reason for keeping you alive. There's a few things I want to know."

"Can't oblige you if I bleed to death first." He motioned at his dusty pantsleg where a spreading stain of red showed above the boot. "I was reaching for something to tie it off with . . ."

"Boy, you get his gun. Go careful."

Jason bent, pulled a .44 Colt from the holster at the tall man's side, and stepped back. The robber took a greasy bandanna from his pocket and knotted it around his leg below the knee.

"That'll do you now. Stand up. What's your name?"

The man grimaced as he heaved stiffly to his feet, holding his weight on his good leg. Big-shouldered and whittle-hipped, he stood an inch or so taller than either Penmark or Jason. He had a hard and dangerous look coupled with a curious dignity and a mannered speech. It made Jason wonder what kind of a cross-dog specimen they'd snared.

"John Heath, gentlemen, at your service."

"Captain Jack Heath?"

"If you like."

Neither name meant anything to Jason. But Penmark gave a slow nod as if it explained everything. "There ain't a judge in the territory would summon me to docket if I blowed you apart where you stand."

"I fancy not."

"You goddam right not. So mister, you do's you're told and don't bat a winker wrong. Or you won't even live to see a hangrope."

Heath's smile flickered and went. "You present a most

engaging choice." He glanced at his dead horse. "You killed a fine animal there, my friend. I set a good deal of store by him."

"You're luckier'n some." Penmark moved his rifle barrel in a short arc. "To your camp. Your other man, the hurt one, he there?"

"Dead. He died less than an hour ago."

"You're still lucky," Penmark said softly. "Get walking."

"Young man, if you'll hand me my hat . . ."

Jason got the black, flat-crowned *ranchero* hat and took it to him. With Heath limping slowly ahead, they moved back to the mottle of scrub oak that hid the camp. The sun had dropped to a flat molten stain on the west rim, shedding a reddish light that barely reached to the gloomy hollow inside the tight-growing scrub. Five horses were tied there; some gear was piled in an orderly fashion to one side. A covered body lay on the ground. There was a half-dug grave, a couple of Bowie knives stuck in the pile of loose earth beside it. Penmark lifted the blanket from the dead man's face, grunted, and lowered it.

"You surprised us in the act of laying a comrade to rest," Heath murmured. "Don't suppose one of you might consent to finish the job."

"Buzzards can have the bastard for all of me," Penmark said. "Drum there, he likes dead folks buried. Ask him."

Heath smiled twistedly. He eased down on his rump, gripping his bloody leg over the wound. "Well, Mr. Drum, you'll only need one of the knives for that. Mind handing me the other? Like to fix that leg a bit. If your friend doesn't object."

Penmark tramped to the mound of fresh dirt and swept his boot sideward, kicking one of the Bowies over by Heath. "You make small moves with that sticker and no sudden ones. Or you be planted in the same hole. Drum, fetch the horses down here. Look for some grass while you're about it. Good a place as any to spend the night."

His muscles leaden with exhaustion, Jason slogged back toward the notch. Scanning about, he spotted a scant lacing of bear grass hard by the east slope. After leading their horses down from the rim, he hobbled them on the grass, then packed his and Penmark's plunder to the camp, got the robbers' horses and did the same for them. He wished he could water the animals, but the bottom of this valley was dry as a bone. His and Penmark's horses had watered at Corazon and so, he supposed, had the robbers' saddle mounts and packhorses. It would have to do them for a time.

Dusk was starting to gray the reddish light as he tramped back to camp, so tired he could hardly lift one foot after the other. Penmark was squatting on his heels, rifle across his knees, eyes half-lidded like a lizard's as he watched Heath finish the job of bandaging his leg. He'd slit his pantsleg to the knee and washed his knot-muscled calf, which the bullet had gone clean through. The wound was a pulpy mess in a dark welter of bruised flesh. Heath ripped up a spare shirt to plug the wound and tie around it.

"Well, you did miss the bone, friend." His jaw muscles rippled with the twisted grin. "Is that what you mean by 'luck'?"

Penmark said flatly, "Fetch wood, boy. Fix some grub."

"Mr. Penmark, I want to know if he's got the money."

"We'll see to that directly. It's drawing dark fast. Get us a fire built."

Jason, on the edge of telling him to go to hell, bit back the words and dragged himself to the task. There was plenty of dead brush close around; in a few minutes he had a sizeable armload. He staggered back to the glade and dropped it, then dug out matches and began to lay a fire.

Heath settled his back against an oak trunk, his leg straight out before him, and pulled a slim black cheroot from his pocket. "Throw me a match, will you, son? Don't know if it's occurred to you, old pot," to Penmark, "but a fire makes smoke."

"It's drawing dark. Anyways, Drum's an ole country

boy. Knows how to make a fire that's 'most smokeless. You *can* do that, can't you, boy?"

Jason nodded, gritting his teeth. He flipped a match over to Heath. The tall man caught it, snapped it into flame on his thumbnail, and fired up his cheroot. His eyes glinted through the smoke. "Apaches, of course, might pick up woodsmoke ten miles off if the wind's right. Freakish thing, a wind current."

Penmark moved his head in negation. "We don't camp with no fire and you to watch. There'll be one or other of us watching you all night long, sonny boy, and he'll have plenty light to shoot by."

Heath chuckled out smoke. "You know, I never thought of that." He gazed at the slow soaking of his bandage as fresh blood dyed it. "Nasty hole, that. Really ought to rest the leg a day or so. And you chaps look as though you might stand a bit of rest yourselves."

"Might be handy for you if I figured so. That greaser who got away, he might just fetch back some help back here."

"Ah yes. Then I'd have a reason for stalling you or at least slowing you, wouldn't I?"

"We followed seven of you out of New Hope. One's dead. You're taken. Say none of the rest are, they will show up at your rendezvous. If the Mex makes it, he can lead 'em back to us. 'Pending how far from here you meant to meet up."

"You're almighty sure we did."

"To split up ten thousand in paper greenbacks. I call that a good reason. Soon's you get that fire going, you can look through his plunder, boy."

"You might save yourself the trouble," Heath said agreeably. "I don't have a plugged cent of the loot."

All the same, Jason felt a feverish glow of hope as he began to rifle through the camp gear. Turning up even a good part of the stolen money would serve his end of things. But a few minutes' search of the bandits' possessions rocked him back into a heavy-footed gloom.

"There ain't nothing in his possibles, Mr. Penmark. Just a few coins. Mexican from the look."

Penmark grunted. "I still lay odds he knows where the loot is. He's the big mucky-muck of that bunch. They didn't have time to split the money, or where's his share? They trust anyone with all of it, I figure it be him. Lay odds he left all of it cached back some'eres along the trail."

Heath grinned. "Now why would I do that?"

"You and the Mex was slowed considerable by the wounded one. You had no idea how many men might be on your trail. Could be two, could be twenty. But even fearful of being overtaken, you wouldn't drop your hurt man. Even a bastard like you's got a code about that. So it'd be insurance, kind of, to hide the money some'eres along the way. Say you and the Mex got caught up with and taken. Say your boys heard about it and also that the loot hadn't been recovered. They would be damn eager to bust you free, seeing you'd know where the money was hid. Even supposing you didn't get caught, be easy enough to pick up the loot later."

"A shrewd guess, old pot. But a guess."

'Hell, I couldn't care less." Penmark glanced indifferently at Jason. "Too bad for you, Drum. 'Less you can make him tell where it is, you are shit out of luck."

Heath showed his strong teeth amusedly. "And of course *you're* not interested?"

Penmark spat. "Mister, I couldn't give less a goddam. I had no money in that matchbox of a bank. Never trusted 'em. You want to make this cocky son of a bitch talk, Drum?"

Jason stared at him a moment, blinking in a fog of angry exhaustion, closing and unclosing his fists. Then he sat down by the fire and looked into it. Penmark made a contemptuous sound with his teeth and tongue. "He's a good Christian boy, Drum is. You had something I want, I'd tear your goddam heart out by the roots if need be."

"I fancy you would." Heath eyed him curiously. "Just what the Sheol *do* you want? I know there was a good-sized posse on our heels at the start. Even assuming you split to take up our separate trails, there must have been more than just the two of you tracking Miguel and Artie and me. . . ."

"Others quit. We had cause not to."

"Huh. And your piece of the pie, young fellow . . . money?"

"My family's whole savings was in that bank," Jason said dully. "All we been able to lay aside in years."

"Huh," Heath said again. "But you, sir, never used a bank."

Penmark was sitting cross-legged. He leaned slightly forward, firelight washing wickedly against his eyes. "My wife did. Had herself an account in that New Hope matchbox. Was in there on business when you and your high-graders held it up."

Heath's eyes narrowed. "Yes?"

"There was shooting. She got a bullet."

"Dead?"

"Straight off. With a bullet in the head."

"There was a spot of shooting," Heath said slowly. "One fool in the bank went for a gun."

"My wife didn't do nothing. She didn't do a goddam thing. All she done was go to the bank to put in some money."

"It must have been a stray shot. Might have been as easily fired by one of the New Hope men as by us." Heath shrugged. "I didn't know. It was a bloody confusion after the shooting began. We had to fight our way out. . . ."

"I tell you what." Canted forward in his intensity, Penmark drove the butt of his rifle hard against the ground. The raised scar of a cut, which had once laid bare the bone, gleamed white across his knuckles. "You shut your goddam mouth about it and maybe you will reach New Hope alive."

"For the hangman." Heath smiled, trickling out a stream of smoke. "So, you know I'm already wanted for a killing or two. It gives you something to think about, eh?"

"No. For you to think about. Every mile of the goddam way. That's why I don't gutshoot you now, you slimy bastard."

III

JASON THREW TOGETHER a meal of sorts but hadn't much appetite for his share of it. Penmark told him to take the first sleep since he was too drag-assed to trust on guard. They'd split the night into four two-hour shifts, two apiece. He rolled into his soogans and fell into a dreamless sleep that wasn't broken till Penmark shook him awake. Jason took up the guard duty feeling considerably freshened. The cool of night was pleasant; it was easeful just to sit and do nothing but keep the fire up. Heath wouldn't bear much watching, for Penmark had tied his hands back of him and lashed them to an oak trunk. A great horned owl belled somewhere in the night. Otherwise, except for Penmark's snoring, it was pretty quiet.

Feeling depressed about the money and all, Jason felt the sight of the covered body start to nag him. Even an outlaw had a right to be laid under like a white man. He knew Penmark would refuse to let him take the time for it come morning. Going about it quiet as he could, Jason got one of the Bowies and began hacking earth out of the unfinished grave. It was tough loosening the stony soil, and after half an hour he'd sunk the hole only a couple feet more. Common sense warned him not to exhaust himself again. He rolled the blanket tight around the dead man and quickly filled the shallow grave, packing the rocks and flinty earth tight to seal it against scavengers.

"Good boy."

Heath spoke softly as he finished smoothing off the mound. Jason jerked around, seeing the outlaw curled awkwardly on his side as he'd been, but his eyes open. Picking up his rifle, Jason sat down cross-legged and watched the man. You could almost see the thoughts crawling behind Heath's eyes. Not what he was thinking, of course. But you could guess. Grunting, Heath tried to ease his position.

"A fellow can't catch much sleep this way. Look, son, you've got the rifle and I've a wounded leg. You wouldn't imperil my captivity by cutting me free of this damned tree. You can leave my hands tied."

"Mr. Penmark wants you like you are. I guess you better stay that way."

Heath's lips quirked upward. "You know, Drum, you're in a worse bind than I am. Letting that crusty old turd run you about like a squaw."

"He don't run me."

"No? From what I've seen, all he'd need do is holler cricket and you'd chirp."

Jason's face began to burn, but he knew what Heath was trying to do. "What I think is you being tied to a tree is sense, no matter who ordered it."

"But his order all the same, eh?" Heath yawned. "Where do you hail from, ole country boy?"

"Outside of New Hope?"

"I mean to start with. Missouri? I thought so. And your people—tater 'n turnip mud farmers, I'd wager."

Jason picked up a short branch and began whittling at it with short angry whacks. "My pap pulled stakes for Arizona three years ago. There was him and Ma and five of us kids. It took all we had to buy up a little cow outfit and make a new start. Didn't hardly clear enough for two years to pay a couple hands while Pa and me learned about beef cows. Typhus took Pa last year. Him and my two little brothers. There's me, Ma, my two sisters left."

"Three women to see after, eh? A tough row for you."

"Not as bad's it might of been. We held on, all of us pitching in and our two hands sticking by. Didn't look to clear no big profit this year but had a piece of luck. Indian agent from the San Lázaro reservation come down looking for cattle to fill out his beef allotment. A rancher up north was supposed to supply him, but couldn't meet his contract. So lots of us small-loop outfits around New Hope was tapped to make up the difference. Got paid in good government cash for our beef. But I guess you know that."

"Oh yes. We heard." A chuckle rippled Heath's jaw. "As your friend said, that New Hope bank's a matchbox. We knew that too. It wasn't outfitted to handle large windfalls of cash from its depositors. No guard, an old-fashioned safe. No town marshal. The county seat fifty miles away and no sheriff's deputy, even, assigned to New Hope. Town almost empty on a mid-week day, hardly anyone about but old codgers dozing on porches. We expected the job to be a plum. Nothing like the spirited resistance we ran into."

"Happened me and a few other people from ranches was in town. Like Mr. Penmark and his wife."

Heath shrugged. "A rum go about the woman, but it's done. Why all the talk suddenly, boy? Trying to arouse my sympathy for your loss?"

"I don't look for much of that from you, mister."

"Wise lad."

"But say you know where the money is, it's no use to you now. You couldn't lose nothing by telling."

"Wrong. I can look for help from my men only if I deal them square. Say I hid the loot as Penmark thinks. Miguel knows where it is too. He'll tell the others. They're my best hope of getting out of this with a whole hide . . . help that won't be forthcoming if I betray where I hid the money."

Jason's teeth tightened together till his jaws ached. "You might be lucky to live that long. Mr. Penmark's on a hairtrigger about you as is. He gets it in his head to do for you, you needn't look to me for help."

"There's head money on me, Drum. . . ."

"I don't know nothing about that."

"I fancy Penmark does. Ask him. All you need do is fetch me to the law intact. A railroad company, several banks, the Territory of Arizona have offered various rewards for my capture. Assuming my men won't overhaul you before we reach New Hope, you stand to collect all of several thousand dollars . . . just for keeping me alive."

An instant suspicion mingled with Jason's flare of hope. "I'd say," he said thinly, "you are trying to set me and Mr. Penmark at odds with each other."

Heath showed the edge of a smile. "I might be, at that. But it's most likely I merely concur with your opinion."

"What?"

"That my chances may stretch rather fine without your help. I'm afraid, Drum, that your companion is a little mad."

The sun was well up as they started north next morning. Val Penmark seemed tired, old beyond his years, his voice a dragging grunt as he gave the order to break camp. In spite of the danger that Heath's men might pose, they rode at a plodding gait, drained by three days of pressing a savage pace on the high-summer desert. Now that Penmark had the gang's kingpin in hand, his driving fury seemed to have shriveled away. He rode in a stiff slump and never looked back. Heath followed behind him, hands tied in front so he could manage his reins. The outlaw was showing the effects of his injury and a near-sleepless night. His face was puffy red with a touch of fever, but he rode with his head up.

Leading the string of pack animals, Jason held the rear, nervously alert. He kept twisting glances back and around. But in all that dun-colored waste he saw nothing that he hadn't been seeing for going on four days, and his alertness began to blur away with the sheer monotony of

it. Flats of gray sage, scatterings of scrub oak and man-
zanita, smoke trees shrouding the zigzag arroyos, all
merged into one scene of neutral desolation. Poppies and
paintbrush, the red stipples of ocotillo in bloom made the
only dashes of color; lemon light hit the redrock ridges
with a raw glare. What's the difference, he thought dully.
Apaches or white outlaws, it would be all the same if they
were attacked—he wouldn't pick up the signs of danger
in time.

Not his kind of country. He thought of Pa, that tough
luckless man who had broken his back and his heart trying to crop the stony, worn-out Missouri acres that his
father and grandfather had tilled before him. The Drums
had always been hardscrabble; they seemed born to be.
All the dedication and hard work of four generations
hadn't improved their line by a lick, and before that their
folks had been tenant people in the north of England. So
pulling stakes never helped either. New Hope. Another
name for old discouragement. Still, a man had to keep
trying. What else was there?

A mother and two young sisters. Which was a good
deal, come down to it. Drums had a deep family way.
They'd be mortally afraid for him, a worry to eat deeper
each passing day. They'd have sent to town for word of
him and would know what he was about and why. Returning empty-handed . . . after all this. It grated like bitter sand in his craw.

Still there was Heath. Penmark had surlily allowed,
when Jason had asked, that there might be a price of sorts
on the outlaw's head. A dim ray in the pan maybe, but it
was something.

Penmark called a stop at noon. They rested on the
bottom of a broad wash where the smoke trees threw a
silky-hot shade. Jason untied Heath so he could look to
his leg. The calf was so swollen that Heath had to rip his
boottop with a knife to pull the boot free of his foot. He
tore the caked mess of a bandage slowly away, pain making the flesh groove white around his mouth. The wound
was draining clean, about all you could say for it. He
looked up, a sheen of sweat on his face.

"I say, Drum. There's a bottle of whiskey in that small pack. Would you break it out?"

Jason rose off his haunches, but Penmark was nearest the horses; he plodded over, undid the diamond hitch, and dumped the pack to the ground. Getting the bottle out, he straightened up. Opening his hand without a word, he let the bottle fall. It shattered to pieces on a rock.

Jason eased warily to his feet, watching Penmark's eyes. "Sir," he said carefully, "there was no cause to do that."

Penmark kept staring fixedly at Heath. "I'll say what's to be, pup. You keep your goddam lip cinched."

"Man," Heath said softly, "the heat's frying your brains. Listen. I didn't kill your wife. Whoever did that shot wild. I don't shoot wild."

"Did or didn't, it's on your head. You head up that scum. You planned it start to finish."

"What's the difference now, old man? It won't bring her back."

"Shut your rotten mouth," Penmark said in a reedy whisper.

Heath's squinted gaze flicked to Jason. "You've a small interest in my staying alive, Drum. Why don't you fetch me some water?"

Jason sidled stiffly toward the canteen he had laid in a rock shadow. Penmark tipped up his rifle. "He don't need water. There's little enough to see us through."

A hot anger boiled up in Jason. "Him too, Mr. Penmark. I had enough of you saying what's to be."

"I'm saying it again, boy. You had your own drink. Leave that water be."

Jason set his jaw and moved on toward the canteen. Penmark's turning stare followed him; so did the rifle muzzle. Halting by the canteen, Jason hesitated. Penmark's eyes were frozen beyond expression. God, would he? Don't think about it, do it. He's got to be stood up to.

Jason bent, reaching for the canteen.

In that moment, with Jason and Penmark fixed on each other, Heath made his try. One moment he was slumped almost prone; the next he was rolling sideways in a long-muscled burst of energy, grabbing for Jason's rifle where the youth had leaned it against a rock several yards away. The move caught Jason flat-footed. But Penmark reacted with a smooth, contemptuous ease, taking three long steps toward Heath.

In those same fleeting seconds, Heath seized the rifle, levered it, and scrambled to his knees. As he swung it up, Penmark's leg lashed out in a powerful kick. His boot smashed against Heath's cheekbone with a force that flung him on his back. Penmark bent and scooped up the rifle and tossed it to Jason, all in one movement.

"You ain't fitten for orders 'cept taking 'em," Penmark said meagerly. "You want to argufy it, now's the time."

Shaken, Jason could only stare at the gun in his hands, then at Penmark. Heath groaned and struggled to a sitting position. A strawberry stain of mashed skin discolored the side of his face.

"You could of shot," Jason began. And let the words die there.

Penmark's taut face seemed to change as he watched it, loosening into tired lines and wattles. His slitted gaze probed at Jason as if he didn't know him. Slowly, slowly, he let the rifle slack downward.

"Too quick." His voice was gray and dull, an old man's voice. "I don't want it quick with him. Tie his hands. Then give him water. One cup, no more."

Nobody said a word through the long afternoon. The sun broiled against their backs and left sides, and finally heeled down toward sunset. All day they'd ridden slowly, covering maybe a third of the distance they had yesterday. They stopped for the night on a sage-dotted flat where they could make a fire between sheltering boulders. Nothing at all was said; the two older men slumped on the ground, and Jason went about the camp tasks.

Heath was feverish, his eyes too bright, his brain still calculating. He broke the silence with a quiet taunt. "You haven't done well today, old man. You've pushed too hard and it's catching up. Perhaps so will my friends before long."

Penmark's gaunt head lifted. "If they do catch up," he said softly, "you're a dead man. No matter how it goes, you're dead."

"Mm, yes. You know, I was afraid of that."

Heath rolled a dead cheroot between his lips, dryly chuckling. He had more cold guts than Jason had ever seen, but it wasn't likely to do him a jot of good. Let it develop he might be rescued and Penmark would shoot him like a dog.

Penmark had a reserve of savage strength he kept digging into; even tired and beat-out, dulled by grief, he hadn't reached the end of it. He put me down for sure, Jason thought, but I don't feel put down noways. Penmark's bereavement had festered in some way that was turning him strange. You couldn't hate that or even resent it much. If it made him dangerous in a way, you felt it as an impersonal kind of threat, like a coiled rattler: keep out of its way and it would leave you alone. Only that might be hard to manage. If their plans for Heath clashed again . . .

.They ate the slight fare of coffee, bacon, and cold biscuits. Then it was full dark, and a wind was rising from the south, tattering the fire. Brush rattled and a coyote called somewhere. Jason said, "Sir, you want to split the watch same as last night?"

Penmark sat by the fire, a blanket around his shoulders. He seemed to be half-dozing, and now, abruptly, he raised his head. But he didn't even glance at Jason. He was hard-faced alert, listening. Suddenly he stood up, shedding the blanket, and kicked sand on the fire. Jason fumbled up his rifle, listening now.

Penmark spoke then, to Heath and very quietly, "You let one peep out o' you and it'll be the last thing you know."

"Mr. Penmark?"

"Shut up, boy. Keep your eyes open. Watch."

Jason sank down on his haunches among the rocks.

For a straining moment he couldn't make out a thing. Remembering an old warning by his father that a man who stared into fire was momentarily blinded when he looked away from it, he'd been careful not to watch the flames. Now, in the wipeout of fireglow, his eyes quickly accustomed themselves to the surrounding dark. It wasn't total; starshine lay faint on the flats and ridges, frosting the gray-silver bunches of sage.

He picked up the sounds first: a creak of leather, a stir of bit chains. The noise carried at an angle against the wind. Isolating its direction as westerly, Jason quickly saw the dark shapes of riders coming slow through the starlight. Two of them, he thought. And a third horse, a pack animal.

"Hellooo, the camp!" a man called. "Friends here. Can we come in?"

"Who are you?" Penmark said harshly.

"Our name's Jamison. On our way from the Panamints. We spotted your fire as she was coming dark. All right if we ride in?"

"You be slow about it."

They gigged their horses forward. Halting a few yards away, the lead rider stepped to the ground. Jason couldn't see his face well, but he was slight and moved stiffly, and his right arm was held at a crooked angle from his body. The other rider got down too, muttering "Goddam." A woman's voice, and her heavy skirt had got hung up on the pommel. She jerked it free, swearing again.

"We're with folks again," the man told her in a dry, mild voice. "You be watching how you talk."

"Surest thing you know, Pappy."

"Nothing like a she-pup for sass," the man said mildly. "Listen, we don't want to horn in on nothing here."

Penmark was on his feet, legs braced apart; his rifle was up and ready. "Depends what you want."

"Well, some of that coffee I smell would go good."

"Build up the fire, boy." Penmark spat sideways. "What you been up to in the Panamints?"

"What I do mostly. Hunt gold. We got a pokeful if you want to look."

"Heading where?"

"For Bodie over west, where the assay office is."

"You picked quite a time for it. There's hostiles out this way. Cayetano's Cherry-cows."

"Jehosephat. We didn't know that. Have been back in the Panamints a good month. Let's see, this here's Saturday, yeah, month tomorrow it's been."

Jason worked the fire up and fed sticks into it till the leaping blaze picked out the newcomers clearly.

They looked tired and dirty and worn. Jamison was a kind-faced man with eyes like smooth pebbles; the hair burred white around his temples under a slouch hat. His crooked right arm had a shrunken look and was probably useless. His daughter was on the short side, kind of, but not small exactly. She filled out her faded duck jacket like the girls you saw pictured on bourbon labels and harvest-time posters and the like.

"I'll have a look at your plunder," Penmark said, motioning at the packhorse. "Throw it down."

"You know, I'd say you're almighty skittery."

"You'd be right. Throw it down and spread it out."

Jamison undid the pack hitch and dumped the whole load to the ground. He nudged the pack open with his boot and scattered its contents some. There were tools for prospecting, all right, and they had seen hard use. Penmark said he'd have a look at the poke mentioned. Jamison dug it out from a deep pocket of his tattered blanket coat, opened the drawstring mouth, and palmed a little of the dust.

"Take a good look, mister. Ain't none o' your low-down pig gold. That's . . ." A slow worry creased his face. "Listen, you boys ain't road agents, are you?"

"Just so you ain't. Put your gold away. You can spread your traps here if you're a mind."

"Thankee." Jamison tilted his chin at Heath. "Him . . . what's he tied for?"

Penmark made a meager explanation while Jamison tended to their animals and the girl set about fixing grub. Jason kept trying not to watch her. Only girls he was used to were his sisters, and neither of them had such free and bouncy movements. He figured this Jamison girl was older than his older sister Gayla Sue, who shaded Jason by a year. Maybe three or four years older. Gayla Sue was generally figured for a looker, but Sue didn't have coppery hair with bronze glints in it or eyes that snapped with greenish sparks. This Jamison girl was surely made to take a man's eye. Heath seemed appreciative.

"What's your name, my dear?" he asked.

"None of your business."

Jamison paused in lighting a stubby pipe. "Christine, you be minding your manners around folks. I ain't going to say it again."

"Good."

He pursed his lips around the pipestem, shaking his head "I got to tell you men it is no light thing to raise a woman-child the way I live. Had us a little place on the Brazos, but after Christy's ma, rest her soul, took the milk sickness and passed on, I went back to gold-finding again. It is a lonesome way to live, and I fear no life for a budding woman. She has taken on a lot of bark, which I am of a mind to larrup off."

"You try it once," Christy said.

"Think you're too old for a hiding, do you?"

"Damn right I am. You try it."

It was strange-sounding talk between them, yet somehow so casual that you got the feel they were merely talking across one another's head for amusement. But people living off in lonesome places were likely to get so, Jason supposed. A little dotty.

Heath showed his teeth pleasantly. "Would you do me a kindness, my dear? Bring me a drink of water?"

"You stay away from him, girl," Penmark snapped. "That man's a killer."

"He is?" She sat on her heels by the fire, stirring crackers and canned tomatoes together in a skillet. "Who'd you kill, mister?"

Heath laughed. "My dear girl, life kills each of us in its own way. Soon or late, quickly or slowly. Pumps you full of ideals and then grinds the ideals to powder. However we reach it, the grave's our goal. Most I've ever done for one or two chaps, a favor really, was given them a premature nudge that way."

"Do tell." She sounded totally indifferent. "Fetch me that slab of bacon from the pack, Pappy."

"Fetch it yourself." Jamison was seated comfortably tailor-fashion by the fire, facing Penmark across it. "You got better legs than me."

"Thanks." She rose to her feet and went to the pack where they had dumped it, crossing behind Jason where he was hunkered, so close that her skirt brushed his shoulder. " 'Scuse me ..."

At the same moment Jamison cleared his throat loudly, then laid down his pipe and reached his bony left hand inside his blanket coat. It came out holding a .44 Dragoon Colt, which he cocked and leveled at Penmark's head. "Now then, mister. You leave your hands where they be. Sit tight and don't wink an eye. Or I'll blow your head off your shoulders."

Jason's hand twitched toward the rifle he'd laid at his side. A ring of cold steel jammed against the back of his neck, and the girl said quietly, "That goes for you too, boy. Hold still."

Penmark sat with his legs folded, rifle across his thighs. He stared at Jamison through the fire, its glare rippling across his gaunt face. His hands were resting on the Winchester, and for an instant they tightened there. He would be dead, Jason knew, before he could bring the piece up. . . .

But Penmark was unmoving then, and Jamison nodded. "That's wise. Christy, I'll watch the young-un too. You pick up his gun, then come get the old man's."

Heath's shoulders jerked with laughter. "Well done, Dallas. But what took you two so damned long?"

IV

AFTER HE'D CUT Heath free, the old man called Dallas whacked some short lengths off a reata and used them to tie up Jason and Penmark, binding them hand and foot while the girl Christy casually held her pistol on them. It was a snub-nosed little Allan that she'd easily carried on her, bringing it out as soon as she'd moved back of Jason. He felt sick with chagrin at how easily the two of them had managed it, bluffing their way into the camp and smoothly putting Penmark and him off their guard. One simple coordinated move and they were masters of the situation. But who'd have guessed an old prospector and his daughter to be allies of Heath?

"Jamison," muttered Penmark. "Jamison, hell. You're Dallas Redmile."

Dallas grunted as he jerked Jason's hands tight behind his back. "Hell, mister, I know who I am." His voice was still mild and tired, but his crooked arm wasn't entirely useless; it was aiding his good one. "That'll do 'em, Jack. They're trussed like a pair of prize hogs."

"Good. Christy, have a look at this leg of mine, will you?"

"Surest thing you know, honey."

The girl dropped the pistol into her jacket pocket, went to Heath, and kneeled down to work off his boot. He leaned back on his elbows, gently rolling the cheroot between his teeth. "I take it Miguel reached the rendezvous at least."

Dallas grunted. Hunkering down by the fire, he scraped some of the bubbling tomato and cracker mess from the skillet onto a plate and began eating hungrily, talking between mouthfuls. As Jason got the sense of it, the wounded Mexican had gone straight to Arrowhead Tanks where the gang was to rendezvous. Dallas and Christy, apparently the only members of Heath's pack who hadn't taken part in the robbery, were waiting there for Heath and the rest. Pure luck, Dallas observed, that the Tanks weren't far away from where Heath had been captured. Miguel had gotten there about midnight. Driving a hard pace, he'd lost a share of blood and was pretty weak, but had enough left to make clear what had happened.

It had left Dallas and Christy with the choice of waiting for other members of the gang to show up or of undertaking to rescue Heath on their own. Any delay might stretch it too fine, they'd decided, and trying to take him from his captors by outright force might get him killed. A simple ruse had seemed the best way. Dallas had his prospecting tools and poke of gold dust: equipment he'd used as a cover for his identity when, somewhat over a week ago, he'd gone to New Hope to reconnoiter the town and particularly its bank for the upcoming job. The same masquerade might enable them to trick Heath's captors without endangering his life. This morning he and Christy had backtracked Miguel to the valley where Heath had been taken, picking up the trail north from there. Having fresh animals, they'd overtaken Heath and his captors by sunset, after which they had simply swung

up on this camp from the west, as if bound from the Panamints.

"Very good—" Heath grimaced as Christy unwrapped
the caked and filthy bandage around his swollen leg.
"Damn it, my dear, go easy there."

"Sorry, honey. Maybe I'd better soak this off."

"Do it then. How is Miguel?"

"He be all right," Dallas said, reaching for the skillet
again. "We left him resting comfortable, food and water
to hand. You hanker for any of this chef's delight, daughter, or can I finish 'er?"

Christy made a sour face. "You can shampoo with it
for all I care, Redmile. But please, no more of that
daughter crap, all right?"

Dallas's smooth-pebble eyes twinkled with sly lights.
"Anyways, you ain't stepping out of character. Good
girl."

Their banter suggested a wry affection between these
two, even if the father-daughter thing had been a sham.
Dallas Redmile's place in Heath's outfit seemed obvious:
crippled and past his prime, he could still turn an old-
lobo shrewdness to good advantage where any subterfuge
was needed, thanks to an unimpressive appearance and
colorless manner. But what about the girl? Maybe the answer was in the gentle care with which she set to sponging
Heath's leg. Tender shades of concern chased across her
face, which tightened to a quick anger as she finally
peeled away the bandage.

"My God, look at it!" She stared at Jason and Penmark. "You bastards don't believe in coddling anyone, do
you?"

Heath laughed. "Don't be too hard on them, angel.
These are men of tenacity and conviction. Who, as it
turns out, have busted their asses, in the argot, for exactly
nothing. I almost consider my score with them evened.
Dallas, old curmudgeon, I hope you thought to pack
along a drop of firewater on this errand of mercy."

"Y'bet."

Dallas produced a bottle from his saddlebag, pulled the
cork with his teeth, and took a long swig before passing it

to Heath, who drank and shuddered. "Well now, that's pure rotgut at least. Undiluted by quality. All right . . . we stay here tonight. Tomorrow we'll pick up the loot, then be on our way to Arrowhead Tanks."

Dallas stroked his chin. "How far we got to go? Miguel mentioned you hid the money a ways out of Corazon."

Heath nodded. "Seemed a reasonable precaution, slowed as we were by poor old Artie. Matter of fact, we're not far from the place now. Just a matter of swinging a few miles west of here . . ."

Christy's mouth compressed; she shook her head, this leg needs attention. You ought to stay out of the saddle a couple days."

"That's fine, angel, but I'm afraid the situation won't permit any luxury of delay. To clarify things a bit—" Heath pulled at the bottle again and wiped his mouth reflectively. "These two chaps were part of a sizeable posse which split up after we did, putting several men on the trail of Miguel and Artie and me, others after Pete Ermine and Cherokee, still others trailing the other two Ermine boys. But all our friends, I'd guess, shook pursuit rather easily, thanks to their spare mounts. While Miguel and I, delayed by Artie slowly dying on our hands, were finally overtaken by the pair yonder. Who apparently had better reasons for sticking to a long chase than did some erstwhile companions of theirs."

"So all them others likely give up by now," Dallas said.

"More than likely. The original posse was hastily formed, badly provisioned. With food and water low, horses tiring and easily distanced by our men, I'd say we can count them out as of a couple days ago." Heath paused. "Thing is, though, a woman was accidentally killed in the shoot-out at New Hope . . ." He motioned at Penmark with the bottle. "That old boy's wife."

"Jesus," Dallas said quietly. "A woman-killing. That's a damn sorry piece of business, Jack."

"I couldn't agree more, old pal, but it's done. And it's a sure bet that the sheriff's office at Longworth, the county seat, will be setting up an organized search for the das-

tards who are responsible. They'll telegraph word all over
the territory. We could become the focus for quite a
manhunt."

"We was heading for Mexico after the job anyways."

"Right. But with all due haste now. Let's assume that
Cherokee and the Ermines have arrived at rendezvous or
will shortly. Miguel will inform them as to what's happened. They might follow you and Christy, but chances
are they'll wait awhile. We'll pick up the whole crew at
Arrowhead Tanks and be on our way to the border. Miguel
and I will have to manage as well as we can."

Dallas tipped his head toward the prisoners. "Them?"

Heath turned a cold measuring glance on Jason and
Penmark. "We'll see," was all he said.

Breaking camp at dawn, they set out westward toward
the outline of a monumental ridge where Heath said he'd
cached the bank loot. Rocking in his saddle, Jason was
blinking and crusty-eyed; he'd spent a near sleepless
night wondering what Heath had in mind for them, feeling with a chill certainty that the man was capable of
putting them both out of the way without thinking twice
about it. On the other hand, Dallas had argued hard
against it, and Christy had added a few equally hard
words. Why not set the pair of 'em afoot? By the time
they reached a settlement, the whole gang would be safely
in Mexico. Heath, tight-mouthed with irritation, had
merely repeated himself: *"We'll see."*

Heath was riding in the lead, his powerful body erect.
Christy had spent half the night putting hot packs on his
leg to draw the first sign of infection. The treatment
seemed to have done its work and he was holding up well.
Jason, parched and miserable, jogged along behind him.
Both he and Penmark rode with hands lashed to their
pommels. The pace was jolting and brutal over this broken terrain, and Jason could feel his wrists being chafed
to a raw agony. Dallas and Christy and the spare animals
brought up the rear.

The sun was high, turning the rocky scape to a sullen
furnace, when they halted at the boulder-strewn base of

the crumbling ridge. Heath dismounted and limped over to a good-sized rock, which he heaved aside, exposing a shallow pit. He pulled out a pair of bulky saddlebags, tossed them over his shoulder, and walked back to his horse.

"All right, Dallas. You can cut these two loose."

"Sure I can," Dallas said dryly. "Then what?"

"Then I'll give 'em what they wouldn't give me. A chance to walk out of this desert alive. Walk, mind you."

"Without grub or water?"

"Give 'em a canteen of water, just one." Heath toed a foot into stirrup and swung up painfully to the saddle, his jaw set with pain. "As for food, let 'em make do. Bodie's the nearest settlement, and they ought to make it in three days." He gave Penmark a mildly relishing grin. "You can find the place, can't you, old pot?"

Penmark was hunched in his saddle, and he raised his head slowly, staring straight at Heath. The deep-socketed eyes smoldered in his haggard face; he didn't say a word.

"You can leave us our guns," Jason said out of a dry throat. "You can do that anyways."

Heath's acid grin twitched wider.

"Listen, those 'Paches who hit Corazon was swinging west. We get caught on foot, two men alone, we wouldn't have no chance."

"Miserable prospect, isn't it? No chance. I know the feeling."

"Jack . . ." Christy nudged her horse over by him. She was seated astride, skirt bunched around her legs, and she handled the raw-boned sorrel with an easy hand. "Let me ask you something. Did you ever pull wings off flies when you were a kid?"

"Going on the prod a bit, aren't you, Christine?"

"You bet your sweet ass I am." Her chin and jaw hardened to one smooth line. "Either you're giving these two a chance to live or you're not. Which is it going to be?"

A sleepy amusement touched Heath's smile. "Why, it's going to be whatever tickles your fancy, my dear. Not a whit less." Hipping around in his saddle, he pointed southward, glancing at Jason. "You see that spire of red sandstone about a mile from here?"

Jason nodded.

"We'll leave your guns there. I'd wait till we're out of sight before I'd start after them. Be a pity if you chaps were too near us when you get weapons in hand again. I'd suggest, therefore, that you not be in too much of a hurry . . ."

They watched the three ride away, each of them leading some of the extra animals. As soon as a crest of land cut them off from view, Penmark began tramping after them.

Jason trudged behind him, the day's heat already dragging at his heels. But Penmark appeared gripped by another surge of that implacable energy of his. He walked erect and tireless, never glancing back or aside, never saying a word. Both men were wearing cowman's half boots. Not the best footgear in the world for a long hike, Jason thought morosely.

"Sir, how far away is this Bodie?"

"Like he said, Hoofing it, about three days."

"I surely hope you know how to get there."

Penmark glanced contemptuously over his shoulder. "Jesus. Be in a dandy fix if I didn't, wouldn't you? We hoof it up to Corazon, then follow the stage road west."

"You reckon we can make it on one canteen?"

"There's water at Corazon. There's Red Jack Springs between there and Bodie. Red Jack don't never run dry. Be water enough to see us through."

The grim hardness of his voice didn't change, and Jason said hesitantly, "What about when we get to Bodie?"

"Me, I'm getting me horses and a good outfit and I'm coming back. You do what you want."

Jason didn't reply, but the idea seemed hopeless to him. Heath and his companions would have pulled a far lead by then, be reunited with the rest of their gang and on their way into Mexico. Why take up the chase again? They'd lost Heath and the money—it looked like for good

—and supposing they did find him again, they'd face impossible odds.

It meant nothing to Penmark, of course. He wanted revenge, pure and simple, and his own life was of no account to him. But Jason wasn't obsessed, only bitterly disappointed that he'd maybe had his bird in hand, only to lose it. He had failed his family for whose welfare he, as its remaining man, was now responsible. Failed himself too, in an obscure way he couldn't quite define. Except that making good at recovering or replacing what had been taken from them had begun, somehow, to resolve itself in his mind as a testing of his manhood. That was the real blow of failing on the edge of success.

Yet, considering it realistically, he'd done all that might reasonably be expected. No cause to feel disgraced. Fact, Ma and Gayla Sue and Josie, worried sick over him by now, would scold hell out of him for foolishly risking his neck far as he had. Privately proud of him maybe, but genuinely scolding too. And with the three of them dependent on him, he had no business risking the neck in question any further . . .

They reached the spire rock.

Scanning to the south, Jason found no sign of Heath and his two friends anywhere on the baking and broken scape. They'd been here and gone on, leaving the guns—both of their rifles and Penmark's Colt .45—in plain view on a flat stone. And something else that was welcome, a sack of jerked meat. Likely Christy's doing. It was her influence with Heath and not Dallas's, as Jason now reckoned, that had accounted for their lives being spared.

Heath couldn't have many such soft spots. He was hard and ruthless and clever, and he talked like he had a tall jag of learning. Jason wondered more and more about him, and about the girl Christy.

Again the two men tramped northward. Jason's feet were starting to pinch and hurt; he could only guess at how long he might keep up this steady hiking. It wouldn't matter to Penmark, who would wear his legs to bloody stumps if he had to.

By the time they reached Corazon around noon, Jason

was gritting his teeth against the pain that shot into his calves. He wanted to rest, but Penmark hadn't once slacked the severe pace he'd set. In light of Penmark's oft-voiced opinion of him, keeping up with the older man had become a matter of bitter pride for Jason.

Penmark had no intention of resting now either. They paused at the Corazon well just long enough to replace the water they'd consumed from the canteen. Jason couldn't stand to look at the three corpses, what remained of them, and the stench was horrible. The bloated carrion birds didn't bother to take flight, but merely flapped and waddled off a few yards from their stinking feast. He fought down an impulse to shoot at them. The buzzards were doing the work that lack of Christian burial made necessary. He was relieved when the two of them had left the place and were continuing west along the hard-rutted stage road, the sun clean and hot on their faces.

About an hour later Penmark did concede a halt, wordlessly dropping on his haunches in some rock shade. The two sipped from the canteen and slowly chewed a handful of jerky apiece. At last Penmark broke his long silence.

"Well, Drum, you decided what you'll do when we raise Bodie? If you're a mind to trail with me, I got money enough to outfit us both."

Jason tried to keep the shock of surprise from his reply. "Thanks. I don't reckon I will." He couldn't help adding, "Don't suppose that'll make you too sorry."

"I don't give a goddam one way or t'other what you do, boy. Had I aught against you siding me, I wouldn't a offered."

"Yes, sir. Thanks just the same."

Penmark was silent awhile, jaw-grinding a hunk of jerky to a fibrous pulp that would slide down his throat. Finally he said, "You done good enough. Sure-hell better'n any of them soft-bellied counter-jumpers we left New Hope in company with. You done good enough for a green hand."

Jason didn't know what to say; he mumbled something or other in reply.

Penmark stared down the dusty ribbon of road, scrubbing a palm over his whisker-furred jaw. "Can't gainsay giving up mightn't be good sense, way things are. Only I can't turn back. No reason to. You understand that, boy?"

Jason nodded. Penmark's tone hadn't softened by a jot; only his words implied a relenting of sorts. This might be the time, Jason reflected, to pursue his curiosity about the outlaws.

"Mr. Penmark, I wonder what you know about this Captain Heath. I never heard of him."

Penmark shrugged. "I know what's common talk anywheres in the territory. Kind you pick up around any campfire or saloon. What they say about Heath, he come of a rich family in Kentucky. Had him a good schooling in England, they say. Later went to West Point. Was there when the war busted out. He joined up with Tierney's Raiders. Bunch of Southern 'cotton aristocrats' who formed an irregular regiment to fight Yankees their own way. No discipline from above. As the war dragged on, the lot of 'em begin to turn crazy mean. Took to raiding settlements on both sides. Burning, looting, and worse. Jeff Davis outlawed Tierney's guerrillas early in '65, and it was Confederate troops who run 'em down and wiped 'em out."

"I heard of that."

"Hell, every schoolboy has. Young Jack Heath and a few others got away and fled to Texas. Heath been mixed up in a lot of shady dealings since. Has turned his hand to everything from hustling wet cattle across the border to knocking down trains and banks. That military training of his allus shows. Way he scouts out a place or has some'un else do it. Organizes everything to the nines. Provisions, spare horses, emergency tactics. Like timing this steal for when Cayetano is got near everyone in the country laying low. Like splitting up his force as he done out of New Hope. That's Captain Jack Heath, what I heard of him."

Penmark paused, tearing off another piece of jerky with his teeth.

"Uh, those others—"

"Redmile, he's an old-time high-grader in these parts. Spent him some time in Yuma Prison. I have heard his name coupled with Heath's now and then. The dead one, Artie, I never heard of. But they're all cut of the same cloth. Them others Heath mentioned, there's Cherokee, he's a half-breed, mean bastard with a knife they say. The Ermines, they're Trask Ermine, a guntipper of some note, and his brothers Pete and Clayt. Try keeping your eyes and ears open sometimes, boy. Way you learn."

"I expect so. I been stuck pretty tight to our place, you know, since we come to the territory. Ain't had a lot of chance to get out and around."

Penmark grunted, tilting the canteen to his lips.

"About that girl, sir . . ."

"What about her?" Penmark swirled some water in his mouth and spat it out. "World's full of female trash like that. Heath's doxie, not his first. Find his kind anywhere, you can bank her kind won't be far away. Fit together like hand and gloves."

"Mr. Penmark, it is my reckoning she likely saved our lives. You got to give her that."

Penmark lowered the canteen, his eyes bleak as flints. "Boy, one thing you'll learn before you get a sight older, there's two kinds of women in this world. Just two kinds. You get lucky at all, you will meet up with a good one. A man can't ask for no better in life."

His voice had dropped to a whisper, tight and cold and bitter. Abruptly he rose to his feet.

"Time we got moving. Should raise Red Jack Springs about sundown by my figuring . . ."

V

SUNDOWN. JASON HARDLY knew when it came. Dazzling heat rocked his eyeballs; he could hardly feel his feet or legs any longer. The rubbery stabs of sensation that remained were barely enough to keep him from reeling off balance. Penmark was starting to limp from his own relentless pace. And Red Jack Springs, Penmark had said, was located only a third of the distance to Bodie! Jason muddily wondered what good it would be having sufficient water when it was probable that by tomorrow the two of them would be too crippled up to continue on.

He almost lurched into Penmark, who had come to a sudden halt. Blinking his eyes clear, Jason saw a broad oasis of scattered cedars lined against the grainy pinkish glow of the last sunrays.

"Are we there?" His voice croaked out, shocking him.

"Yeah. So is someone else."

Jason blinked again. Now he spotted a ragged plume of smoke rising from somewhere in the trees. "That ain't? . . ."

"It's a white man's fire." Penmark clucked his tongue disgustedly. "Maybe he wants to smoke himself up a pile of trouble. That's how to bring it. Let's go in, but slow."

They approached through the thin line of trees. Grass grew thickly underfoot, and the ground had a feel of damp seep-fed chunkiness. Jason saw a glimmer of water; it reflected the orange blaze of a good-sized fire. He saw a man's dark shape standing close by; light raced faintly along a rifle barrel as it swung up.

"Who is that?" the man called. "You out there—"

"White men," Penmark growled. "Hold still. We're friendly."

A second man climbed to his feet now and stood by the other, both of them holding their rifles half-lifted. Jason and Penmark hauled up several yards away, facing them across the fire.

"What you doing way out here 'ith no hosses?" one of them asked.

Penmark took his time about replying, sending his gaze touching slowly over the camp without moving his head. The men's gear, most of it new looking, was scattered carelessly about. There was a brush lean-to with some rumpled blankets inside. Four horses were hobbled a ways back in the cedars. A coffeepot and a copper kettle bubbling with something that looked like a grayish stew stood askew by the fire.

"You see anythin' you like?" asked the man.

Maybe he meant it humorously. He was thin and middle sized with a balding saddle of sandy hair. A mesh of crow's feet radiating from the corners of his pale eyes gave him a slyly secretive look. His big horsey teeth showed completely when he spoke; one of them was solid gold.

"Nothing much." Penmark fixed him with that flat uncompromising stare.

"Heh heh heh," the man said. "Can't take a joke, hey? I'm Hub Quitlow. This here's my nevvy Lafe. We're fresh outen Bodie. Got newly outfitted there. Are goin' for the Panamints to prospect some, we are."

" 'Pache trouble · don't raise your short hairs none, I see."

"Oh, the Cherry-cows, hell, they done been raiding way south o' here."

"Was," Penmark said. "They hit Corazon two day back. Wiped out the Mexes who run the station there. Looked like they swung this way after."

"Well, we ain't raised no 'Paches."

"Cory-zone," muttered the other man. His cloudy eyes brightened. "Mexes, huh? Say, Uncle Hub, mebbe that be where—"

"Yeh." Hub cut him off in a flatly tolerant way. "That be where we're gonna strike out for the Panamints from. That is sure enough right, Lafe."

Like the other'd been about to say something he didn't want said. Lafe grinned in a foolish kind of way that was accented by the cleft of a deep harelip. By far the younger of the two men, he was burly and round shouldered with hair like matted straw.

"Lafe, he is slow between the ears," Hub said by way of explanation. "My brother Newt's boy. Got the care of him when Newt passed along. Be pretty much lost, Lafe'd be, if not for some'un to see after him."

That was fairly obvious; there seemed no particular call for stressing the fact. You had the feeling that Hub Quitlow wanted to be sure his nephew's remark was shuffled aside. Penmark merely nodded indifferently and said, "Trust you got no objection to the pair of us laying over by these springs tonight."

"Why shoot no, cousin, it is a public road." Hub's gold tooth flashed. "You welcome to share our vittles iffen you're mind."

Jason sensed a stiff-held wariness behind the man's accommodating manner. There was something ratty and shifty about the pair despite the newness of their gear. But could be it was just their way. He'd seen men of the same clannish, strange-acting ilk before. Hill-country scourings of an older frontier that was vaguely Southern, inbred by generations of isolated living till the features of any one could top those of any other almost twinlike. It showed in these Quitlows.

"Come from Corazon, did you?" Hub was saying. "All on foot, hey? Fancy that. . . ."

Grass rustled among the darkening trees. A girl's slight form came limping into the spread of firelight. She stopped at sight of Penmark and Jason, gazing at them dumbly. Her thin arms were clasped around a bundle of sticks she must have been gathering.

"Jest drop the wood over here, honey." Hub grinned at them. "Lafe's woman. She's a dummy too, manner o' speakin'. Cain't talk noways. Cain't speak a word."

The girl hobbled over by the fire and knelt, easing her armload of wood to the ground. She was Mexican or Indian from the look. And she'd been ill used, that was plain. Her rag of a calico dress was torn in several places; her black hair hung in a dirt-matted tangle. A shiny bruise purpled one high cheekbone. She was a little thing, thin to gawky in a coltish, adolescent way, and Jason had the shocked realization that she wasn't over sixteen, maybe less. Her brown legs were dusty and scratched below her calf-length skirt; one of her *huarache* sandals dangled with a broken strap. After that one long stare at them, she kept her head meekly down.

"Dish up the stew, honey girl," said Hub. "These here gents be hungry."

"Not right yet," Penmark said gruffly. "Feet're in bad shape. Gonna soak 'em in that cold spring."

"Jest the thing," Hub grinned, "long's they don't pizen the water."

Lafe rolled his dull eyes and cackled. Jason moved after Penmark as the older man tramped slowly around the fire toward the springs. The girl's head lifted furtively, her dark eyes briefly locking his. Then they fell away. Jason's spine began to crawl. He might have been mistaken as to what he'd seen in that first long look of hers. Now he was sure he hadn't been.

What he'd seen was fear. Naked and shining fear that

—he was almost sure—mingled with a kind of dumb pleading. What did it mean?

Several saucer-shaped depressions where water pooled cold and fresh to the surface gave Red Jack Springs its name. Penmark eased down on his rump by one of these and proceeded to work off his right boot, grimacing with pain. "Goddlemighty, my dogs are swole all to hell. Be easier to cut the sons a bitches off . . ."

Jason plunked down beside him, muttering, "Mr. Penmark. There's something dead wrong here."

"That young'un, yeah. Something amiss with him for sure."

"I mean that girl. She is been harshly used."

Penmark grunted as he jerked his foot free of the boot. "Looks to be, all right. Sorry thing to see. But she is wife to a man, and he got whatever use of her it suits him. You don't meddle between a man and his wife."

"Supposing she ain't his wife?"

"Hell, his kept woman or whatever, then. Either way it's no mix of ours."

"Sir, that girl is plain-out scared. The way she looked . . . I never seen the like of it in a human face."

"Like you said, Drum, you ain't been out and around much."

Penmark had wrestled off his other boot and removed the remnants of his socks. Groaning with relief, he sank his reddened feet into the water. "Ahhh . . . that's the ticket, by God. Get off your boots and soak your dogs. Feel a sight better, I'll tell you."

"Suppose—" Jason hesitated. "Suppose they are keeping her against her will."

"Reckon you can ask her."

"That Quitlow said she can't talk."

"Can't tell you nothing then, can she?"

Jason could no longer bite back his anger. "Damn you! Don't you care about anything?"

"Yeah," Penmark said softly. "One thing. I care about one thing, boy. I told you what that be. Now you hear

me, Drum, and hear me goddam good." He fixed Jason
with his dead graystone stare. "This situation is no mix of
mine or yourn. You want to brace that pair over a miserable greaser wench, you do it alone. I ain't lifting a goddam finger. You hear me?"

Jason nodded dismally. Might as well try to sway a
stone wall as Val Penmark. He ought to know that by
now.

Bitterly he began tussling with his boots. When he
plunged his bare feet into the water, its icy clasp almost
made him yell. But the cooling relief then came close to
chasing everything else from his thoughts. The two men
scrubbed their socks clean and laid them out to dry. Afterward they hobbled barefoot back to the Quitlows' fire.
Hub and Lafe sat cross-legged with tin plates on their
laps, spooning stew into their mouths as fast as they
could.

"Sit yourselves and eat," Hub Quitlow told them ge-
nially. "Honey girl, serve these men up some o' this good
stew. You boys ain't said your names."

"Val Penmark from up New Hope way. This here's
Jason Drum, same place."

"New Hope, hey? You be a long ways from home."
Hub got his words out between mouthfuls, some of the
stew spilling down his chin. He sleeved it away, bending
forward with a show of real or feigned interest. "And all
afoot, hey? That be a caution. You meet with a mishap?"

Speaking in his terse way, Penmark told most of what
had happened during the past four days. The girl, meantime, was dishing up plates of stew for Jason and him.
When she handed Jason his, he met the high luminous
shine of her eyes once more. Again he saw the stark animal horror that seemed to tunnel back into her soul. He
stared down at his plate, his palms sweating against its
warmth. God, a man couldn't just sit and ignore that
nameless, silent plea. But what else could he do? He
wasn't sure of anything except that the poor creature was
gut-deep frightened. . . .

The dilemma sat in his belly like solid lead as he began

to eat. The stew was a lumpy, tasteless concoction of dried meat and watery broth that was way undercooked. Penmark ate his share with unconcealed distaste, mouth puckered as though he'd bitten into a briny pickle. The two Quitlows called for seconds. When the girl had refilled their plates, they fed their faces with undiminished appetites, wiping off dribbles on their filth-crusted sleeves. The sight by itself was enough to spoil a body's eating.

"Do tell, do tell,' Hub mumbled around a full mouth as Penmark finished talking. "Too bad about your woman. Buried a couple myself back in Tennessee. Say, you two got some tall walking ahead o' you yit, you know that?"

"We know," Penmark said in a clipped voice. "Wonder if you'd be interested in making a dicker."

Hub raised his sly pale eyes. "Dicker f'r what?"

"You got fresh animals and a new grubstake. . . ." Penmark leaned forward with a sudden intensity. "I can use both, and straightway. If I can backtrack from here without delay, good chance I can overhaul Jack Heath in a day or so. He won't be looking for no pursuit this soon."

"That mought be a handy trade for you, cousin, but it 'ud leave Lafe 'n me short of hosses and vittles."

"I can make it worth your while."

"Uh-huh. Well, we ain't in no almighty rush, a course. Just we'd have to mosey back to Bodie to fetch us more hosses and what-not, and that be a sight o' bother."

"I'll give you five hundred dollars for a saddle horse and a packhorse and some of your grub."

Hub spooned up the last of his stew and laid his plate aside, rubbing his belly. "Well now, that has an uncommon generous ring to it. You got five hunnerd dollar on you?"

"I got fifty in greenbacks in a belt under my shirt. Will get the rest for you later. You want, I can write a letter for you to give my lawyer. Case I don't come back alive, it'll serve as a codicil to my will, directing him in my own hand to pay you four hundred and fifty dollars."

Hub was already shaking his head. "No deal," he said affably. "A Quitlow don't bargain for no empty poke. It's cash on the barrelhead or nothing."

"Goddamit." Penmark's voice shook; muscle ridged along his jaw. "Don't you know when to trust a man?"

"Shoot, cousin, you trying to dicker on a busted chip." The gold tooth glimmered. "Fergit it."

Slowly, still staring at Hub Quitlow, Penmark settled back; his mouth twitched. "All right. All right then," he said softly.

"More stew cousins? No?" Hub smacked his lips. " 'Y God, that 'uz prime eatin'. Honey girl, you fetch us some o' that coffee now."

The girl brought some tin cups and handed one to each man, then wrapped a piece of cloth around her hand and picked up the coffeepot and carried it over to Hub and Lafe's side of the fire. Hub shook his head. "I declare, girl, body'd think you was raised in a sty o' some kind. No proper manners atall. Them two yonder's our guests. You serve 'em first, *comprende?* You snap to with dispatch now, or Lafe, he's like to swat you one."

The girl came limping around the fire. Her hands were trembling so much that she had to grip the handle of the coffeepot in both fists to steady it as she poured for Penmark, then Jason. Young Lafe began banging his cup on his empty plate, grinning a wide stupid grin.

"C'mon dummy," he chortled, "gimme some coffee. You best snap to with dispatch there, or I gonna swat you so *goddam* hard. . . ."

The girl hurried around the fire, and Lafe held up his cup. She tilted the pot to pour, her badly shaking hands causing it to chatter against Lafe's cup. Some of the boiling brew splashed on his wrist.

Lafe let out a howl of pain. He scrambled to his feet, yelling, "Jeezus, looka there, Uncle Hub, what she done! Burned me all to hell! Goddam dummy—"

He turned on the girl, his meaty hand swinging back. More of a blow than a slap, it knocked her clear off her feet. She hit the ground on her side, the coffeepot jarring its scalding contents across one bare arm. She screamed.

Lafe's pink face split in a distorted laugh. The girl lay huddled as she'd fallen, moaning with pain.

Jason's right hand had already closed on the rifle by his knee. Now he lifted it to his thigh, holding it pointed down but ready.

"That's enough," he said tightly. "Don't lay a hand on her again."

Lafe quit laughing. His jaw hung open. Hub Quitlow's mild eyes began to harden and narrow. He picked up his own rifle and climbed slowly to his feet, holding it cradled on one arm. Jason matched the movement, getting up at the same time.

"My nevvy is troubled in his head," Hub said. "You don't hard-mouth a troubled man that way."

Penmark laid his plate aside and rose too, uncoiling like a big snake. Jason snatched a glance at him, but Penmark was quietly studying the two Quitlows. His stance was relaxed, his face expressionless. He said nothing at all, as though he were letting the rest of them determine the next move. But in that instant, Jason knew that Penmark would back him.

"You best say your pardons," Hub said softly. "Then you pack out o' here, the both o' you."

"We're taking that girl with us," Jason heard himself say.

Hub's eyes half-lidded. "Young'un, you're twisting a wildcat's tail. You talking about another man's woman."

"I say you're a liar." The blood was pounding in Jason's ears. "A man don't use his wife the way—"

Aroused to a sudden combative rage, Lafe broke his silence. A crazy light quivered in his eyes. "Jeezus!" he bleated. "You hear him? He comes sits by a man's fire and eats his grub. Then he tells him how to fetch his woman about—"

Bending over fast, he came up with his rifle, snapping the finger lever down as he brought it to bear. His face was twisted and snarling. Jason's Winchester was already level, his motions smooth and unthinking as he levered it and fired. The bullet slammed Lafe half-around.

No time for Jason to even begin swinging his attention

to Hub; the older Quitlow's rifle muzzle was already fixed squarely on him. But he never pulled off his shot. Steel winked in Penmark's fist as his hand slapped down and up. He fired. The slug's impact flung Hub backward like a broken doll.

Lafe was still on his feet, fighting to bring his rifle up again. His eyes blazed crazily at Jason. For a long moment Jason could only stand rooted as he was; then he began wildly to jack another shell into his chamber. But Penmark shot first. Lafe's snarling mouth dissolved in a crimson welter. He crashed forward across the fire, his body exploding a cloud of sparks.

Hub pulled himself up to his knees, blood pouring from his belly. He tried to lift his rifle and failed. The rifle dropped; and he stayed on his knees, hands clamped over his belly.

Deliberately, Penmark thumbed back the hammer of his .45.

Frozen by the sudden and senseless smash of violence, Jason found his voice. "Don't!" he yelled. "My God, you finished him! He'll be dead in a minute!"

"I think he will," Penmark said, letting his pistol off-cock. "Well, I didn't think you had it in you, boy. But reckon you'd a been in a pretty fix if old Val Penmark hadn't took a hand in this ruction you started."

Penmark was, Jason saw with a shock, as near to smiling as he'd ever seen him.

VI

JASON SPOKE TO the girl, making his voice quiet and
gentle. She no longer seemed scared, but she was sure
enough mute—quick-witted though, shaking her head
and motioning at her mouth to indicate her lack of
speech. He wondered if she'd been born that way or
whether some mishap, or maybe scarlet fever, had taken
her voice. The Quitlows had abused her, as the freshness
of her bruises testified, but he couldn't be sure how badly.
Anyway, she didn't have any crippling hurts, save for the
slight limp.

Searching through the Quitlows' effects, he found a can
of patent medicine salve. This he smeared on her scalded
arm while she held it out. She understood everything he
said all right, but he noticed she watched his mouth carefully as he talked, as if she had only a smattering of English. He asked her questions that could be answered by a
nod or a shake of the head, but outside of ascertaining
that no, she wasn't wife to Lafe Quitlow, he didn't learn

anything that was helpful in regard to who she was or how she'd come into the company of this blue-ribbon pair.

Even if her hair were combed out and her filthy rag of a dress neatened up, he guessed she wouldn't be much to look at. Still, she was slender rather than bony, and had nice movements; she couldn't be over sixteen, and like his younger sister Gayla Sue, she was still teetering between girl and woman. Her face was thin and snub-nosed, but had less of an Indian look than he'd first guessed. With her dazed fear relaxed, he could see a fine structure to brow and cheekbones; her eyes were strong and expressive. She never took her gaze off him. Jason felt a growing embarrassment.

Hub Quitlow lay on the ground with his hands pressed over his belly, groaning, letting out a hard grunt of pain now and then. He rolled his eyes toward Jason. "Water," he croaked. "Water, please."

Jason shot a glance at Penmark who was crouched by the fire, examining Hub's rifle. "Forty-five Sharps," he murmured. "Telescope sight too." He raised it and lined his eye along the barrel. "Ain't that a dandy thing, though."

Again Jason felt a surge of weary disgust, but it was blunted by too much that had happened already. He didn't reply. No point saying anything to a man who was impervious to plain talk. Tiredly Jason filled a tin cup with water and kneeled beside the dying Quitlow, lifting his head and tipping the cup to his lips.

Hub had a hard time getting the water down, and his body gave a wrench of pain at each swallow. It wouldn't do him any good, all torn up inside as he was, but it couldn't make any real difference either. His eyes were dimming, the color graying out of his face.

"Bless you, boy," he whispered. "God bless you."

"There ain't nothing I can do," Jason said. "I'm sorry."

Hub began talking faintly. The words were disjointed and faltering, and Jason had to bend his head to catch them. What sense he could piece together from Hub's mutterings was that the Quitlows had found the girl this morning. She'd been wandering along the stage road in a daze, apparently headed for Bodie. They hadn't been able to fetch a word out of her. Anyway, Lafe had taken a shine to her, being full of sap and vinegar, his cub fancies easily tickled, and it hadn't seemed no harm letting him have his way, seeing the girl was just a greaser. . . .

Jason eased the man's last moments as well as he could. Then Hub was gone, and there wasn't a thing more to be done but the burying. Jason dumped out a pack that held the Quitlows' prospecting tools so he could get at a shovel. He wrestled out the residues of his gutted anger and disgust by tying into the flinty ground, forcing his rubbery muscles into motion as he widened out a double grave. Then he wrapped the bodies in a blanket apiece and laid the Quitlows side by side and covered them.

Finished, he straightened up, shuddering and sweat drenched, and met Penmark's cold stare. The older man sat cross-legged, Hub's rifle across his knees. "Good thing you got a strong back to go with your weak head, Drum," he said mildly. "You do like planting folks so damn much."

Jason's aching hands tightened around the shovel. He tramped over to Penmark and stood above him, swaying a little. Penmark didn't stir a muscle. "Like to lay into me with that, eh? All right, Salty, you think on just what happened here. You think on it a minute."

"Two men are dead, that's what—"

"Scum," Penmark said dispassionately. "A pair of low-down graybacks the world is better off shed of. Take it in their heads, they'd a killed you or me for a few dollars. Or no reason at all."

"They were men, damn you!"

"All right. I see I'm the one who's got to say just what happened. You started a ruction over that wench, and it got a couple *men* killed. You started it, Drum, but it took me to finish it." Penmark's lips pulled back till the flesh tautened skull-like to his jaws. "How you like it now, boy?"

Jason sat down and dropped the shovel at his feet. He looked at the girl as she wrapped a piece of cloth around

her burned arm, her eyes still on him, and then he rolled
his shoulders exhaustedly. "I don't know," he muttered.
"Thanks for the help."

Penmark grunted. "What did he say?"

"Not a lot. They come on the girl this morning. Guess
she was pretty much this way when they found her. All
the same they used her rough." Jason's voice climbed a
notch. "I done what had to be, Mr. Penmark. It was the
right thing."

"Just so you're satisfied to that," Penmark said sardonically. "Now you got her, what you going to do with her?"

"Take her to Bodie, I reckon. Have a doctor look at
her. No telling what's been done to her. Might be hurt
some way we can't tell."

"You won't find no doctor in Bodie. What I heard, it's
a hardrock camp with a store, a saloon, an assay office,
and nothing much else."

"Well, maybe she got some people there. Anyways,
someone might know her. Who she is, where she's from."

"I hazard them dead Mexes back at Corazon could of
told you."

"You think she come from there?"

Penmark beckoned to the girl. "You. Come over here."

Slowly she moved up by the fire. Penmark smoothed a
patch of ground with his hand, then picked up a stick and
marked a small cross in the dirt. "Corazon, *comprende?*"
The girl nodded. He drew a line west from the cross, adding, "*Camino,* eh?" And marked another cross at the
line's end. "Bodie, all right? You was heading for Bodie."
Again she nodded. "*¿Donde vive?* You live at Corazon?"

Her face tightened; she opened her mouth. The ten-
dons of her throat stood out as she tried to speak, but all
she could manage was a kind of moan. She struck her
mouth with the flat of her hand and fell to her knees,
shaking her head back and forth.

Penmark spat into the fire. "Well, that says something.
Seems she could talk before."

"Before . . . something happened?"

"Yeh. Could of got shocked speechless, I reckon.
That's happened to folks."

Penmark talked quietly, forcing the girl's attention back. Her eyes followed the stick as he drew more marks in the dirt, at the same time putting further questions to which she could indicate yes or no. Bit by bit her story came out. The Apaches had come while she was off in the brush picking berries. It was almost over by the time the noise of a ruckus had drawn her partway back. Huddled in the brush nearby, she'd watched the tail end of the little massacre. Then the Apaches had fired the station and driven off the stock. She didn't remember anything after that except walking for a long time, till the Quitlows had found her.

Did she have live kin anywhere? People she could go to? She shook her head no, her eyes shifting between Penmark and Jason as if she expected them to have the real answer.

Penmark gave a disgusted grunt. "Well, that's 'bout it, boy. She'll be your lookout. Leastways I reckon that's how you'll want it."

"Ain't a question of what anyone wants," Jason said coldly, "it's—"

"Yeah, Christian goodness, I know. Ain't saddling myself with no greaser girl, that's sure."

"Then you don't need to worry about it, do you?"

Penmark shrugged. "I 'low to a hope you'd be inclined to trail 'long with me after all. There's Heath and I mean to get him. Am starting after him first light." A sudden twist of his hands snapped the stick. "I don't quit till I get that bastard. And this time I get him dead."

"Your business," Jason said in the same cold voice. "I don't give a damn about Heath."

"Still give a damn for that money, don't you? You was itching after it fierce enough before." Penmark paused, his slitted gaze locking Jason's. "We got horses now. And grub aplenty. Think about it."

Jason didn't reply right away. A dark suspicion had touched him, and now it ballooned full-blown in his mind. "Mr. Penmark. You said you wasn't going to take my part against these men."

"Hell, nobody in his right mind gets tolled into a

ruckus that's no mix of his. But you had to push it."

"That ain't the point," Jason said thinly. "You wanted no part of it. That's what you said. Then you lent a hand anyways. You ain't gonna tell me you done it to save my hide."

"Ain't told you a damn thing of the sort, have I?"

"You don't need to." Jason hunched his body forward, taut on the balls of his feet. "That's why you changed your mind. With the Quitlows dead, you'd have their horses and grub. Then you could set straightway after Heath like you want."

"You're the one's saying it, Drum." Penmark's face was like a metal mask. "It don't make a damn lick of difference why I done it. I hadn't, you wouldn't be sitting up talking about it. And don't you forget it."

Jason bit back a hot reply. What good to argue with this man? He was hard enough, a man of his times. Yet like all such, he'd lived by deep-grained principles of his own, and his handshake was as good as his bond. The killing of his wife had snapped Penmark's iron code and swept the pieces away. All he cared about was getting the man he deemed responsible, Jack Heath. If Hub Quitlow wouldn't sell him horses, there'd remained one way to get them.

It had been, on Penmark's part, an act of simple murder. But if the man was no longer capable of seeing it that way, what could you say to him? Nothing. Particularly when it was sure as sunrise that Penmark, just as he'd said, had saved Jason Drum's skin. Whatever his reason, that cold fact couldn't be denied.

Penmark ended the long silence. "There's still the money. You don't argue what getting it back 'ud mean to you and yours."

"No," Jason said dully.

"Then you look at it that way, boy. You fix your mind to that and nothing else. We got the horses and the grub. Right now Heath got no more'n a day's lead on us. Thinking he's shed of all pursuit, he won't push too fast. We got that edge and another too." He leaned forward and tapped a finger on Jason's knee. "They won't be expecting us. We catch up before they raise the rest of Heath's crew, two of us can handle 'em sure. I'll have Heath. You'll have your money."

Jason gnawed the corner of his lip. Penmark's words held a cold persuasion that swayed him. The Quitlow horses, illgotten or no, put a fresh handle on the whole business. It was hard to thrust the temptation aside and shake his head.

"All right," Penmark said flatly, "there's the girl. What can you do for her she can't do for herself? There's four horses. Gives us two saddle mounts and a packhorse. That leaves one animal for her. There's the road. All she got to do is follow it to Bodie."

"I aim to see she gets there safe," Jason said stubbornly. "I—"

A quick sound from the girl. She was motioning with her hands, shaking her head vehemently. She had followed enough of the talk to get its gist. No, she painfully made clear, she wasn't going to Bodie. A few questions by Penmark clarified what she intended to do: return to Corazon and bury her family.

Jason tried to argue her out of it, but he might as well have tried to talk down the wind. She held her mouth tight and kept shaking her head.

"Tough little beggar." Penmark's tone was touched by a bleak amusement. "You going back to Corazon with her, Drum?"

Jason gave a helpless shrug. "Seems I'll be obliged to."

"All right, then. I am going on Heath's trail by way of Corazon. You and her ride along that far. Give you time to think on it. Might just be you'll change your mind. Meantime, sleep on it." Penmark looked down at the rifle; his hand stroked along its barrel. "Yes sir . . . that is one dandy weapon for certain."

When he woke next morning, Jason was surprised to find it was past full dawn, the sun slanting bright against his eyes. He smelled bacon and coffee cooking and saw the Mexican girl already up and fixing breakfast—and was surprised all over when he saw Penmark still snoring in his blanket. It was long past first light. So pure exhaustion had finally overcome Penmark's iron determination and his impatience. Even he needed to rest sometimes.

It was the first real sleep Jason had known in days; he felt restored and finely alert. He went to the spring and took his time washing up. As he pitched into the meal the girl had put together, he found he was keenly hungry. They ate in silence, the morning pleasantly quiet around them, till Penmark roused out in a muttering, savage mood because he'd overslept. Stiff and haggard-faced, he gobbled down his breakfast while Jason and the girl saddled the animals and rigged up a pack.

They rode briskly east toward Corazon. Jason did a lot of thinking about what Penmark had said last night. Maybe it would be as easy as the older man thought, overtaking Heath's party and getting back that money. Heath was injured; his companions, an old man and a girl, weren't likely to offer a very tough resistance. Feeling chipper and renewed, Jason also felt his confidence stoking up, the fever of purpose gripping him again.

There was the Mexican girl, of course. That was the troublesome part. He'd been raised to a strict feeling in such matters. Man's part was to cherish and protect the distaff side. Plain conscience pointed to his proper course: see that she was gotten to a place of safety. But it would mean abandoning the pursuit for good, and that wasn't right either. He had an obligation to his own—who were on the distaff side too. He had no obligation at all to this little waif of a Mexican. Also, she was proving to be a sight tougher than her physical slightness would indicate. No reason she couldn't make it alone to Bodie, given a horse and supplies and a gun.

Danger? Odds that way cut pretty slim when you thought on it. The Apaches had made their swing across this territory three days gone; that threat was surely past. Wasn't much chance, either, of her meeting up with any others like the Quitlows. They had been the scum Penmark had named them; few Western men ever sank that low. No matter how hard a Western man of any stripe might be, he most always respected women.

By the time they came in sight of Corazon at noon, Jason had taken the fever of pursuit again. Penmark, who had neither youth's optimism nor its second saving strength, only a grim and driving impatience, motioned for a halt just before they reached the fire-gutted station. Hands crossed on his pommel, he looked bitter-eyed at Jason.

"All right, Drum. You had your time to think on it. What's it to be? You fetching up here or you coming with me?"

"With you. But I'm going to help the girl lay her kin to rest. It won't take long. You can ride on if you want and I'll catch up."

Penmark grunted sardonically. "All you do without me alongside is get yourself lost. I'll help with the burying. Don't reckon there'll be a whole lot to lay away. . . ."

Digging a wide common grave was easy enough. The rest of it was the trying part, gathering up the carrion remains of three people and setting them in a proper order of sorts before filling in the grave. Jason had to fight his squirming innards through the ordeal and couldn't remember a feeling of relief as overwhelming as he knew when the job was over. He also felt an awed admiration for the girl, who had remained still-faced and contained through the whole business. She had refused to hold back, pitching in without a blink or a whimper beside Penmark and him until the last spadeful of earth had been patted into place.

While Penmark filled a small cask of water at the well and lashed it onto the packhorse, Jason talked haltingly to the girl, telling her he was going on with his friend and why. She listened carefully, then made some rapid gestures that he had a time making sense of. When he got her meaning, he shook his head vigorously.

"No, you can't come with us. That's out o' the question! You go on to Bodie. All you got to do is follow the stage road, understand?"

He felt foolish under her bright demanding stare; a slow heat washed into his face. "Look, that is how it's got to be. If you want, you can wait for us here. We will be

back in a couple of days, about. Then I will see you to
Bodie. You can go on alone if you want or you can wait
for me. But that is how it's got to be!"

A gritty wind flapped Anita Cortinas's ragged skirt
around her legs as she stood watching the two gringos
ride southward. She watched till they were only diminishing dots on the vast *playa*. Then she looked down at the
freshly smoothed mound at her feet.

Kneeling beside it, she crossed herself and folded her
hands on her lap. There was no priest to offer a committal
prayer, to give the office of the dead, or say a Requiem
Mass. She knew these things should be done, but of them
she knew only what she had heard at one time or another.
She had a mere gray memory of attending Mass in a white-
washed village church when she was very small. 'Nita
wasn't sure just where she stood in the matter of religion.
It had never been a great thing with her father or mother,
and *Abuelito*, her crotchety grandfather, had been very
outspoken about believing in nothing at all. Voiceless, she
couldn't utter a simple Hail Mary; even a silent prayer
refused to shape itself in her mind. She couldn't weep, either, past the unyielding grief that knotted her throat.

Maybe it would all come later. The dazed numbness
that had held her mind for so many hours had lifted. That
was something.

She rose and brushed her hands over her dusty dress,
then looked again after the two gringos. They were almost
lost to sight now.

'Nita Cortinas was very sure of what she was going to
do, though she barely knew why. Perhaps it was enough
that she did not want to remain in this place, alone with a
silent grave and the burned remains of her home. And
somehow she did not want to lose sight of these two
gringos. Maybe they would return, or at least the young one
would, for he had said so. But maybe he would not.

Vaguely she thought of these two as a line to life: the
only one, for now, that she knew. Here were only the
dead and the memory of her last sight of them, to which

she could not close her mind. For them, there was no more she could do.

She limped over to where the horse the gringos had left her stood in the shade of the station wall. Her right leg was still painful; she couldn't remember how it had gotten hurt. But she could get about on it; no bone was broken. The horse was a wiry paint mustang, who would bear her slight weight as far and as fast as the gringos' mounts would take them. The food and canteen and blankets that they had left with her would be little additional weight. Of these she made a small bundle, tying it to the saddle cantle. On the ground nearby lay a dirty piece of muslin, charred at the ends; picking it up, she recognized all that remained of some bolt goods from which her mother had planned to make a dress. Tucking in the ends, 'Nita wrapped the strip of cloth around her head and throat to shield them partly from the sun.

Holding the rifle in one hand, reins in the other, she essayed to climb into the saddle. She made it on the third try. Her skirt was hiked above her knees, and she spent a few awkward seconds trying to adjust the wide hem over her legs without much success. Afterward, she kneed the paint horse into motion and headed away from Corazon.

She did not look back.

VII

THE COUNTRY WAS a monotony of pinks and browns, largely flats that were stippled by silver-gray sage and broken up by sand-colored formations. A day of pushing steadily across it into more of the same wore Jason's eagerness back to a frayed nub. He wondered sourly why he always forgot that a body's moods pretty much depended on his general physical being, his digestion and the like; moods never lasted. One hour you were sitting on top of the world; next you were way down in the mouth. "Won't get no better as you get older, boy," Pap had once assured him. "You just take on more aches to plague you. It's in the way of nature, same as hot weather is and being tired is. Only them you learn to live with."

He guessed he had a sight to learn yet. Heat and weariness—the doses he had gotten on this trek were enough to last him a long while.

He and Penmark had backtracked to where they had split off from Heath's party yesterday morning, taking up the trail from there. Arrowhead Tanks, which had been mentioned as Heath's destination, where he was supposed to meet the rest of his bunch, was just a hop-skip from the line with Mexico, Penmark said. He didn't know exactly where the place was, but it was a well-known waterhole and a favored campsite of Indians. Anyway, it was at least a couple days' ride; with any luck they should come up on Heath and Dallas Redmile and the girl Christy before they got that far.

That was the important thing. Overhauling 'em before they reached the Tanks and were reinforced by the rest of their outfit. Odds against successfully taking 'em then would be impossibly steep. As it was, prospects seemed better'n fair. The Quitlow horses were tough Indian mustangs and were still fresh. Also the track showed that Heath wasn't pressing along fast. Chances of overtaking him by, say, early tomorrow looked good.

They made fair time all day; even Penmark was halfway satisfied when darkness forced them to halt and make camp in a narrow swale. They cooked some grub and sought their blankets, and were up before sunrise.

As they packed up and saddled the horses, Penmark was as edgy as a hunting dog: hot on the scent and keen to draw blood. "We be onto 'em by noon," he muttered, "or I miss my guess. . . ."

Jason merely grunted.

"Tricky part'll be when we take 'em. Depending on the lay of the land, maybe we can get 'em by surprise. We can't, it'll be rough. But either way, we are taking 'em right off."

Penmark cinched up his saddle, then stepped around his horse and halted beside Jason. "One thing I want to get said so's there's no mistaking it."

Jason, frowning at his latigo, said "What?"

"You bucked me when we had him square in hand before. Don't do it again."

Jason nodded indifferently.

"I mean it. You try to stop me from fetching that bastard his just deserts, I'll bust you, kid. I'll bust you cold. You understand?"

"Uh-huh."

Penmark scowled. "What the hell's eating you now? We stand the best chance yet of getting your goddam money. What you want, ain't it?"

"I been thinking about that girl at the station. It wasn't a good thing we done, leaving her that way. Can't be sure she—"

"Jesus." Penmark shook his head; he was near to smiling for the second time. "I never see a good American boy sweat his balls over chilipickers like you do. That's something."

Jason took a step away from his horse and turned, squarely facing the older man. "Mr. Penmark, now I want you to get this. I heard all the talk of that sort I'm going to from you. If there is any more of it, you won't need to worry about us having a set-to over Heath. Next word you drop about greasers or spicks or chilipickers or pepperguts, we are going to have one right then and there. And it will be the damnedest ruction you ever walked into in your fifty-odd years."

Penmark eyed him a long moment, then nodded slowly. "You taken some bark in your craw since we started out, ain't you? Just so's we understand each other. . . ."

As they rode steadily through a long morning, the monotony vanish in a keen stir of anticipation. Some of what Jason felt was plain nervousness, but he realized with a kind of detached surprise that he wasn't coming up skittish or queasy as had been the case before. No danger, this time, of his taking buck fever. What he felt more than anything was the high excitement of the chase, closing on their prey. No justifying the feeling; just now it was a good way to feel, that was all.

A little before noon, they spotted a tendril of smoke curling up beyond a tall and craggy-topped ridge. The two men looked at each other but didn't say anything. They pushed straight toward the odd-shaped promontory. When they halted a short distance from it, the smoke seemed pretty close, only the bald height of land cutting them off from its source.

Stepping to the ground, Penmark pulled the .45 Sharps

that had belonged to Hub Quitlow from his saddle boot. Then he got out the telescope sight and his field glasses. As he fitted the scope sight in place, he said "About time we fell into some luck. That ridge is lucky for us. . . ."

"If it's them."

"Track goes straight on around the ridge. It's them. We got a prime chance to take 'em unawares, but I want a good sight on the layout first. Then we'll settle how we're going to handle it." He peered up at the ridge. "She's a good hard climb. I'll go up alone, you wait by the horses."

Jason hesitated. Penmark's state of mind bothered him; no telling just what he might do. Be wise to stick close to him. "Reckon I'll just go up with you."

Penmark gave him a raking glance, then turned on his heel and tramped away toward the ridge. Jason was right behind him.

The lower scarp of the rise wasn't too difficult to negotiate. It was sloped with ramps of crumbled rock that had weathered away and fallen from the upper height, forming a rough surface that could be climbed easily but slowly. They worked their way around the larger boulders, careful of their footing on the loose stuff. Had to be watchful of one's hand supports too, never touching one of the oven-hot rocks for more than an instant. Higher up, the formation grew quite steep, finally rounding off abruptly at its crown.

Both men were pouring sweat as they came onto the top, a sun-baked sprawl of blocky boulders and spires. The sun banked off the naked rocks with a furnace fury that beat at their bodies and rose through the soles of their boots. Not pausing, Penmark clambered over the rubble till he reached the shade of a giant boulder perched on the rim's south end. Moving up beside him, Jason saw that the ridge tipped off at their feet in an uneven, almost straight-down drop. It was forty or more yards to the bottom. From here they had a clear view of the sage flat that stretched away from it.

The huge rock was only middling warm in its pocket of shadow; pressed against its flank, they were merged with

its shape, concealed from any but a close observer below.
A good thing, for the camp wasn't over five hundred
yards distant.

Jason made out six people ranged around a fire. *Six?*

"Mr. Penmark, there's—"

"Shut up."

Penmark set his glasses to his eyes and studied the
camp. Jason was tasting the brass-bitter significance of
what the number of the party meant as, slowly, Penmark
lowered the glasses.

"Seems their friends didn't wait at the Tanks," he murmured. "The Mex told 'em what was up and they come
north following his back-trail. I hazard they just now met
up with Heath, Redmile, and the girl."

"Mr. Penmark, there's only three of 'em."

Penmark rasped a hand across his jaw. "I never seen
the Ermine boys, but that'd be them. Three gringos.
Means the Mex stayed behind and I reckon that Cherokee, the breed, he did too. Well, it don't make much difference. Three and three makes six." He swiveled a
wicked stare at Jason. "Means the odds have got a sight
too steep. Only way to surprise that many 'ud be to sneak
in close. Can't manage that on no open flat."

"Then there's nothing we can do."

"Oh yes," Penmark said gently. "There's still one thing,
boy. There's Cap'n Heath." He patted the Sharps. "This
old gun has the range. With a scope sight, be as easy as
nailing a fish in a barrel."

Jason looked at him in disbelief. "Mr. Penmark . . .
you do that, you will pull the rest of 'em right up here
onto us. We never make it down this damn ridge before
they cut us off."

"Think of that, now."

"Listen," Jason said heatedly, "you don't give a sorry
damn about your own neck, all right! But it ain't all right
you run mine into a noose too."

"I ain't about to, shorthorn. What you do, you get
down off here and get clear away. Take my nag and the
packhorse too. Time I let this gun off at Heath, you'll be

good and gone." Penmark's mouth twisted faintly. "I'll give you time."

"Sir. Look." Jason blinked sweatily; he rubbed a shaking hand over his face. "If you won't think about your own life, think about this. You ain't even fired that Sharps, much less got it sighted in. This far a shot, you can't be sure. You just can't be."

Penmark palmed his watch in a quick gesture; he snapped open its case. "You got twenty minutes. Less'n that if they break camp and start to pull out before time's up. They do, I ain't waiting."

His voice was unchanging, his face still as stone. A peculiar shine had surfaced on his eyes. And Jason knew that the time for talking was past.

He turned and started away from Penmark, stumbling across the rubble toward the place where they'd ascended. Suddenly a shadow stirred in his path. Jason came to a dead halt, his heart almost stopping. Then he turned his head.

For a moment he didn't believe what he saw. A dark-faced man had stepped noiselessly from behind a leaning spire not five yards away. A short fellow, hard and squatly built, his black hair closely cropped to his head. His face was square and primitive under an old horse-thief hat. His strong scarred hands held a Winchester that was negligently aimed at Jason's chest.

Jason stood stock still, his muscles bunched with tension, as the man moved close, then reached out and took the rifle from his hands. For a wild moment Jason didn't know what to think. Then it came to him who this man was. Cherokee, the half-breed. He laid Jason's rifle on the ground, then made a tight menacing motion with his Winchester, indicating that Jason was to move back toward the rim.

Jason slowly wheeled and tramped back that way, his boots crunching on crumbled stone with what seemed an abnormal loudness in his ears. He knew Cherokee was right behind him, though the half-breed's moccasined feet made no sound.

Crouched by the big rock, Penmark was sighting along the Sharps as he drew a bead on the camp. Jason's throat tightened with the impulse to yell a warning. Then, hearing his footsteps, Penmark turned his head.

In the same moment the half-breed's rifle slammed into Jason's kidneys and knocked him sprawling. Penmark whirled to face them, moving away from the rock as he whipped the rifle around in a tight arc.

The crash of Cherokee's weapon came even as Jason was skidding on his face in the rubble. Penmark jerked with the bullet's impact. Reeling backward, he toppled over the rim.

Jason, curled up with pain on the ground, had only a distorted glimpse of Penmark as he plunged from sight. A dim clatter of falling rubble followed. Then silence.

"Get up," Cherokee said.

Jason climbed shakily to his feet, half-doubled with the pain of his back. Cherokee jabbed him with the rifle, nudging him ahead, and together they moved over to the brink of the drop. A third of the way down its rough steep slant, Penmark's body lay hung across a projecting spur which had broken his fall. He was twisted and motionless, one leg hanging over the ledge. Blood dyed his gray hair and made a spreading brightness across the dust-colored rock where his head rested.

"I don't think he listen, that one," the half-breed said. "So then I shoot fast."

Jason looked at him.

Cherokee showed his strong yellow teeth. "Me, I'm sent up here for lookout. He don't take no chance, Heath. I see you and him coming long way off. I get out of sight and wait. Now you know, eh?"

The men down in the camp were on their feet, watching the ridge-top. One of them yelled something at Cherokee. In reply, the half-breed raised his rifle above his head and waved it once. Then he pointed it at Jason again.

"You go on down, boy. Stay ahead of me and go slow."

He retrieved Jason's rifle and brought it along. They clambered back across the crumbling top of the ridge and descended its sloped flank. Cherokee prodded him over to the three horses and told him to pick up the reins and bring them along. They tramped across the sage flat to the fire where Heath and his men waited.

Heath stood with his arms folded, holding his weight hip-shot away from his hurt leg. His pale stare held on Jason while Cherokee briefly explained what had happened. Afterward Heath's gaze moved to the low scarp where, from here, part of Penmark's body was visible along the spur rock.

"So he had to get me," he murmured, "and you had to get your money. Too bad. How did you come by the horses?"

Jason told him. Wasn't any reason not to. But he felt a cold dread even as he talked. Heath had ample cause to settle him too. Christy moved over to the leader and laid a hand on his arm.

"Jack . . . let the boy go, why don't you?"

"You know what, angel?" Heath said mildly. "I think the heat is scrambling your brains. Mine too, apparently. I let them go before on your say-so. I rather doubt the old man was drawing a bead on you or Dallas, up there."

"All right," she said coldly. "Go ahead and shoot him. While you're about it, remember he's the one who stood between you and the old man's gun before. Or so you told us."

Heath nodded bleakly. "True enough . . ."

"All he wants, from what you've said yourself, is to get his family's savings back. That right, Drum?"

"Yes'm."

One of the Ermine brothers rumbled a slow chuckle. About thirty, he was built like a great chunky wedge, tub bellied but solid. His wreath of jowls sparkled with a burr of blond whiskers; his clothes were stiff with filth, and he gave off a sour aura of sweat and tobacco. His shirtfront was tracked with tobacco stains. He fired a squirt of brown juice at the fire now.

"Boy howdy, that's something," he said. "Maybe we oughta pat his rosy cheeks and give him back his money while we're about it."

"Not a bad idea," Christy said calmly, "considering the source. I'd say Jack owes him that. How much of your money we got, Drum?"

"Eight hundred—" Jason cleared his throat. "Eight hundred seventy-five dollars."

"Well, you do go for the big bucks, don't you? Jack, give him his money, it's a piddling piece of change we'll never miss. Then send him on his way. He won't bother us again. Will you, Drum?"

"No, ma'am."

The tub-bellied man shook his head, grinning. "Sister, you're something. You know that?"

"Careful what you say, Pete." Heath's voice had a warning edge. "Forget it, angel. This fellow's given me enough trouble, he and his friend. I'm taking no more chances with him. What we'll do, I think is take him along with us."

"Why?"

A flat, single word from the tallest Ermine brother. Just looking at this fellow, you got the feeling he never wasted speech. A raw-boned lath of a man in his mid-thirties, he wore his yellow hair long, curling over his collar. He had a bony clean-shaven face with a blade of a nose and eyes as chilly as Penmark's. A gaping pink scar that was six inches long laid open the side of his face; its edges had never healed together. The way he wore his gun, holstered at a jutting angle so that the wrist of his straight-hanging arm alway's brushed the butt, was what you noticed most.

"A hostage, Trask," Heath said. "A hostage to the border. I've been fetched enough surprises on this trip. Had thought we'd shaken his friend and him, and by God if they didn't show up again. I think Mr. Drum's presence might provide a splendid warranty against any more surprises."

"Thought you said we thrown off the rest of that posse."

"They all turned back, yes." Heath moved his weight to his stiff leg, grimaced, and shifted back again. "But word's gone out by now. No telegraph out of New Hope, but Longworth isn't too far from there. Longworth has wires to Bisbee and Tucson. From there word would be sent to the border. Of course there's not enough law down there to start to cover the whole Mexican line, particularly where we'll cross. But as I say—I've had enough surprises this trip. Should we run into any more, Mr. Drum will be our passport."

"That makes sense, all right," Dallas Redmile said mildly.

"Shee-it," said the third Ermine. "Whatever be it Jack says, you go along, old man."

"So do you." Heath gave him that flat-edged look of his. "And don't forget it."

Clayt Ermine, this one would be. He was a lot younger than his brothers. Not much older than Jason, in fact. Callow-seeming and close-eyed, with Trask Ermine's blade nose, he was sort of a pale copy of his oldest brother. Held his lank body the same way and wore a jut angled Colt. But he dressed a lot fancier, wearing a costly looking calfskin vest and flowered sleeve garters. Under Heath's stare, a pale rage flared in his eyes, then veiled over with a thin caution. He remained fidgety as hell, and Trask gave him a warning look.

"All right," grunted Pete Ermine. "We all taken your orders right enough. Job's done and you still holding all the money. Time we made the split."

"That'll wait." Heath limped to the fire and swept dirt over it with his foot. "Right now—"

"Hell no, it won't wait," Pete said truculently. He set his hands on his hips, a massive hogshead of a man with no softness about him. "Suppose'n we got to break up again like we done out of New Hope. There we was kiting off in different directions and you had our shares. All right, it was needful, how you done it, posse hot on our asses and no time to divide the loot. But I don't see no odds we let that happen again."

"Well, well," Heath murmured. "I've rather a suspicion that Pete doesn't trust me. Could that be the case with all you bucko lads?"

Trask Ermine had the makings out and was building a cigarette. Not looking up, he raised one shoulder in a lazy shrug. "You never dealt a partner crooked that I heard of. All the same, Pete got a point. You got taken by this young'un and the old man. Hadn't been for Redmile and your woman, you be cooling your butt in the *calabozo* up at New Hope and we be out our shares."

"To state the matter flat out," Heath said pleasantly, "are you saying we divide the money here and now? Is that it?"

Trask lifted his cold and colorless eyes while his fingers kept shaping the smoke. "That's it."

"Well, I'll tell you, gentlemen. . . ." Heath took a cheroot from his pocket, stuck it in his mouth, and bent over, picking up a thick short branch at the edge of the half-doused fire. He held the glowing end to his cheroot and lighted it. "Pete may indeed have a point. But the sole point which concerns me is where authority resides in this outfit. Doubtless you've heard of me as an arrogant bastard who's accustomed to having his way, and I assure you that you've heard correctly."

Grinning faintly around the cheroot, he squinted against the smoke, meeting Trask's eyes. "In other words, old pot, we divide the money when I damned well say we do and not before then. Clear?"

Pete Ermine heaved forward, his thick trunk swaying, his chin shelving out. "Your goddam say-so don't cut no ice on my pond, mister."

Trask said gently, his eyes on Heath, "Let it ride, Pete. Let it ride."

"Bullshit. Listen, Heath. Me 'n my brothers and Cherokee been trailing together a long time. We come in with you, we taken your orders all right. But we come in for one job at a time. This one's over. We want what's coming to us and you gonna fork it over. That's how it is."

"My, my," Heath murmured. "How it really is—"

Jason would never forget what Heath did next or how

he did it. He looked down at the smoldering branch in his
fist with a quiet, even disarming smile. Then he took two
steps, swinging the heavy chunk of wood back and forward in one savage clubbing motion. Pete Ermine stood
flat-footed, his jaw opening, and then flung up an arm to
intercept the blow, too late. The chunk took him stiffly
across the jaw. His knees folded, his eyes rolled; he
pitched forward without a sound. Heath simply stepped
aside and let him fall, his outflung arm almost landing in
the fire.

Dallas Redmile had moved at almost the same moment. He was edging quietly backward even before Heath
took a step. Now he swiftly levered his rifle and said in
his mild voice, "Don't nobody twitch a finger."

He was standing slightly behind Trask and Clayt, and
his rifle was pointed loosely at Cherokee, whose hand had
dived instinctively to the Bowie knife at his belt. Even the
half-breed, alert and cat quick, had been caught flat-
footed by the suddenness of it.

"I'm sure nobody will, Dallas," Heath said idly. "Will
you, Trask?"

Trask Ermine hadn't stirred a muscle. Eyes still on
Heath, he finished shaping his cigarette. "That was taking
a pretty long chance, Cap'n. I could of dropped you before the old man got me."

"Part of the game, old pot, living one's chances close to
the nerve." Heath laughed softly, his eyes alight and
sparking; he tossed the branch away. "I keep my bar-
gains, Trask. We'll split the money when we reach Arrowhead Tanks. That was the agreement to start with. I
don't see any reason to change it, do you, now?"

Trask shook his head. He dropped to one knee by his
unconscious brother, turned Pete's face out of the dirt,
and felt along his jaw. "Leastways you didn't bust it."

Heath raised his brows. "Really? I meant to, you
know."

Trask stood up slowly. He flung his cigarette in the fire.
"Could be," he said softly, "Pete asked for that. But I
want you to know something, Cap'n. No man'd ever do
that to me."

"Fine, old pot. And I want you to know something. Next time I have to remind any of you sterling specimens who is top dog of this outfit, the outcome is going to be a lot more permanent. Now let's get moving. We've a good many miles to cover. . . ."

VIII

'NITA CORTINAS KNEW the desert country to which she had been bred. She knew about its teeming and tough-fibered creatures and plants; they held no terrors for her. She had lived next to its threats of death and pain all her young life: sudden and fanged death in a rattler's strike; pain that barbed the needles of the *cholla,* which sprang and hooked to a touch, working a throbbing agony into the flesh. But there were gifts of life too, in certain healing herbs and in the watery contents of the *bisnaga* cactus. The difference between living and dying in desert country was a difference between choices; one learned to make the right ones. One learned by mistakes that were painful and toughening. And always there were vistas of fierce beauty from the small to the large, of vast and contemplative silences, that made it all worth the while for one who could see, who could feel.

So 'Nita had found in her sixteen years. She had more than her share of quick and restless curiosity; once or

twice it had led her into situations where only luck and
native ingenuity had bailed her out. There was the time
when, at eleven, she had saddled a mule without telling
anyone and had ridden off toward the Santa Catalinas to
the north to see if she could find some of the gold of
which she'd heard an Anglo prospector tell. Aside from
the stage passengers who quickly came and went, a blend
of anonymous faces, visitors were rare at Corazon's lonely station. 'Nita had always listened avidly to the talk of
these few, and the old gold-hunter's tall tales of riches
to be found in the north peaks had fired her young fancies. Thinking of the wealth she might bestow on her
family, she had set out for the Catalinas. At first she had
been surprised, then uneasy, and finally terrified to find
the blue wavering line of the mountains still retreating
steadily before her after long hours. Turning back, she'd
soon realized she was thoroughly lost. But she'd had the
sense to stop where she was, waiting through a long cold
night and another long hot day till her father and grandfather had found her. Sun-blistered, half-dead of thirst,
and thoroughly chastened, she'd afterward come to a
deep respect for the desert, but the experience hadn't
quelled her curiosity. 'Nita was sure she could cope with
anything; it was just a matter of watching and learning.

She'd been encouraged in such pursuits by a leathery
maverick of a grandfather who claimed that she reminded
him of him—this to the dismay of her parents, who had
spoken much of sending her to the home of a distant and
wealthy cousin of her father in Mexico City, where she
might be schooled to demure and proper ways. A letter
requesting the favor had been sent, along with an offer of
payment, for a poor Cortinas was no less proud than a
rich one. But the cousin's reply, when it had finally come,
had been discouraging, which had secretly pleased 'Nita.
She was curious about the wide world beyond her small
one, but *Abuelito*'s disgusted assurances that all existence
there was stiff and stuffy, no better than a prison, had
damped any desires in that direction. Here was the freedom of a carefree girlhood with many things remaining to
be explored and learned of. To her it was a way of life

deeply satisfying, rather than one full of harsh privations, for she had known nothing else.

Now it was done with, wiped out as cleanly as the stroke of an ax might ready a chicken for the pot. The 'dobe-walled station at Corazon was no longer home; it was a place of strangeness and desolation on which she turned her back without regret, except for the sodden lump of grief in her throat.

It did not blunt the keenness of her senses. She rode straight-up and studied with minute care the land she was crossing. 'Nita felt confident, but not foolishly so. She knew her experience as a desert-dweller must be tempered by her ignorance of the desert at large. Not yet six years old when her parents had brought her to Corazon, she'd never traveled over ten miles from it since. She knew that there were other kinds of country at no great distance, that in such places conditions were very different from what she'd always known. The mountain ranges she had seen only from a good way off cradled tall timber and wide grasslands and rushing streams, and there was wild game in abundance and great ranches where *vaqueros* tended herds of white-faced cattle.

Of these things she had often wondered, but she barely thought of them now. Her way was taking her across the powdery white glare of alkali flats and flinty terrain mantled by such scrubby and thorny vegetation as she knew well. This was the way her two gringos had gone, and there she would go. She thought of them that way—her gringos. She had many thoughts, both puzzled and understanding, about the pair. She had a rough comprehension of their mission, though the purposes of each weren't entirely clear. They were very different men, so different that only strong reasons would have brought them so far together on a long trail.

Since 'Nita did not want them to catch sight of her for a while, she rode at an inheld pace, following their sign. This was easy enough in most places, and wherever it was not, she dismounted and had little difficulty studying the sign out. Eventually, of course, she would have to show herself to them, and she guessed they'd be anything but overjoyed. What would they say? It did not matter, she thought stubbornly, except of course that she could say nothing in return, a thought she found quite depressing.

She loosened her headcloth and let the warm wind cool her sweaty throat. Fingering her neck and feeling no pain there, she wondered once more what had happened to her voice. She couldn't recall injuring her throat any more than she remembered hurting her foot. Instinctively she knew that the injury was not physical, that the effort to form words, no matter how hard she tried, was useless.

After riding a long time across sage-covered flats, she halted to rest her mount. As she unslung her canteen, she heard a distant slam of gunfire. She listened awhile, but there was only the one shot, no more. Uncapping the canteen, she took a small drink, then glanced at the sun. It was lowering, but still hours short of setting. It might be a good idea to overtake the gringos before nightfall.

Pushing on a bit more quickly, she speculated on that single gunshot. Perhaps it meant nothing. A man might fire one shot to bag a quail or jackrabbit. But she was doubly watchful now.

Coming onto the brow of a short rise, she pulled up and shaded her eyes with a hand. There was an oddly shaped ridge somewhat off to her right; a couple of buzzards were wheeling and dipping above it. Something was dead or close to it. Nothing remarkable in that, but the memory of the gunshot gave her a tingle of apprehension.

She gigged her paint swiftly on, hardly bothering to check the horse tracks anymore. They led straight to the ridge; at its base she plainly marked where the two gringos had dismounted. Stepping to the ground, she followed their tracks to where they faded out on the ridge's lower slope. Both horses and men were gone now, but the gringos must have gone up on the ridge for a reason. And there were the buzzards circling insistently above. . . .

She started laboriously up the slope. It was slow going, her sandals in bad shape and flapping loose, her foot catching painful twinges. When she reached the summit, 'Nita saw nothing but a stretch of crumbling rock. She moved carefully across to the far rim and a sharp drop-off. Below was a rolling sage flat; she saw smoke wisping from the site of a recent fire.

Cautiously edging onto the rimrock, she looked straight down. Yards below her, a man's body was hung precariously on a thrust of rock. Though he lay face down on the narrow shelf, grotesquely sprawled, she could tell it was the gray-haired gringo, Penmark.

Dried blood stained his hair and darkened the rock beneath his head. It seemed likely he was dead. If he had fallen from up here, his head must have cracked on the rock. Would his young *compadre* have left him if he were yet alive? Even if he thought the old man was dead, she reasoned, he would not leave the body like this. But what of that shot? Perhaps the men's enemies had shot the old man and had taken the young one prisoner.

Yes, that seemed the answer. The enemies had been camped below, where the fire was, and the two gringos had seen its smoke and had come up here to spy on them. But something had gone wrong; the old man was shot, the young one captured.

'Nita sat down on her heels, studying the almost straight drop below. The cliffside was very rough, and it slanted outward only a little. Could the old one have fallen so far and still be alive? Maybe he had been dead before he fell; they had shot him and thrown his body over. But she could see his hat and rifle at the bottom of the drop. Would they have thrown his rifle down too?

She doubted that she could climb down to him; even if she were able, how would she get his body up? She could think of but one way, and was not at all sure she could manage it. But she must try. If the old man were still alive, if there was the faintest chance he lived, she must try.

'Nita descended the ridge and set to the task of leading her horse up its crumbling flank. She had to fight him all the way, leaning her slight weight against the reins. The final precipitous yards were the worst; the animal balked and shied as rotted rock scaled away under his hooves.

When they reached the top, he was lathered and trembling. 'Nita's palms were slick with blood where the reins had cut them.

Taking the coiled reata from her saddle, she secured its noose end around a great block of stone that rested near the rim. She let the other end tumble down the cliff wall; it extended more than a yard past Penmark's body. That was little slack to spare, but it was enough.

Studying the distance to the cliff base, she thought about what would happen if she made a misstep. Then she knew that the best thing was not to think about it. Drying her bloody hands on her skirt, she gripped the rope with all her strength and threw her weight tentatively against it a few times to be sure the noose was secure. The anchoring rock itself was at least six times as heavy as she.

Setting her back to the drop, she slipped gradually over the rim, walking slowly backward and down. The escarpment slanted just enough that her feet could help steady her descent, and for once 'Nita had cause to be glad she was skinny and had wiry muscle in her arms. This was something she could do, she guessed, as well as any boy might do it.

Descending the rope was quite simple, so long as she didn't glance down too often, any more than was necessary to locate footing and to guide her feet onto the ledge. There was less than a foot of space between the wall and Penmark's sprawled form, leaving barely enough room for her to stoop down. She managed to do so, holding the rope with one hand, clasping Penmark's wrist in the other, and moving her fingers till she located a pulse.

It was a good strong pulse. Relief flooded her.

The tricky part now was to let go the rope, freeing both her hands to do what must be done without losing her balance. Penmark's right leg dangled over the abutment, pulling his whole body precariously toward its edge. She'd have to move a little to set the rope; hardly any movement at all would shift his weight slightly toward his overbalanced side. Another inch or so might tip his body over the edge. But the risk must be taken.

'Nita grasped his belt in her right hand and strained with all her strength to raise his body enough to slip the rope end beneath his stomach with her left hand. It was the work of many minutes for her to maneuver the rope to his other side, heaving his belly up a fraction of an inch for a couple seconds at a time, resting briefly between each effort. Meantime she could feel the little telltale jerks as his weight slid outward on the shelf.

Finally she could reach across him and grasp the rope's end. Giving more sporadic tugs on his belt, she hauled several inches of slack into the rope. Enough to enable her to knot it securely around his waist.

That done, there was no danger of his slipping over. 'Nita wiped her palms dry again, then seized hold of the rope and climbed back to the rim. When she stood once more on solid rimrock, a wild quivering seized her; she sat down on the rock, sweating and shaking, till her muscles and nerves steadied.

The paint was reluctant to venture near the rim. It was necessary, however, to urge the fiddlefooting animal close enough for her to slip the noose off the rock and over her saddle horn. Once she'd accomplished this, the rest was comparatively easy. She mounted and reined the paint sideways. He sidled against the rope's taut resistance with the skill of any trained cowpony; Penmark's limp body slowly bumped and rasped up the side of the cliff.

At last the gray-haired gringo lay doubled up on the rimrock. 'Nita removed the rope and then, grasping his wrists, dragged him over to the deep shade of a boulder. Ignoring her own exhaustion, she went over the unconscious man with sensitive hands, trying to determine the extent of his hurts. All his bones seemed to be intact, even his skull. He bore a multitude of bruises and scratches, as well as several great raw abrasions where flesh had scraped away in his fall. Using a strip torn from her skirt and a little canteen water, she soaked away the clotted blood that matted his hair, discovering a straight furrow in his scalp that bared the clean white bone of his skull.

That, she thought, could have been made by a bullet.

She could find no other serious hurts, except the mashed flesh and purpled swelling of his forehead where it must have struck the ledge. It was bleeding a little. He was a tough, strongly muscled old gringo; nevertheless, 'Nita felt a deepening anxiety. A fall such as he had taken could very well jar a man's vitals loose, and there was no telling what had been done to him internally. At least not till he was conscious again, and so far he hadn't twitched an eyelash.

'Nita bathed his face and scalp sparingly. Then she descended the ridge and hunted up a patch of prickly pear. She hacked off several of the flat paddles and, having pared away the spines, carried them back to the ridgetop. After macerating the cactus paddles between a pair of stones she applied the resulting mash to the wounds on Penmark's scalp and forehead. A couple more strips, these torn from her bedraggled petticoat, made bandages to tie the poultices in place.

The sun had tipped low; it flattened to a molten stain along the rim of earth. Wearily the girl spread a blanket over Penmark, then went down the ridge to scour up an armload of brush and carry it up. She built a small fire between sheltering rocks where it wouldn't be seen when darkness came. She carried up several more armfuls of dry wood. Then she cut strips of bacon and laid them in her small skillet. While the bacon was frying, she kneaded cornmeal and salt and a little water together on a flat stone. Cooked in bacon grease, the mixture baked to a crisp gold-brown. She ate half of the bacon and johnny cake and wrapped the rest in an oilcloth.

By now it was full dark and still the gringo had not come to; she wondered if he ever would. She had heard of people staying alive and unconscious for a long time until, for lack of nourishment, they expired. 'Nita shivered as she sat resting her chin on an updrawn knee, studying Penmark's haggard face, its weathered brown gone sallow and bloodless in the firelight. No matter what, she thought with a kind of numb determination, she would not desert this man. If he did not revive, she would stay with him till he died.

She had found *Abuelito's* clasp knife on the ground near his body and picked it up as a sentimental token, but it would be of use for effecting repairs on her disintegrating sandals. It contained a fold-in leather punch as well as big and small blades. She used the tiny awl to poke ravels of cloth through the rope-soles of her sandals, tying them so they would reinforce the fraying straps.

As she worked, she felt her throat lumping painfully with a hundred memories of *Abuelito*, his deft sinewy hands engaged at the leather craft he knew so well. The lump softened like warm wax, and something cold in her stomach seemed to melt; her eyes misted. The tears came at last, crawling down her cheeks, but she couldn't manage to cry aloud, not truly. The sounds she made were more of sodden belchings that rolled up in aching spasms from her throat, hurting clear to the pit of her stomach. She dropped her work, pressing her hands over her mouth and throat, trying to control the ugly sobs that were not sobs.

Penmark groaned quietly. Weakly he moved a hand, lifted it, let it fall to his chest.

'Nita reached with all her will for self-control; she moved on her knees to the gringo's side. She raised his head and rubbed a wet cloth over his face; she rubbed harder. His eyes opened; his cracked lips stirred.

"What is it, girl? Wha? . . ."

She held the canteen to his lips; he rolled the water slowly in his mouth and slowly swallowed.

After a few minutes he essayed to sit up, clasping one hand to his head. His jaw was gritted; beads of sweat stood on his face. 'Nita made one effort to press him back, and he pushed her hand weakly but roughly away. Finally he achieved a sitting position. And then he grabbed at his belly.

"Gawd! . . ." His face was gray and twisted; 'Nita dreaded the worst. But as he steadily rubbed a hand back and forth across his belly, his face relaxed to a tight grimace.

"Feels like I got stomped by a crazy bronc," he muttered. His eyes moved to her face; his brows drew together in an effort at concentration. He looked slowly around him, then back at her. "Fell off that rim . . . all I remember. Christ. How come I ain't busted to hell? How you get me up here?"

She did her best to explain, making careful motions with her hands. Penmark shook his head impatiently, grimacing again. "Leave it go, girl. . . . I'll puzzle it out later."

He settled his body back on the ground, staring upward. His eyes were clear once more, full of the chill purpose that she remembered. It was a look that might frighten some, but it had never frightened her at all, not even at first.

"Feel like I'm one solid bruise. But don't seem to be nothing broken." His eyes flicked to her for confirmation.

She shook her head, though she didn't really know.

"Good . . . good. I'll make it all right. There's a man I got to find." Again a flicking glance at her. "You come this far. You want to come along?"

'Nita smiled. She was surprised to find that a smile was easy to manage when words were not.

IX

HEATH AND HIS people pushed south with no particular haste. Jason judged that this was deliberate on Heath's part: the Ermines were impatient to get to Mexico, and so Heath dawdled. He had quelled one small rebellion, and he meant to keep control of the situation by making no concessions. But he seemed to be riding his luck on a god-awful tight edge. And he seemed to have no better reason for doing it than arrogant pride and the plain hell of it. If the Ermines and Cherokee all turned against his authority at once, it would be four tough hardcases against Heath, old Dallas, and the girl Christy. With his own chance of coming out with a whole skin hanging on the favor of these three, Jason felt anything but comfortable about the odds.

Trask Ermine didn't appear to be cowed by Heath; he simply didn't consider that the question of when to divide the spoils was worth a squabble, much less a shoot-out.

And he had the say-so, more or less, with his brothers
and the half-breed. In going against Heath, Pete Ermine
had also defied Trask's warning, so Pete had got the
come-uppance he deserved. That was how Trask seemed
to look at it. All the same he was no man to run afoul of,
Jason decided glumly. You never knew what someone
like Heath might take it in his head to do; he was that
kind. If, just for the hell of it, he sat on Trask Ermine too
hard, there would be fireworks for sure.

For that matter Jason felt far from secure about his
own prospects where Heath was concerned. So far it had
suited his whim to yield to Christy's wish, but Jason
sensed that this was pretty thin insurance. There was a
vital, restless power about Heath that wouldn't shape for
very long to any mold, including any to which a woman
might attempt fitting him. Christy knew it too. After vehemently arguing that Jason be turned free, she hadn't
opposed Heath's decision to take him along as hostage. It
must have been her shrewd intent, by asking more than
Heath was likely to grant, merely to prevent Jason's
throat from being cut on the spot. And it had worked.
She knew how to handle Heath. But that sort of female
ploy had its limits. The real test of Christy's influence
would come once they reached the border, when Heath,
no longer needing a hostage, had the choice of turning
Jason loose or belatedly cutting his throat.

Jason was grateful to the girl and puzzled by her too.
She was something outside of his experience. To Penmark
it had been as simple as A and B: there were two kinds of
women and she was the wrong kind. Two kinds of women
—all the older men Jason had ever heard offer opinion on
the subject, including his father, thought the same way. If
the years had given any of 'em an inkling it might be otherwise, they weren't admitting it. The lines were firmly
drawn in their own heads and wasn't nobody going to tell
'em different.

But Christy was different. Different in a curious, excit-
ing way. It was hard to keep his thoughts, no matter what
tack they took, from circling back to her.

Besides, how else did you occupy yourself under the

conditions? Jogging along between armed captors across
the desert's baking monotony, its heat rolling sullenly
against your body, your skin drying and your eyes aching
with spotty flickers, all you could do was let your mind
drift in weary circuits that got nowhere. Your hands were
free to handle your reins, but any break for freedom
would be fatal.

Maybe there'd be a chance when they made camp . . .
after darkness came. Jason doubted it, but the hapless
swing of his thoughts kept hitting a fine edge of desperation. As long as he couldn't be sure of his fate at Heath's
hands, it seemed better to watch for any chance that offered itself, whatever the risk.

There was Penmark too. Though he'd had mixed feelings toward the man, Jason felt a sick and genuine regret.
If Penmark hadn't been killed outright, he must have been
close to death after being shot and falling off the rim, his
body snagging up hard. If still alive, he would face a slow
and helpless dying, stranded on that naked shelf of rock.

If I get out of this, I will go back there, Jason thought
dully. It won't do no good, but I'll go back. His dust-
caked lips twitched; it would be exactly the sort of gesture
on which Penmark would heap biting ridicule. But Jason
had his own way. And that, at least, was one thing that
Val Penmark had come to understand. . . .

There wasn't even a remote chance of escape that
night, because as soon as they made camp, Jason was tied
hand and foot with tough rawhide *peales*. He was briefly
unbound so he could eat supper and afterward relieve
himself, then tied up again.

Next day, a little before noon, Heath's party reached
Arrowhead Tanks.

They were located amid lava beds that ages ago had
cooled into contorted swells and spires of bluish-black
rock, laced by treacherous chasms and potholes. The
tanks took their name from a cluster of natural catch basins where runoff water accumulated. Such basins in desert country were usually unreliable; they might dry up in
the summer heat or be reduced to puddles of rancid scum.

It was always a matter for concern in a land where travel
was circumscribed by the availability and quality of
water. The ancient trails worn by animals and nomadic
tribes converged on such places or pointedly skirted them.
Arrowhead Tanks, despite the harsh and burned-out
country that surrounded them, had a reputation for staying wet and drinkable the year around. For that reason,
and because antelope and bighorn sheep came to water
here, the place had long been a favored camp of Indian
bands.

So Heath and his group, picking their way slowly
across the lava field, approached the Tanks with their
weapons ready. Nearing the cordon of basaltic boulders
that surrounded the catch basins, they saw a man tramp
out to sight and wave his arm. It was the chunky Mexican
Miguel; grinning widely, he motioned them on. They rode
into the circle of rocks and dismounted with stiff and
weary movements.

"How are you making it, Miguel?" Heath asked.

"Good, *jefe*, good." The Mexican patted his left arm in
its dirty sling. "The arm, she's hurt like hell, but the fever,
she's wear out. *Dios*, is good to see you! I'm think maybe
we see each other in hell next."

Heath chuckled. "A premature thought, I'm glad to
say."

He gave orders for setting up camp. The packs were
dumped in a sandy clearing between the huge-slabbed
boulders. The horses, including Jason's and Penmark's,
were led to drink and then picketed on some bear grass
that grew sparsely among the rocks. Jason was trussed up
again and left in a patch of rock-flung shade. He sat glow-
ering at the outlaws, nursing a mighty thirst along with
his bitter worry, but damned if he was going to ask 'em
for anything.

Trask Ermine stood hip-shot, right arm dangling along
his gun butt; lefthanded, he smoked a cigarette, bringing
it to and away from his lips in a kind of deliberate
rhythm. He was watching Heath.

Pete Ermine sidled up to Trask at his thick rolling gait.
The whole side of Pete's face was swollen purple where

Heath had walloped him. His eyes were bloodshot with
pain and lack of sleep; he could hardly manage to talk.
He mumbled something in his brother's ear. Trask shook
his head, giving a brief irritable reply.

Jason wondered if things would break wide open here
and now. They were all conscious of the tension, both
factions casually wary of one another, but not ready to
push it unless the leaders gave a signal. Heath was talking
quietly with Dallas, who was watching Trask and Pete.
Cherokee and Clayt Ermine stood off to one side, Miguel
quietly keeping an eye on them both. Christy was on her
knees building a fire; she was tired, her eyes dark circled,
but alert to all that was going on.

"Cap'n," said Trask.

Heath ignored him and he repeated it; Heath gave him
a careless nod. "What is it, old man?"

"Time for a divvy, I reckon. You said Arrowhead
Tanks. We're here."

"Ah yes. . . ." Heath touched his mustaches. "Well,
now we're here, no rush, eh? We'll make the split before
we leave."

"How long you mean to lay over?"

"We can all use a spot of rest. A day. Perhaps two
days."

"This don't seem a likely time for it. We're close to the
border. Can raise it before nightfall if we hustle."

Heath lifted an eyebrow. "Yes, old pot, but the horses
are about done in. Wouldn't want to ride 'em to death,
would you? Bit of rest will do wonders for 'em, don't you
agree?"

Trask flicked his cigarette butt to the ground. "I tell
you, Cap'n. I got a place between my shoulders itches like
hell. Only thing's going to scratch it is getting clean across
that line. Maybe we thrown off pursuit, maybe not. But
you said it yourself. There's law down this way too. It
might of got word on us. Could be the damnfoolest thing
you ever done, holding us here without need."

Heath was standing side-on to the brothers; he swung
on his heel to face them. "Apparently, old pot, the details
of our arrangement haven't quite penetrated your skull.

Let me clarify them. Once we are across the border, you are free to follow your fancies wither they take flight. Until then, you are under my command."

"Is that right."

"That's right, laddie, and if you're curious as to what I'd do should you chaps take it in your heads to pack up and clear out now . . . why, nothing. Absolutely nothing." Heath slightly spread his hands, smiling. "Of course you'll leave here without your shares. A broken agreement is no agreement, as I see it."

His eyes were wickedly alight and sparking again. He was tough-cored and fearless; he liked the play of power and of matching his wits against an established order of things. But at the heart of it all was a reckless willingness to throw everything on a single cast of the dice, a momentary turn of the cards. That was the real meat and drink of living for Heath. And it was the no-man's territory where Trask Ermine, just as fearless, just as tough in his way, did not tread. These two men understood each other, and Jason vaguely understood that this was why a real confrontation, a testing of mettle, might be inevitable between them. For understanding or not, there was always that hair-breadth margin of doubt where each man, one boldly, the other cautiously, couldn't help asking himself: *What will he do—if?*

Trask didn't rise to the bait. His scarred face twitched; he said "Shit!" in a flat, positive voice. Turning on his heel, he walked stiffly over to Clayt and Cherokee, saying something to them in a low, angry tone. Pete stared red-eyed at Heath for a long moment, then moved over by his brothers.

There'd be no showdown—at least not yet. . . .

Christy prepared a meal of bacon and tomatoes and pan bread. Jason watched her covertly; she was free striding, her movements quick, firm, and bouncy. Even in a man's shirt, a shapeless calf-length skirt, and tall moccasins, her body curved like a milkmaid's. Her features were clean angled and striking, too sharp for mere prettiness; her hair was cropped boyishly close to her head, shaping it like a smooth coppery helmet. She had a wide, soft-looking mouth and the boldest eyes Jason had ever seen; they shone softly or hardened like green flints, no in-between.

The men ate in silence, bleakly watchful of each other. They ignored Jason, and he, stretched out in the shade, tried to ignore his thirst and hunger. When they'd finished eating, Christy said, "How about feeding the boy, Jack?"

Heath nodded. "Untie him, Cherokee. And watch him."

The half-breed loosened Jason's hands and stood by while Christy brought him a plate of food and a cup of coffee. As she set them beside him, she leaned close and whispered, "You keep looking so hard, Buster, you'll get sunstruck."

Bending his hot face above his plate, Jason ate hungrily.

When he'd finished, Cherokee escorted him a short ways from the camp so he could tend his needs. The half-breed wore a gun but disdained to draw it; Jason had the feeling his real weapon was the knife at his belt, its beaded sheath cocked at a ready angle. His dark, contemptuous stare said plain as words that he wouldn't mind a reason to use it. Jason was careful not to give him one. Cherokee was compact and hard knit, with muscles like wire rope.

Jason was permitted to wash up at one of the pools; when they returned to camp, Cherokee tied his hands in front of him, not in back, and left his feet unbound. With their bellies full and the midday heat working into them, the men gradually relaxed their bitter vigilance. Cherokee and Miguel and Pete Ermine stretched out for siestas; Heath and Dallas idly conversed; Clayt Ermine dug out a bottle of whiskey and a greasy deck of cards and cajoled Trask into a game. Christy gathered up the dirty utensils and carried them to a pool for washing; she winked at Jason as she passed him, strutting her hip movements more freely than usual.

Clayt took a long pull at the bottle, following her with his eyes. Trask jogged him back to the game with an irritable word. Clayt had no belly for liquor; he became flushed and talkative and finally, when Trask told him to shut up, lapsed into a surly silence. Then he broke out again, accusing his brother of belly stripping; with a disgusted curse, Trask threw down his cards, got up, and walked away.

The afternoon wore drowsily on. Pretty soon everyone but Dallas and Christy was napping in the shade. The girl sauntered over to Jason and halted by him, resting a hand on her hip as she sipped a cup of watter. Her green eyes were amused and teasing.

"Want a drink, Buster?"

He nodded. She bent a little to hand him the cup, her breasts stirring gently forward; they formed two firm springy cones against the man's shirt. Face burning, he held the cup awkwardly between his hands and drank, taking a wrong-way swallow that made him cough, spilling the water. Christy took the cup from him, laughing quietly.

Dallas was sitting cross-legged against a rock, mending his bridle. He grunted and stretched his legs, saying mildly, dryly, "Missy, you do like to play hell, don't you?"

She yawned, making a face at him. "You know a better way to pass time?"

"Well, you looking to keep that boy alive, you best watch your fooferawing. Jack's got a jealous eyes."

She walked over to Dallas, lifted his hat, and playfully ruffled his gray hair. "You're the jealous one, you old booger. Admit it."

Chuckling, Dallas grabbed back his hat, giving her a slap on the flank. "Go on, quit your deviling. Go take a bath or something."

"That's a grand idea. Want to join me?"

"Honey, was I twenty years younger, you wouldn't offer."

"You was twenty years younger, old booger, I wouldn't have to."

"That's a thought."

Christy laughed. She got her sack of possibles and dug out a towel and a piece of soap, then headed for one of the rock-sheltered pools.

Jason curled up on his side, bound hands tucked against his chest. He pretended to sleep, but he was fiercely alert, his heart pounding. With his movements hidden from Dallas, he began to work his hands slowly back and forth, twisting against the rawhide strands. The spilled water had drenched his wrists, soaking the dry and flinty *peales*. They were slick and greasy now, and he could feel them gradually, almost imperceptibly, start to stretch with his efforts.

Meantime his head was tipped so he kept Dallas just inside his line of sight, watching him from slitted eyes. The old outlaw was yawning as the sun worked into him, making him drowsy. Finally his hands grew still, his chin sank to his chest.

Jason fought his bonds with a silent fury now, using his teeth as well. His wrists were rasped raw, the skin broken and bleeding, before he finally jerked a hand free of the loops.

Lying motionless, he studied the sleeping outlaws. He needed a horse. Try to sneak one away, he was bound to rouse them. Could maybe get his hands on one of their guns and get the drop, but there were seven to face, seven tough and violent men. If just one tried to fight the drop, so would the rest; most he could hope was to take out one, maybe two, before they got him.

His only chance was with a hostage. One he could handle.

Edging noiselessly to his feet, Jason slipped across the camp and into the boulder-flanked aisle where he had seen Christy disappear. Bending low, he crept between the looming basalt slabs into a brush-grown gully. He heard a faint splashing of water; then it ceased. He paused, listening, then worked upward from the gully toward a corner of angled rock. Beyond it he caught a glint of water at the pool's rim.

Jason came quickly around the rock. Christy was sitting on the edge of the pool, wet hair clinging to her head; she had donned her shirt and skirt and was pulling on one of her long moccasins. She looked up, her eyes rounding.

Jason had eyes only for the jacket on the ground beside her, thinking of the little gun she carried in one of its pockets.

He took a long stride forward and dived for the jacket. Landing on his belly with a grunt, he made a wild grab at it. At the same moment Christy snatched it up and rolled away, tearing the jacket from his grasp, then scrambling to her feet. Jason made another wild grab, this time at one of her ankles, but his fingers skidded on her damp skin; she spun away, quick as an eel.

She plunged a hand into the jacket, trying to find the gun in its tangled folds. Jason floundered to his feet as she gave a ripe oath, then tried to dart past him to the gully. His arms flung around her and whirled her off her feet.

She let out a screech, writhing and kicking, and the two of them tumbled to the ground. It took Jason several precious, struggling moments to subdue the girl, pinning her wrists with one hand, trying to push her face in the sand to muffle her cries and unpry her fingers from the jacket, all at the same time.

As he got the jacket away from her, he heard a crunch of running feet in the gully. Frantically he tried to shake loose the pistol, whose weight he could feel in the jacket's folds.

Then Cherokee came pounding around the angled rock. He was on them in a moment, his foot sweeping up. The hard, curled toe of his moccasin slammed Jason in the face and knocked him over backward.

He crawled to his hands and knees, dimly aware of the men pulling around him, a jumble of voices. Then a boot drove into his ribs. The knifelike pain of the kick was lost in a rain of other blows, booted feet smashing at him from all sides. Dark light exploded in his head; he felt nothing more.

X

PENMARK SPENT A bad night, and so did 'Nita Cortinas, kept awake by his groanings and mutterings. Neither of them got much sleep. When a sickly daylight crawled across the sky ahead of the sun, the gringo was on his feet —swaying dizzily, hardly able to stand, but standing.

His body, 'Nita knew, was pummeled to a mass of bruises; his shirt was stiffened by patches of dried blood from many cuts. His face was pasty except for a dull burn of fever in his gaunt cheeks. His eyes were glassy with fever. He kept holding his stomach, which, she guessed, had taken most of the impact of the fall. If anything was broken inside, he would probably be unable to stand; but with this gringo, it was hard to be sure.

He was iron tough and full of a grinding purpose such as she had never seen. And, she realized, perhaps he was a little mad. Thinking of this, she felt for the first time a small lance of fear.

"All right, girl," he said hoarsely. "Let's be packing.

Get the stuff together. . . ." His brows puckered in sweating concentration. "Had a rifle, a good Sharps rifle. It must of . . ."

He hobbled over to the rimrock and peered downward, so heedlessly near its edge that a noiseless cry welled in her throat. "It's there. You get the stuff readied, meet me below."

Moving slowly, as if each step was agony, he clambered across the ridgetop and began to descend. Quickly 'Nita saddled and bridled the paint horse and crammed the saddlebags and blanket roll with her slender gear and provisions. She coaxed the paint into a painstaking descent of the ridge, then led him around to its other side. Penmark was sitting on a rock, examining the rifle.

"It's all right," he muttered. "It'll do." He picked up his crumpled hat and beat it into shape, then set it on his bandaged head. Then he stood up, swayed for balance, and stumbled over to the paint horse. Grasping the saddle leather, he looked at her glazedly and said, "There's just the one horse. We ride him by turns, eh? That all right with you?"

She nodded.

"Jesus, I'm dizzy . . . hold him steady."

'Nita gripped the rein close to the bit, anxiously watching Penmark toe into the stirrup. He set his weight and heaved himself upward, pitched astride with an agonized grunt, swayed over, then caught his balance. He straightened in the saddle, holding to the pommel one-handed, his eyes stark as slate.

"How you on track?"

She wanted to cry at him that this was no good, he was too sick, knowing that if she could shape the words, they'd be futile. She gave a small nod.

"Then you follow it. From there, see where that fire was? All right, get moving now. Lead out."

Walking slowly, 'Nita led the paint horse across the sage flat toward the broken country beyond. The people they were following had many horses; the trampled sign was so clear she did not even think about it. She didn't see how they'd ever overtake the people at such a pace as this. But if the sick gringo would not have it otherwise, she must follow the trail until . . . until he could continue no farther.

Maybe he would not be willing to stop till he was dead. But what could she do?

She looked back at him often and anxiously. He held to the pommel with one hand, the other gripping his rifle as if frozen around it. He swayed and rolled dangerously, his chin bouncing on his chest. How long could he keep it up? *El viejo,* she thought wryly. With such a *viejo,* there was no telling.

The immediate country changed as she moved on, but 'Nita easily held her general bearings. At her back were the bald heights of the Santa Catalinas; southward rose the purple sawtooths of the Santa Ritas, while south and east the San Ignacio range bent into Mexico. She thought that, given time, she could find her way to any place whose general location she knew, even if she hadn't been there. Towns and camps were widely scattered in the region, but many were linked by roads that she could follow. Either the gringo would drive himself to death or he would become too sick and helpless to resist her, and then she would look for a town. And help for the gringo, if he still lived. . . .

As there was no question of taking turns with the horse, she must walk for as long as she could keep going. Her big worry was water. They had a single small canteen of it to divide between them; she was determined to manage without water herself as long as possible. Several times she made a halt to give Penmark a drink; pretending to drink from the canteen, she barely moistened her lips.

Noon came and went. By then Penmark was in a terrible way. She didn't know what was holding him in the saddle. His color was ghastly, his fever climbing. Yet he refused even to pause for a rest, perhaps knowing that if he left the saddle, he wouldn't make it back up. She knew from his mumblings that he had lost all sense of time; he spoke of sunset being an hour away, though it was early afternoon. She guessed that the end of his endurance was close.

It came suddenly. One moment he was riding head up, briefly and relentlessly erect. The next, he was canting sideways, pitching heavily to the ground. He fell face down and then, groaning, struggled to push himself up. He managed only to roll onto his back.

"Help me, girl . . . get me up again . . . tie me on."

'Nita shook her head.

"Goddam . . . your . . . bead-counting heathen soul."

His eyes closed; he didn't move again. She knelt by him and shook him gently. Then laid her ear to his chest. He was alive and unconscious, and hopefully would stay that way a good while.

They had stopped in a vast rock field, a raw and broken sweep of splintered red boulders and slablike monoliths. Seizing hold of Penmark's arms, she tugged him into the shadow of a boulder. It was a few minutes' work to hobble the horse and to make the man as comfortable as she could, digging a hollow in the sand for his hips and covering him with a blanket. 'Nita gave the canteen a shake, finding the water nearly gone. Taking stock of her dwindling provisions too, she knew she must find a way of stretching them for two people. That she could manage, but water was the real concern.

She set out to explore the area, working outward in a slow circle. The vegetation was scanty, but she found enough to serve her purpose: squaw cabbage and puffballs, mesquite beans and juniper berries. Continuing on, she stopped often to rest and to rub her aching legs. Oddly, a half-day's grueling hike had worked out her limp. It was almost gone, but her feet wouldn't last through another trek like today's. They were lacerated by rock and thorn, raw with pain that shot into her calves at every step. The pebbly, baking soil felt like a red-hot plate on her soles. Her sandals were nearly finished, beyond repair.

She came to a shallow dry wash laced with brush that was full of quail runways. It was a good find, but she came

on a better one a little way down the wash. Scraping
noises attracted her to a low spot where a couple of por-
cupines were busily digging. The animals waddled off at
her approach. 'Nita dropped to her knees by the hole
they'd made and clawed out more earth to deepen it.
When her fingers touched moist sand, she worked feverishly to widen the bottom till a broad cup was formed.

She sat back on her heels, watching water seep up in a
cloudy puddle. It would take time for the hole to fill and
the water to clear, but she knew with a surge of relief that
the most pressing need was solved. . . .

Before the day was over, 'Nita had snared two quail in
running nooses she'd set in the runways; these she spitted
on a stick and slow-roasted over a good bed of coals. She
sliced up a puffball and fried the pieces in bacon grease;
along with roasted root of squaw cabbage, it would
stretch out to several good meals. She'd cooked up mesquite beans to make a palatable coffee. The paint horse
was well fed on mesquite beans and juniper berries, his
thirst satisfied.

She mashed up more prickly pear and changed the
poultices on Penmark's head. His fever peaked swiftly; he
thrashed about and raved disjointedly. 'Nita built the fire
to a roaring blaze and kept him covered with blankets to
help sweat out the fever. She got him to take a little
water. Finally he quieted down; he slept. By then it was
sunset, and she was too exhausted to do anything but sit
by the fire and stare dully at the flames. From the gringo's
delirious talk, she could put together in a rough way the
story of his wife's death and the reason of his bitter mission.

She rested her crossed arms on her updrawn knees,
gazing at the sleeping man's face—a harsh and craggy
face even in repose. What would he do when he came to
his senses? She dreaded the worst, for even drained by
fever, he might be more than she could handle. He would
get well only if he stayed quiet; even great weakness, she
feared, would not abate the iron fury in the man.

'Nita's face sank gradually onto her arms. It would do

no harm to sleep, but she did not want to sleep too soundly; she must wake quickly if he needed her.

She woke with a start. It was full dark, and she knew that she had slept for hours. The night chill had crept into her flesh; the fire had died to a handful of cherried embers. She rubbed her arms, shivering, and then built up the fire. The wash of light glanced on Penmark's face, and she saw it was turned toward her. His eyes were open, half-lidded but clear.

" 'Lo, sis," he whispered.

Her throat worked convulsively. *¡Santa Maria!* If only she could get out the words she wanted to. Tell him he must be still and not excite himself. Maybe it would do no good, but what a thing it would be to say the words.

"Reckon . . . I damn near killed myself . . . and you. Damnfool thing to do. Must of been way out of my head. Well . . ." His eyes tipped away from her face. "I want to last awhile yet. I got to last. Jesus, I got me a thirst. Could drink a river dry."

She wasn't slow in making him understand they had plenty of water; she showed him the food she had improvised. And then she found him looking at her strangely, as though he were seeing her for the first time.

"Been busy as a bee in clover, ain't you?" His lips barely stirred, but she had the startled thought that he wasn't far from a smile. "Well, that's fine. You been plenty lucky for me. We're going to make it all right, sis. We're going to make it out together."

Penmark didn't rouse next day until nearly noon. He had slept like a log; he moved stiffly and slowly, but his dizziness had abated with the fever. According to him, he'd gotten as much rest as he needed; it was time to move along. When the paint was readied, he mounted and swung 'Nita up behind him. And they took up the two-day-old trail.

They made better time now, but as the day waned, so did the paint's stamina. 'Nita's hundred pounds and Penmark's two hundred, plus saddle and gear, added to a stiff burden. Penmark chafed with impatience, but was cold-

headed enough to hold the paint to a reasonable pace.
Still, the heat and the weight were wearing the animal
down.

In the late afternoon, they halted on the summit of a
rise thinly forested with mesquite that stood almost head-
high to a man. Penmark grunted, "Rest," and they dismounted. Wincing a little, he hobbled to the edge of the
ridge and hunkered down, studying the land south and
west. 'Nita broke out some cold grub and sat down on the
warm sand beside him, setting the food between them. He
ate slowly, not looking at her. She watched him covertly,
thinking he was like a gaunt gray lobo, a grim wolf of a
man empty of everything but his driving purpose. Under
control now, it still seethed in him like cold acid.

"Losing time to beat hell," he muttered around a
mouthful of food, "but no help for it. Horse'll founder,
we keep this up. We better walk a spell." His eyes turned
coldly on her. 'Nita lowered her gaze self-consciously,
rubbing a long scratch on her bare leg. "Hell," he said
abruptly, "you can't walk on them feet. You ride."

He washed down a last mouthful of food with a drink
from the canteen, then started to get up. Swiftly then, he
pulled back down, closing a hand around 'Nita's wrist to
hold her beside him. She followed the direction of his
stare toward a crumbling height some distance off right of
them. For a moment she couldn't discern what had caught
his attention.

Then she fixed on a flicker of dull color. This resolved
itself into a pair of riders. They were picking their way
down the rocky, angular face of the height.

"We'll keep down," Penmark murmured. "Wait."

She felt a touch of apprehension as he fingered his rifle.
They waited for endless minutes, watching the horsemen
move off the high scarp and onto the desert floor. They
were heading generally this way; their line of advance
should bring them within a few hundred feet of the
mesquite-covered ridge.

As they came clearly into sight, 'Nita felt the slow,
crawling terror of recognition. These were Apaches. She
could see their breechcloths and long leggin-moccasins

and the red kerchiefs tied around their heads. Even under a bright blaze of sun, fear stabbed her flesh like icy quills; her tongue went thick and dry and seemed to fill her mouth. The screams of her murdered family echoed in her head.

"Hostiles," Penmark said quietly. "Tell you what I'm going to do, little girl. I'm going to get us a horse. Maybe a couple of horses. You sit tight now. . . ."

He brought the rifle to his shoulder and set his eyes along the sights. But he didn't fire. He waited through another endless drag of time while the two Apaches slowly angled this way. They were in no hurry. In addition to their mounts, they had a packhorse with the carcass of a bighorn sheep tied across it.

'Nita's mind was numb to everything but a chill clarity of physical detail. She felt a hot wind press across the ridge and saw it skirl up dust along the flats beyond; she saw the men's dark-copper skins and the bright warpaint that barred their faces. She knew a sickness of cold panic held in leash only by the paralysis that gripped her limbs.

The drumroll of her pulse filled her ears like thunder. If she were not voiceless, if a scream could have forced itself from her swollen throat, she would have screamed.

Penmark's rifle shifted almost imperceptibly to the men's approach. They were crossing directly in front of the ridge's south flank. If they had any intimation of danger, they gave no sign of it.

The rifle made its sullen boom.

As if a trigger had been touched in her too, 'Nita fell on her hands and knees; her mouth opened wide to scream. But if she made any sound, it was lost in the waves of gunroar that crashed and beat in her ears. She saw the buckskin horse in the lead fold down as if pole-axed, and his rider pitch forward over his head.

The other Apache reined up, throwing a wild glance around. Penmark was already ramming another shell into his breech; this time he took only a fleeting instant to pull his bead.

The shot wiped the second brave from horseback as if

he'd been struck by an unseen fist. He hit the ground like a bundle of brown rags and lay unmoving.

The first man had lit on all fours and had promptly scrambled to his feet. He paused only momentarily as he saw his companion hit the dust; then he made a wild leap for the second Apache's horse. He caught its rein and swung astride. Whirling the animal around, he kicked it into a run toward the west, bending low to its neck and drumming his heels. He was racing for a deep gulch whose banks were flanked by heavy mesquite and cat-claw.

Cursing savagely, Penmark breeched another shell and settled his sights. He pulled trigger. 'Nita saw the bullet kick up dust in front of the running horse. The Apache slowed as he reached the steep-sided gulch, then plunged his mount into it. He cut swiftly away along its bottom, half-concealed by the banks; only fleeting glimpses of him showed above its brush-laced rim.

Penmark fired twice more. Then the Apache was lost to sight where the gulch curved into a jumble of sandstone rises; he was gone.

"Goddam it!" The oath slashed from Penmark's lips like a knife; he straightened up, swiping a fist across his sweating face. "Got clean away. . . . If he makes smoke, we got trouble."

He started down the rise at a stiff trot. 'Nita crawled to her feet; her trembling legs threatened to give way. Stumbling painfully over the rough ground, she followed him.

Penmark's bullet had creased the buckskin horse at the exact point where his neck swelled into his withers. Momentarily stunned, he was thrashing his legs now, struggling to regain his feet. Penmark ran to him and seized the trailing horsehair halter that was the Apache's only rein. The buckskin lunged upright and reared, and Penmark hauled him down with an iron hand.

"Whoa there . . . whoa!"

Gradually the horse calmed, tremors rippling over his glossy coat. Another rope trailed from the buckskin's neck to the halter of the packhorse, a solid and short-coupled bay. Unable to bolt, this animal had stayed quiet, shuffling a little, his ears laid back.

Penmark was talking to both animals, soothing horse-talk, as 'Nita came up. She halted a few yards away, her arms limp at her sides. She looked at the sprawled body of the Apache, twisted half on its side; her throat worked silently. Then she saw the man's arm move—only his arm, inching stealthily around to his hip where a knife was sheathed. Penmark's back was to him.

'Nita opened her mouth to cry at Penmark. Nothing.

The Apache's quartz-tipped lance lay about two yards from her feet, flung there when the bullet had driven him backward. She bent and snatched it up. In the same instant the Apache pulled his knife and rolled slowly and painfully onto his rump. She saw the ripple of long cordy muscles under his skin, which glistened with blood and sweat; and the dark-copper face, fiercely barred with blue and vermilion, squeezed into a savage grimace.

He got one knee under him and lurched to his feet.

'Nita ran forward. A cry burst from her lips. She held the lance in a two-handed grip, straight out before her and thrust blindly and without conscious volition. She saw the Apache's eyes focus on her in that last second. And then he toppled back like a falling tree, the lance sticking up from the arch of his belly where it met his barrel chest.

He twitched and groaned, chopping his knife into the earth. Then his fist balled hard around the hilt and he was still. . . .

'Nita stood as she was, gazing at the dead man, till she felt Penmark's hands on her shoulders. He started to say something, and she turned blindly against him, her cheek pressed to his chest, her fingers closing and opening and closing again on his arms. Her body shook with a wild, convulsive sobbing.

Penmark didn't say anything for a time. When he did, he wasn't so much speaking to her as spelling his thoughts aloud. "Them two was out hunting . . . main band can't be far away. Cayetano's crowd, I reckon, and they are swinging back south. And," he added grimly, "we killed one and let one get away. That'll fix us 'less we make tracks."

Moving 'Nita aside, he tramped over to the Apache, kneeled down, and peeled off the dead man's tall moccasins. He walked back to the girl, holding the moccasins out. "Here. Pull these on. Don't lose no time about it. We—"

"No!" She shrank back a step, her eyes fixed on the moccasins. "No!"

Penmark was silent for a surprised moment; flesh crinkled quizzically at the corners of his eyes. "So. Found your voice at last, huh? You understand me all right?"

"*Sí* . . . yes." Her voice was a strained whisper.

"Then you get them things on. We got no time to waste."

Her lips thinned; she shook her head.

Penmark's voice deepened harshly. "Sister, I ain't going to tell you again. Put 'em on. Or I'll put 'em on you, if I have to bust both your legs to do it. *¿Comprende?*"

She reached out a hand and touched the stiff leather, shuddering. Then she took the moccasins from him and sat down to tug them on.

XI

THE SKY AT dawn was a strange color. Jason had never seen anything like it: a grimy yellow overcast that filled it from horizon to horizon. The sun had a weak and hazy glow, as if its strength had been dissipated into the brassy stain that overlay the sky and land. The men roused sluggishly from their blankets, looking owlish and tired. The half-breed Cherokee was restless and uneasy; he prowled around and outside of the camp, muttering to himself.

Trask Ermine spoke to him, then approached Heath.

"Cap'n, he says there's a storm coming. A bad one. High wind and a lot o' sand."

"Sandstorm, eh? I've heard of 'em."

"I been in one," Ermine said curtly. "Like to tear all hell loose when they hit. It's coming fast and we're in a bad place for it. Could of been out of its way, maybe, we'd kept moving yesterday. Now all we can do is lay low and wait it out."

They did everything that could be done in the way of

preparing for it. The horses were herded into the deep
cover of an arroyo; the canteens were filled. A rude tent
of blankets was arranged in a pocket among the bulges of
lava, and they lugged their belongings under its shelter.

Huddled on his side, Jason watched their preparations.
He was so sore from the savage beating they'd fetched
him yesterday that he doubted he could move a muscle
even if he hadn't been tied hand and foot. Raging at his
attempt to escape, the men had worked him over with
fists and boots till he'd lost consciousness. Since that time
they had simply ignored him; nobody had offered him
water or food last night or this morning. His mouth was a
furry kiln, his head buzzing; it was hard to fix his
thoughts on anything. Stabs of pain in his sides made him
numbly wonder if some of his ribs were busted; sick as he
felt, he almost didn't give a damn.

A brooding silence had settled on the desert. There was
no stir of wind, no movement of any kind. No lizard scut-
tled; no bird flew. Even the occasional calls of quail from
brush and stunted trees had died away in the vast quiet.
Over everything lay a pall of yellowish heat that throbbed
all around, making you feel like a scorched ant trapped at
the bottom of a limitless bowl.

Far off and faintly, Jason caught a dim roar of sound.
He had no idea where it was coming from, nor could he
make out any change in the sickly sky. Yet the noise was
steadily swelling in volume; he fancied he could feel it vi-
brating through the hot earth. And then he knew a first
icy crawl of panic. As a boy, he had huddled in a root
cellar on the edge of a tornado; he remembered clinging to
his mother, and he remembered how the awesome roar of
wind had shattered all your perspectives and your judg-
ments, causing the whole world to shrink to a few square
feet of terrifying darkness.

And he sensed how this might be worse, a hundred
times worse, and why they were likely in the worst possible place to encounter it. Vast dunes of naked sand lay to
the east and south, and some to the north as well. Thinking of the destruction wrought by that long-ago tornado,
how it had uprooted great trees and hurled building

timbers about like baby's toys, he had an inkling of what a powerful wind would do to tons upon tons of loose sand.

Did the others intend to leave him out in the middle of it? Something akin to pure horror seized Jason; he kicked feebly with his legs, trying to croak out a yell from his parched throat.

Christy was heading for the shelter, a pair of bulging saddlebags slung from her shoulder. She halted and gave him a long look. Since his rough manhandling of her, she'd ignored him as completely as had the others; he felt a sinking conviction that she was in no mood to do him more favors. Whatever her mood was, though, she dropped the saddlebags and came over, knelt by him and cut away his leg ropes. Then she helped him to his feet. Leaning heavily on her, hardly able to move one foot ahead of the other, Jason stumbled to the hollow between the lava slabs, dropped to his knees, and rolled into it under the blankets.

Nobody said anything. They were all occupied with shoving saddles and other plunder into the space. One by one now, they crawled under the blankets and sandwiched themselves side by side with their backs to the rocks.

Even in this jammed closeness, pressed in a corner with Cherokee crouched sweatily beside him, Jason was aware that the pulsing quilt of heat had loosened, drawing up from the ground as if pulled by invisible strings. All of nature seemed to pause in a lull of sullen suspense, and still the thunder of approaching wind grew constantly. He felt static charges prickle the hair at the back of his neck.

Now the patch of sky he could see through a gap in the blankets was hazing from yellow to tan, the weird glow fading, darkening under a turgid front of sand particles that towered thousands of feet high. Not a mile away, it was rushing toward the lava beds. Out on the flats, tumbleweeds bounced like jackrabbits, riding the first sweep of wind—an icy wind that flicked under the shelter in gusty whips, chilling to the bone with a swift fury that was startling, frightening, in the wake of that furnace heat.

They grasped hold of the blankets and clutched them

tight. The pocketing hollow was partly exposed to the
blast of wind-borne sand as it struck; it took their com-
bined strengths to hold down the flapping soogans in
those first wild moments. Then the fierce torrent of wind
and sand became a howling pressure that built up against
the flimsy barrier, and their efforts were turned to forcing
a space around their heads. The wind blew colder and
colder. Its thunderous din increased till all their senses
were drowned in a blind maelstrom where time and space
meant nothing, where body and mind became suspended
in a nightmare cocoon somewhere between solid earth
and boiling sky.

That was the worst of it for Jason—not the pounding
violence of wind and sand, not the marrow-eating cold,
not the gritty tempest of sand that beat through the mesh
of thick-weave blankets, scouring his nose and throat,
searing like sandpaper between his tight-shut eyelids. No,
it was the loss of all direction, of near and far, of high
and low—of everything but the seething malevolence of
nature gone out of control, righting some timeless imba-
lance in its mysterious chemistry with one screaming
drawn-out surge.

So the storm wore on, for a numbing and measureless
space of minutes into hours. Finally its savage eternity
was spent; it died away. But long before that happened,
their flesh and nerves had been battered beyond feeling
and beyond caring. . . .

When they began to stir at last, it was with the frayed
and uncertain motions of drugged people. Sand had
mounded against the blankets, half-burying them; it cascaded away from their bodies as they pushed free.
Christy straightened up cautiously, easing the cramps
from her legs, her arms. A tinny ringing filled her ears;
her mouth and eyes were sore as the devil. Her skin felt
gritty all over, and her only thought at the moment was of
washing up.

"Well, what about it now?" Trask Ermine said harshly.
"Do we ride or not?"

"We ride." Heath stretched his arms, yawning. "Let's

get our plunder together, folks. Cherokee, have a look at the horses. See how they weathered it out."

The half-breed tramped away toward the arroyo. Christy tried shaking the sand from her clothing, then gave it up. "Lordy, Jack, I need a bath."

Heath gave her a faintly amused look. "Well, make it quick, angel. That's if you've a taste for another sand scrubbing."

"What?"

"Go see for yourself."

She slogged through the loose, ankle-deep sand to one of the lava basins. She halted and stared, then eyed Heath with a cool disgust. "It's half-full of sand. And dry as a bone, no less."

"Naturally it is, my dear. Sand particles in a storm like that one are so charged and dry, they literally draw up moisture like a sponge."

"Got that out of some fancy-ass book, didn't you?"

Heath laughed.

Christy was in no mood for what he considered humorous. She went back to the hollow where they had taken refuge, dug her saddle free of the sand, and shook her soogans out. Jason Drum was sitting against a nearby rock, dust caked and dazed. Christy regarded his bruised face without much sympathy; she was still sore from his roughing her up. Then she noticed his hands, the fingers discolored and swollen like sausages from the brutally tight ropes on his wrists, and had to steel herself against pity. He had it coming, she thought. She'd been sure of persuading Jack to set him free at the border. Now, she was far from certain. . . .

Cherokee came up from the arroyo, leading two horses. As always his dark face was unreadable, but Christy thought he looked glummer than usual. He halted, looking at Pete and Clayt Ermine as he spoke.

"Horses all gone. All but these."

"Gone?" Heath paused in the act of lighting a cheroot. "What do you mean, gone?"

"They pull pickets, drift away with storm. These two deep in rocks, they stay. All others gone."

Everyone looked at the two Ermines now, and Miguel murmured, "*¡Jesus Maria!*"

"Pulled their pickets," Heath echoed. "You two had charge of . . . for the love of God, didn't you put proper hobbles on the beasts?"

Pete Ermine's jowls had whitened under his whisker stubble; he cleared his throat. "Well, Christ," he muttered, "we ground-tied 'em good, and they was sheltered good in them banks, that should of . . ."

"You . . . stupid . . . bastards." Trask Ermine spoke with an ominous quiet, staring at his brothers. "Something that simple, you can't do it right. Too damn simple for you jugheads!"

Heath gazed at the tip of his cheroot. "Well, gentlemen. You've landed us in a pretty fix. What do you think happens now?"

At once Trasks's anger veered; his stare pounced at Heath. "Way I reckon, that ain't for you to say. Much your doing as anyone's, holding us here till that storm hit. You want to spike any Ermine's gun on that score, why, you just start with me."

Christy tensed, glancing quickly at Jack. Now it happens, she thought. But Heath only smiled; he flicked a match alight on his thumbnail and touched it to his cheroot. "Ah," he murmured, "the old clan fealty never falters. Charming. But recriminations are rather futile now, aren't they? Assuming that even the sawdust brains of an Ermine can grasp that elemental fact, I'd suggest we save our energies for dealing with the problem at hand."

Dallas Redmile moved between the two men casually, not looking at either of them. "How you size it, Cherokee? Any chance o' catching up them horses?"

The half-breed shrugged. "We go look, mebbeso. But I think no good. Long gone, horses, hours gone. The sand, she's cover all the track."

"Well, then," Dallas said quietly, dryly, "reckon on a maybe that sizeable, we best not waste our strength looking. There's Tubac over by the border, closest place I know of we might get horses. We got a full canteen o' water apiece, that's something. Will hold us for a day or so. Got two horses for two people. They can ride to Tubac and fetch back mounts for the rest."

Heath rubbed his chin. "It'll be chancy, old pal. There's law at Tubac, and I'd wager it has the word on us. Even a pair of strangers who ride in might be seized and questioned. And if even one person in the place could identify either of 'em . . ."

"Well, reckon my face be the least known. And Christy, ain't nobody likely to spot her. Supposin' ole Jamison the prospector and his she-whelp handle this job? Seems the best bet, Jack."

"Un momento," Miguel put in. "Maybe there's a better way, eh? A cousin of mine, he got a place over east on the San Cruces, little ways above the border. He raise horse to sell. Is a longer ride than Tubac. But a couple of us start now, we get back tomorrow night with the horses, I think."

"This cousin," said Heath. "He knows all about you?"

"Sí," Miguel grinned. "All. But he is the son of my mother's brother. His little boy is name' after me. He sell us horses and keep his mouth shut, *jefe.* His *vaqueros* too, they say nothing."

"Good, good. That's settled. We'll set out at once, you and I. . . ."

"Cap'n," Trask Ermine said gently, "you don't ride out of here with that poke of money. Not before we split on it, you don't."

"Did I say I was?" Heath clucked his tongue sadly, shaking his head. "No trust. That's the trouble with this trade. Absolutely no one trusts an honest thief. Get those saddlebags, Dallas, and we'll set about satisfying the common avarice."

Dallas brought the saddlebags, hunkered down, and spilled the packets of greenbacks out on the sand. With everyone watching, he counted out the notes by denominations, an equal share to each of the men and Christy.

"There you are, Trask," said Heath. "Exactly as we agreed. Satisfied?"

Ermine bent down and picked up a stack of greenbacks

and handed it to Cherokee. He handed two more to his
brothers and then straightened up, pocketing his share.

"I'm satisfied. I surely hope you are, Cap'n, for that
settles our bargain, far as I'm concerned. Soon as you get
back with them horses, we are dusting out of here. We
ain't doing it in your company. That understood?"

"You strike me to the quick, Trask. You really do.
Haven't I dealt on the square with you fellows?"

"Yeah, in a backhanded way," Trask said softly. "You
just rub me against the fur, Cap'n. You're hard-nosed
when there's no call, then you laugh up your goddam
sleeve at a man. I don't like that. I don't like you. So we'll
just call it quits hereafter."

"Soon as I've brought you horses, don't you mean?"

"Yeah, that's what I mean. You won't run no sandy either, not with your woman and Redmile left with us."

"Why, that's quite perceptive of you, Trask," Heath
said with open sarcasm. "You'll get your horses, you and
your rancid brotherhood. You'll pay for 'em out of your
shares, too."

The Ermines and Cherokee pulled off by themselves,
while Christy and Dallas helped Heath and Miguel ready
their gear and saddle up. They packed their bedrolls,
some provisions, and a canteen of water each.

"How's your arm doing, Miguel?" Christy asked.

"Ha. It hurt some, but I'm think it be good enough."
The Mexican chuckled. "I don' ride on my arm."

"What about your leg, Jack?"

"Better than it was. I'll hold up all right."

"I hope so. You think we might have a minute together?"

Heath nodded. "I mean us to, angel. Let's find some
privacy. . . ."

They walked down the arroyo till they were cut off
from the others. Then they stopped; Heath reached for
her, but she pressed lightly away from his arms.

"Jack, what will you do with the boy when we get to
the border?"

He smiled crookedly. "Angel, I'm just not of a mood
for talking about boys."

"All the same—" She tightened her arms against him, holding him back. "We'll talk about it."

"What he deserves, after yesterday, is to have his neck wrung. I don't like a man roughing you about."

"I don't cotton to it myself," she said dryly. "But I can't blame him for trying to get away. So would you, if you felt like a lone virgin in a gang of rapists. Never felt that way myself, of course. . . ."

Heath threw back his head and laughed. "All right, angel. Have it your way. No harm letting him go free, I suppose . . . at the border." He eyed her quizzically. "You haven't let that kid get under your skin, have you?"

Christy felt her face warm a little. "Well, you know I was a mother once. Not for long, but I know the feeling."

He laughed again. "You're saying the lad touches your maternal wellsprings? Well, so long as that's all he touches. . . . Funny thing with you, Christine. You've never really lost those nice shiny stars in your eyes, have you?"

"I dunno. . . . I suppose in a way not. I suppose I'd like to stop sometime. Just stop and live awhile. Haven't you ever thought of stopping, Jack?"

"Never for long, angel. To keep moving, to keep going always. That's all of living, for me. You know that."

"I know. But why is it?"

"Does it matter? Call it excitement. Call it a living. Call it any damned thing you please." He smiled, but his eyes were hard and unamused. "You haven't talked like that before. How deep does it go, Christine? Are you thinking of cutting loose?"

"Who doesn't, sometimes? When there's one too many stones in the beans. One too few drinks left in the canteen. Sure, I think about it."

"Perfectly all right. To think about it."

Again the smile streaked white across his dark face. His hands reached and settled lightly on Christy's supple waist, then sleeked down over the swelling flare of her hips. Gently, insistently, those hands pulled her in until the tips of two firm, pointed breasts nudged against his chest. As always, the hard animal vitality of him sent a taut throb of desire through the girl.

She threw her head back, lips parting. "Jack," she whispered. "Oh Jack. . . ."

He kissed her shut eyes, her nose and cheek and the hammering pulse in her throat. Then his mouth sought the wide soft lips. For a time Christy let herself surrender to the fierce sweetness of lovers' kisses. Then she twisted determinedly against his arms and pulled free.

"Don't get carried away, boy. Not now and not here."

"Why not?" he chuckled. "All right. There'll be time, plenty of time. . . ."

Christy stood at the edge of the lava beds, watching Heath and Miguel ride toward the southeast. When a lopsided dune cut them from view, she turned back toward the camp, feeling a kind of weary despondency.

There was, she knew, no way of changing Jack Heath. Other women—he'd never been shy about letting her know—had tried it before her. You went along or you dropped out. I want to stop, she thought, so bad I can taste it, but I want him too. Oh, damn damn damn!

Dallas had untied Jason Drum, letting him sit on the ground and rub feeling back to his mangled wrists. Dallas sat on a rock a few yards away, idly holding a gun on him. She walked over and halted by Jason, saying stonily, "You'll be set loose. Jack give his word. Think you can manage to be a good boy till then? Because if you cut any more capers, you'll be a dead one sure."

He lifted his head, eyeing her silently.

"You're welcome," she said coldly.

"Thanks."

He said it with a soft irony that surprised her a little. He wasn't a good-looking kid, but his eyes, dark and oddly brooding, got to her somehow, as they had from the first. Dallas gave her one of his dry, probing looks. Turning away, she was aware that her face was warming again. Damn them, she thought, suddenly and bitterly unsure of herself; damn all men.

XII

THE STORM WAS over; but the dust-laden sky continued
to diffuse the sun's rays into a sallow glow, and it threw a
silent gloom over the camp as the day wore on. A fire was
built and some grub was cooked. Jason felt a little better
after he was given something to eat and a few swallows of
water. Then Dallas tied his hands again, but not so tightly, and left his legs free so he could walk slowly up and
down under Dallas's watchful eye. They'd take no more
chances with him, but it didn't really matter; he was still
so sore from the beating that any wish to attempt escape
was pretty well dampened. It seemed his best hope was to
follow Christy's advice and not tempt the outlaws' anger
again. If Heath had given his word to free him eventually,
he might as well accept it as the best of bad choices.

There was nothing to do now but wait, and the Ermine
brothers began to chafe with waiting. Pete and Clayt
broke out bottles of whiskey, taking long slugs of the stuff
that did nothing to sweeten their dispositions. Both were

growing ugly and restless. Trask merely walked up and down, smoking one cigarette after another, and staring off toward the saffron horizon. Cherokee stretched out on the sand, tipped his hat over his face, and went to sleep. Christy and Dallas kept apart from the four of them, remaining on one side of the camp with Jason.

"I hope to God Jack and Miguel don't delay getting back," Christy muttered. "Sooner we're shed of this crew, the better."

"Yeh, they're a sore-footed lot." Dallas dug out his stubby pipe and chewed the stem ruminatively. "Course Jack didn't help matters none, rubbing 'em all ways to Sunday."

She smiled thinly. "Seems he just can't help himself."

Clayt Ermine came lurching their way. He halted and looked carefully at Christy, his eyes inflamed and out of focus. He said, "Have a drink," and held out his bottle.

"Go away," she said coldly.

"It's gonna be a cold wait, Red. You oughta warm up a little."

"Listen, you miserable—"

"Clayt!" Trask Ermine's voice came flat and warning. "No more of that. You hear me?"

"Hell with you, big brother. I do what I goddam feel like."

Trask came stalking across the camp. He grabbed the bottle away and flung it against a rock. Then he doubled up Clayt's shirtfront in both hands, shaking him. "Damn your weasel guts, we got enough troubles! You ain't stirring up more!"

He flung Clayt stumbling back across the camp, hustling him along with a hard kick. Walking over to Pete then, Trask held out his hand. "Let's have it." There was a dangerous edge on his tone, and Pete silently and sullenly handed over his bottle. Trask sailed it into the rocks.

"I can handle my snake juice all right," Pete grumbled. "Wa'n't no call for that."

"That's right. Hell, you don't need hooch in you to go on a pizen-eyed mean. It just gets you worse. You two got ants in your asses, why'n't you go hunting or something?"

Pete blinked owlishly. "What we hunt for?"

"Some brains, maybe. Hell, I don't know. Ask Cherokee."

The half-breed lifted his hat off his face. "You want hunt? Bighorn, maybe antelope?"

"Bet your ass," said Pete. "But I ain't see no game like that about."

"Plenty track around tanks before sand come. Plenty game water here, but not come when man around. You want hunt, you walk. Maybe walk long time, we find game."

"Good," Trask grunted. "We'll walk, then. Get our edges off, maybe get some meat into the bargain."

Clayt had slumped down on his heels, rubbing his belly. He had a sickly look. "You men go on. I don't feel good."

"Jesus," said Trask, shaking his head wearily. "I knew it. All right, get it up if you can. Then you best take to your blankets and sleep it off. Heath gets back, we are losing no time dusting away from here. Don't want you dragging along sick. Recall once you drunk too much shitty rotgut, you was sick for three days."

Clayt didn't reply. He climbed to his feet and went hunching away, his head down. Off behind some rocks, he began retching sickly. Pete gave a coarse chuckle and picked up his rifle, checking the action. "Let's get hunting, all right? Man, my mouth's watering already. Could put away 'bout a dozen juicy rump steaks by myself."

"You could put away the whole carcass yourself, you damn hog," said Trask. He watched Clayt come trudging back and throw himself on his bedroll. "You be all right, kid?"

Shuddering, Clayt pulled the blankets around him. He managed a nod.

"We fetch you back a nice feed, kid," leered Pete. "Ha-ha! Good juicy rump steak, how's 'at sound?"

Trask gave him a savage prod. "Come on, let's go. Cherokee, you lead out. Find us some track."

The three of them tramped away. For a while there was silence, except for Clayt giving out a muffled groan now and then. Finally Christy yawned. "Dunno why, but somehow all this has made me very sleepy."

"Catch yourself some shut-eye," said Dallas. "I'll keep a watch. Till Jack gets back, might be a good thing if one or t'other of us is allus awake. We can spell each other, how 'bout it?"

"Considering the company, I call that a dandy idea, old booger."

Christy spread her blankets in the shade and lay down. Dallas said, "Got your kinks worked out, kid?" Jason nodded. "Catch some sleep yourself, then. Anyway sit down. Sight o' bother watching you on your feet."

Jason stretched out. He felt drowsy almost at once, warmth of sun and sand working into him. And he dozed. He wasn't sure for how long. A sharpness of voices roused him. He raised his head. Dallas had gone to sleep, head resting on his shoulder, and Jason's gaze moved past him.

Clayt Ermine was kneeling by Christy, and she was pulling away from him. He laid a hand on her. "C'mon, Red, you know what a man needs, you been up the hill and down again. Hell, you been shaking it at ever'body in camp. C'mon now, be nice to a man, nobody got t' know. . . ."

"Get away from me, you drunken slob!"

Her hand fetched Clayt a slap across the jaw that jolted him back on his heels. The pistol-shot impact of it made Dallas's head jerk up. "Huh? . . ."

Clayt lurched to his feet, holding his jaw. His drink-mottled face wore the imprint of the blow, one hard enough to half-sober him. Slowly his look changed from disbelief to hot rage.

"You barnyard bitch!" he bawled. "You get what-for now, by God!"

Abruptly Christy squirmed sideways out of his reach, trying to get to her jacket and the gun a couple yards away. Realizing her intent, Clayt made a stumbling dive; he pinned her flat to the ground. Dallas, on his feet now, was moving toward them with a stiff haste. He jammed his rifle into Clayt's back.

"Quit that! Get off her, you bastard, or I'll open you up like a can o' tomaters. . . ."

Clayt rolled half-upright, his face twisted in a mindless snarl. Suddenly his hand shot out and grabbed the rifle, twisting the barrel aside. Then he was fully on his feet, wrestling Dallas for the weapon. Wrenching it from the old man's frail hold, he knocked him staggering. Dallas kept his feet, and then he went back to the attack like a feisty terrier.

Clayt swung the rifle up and down, smashing the butt against Dallas's head. It was a full-armed blow dealt with crushing force. Dallas reeled aside, took a couple of faltering steps, and fell on his face. He lay with arms and legs flung out, his body twitching.

Jason sat up, savagely twisting his wrists against the ropes. Christy screamed and went for the jacket again. Wheeling around, Clayt flung the rifle aside and seized a handful of her hair. As he hauled her to her feet, she turned on him, kicking and clawing. Clayt held her away one-handed, pulled back his other hand, and gave her a wicked clout. Half-stunned, she sagged down against his hold.

Jason quit fighting his ropes. He braced his back to a rock, pulled his heels up beneath his rump, and shoved himself upright. Clayt's back was partly turned to him. Jason balled his whole body and barreled at him in a low lunge. Clayt caught movement from the tail of his eye; he let go of the girl and started coming around, too late. Jason's head was sunk tight between his shoulders; he turned one shoulder for the impact as he slammed sidelong into Clayt.

His weight knocked Clayt sprawling. Unable to halt his momentum, Jason tried to hurdle the downed outlaw but tripped and went down across him. Clayt heaved Jason's legs away and scrambled to his feet. His hand dived for the knife at his hip. Jason kicked wildly; his heel cracked against Clayt's shin and drove his leg from under him, Clayt hit the ground again, spun on his side to get clear of

Jason, and then sprang to his feet. He whipped out the knife.

Desperately throwing his strength into one muscle-cracking effort, Jason surged up onto his heels. He straightened his legs and floundered up, tottering wildly for balance. In that instant Clayt took a long step, his knife snaking in and out. Jason felt his shirt tear and the burn of cold steel; he saw Clayt's red-streaked blade pull back for another thrust.

Jason leaped blindly aside, still off balance, and his foot struck Dallas's leg. He fell heavily, lit on his side, and then twisted over on his back as Clayt came after him.

Jason lashed out with both feet, but Clayt kept just out of reach, swiftly circling now. Not quite as helpless as an upended turtle, Jason tried to turn with him, but he couldn't turn quickly enough. He jerked his head away from Clayt's vicious kick, but it caught him at the joining of neck and shoulder.

It flooded his brain with a black pain that was sickening, literally paralyzing; for a moment he couldn't see. He lay helpless, open to the knife thrust he expected.

Then gun-roar filled Jason's ears. He felt the jolt of a falling weight.

When he could see again, he realized that Clayt Ermine's body lay crumpled across him. Christy stood there, looking dazed as she lowered her pistol. She had shot Clayt in the back of the head.

Jason heaved upward; ragged pain blazed in his side. He pushed up again, and this time succeeded in rolling Clayt off him.

Dallas quivered and groaned. Christy dropped the pistol and fell on her knees beside him. She managed to turn him on his back. Dallas lifted his head; blood streamed down his face, but more than a blow on the head had felled him. He was hemorrhaging; blood flecked his lips. His eyes seemed remote and sunken as they looked toward Clayt's body.

"Don't mind me . . . sister . . . get out. Get out o' here . . . or you be dead . . . boy too."

His head sagged back.

"Dallas!" Christy wept. She shook him by the shoulders. "Dallas!"

Jason maneuvered slowly and laboriously to his knees. "Cut me loose," he said huskily.

She didn't seem to hear him. He yelled the words. She looked at him blankly and then, moving in a daze, came over and sliced away his ropes. Staggering to his feet, Jason stood swaying dizzily.

"He's done. We got to get out of here."

"We? . . ." Christy stared at him. "No."

She touched Dallas's face; its color was ebbing to a slow grayness. "I can't just leave him, he's . . . he's not dead."

"He be dead in a little while. He's dying, can't you see that? We got no time to lose." Jason reached for a reserve of strength and raised his voice to a shout, hammering the words at her. "Didn't you hear what he said? They come back, we be dead people for sure! That shot'll fetch 'em—and you just killed their brother!"

As simple as that. There was nothing else to do, and the sense of it reached her then. As they hastily threw together two small packs of grub, water, and blankets, Jason's mind was working coldly. Packing light, they could carry two canteens of water apiece. Deliberately now, he gathered up the other canteens, unstoppered them one by one, and poured the water out. Then he hurriedly dumped all the excess grub on the ground and began savagely stamping it into the sand.

"They follow us," he muttered, "they'll do it dry and hungry."

Christy watched him dully. "They'll follow, you can bet on it. They'll follow us all the way to hell."

"It ain't far away, I reckon," Jason said grimly, bitterly. "I been living on the hot edge of it since I met you people."

He tramped over to Clayt, knelt down and ripped his shirt open, then uncinched the bulky money belt around the dead outlaw's waist.

Christy said shrilly, "What're you doing?"

"What's it look like? Getting what's mine. What I started out for."

"Oh sure, your money." She gave a harsh peal of laughter. "Your goddam money. Eight hundred seventy-five dollars! Not a cent less, right?"

It was easy to follow the tracks left by Heath's and Miguel's horses in the fresh-drifted sand. If there was any place of refuge close by, ranch or town or mining camp, neither Jason nor Christy knew how to find it. So they followed the tracks. On foot they couldn't hope to overtake the pair, but if they could keep ahead of any pursuit long enough, they might meet up with Heath and Miguel on their way back, maybe sometime tomorrow.

For about an hour they tramped at a hard, steady pace, hoping to pull a good lead. The big question was whether the Ermines and Cherokee would take up their trail at once, gambling on catching up before they got far, or whether they'd place first priority on finding food and water. Christy pessimistically allowed that they'd be in such a sweat to avenge their brother, they'd make the former choice. Even if they didn't, she pointed out, locating water and edibles might not take them long. Cherokee knew the country well, knew where good water could be found or dug for—perhaps along this same route. A tracker of uncanny ability, the half-breed could find game or improvise food from desert plants. At least he hadn't come on game by the time Clayt was killed; they'd heard no shooting.

The lemon-colored haze was fading, the sun burning low to the west. But darkness was still hours away, and Jason wondered if he could keep going that long. He had balled a piece of cloth torn from a blanket, pressing it tight to his side as he tramped along. Clayt's knife had entered shallowly between two of his ribs; he didn't think it was much of a wound. But it continued to bleed steadily, soaking the whole side of his shirt, then his trousers; finally he felt blood puddling in his boots.

Christy was watching him, and she said abruptly, "Let's stop. I'm going to tie that off."

Jason didn't argue. He peeled his shirt off and settled wearily on his hunkers, keeping an eye on their back-trail while Christy cut more strips from the blanket. Then she swabbed the wound clean. Opening a small sack of flour they'd packed along, she plastered handfuls of its cool whiteness over the cut. With the bleeding checked, she applied a thick compress to his side and tied it in place.

"That'll have to do you, boy. Afraid it won't help for long. What you need is rest."

Jason shook his head doggedly. "Got to keep going till dark. We don't know how close they are."

Christy straightened up and studied the sky. "Funny," she muttered. "The sun was clear awhile there, after the dust settled. Now it's darkening over again."

"Uh-huh. I think it might be brewing up a storm. A wet one this time."

"Just what we needed. Let's fix our stuff so it'll carry better, all right?"

They took the time to wrap their grubsacks in their soogans; tying them up again, they lashed their rifles to the outside of the blanket rolls. Slinging these compact bundles to their backs, they found the going a good deal easier.

They pushed on, scanning the back-trail often. The land was inclining slowly upward; its barren scape was rock studded and lifeless, except for more kinds of cacti than Jason had ever seen and, here and there, the spiky clustered canes of ocotillo. A black bulge of sheer rock grew out of the skyline ahead: a massive tilted shelf where the earth's crust had buckled in some bygone age, it formed a long rambling cliff that ran north and south. Didn't look as if it could be scaled, yet the tracks headed straight for it.

Meantime the heat had built oppressively, piling around them like layers of damp wool. A wind kicked up, hot and gritty. The clouds driving out of the west were swollen and dark bellied, and Jason guessed they were in for a genuine cloudburst. There was no cover here, but there might be some up by that cliff.

Jason felt a weary drag in his muscles; he was growing
light-headed. Pain shot knifelike through his side, and the
wound was starting to leak again. He'd never last till
dark, he knew. But he slogged on, letting Christy lead the
way now.

Nearing the black cliff, they saw that several deep
chasms split it from top to base. The horse tracks led into
one of these. They entered it, finding themselves in a narrow defile whose rock-littered floor tended gradually upward. Its walls tapered so tightly overhead that the rims
almost met. The place felt like a gloomy trap. Jason was
glad when the sides widened out above, though the bottom of the cleft remained so cramped they had to proceed
along it singly.

Thunder cannonaded, shaking the earth. The first fat
raindrops fell. With unbelievable swiftness then, the sky
split open and drenched them to the skin. In less than a
minute the floor of the gorge was roiling with ankle-deep
water.

"We better hustle," Christy said. "Come on, hurry it
up!"

"What's the difference?" Jason said tiredly. "We're
soaked through. . . ."

"It's a bad place for us, bub. You ever been caught in
the open during one of these . . . an Arizona cloudburst?
Well, I have. Flats miles wide covered with water in a few
minutes. Think of that much water pouring into a little
old gully like this, you can figure what'll happen. But I
never thought this damn gorge 'ud go on near so far.
Come on, shake into it now."

The gorge bottom grew rougher and steeper as they
climbed, and the water deepened at an alarming rate, ca-
scading in torrents off the steep-sloping walls and funnel-
ing into the passage. As it swirled knee-high around their
legs, Christy splashed to a stop. She whirled, grabbing Jason's arm. There was pure terror in her face.

"God, I can't even see the end of this thing, and we'll
be rushed off our feet in another minute!" She yelled the
words over the roar of thunder and water. "We got to
climb . . . climb out of it. That way!"

She pointed at the rugged slant of one wall. It was a little less precipitous than the other, and by now the rimrock had tipped a lot lower, rounding off along its upper half. If they could make it that far, they'd be safe. But those few yards of treacherous lower wall might be unscalable unless they could lend each other a hand.

Jason sized up a ledge a couple feet above his head; it appeared solid enough. He didn't say anything, just pointed at it, then stooped and cupped his hands together. Christy set her heel in his palms; he boosted her as high as he could, then braced himself against her weight. The exertion slashed red pain through his side, and now the water was sweeping higher than his knees. From up-canyon came a sullen bellow as the full force of the flood came boiling down toward them. Once it hit, if he were still on his feet, he'd be carried away like a cork, drowned or battered to death on the flinty walls.

Christy was clawing frantically at the ledge, trying to gain enough purchase to hike herself atop it. Her effort scaled away pieces of rotted stone that pelted down on Jason. "Hurry up!" he yelled. His arms numbed into his shoulders against the strain of her weight; the agony of his side blazed into his chest.

Then the weight left his hands, as Christy succeeded in scrambling onto the shelf .

A moment later, sprawled flat with only her head and shoulders showing, she thrust an arm down to Jason. He gripped her wrist; he found a slight foothold and began inching himself upward. He used Christy to steady rather than support him, picking holds with his feet and one hand carefully, knowing his full weight would yank her off the ledge.

The stub of rock broke under his foot; his holds slipped, and he dropped back into the water, falling to his knees. He was almost swept under before he fought back to his feet. The water reached nearly to his waist, and its increasing roar yanked his glance up-canyon. The flood's solid front was bucketing down toward him, raging and frothing between the walls.

Panic fed Jason's muscles as he seized Christy's arm

again, barely picking his holds now as he climbed with a furious haste.

His free hand grabbed the projecting rock, and he clung desperately to it. Then Christy's other hand caught hold of that wrist. Crouched above him now, heels braced, leaning back to take his weight, she yelled "Hold on!" as the savage crush of water struck his body. It churned up to his waist, chest, armpits; it would have wrenched him away but for Christy's holds.

Then the first giant thrust of flood was past him, and Jason could partly brace himself against its powerful tug. The water climbed no higher, but for a frightening moment he wondered if Christy's strength would be enough to pull his body free of it.

For the moment it was all she could do just to hold on. Jason treadwheeled his legs wildly, trying to gain some traction with his feet. His right toes hooked solidly in a crevice; he pushed suddenly upward. Christy fell over backward, still gripping his wrists.

Inch by inch, fighting against a leaden exhaustion, he hauled himself up beside her.

For long moments they crouched in the driving rain, just resting. Then, holding onto each other, they tackled the last yards of the wall, which curved roughly inward now. After collapsing on the rimrock, they looked dazedly around them. The summit of this tilted height was a tortured jumble of rock wrenched loose by ancient convulsions, scarred and pitted by erosion.

Spotting a kind of hollow formed by the gap between two tilted slabs, they crawled over to it. Wedging themselves side by side within it, they were partly cut off from the slashing rain. There they huddled, shivering like a pair of drenched rats, and waited for the storm to play itself out.

XIII

VAL PENMARK AND Anita Cortinas were crouched under an overhang in the lee of a high-shouldered ridge that pretty well cut off the blast of wind and rain. Taking shelter here before the storm had hit, they'd found a pack rat's nest that had yielded a good store of wood, enough to keep them supplied through the night. Their three horses, the paint mustang and two Apache ponies, had been restless and skittish when the thunder and lightning began, but the fire had its calming effect. Horses accustomed to campfires generally found something soothing in them, and Penmark hobbled the animals close in, so they could move toward or away from the fire.

Heading south away from the place where Penmark had ambushed the two Apaches, they had made good time. There was sound reason for wanting to, one of the Apaches having gotten away. Penmark had guessed, from the sheep carcass on their packhorse, that the pair had been sent out from Cayetano's band to get fresh meat. So the main bunch wasn't far away, and going by what he

knew of Cayetano's habits, Penmark had figured it likely
the war chief wouldn't find it inconvenient to seek retri-
bution for the killing of a warrior of his. The one who'd
gotten away would lead the band to the spot in no time. It
was important for the good of the dead man's soul to see
him properly buried; then they'd set out to punish the
ones responsible. The sign would tell his comrades that
one white-eyes had done the job and that his only companion was a woman. Overtaking the two would be a
matter of pride and anger, for Apache war bands were
small; a war chief couldn't afford the loss of even one
seasoned brave. Since Cayetano was swinging generally
back south anyway, it seemed a good guess he'd pick up
the southward trail of his man's killer.

At least that was how Penmark sized it, and his blunt
reasoning had convinced 'Nita too. She felt a numb terror
of the Apache menace that might be dogging their trail,
and she thought of the outlaws ahead of them. It was like
feeling caught between two fires. But at least they had
horses; they had plenty of food and water, and somehow
the presence of the big grim-eyed gringo gave her a sense
of assurance that helped keep fear in its place. His mad
intent made her more than a little uneasy, but that was
another thing.

Earlier today, they had seen the sandstorm from a distance, a brown shroud that yellowed the far sky, and
Penmark had guessed it would blanket the whole region
of Arrowhead Tanks well to north and south. But he
knew the outlaws had been bound for there, remembering
their mention of the place. So he wasn't greatly perturbed
by the fact that sand would obliterate the track he'd followed this far. He knew where the Tanks were, not much
over a day's ride now. If Heath's gang had gotten no farther before the storm came, he could pick up more sign
from there, or maybe catch the outlaws still encamped
there.

'Nita wasn't at all enthused by the prospect, but her
mind had settled into a resigned fatalism by now. She had
cast her lot with the big gringo's; she was willing to share
his fate come what might, even die by his side if she must.

Wind snaked in beneath the overhang and guttered the fire, throwing a wild blend of light and shadow beyond its pocketing glow. Except for the occasional chill of wind, 'Nita felt snug and dry, and there was something companionable in the way the horses had pulled near, sharing an oasis of light and warmth with two humans. She and Penmark had made a good meal of wild mutton, frying strips of it in the skillet and wolfing it down hungrily. The meat was tough and greasy, it had a strong wild flavor she wasn't used to, but it was hot and filling as nothing she'd eaten in days had been. 'Nita felt stuffed and relaxed.

She made small rambling talk, telling Penmark of little things in her past life. Matters she might contemplate with sadness, but no longer with that first tearing sense of loss. So much had happened to her in a few days, a violent succession of events rocking her world apart, that already her past had blurred at the edges, taking on something of the unreality of a dream. Later it might all return with a bitter sharpness. But here and now, soothed by a sum of simple animal comforts, she could speak of trivialities with a wistful pleasure—of *Abuelito's* handskills with wood and leather, of a pet lizard she had once kept, of a red dress she'd prized and had liked to put on sometimes, though there were no holidays to celebrate and no company in which to wear it at lonely Corazon.

So she chattered idly, not knowing whether Penmark was listening or not. He stared at the silvery gouts of rain dripping from the overhang, never moving except to throw more wood on the fire. His thoughts were his own, grim and forbidding thoughts from his expression; but then his expression was always the same. Maybe he was thinking of how the rain could add to his tracking problems.

Talking in her own language gave a freer rein to her thoughts, and she knew that *el viejo's* Spanish was much better than her English. In their time together he'd unbent enough now and then to clarify in her own tongue a point which she found difficult to grasp in his, but always with a sour impatience that let her know he resented the doing.

So they did nearly all their conversing in their own languages, and it worked surprisingly well.

'Nita could be just as stubborn, and also she enjoyed exercising her voice again. She was satisfied when, finally, she stirred a grunt of annoyance from him.

"I don't know it's so grand you lost that cinch on your tongue," he growled. "You ain't hardly quit wagging it."

"I like to talk. Is that so bad?"

"Best women know when to keep their mouths shut."

"When is that?" she asked innocently. "For you, *viejo*, I think that is never."

He hitched a cramp out of one haunch, scowling. "I tell you one thing—I am getting a crawful of being called that. How'n hell old you think I am?"

"I think you are as old as *Abuelito* was. He was fifty-nine."

"I ain't no fifty-nine," Penmark growled.

"It must be you remind me of *Abuelito*." She smiled a little. "I did not think of that before, but yes, some ways you are like him."

"Jesus. Like *your* grandpa?"

"*Sí.*"

"I never been nobody's grandfather," he snapped, "and I sure to hell ain't yours."

"Maybe you were not lucky then."

"Ha!"

For a time the two of them were silent, looking out at the rainy murk. Except when sheets of skyfire lit up everything brighter than day, all objects such as trees and rocks were an anonymous blur. It was as if the storm and night had cut them off from the world. Somehow the feeling increased 'Nita's sense of security in this crude oasis of theirs. She wiggled her feet comfortably inside the tall Apache moccasins, very glad now that Penmark had forced her to wear them.

Not that the gesture had implied anything but a cold practicality on his part. He simply didn't want her slowing him down for lack of being decently shod. Whatever streaks of tenderness were in the man lay buried and unreachable, she was sure. At best he felt a sense of bitter obligation toward her, mixed with a fleck or two of guarded gratitude. He had no room for any strong thought except vengeance on the man Jack Heath.

But I like him, she thought. I like this old gringo and I do not care what he thinks.

Penmark lowerd his head so the brim of his hat put his face in deep shadow. Then he said slowly, "I tell you, I don't know what's going to happen in the next day or so. It is going to be a damn tight thing when I catch up with them men. And them 'Paches may be at our backs somewhere, we don't know how close. It is a damn bad situation for you."

"Do not blame yourself for that. I—"

"Hellfire!" His face came up, his eyes steely with anger. "Who said a whit about blame? Ain't my fault if you dealt into my affairs. All the same, I'm beholden to you."

"You owe me nothing," she said stiffly.

As if he hadn't heard her, he went on, "Soon as any trouble shows, if we find it or it finds us, what I'll do is try to hide you. Put you in a place you'll be safe. I can't do no more."

"I have a rifle," she said quietly. "I can shoot. *Abuelito* taught me to shoot."

He did not reply. After a half-minute of trying vainly to read past the hard set of his face, 'Nita gave up. She was tired; abruptly she realized how tired, and there was no more to say. . . .

After the rain had slacked off to a steady drizzle, Jason and Christy looked around for better shelter. They were wet to the skin and bitterly chilled, and their only thought for the moment was of a place to get warm and dry. It would be dark before long, and once night closed down, they would have to stay where they were till morning. If the Ermines and Cherokee were anywhere behind them, they'd be occupied with the same problems. Meantime the rain would have wiped out all track, and any way out of their dilemma would have to wait till morning.

They stumbled along the ragged rim of the pass that

had almost claimed their lives, working across the tilted height till the gorge petered out. Then they were descending the far side of the vast rise, finding that it slanted off gradually on its east flank. But it was still rugged going, and the rain-slick rock made for treacherous footing. The gray daylight was starting to fade when Jason spotted what looked like the black mouth of a cave in the pitted scarp. They clambered over to it.

It was a cave all right, a fairly shallow one, so low-arched that even Christy had to bend over to enter it. But it was dry inside, floored with soft sand, and scattered with pack rats debris that would make a fire. Jason carefully beat every corner of the place with a stick in order to roust out any rats or snakes. Apparently there were no tenants in or out; the only animal droppings he found were old and powdery.

Christy had a packet of matches wrapped in oilcloth; it didn't take long to get a lively blaze going. When the two of them had thawed out, they peeled off their outer clothes and footgear and propped them on sticks by the fire. Their blanket rolls were dry enough, thanks to the waterproof tarp sheets they were wrapped in.

"We better look to that cut of yours," Christy said.

She knelt beside him and started to undo the bandage. Jason's face got warm; he said, "Uh, look, I'll take care of it."

"Stop fidgeting, dammit. You got your drawers on, haven't you?"

All the same, he didn't feel decently covered, and she wasn't by a far sight—not in a wet short-skirted chemise that hugged every nubile curve and hollow. But he sat still, looking self-consciously away as she peeled off the bandage. The compress was stuck fast to his flesh with blood-caked flour, and he gave a yowl as she jerked it away. Fresh blood welled over the livid edges of the wound. Christy washed it clean and bent close to inspect it, making him too aware of her body warmth.

"We got to close that off," she muttered. "There's something might help. Seen some of it growing close by this cave."

"What's that?"

"*Sangre de Cristo.* It's a plant with sap in it that dries quick. You can seal a wound with it. I'll fetch some."

Taking her knife, she stepped out in the rain. In a couple minutes she returned with a handful of half-coagulated fluid. The stuff burned like fury as she smeared it along the cut, but the bleeding was checked almost at once. As she put on another bandage, Christy said, "That ought to fix it all right. It's a clean wound, not like a bullet 'ud make. Jack showed me that trick with the plant."

"He's a smart man."

"Oh, he's that," she said dryly. "He has more twists in him than a sidewinder." She touched his forehead. "You cooking up a little fever there, Mr. Drum. Let's wrap you up nice and comfy, and you get some sleep."

Jason nodded dully. He was shivering despite the fire's warmth; his head throbbed sickly and his belly churned. Blood loss and the ordeals of the past few days were catching up. Christy spread out a groundsheet and a blanket and motioned him to lie down, afterward tucking a couple more blankets around him. Like a mother bundling up her infant, he thought, feeling downright foolish. But the feeling faded as a vast weariness crept over him. He shut his eyes. . . .

A fresh sputter and crackle of flames penetrated his last shred of consciousness, pulling his eyes drowsily half-open. Christy had dropped more wood on the fire, and now she straightened up. Standing sideways to him, she slipped the straps of her chemise off her shoulders; the wet garment slid down her legs and she stepped out of it.

For a heart-stopping moment he saw more naked loveliness than he had ever dreamed of. The high wash of flamelight made a pink witchery of the girl's creamy flesh, of her ripe and conical breasts stressed by two circling shadows, of the red-pink nipples tautly pointed from the rainy chill, of the flat belly and the flare of her mature hips, of the smooth beauty of her rounded thighs and the secret darkness where they joined.

She was so for only a moment; then she picked up a

blanket, threw it around her, and turned back to the fire.
Jason quickly closed his eyes again.

For a while his sleep was plagued by a succession of
bad dreams. Then he slept soundly. When he woke, it was
suddenly, and he lay blinking at a hint of steel-gray light
from the cave mouth. Then he raised his head. Christy
was sitting cross-legged on the other side of the fire, fully
dressed except for her moccasins.

"How you feeling?" she asked.

Jason sat up carefully and felt of his side. There was
hardly a twinge of pain—and the bandage was dry.
"Pretty good." He didn't quite meet her eyes. "Didn't you
get no sleep?"

"Enough." She yawned and raised a hand to pat her
close-cropped hair. "Much as I could with you sawing
wood all this time. It's 'most daylight. You hungry?"

"Yeah."

"I cooked up some bacon and bannock." She nodded
at the skillet beside him. "Go ahead. I ate. Our clothes
are dry, 'cept for your boots and my moccasins. You got
any ideas?"

Jason, about to set his teeth into a chunk of pan bread,
gave her a wary look. "Uh, ideas?"

"Yes, like how we'll pick up Jack's trail. That rain
pretty well done for his and Miguel's tracks."

He bit into the bread, frowning. "Maybe we ought to
stay where we are. They be back this way with the horses,
won't they?"

"Sure, but meantime there's our three friends back
there. Course our track's been wiped out too, and I
doused the fire before it begin turning light so's they won't
have any smoke to find us by. But they know the way we
was going, and that damn Cherokee knows this country
like you know your own bee-hee."

"We never raised no sight of 'em before the storm hit.
Maybe . . ."

"That's a big maybe, boy. They could be closer than
we know. Anyway, those damned Ermines will be out for

blood—ours. And you can bank they will start looking soon's it's full light. This cave is close to the head of that pass, and they'll be coming through it. You want to gamble that half-Injun don't spot it and come looking?"

Jason shook his head dismally. God, he felt used up. He was rested and cool-headed again, but plain used up where it counted, in the mind and guts. These past days had been an on-running nightmare of chasing or being chased, more brutally harrowing business compressed into a week than he'd known in his life. It was a nightmare from which there was no pinching himself awake. Where would it end? How?

"I reckon, soon's there's light enough, we best try to get our bearings and move on."

"Right you are, Drum." Christy grinned and reached over to pat his hand. "Maybe we'll get lucky for a change. Go on, wrap yourself around that grub."

Jason ate in silence for a moment. Then he said, "How you fall in with him anyway . . . Heath?"

"You might call it my destiny. As Jack says, 'It was jolly well your destiny, old girl.' " She made a face, letting her shoulders lift and settle. "I dunno. Does it matter?"

"It matters, sure. I mean, I want to hear it."

She made a pretty sketchy account of it, so that mostly he had to read between the lines. Her folks had lived on a busted-down farm in Illinois, and she supposed it was hating dirt and poverty—as much as getting with child by a neighbor lad—that had made her run away from home when she was sixteen. She'd had a notion of heading California way, but penniless and making her way by hook or crook, as she vaguely put it, she hadn't gotten farther than Tombstone before her baby was born. Some kindly people had helped her, and she'd set out to repay them by taking a job as entertainer at the Lady Gay Saloon.

"I could of made lots more at one of the girls' boarding houses, and believe you me, there was plenty of 'em in that place, but . . ." She shrugged. "Somehow it never seemed worth it."

"Boarding houses?"

"Uh-huh. Take it your daddy never told you about boarding houses."

"I reckon I know what you mean."

"Well, that's quick and bright of you, Jason." She patted his hand again. "Anyway . . . oh, what's to tell? My baby was sickly, he died after a year. And I started drifting. One place and then another. I was a gambler's shill for a spell. Then I met Jack. I guess," her mouth gave an ironic twist, "it was love at first sight."

"I just don't see . . ."

"What don't you, honey?"

"How you can have a feeling for a man like that."

"You don't, huh? Well, you have a lot coming to you." Her green eyes went flinty; she pressed her palms together and gazed down at them. "It don't matter what you call it. When you have a man, you stick by him, no matter where he goes or what he does. You maybe don't like much of what he does or the places it gets you into, but that's how it is." She smiled bleakly. "How's that for a declaration of principles?"

"I guess you're right," Jason muttered, looking away from her. "I got a lot to learn."

"You have, bub, you really have. You don't know anything, do you?"

A gently teasing note in her voice made him look at her again. She was smiling a little, her eyes softening. Then she came to her feet and moved to his side; she knelt in a quick movement, laying her hands on his shoulders. "It's time you learned," she whispered, and tipped her mouth into his. The soft wetness drew his senses like a drug, and he reached for her then, awkwardly. It was an embrace that began gently and turned swiftly, fiercely passionate.

Christy drew back a little in his arms, her face flushed. Her fingers brushed his cheek in a wondering, strangely tender way. "Honey, haven't you ever held a girl before?"

"I guess I ain't. Not like this, I mean. I don't much know what's to do."

"What you do," she said huskily, "is go on doing and don't stop. Do it, Jason."

XIV

THEY HAD RIDDEN steadily through the cool hours of false dawn. A little after sunrise they saw the black field of lava rock where Arrowhead Tanks lay. Penmark rode in slowly with his Sharps resting on his pommel, and 'Nita kept her rifle ready too. There was no smoke or other sign of life; nobody raised an alarm at their approach. They rode cautiously into the place and found it deserted.

The basins that had held water were filled with sand, 'Nita saw; sand had piled in deep fans against the rock slabs. People had been here after the sandstorm had swept over the place, as the wet char of a fire showed. But they had left before the rain came, for there was no other sign that she could see.

There was, however, the body of a man. It lay in its sodden clothing at one side of the sandy clearing between the tanks. Penmark dismounted and walked over to the body and bent down by it.

"Dead for a day anyways," he muttered. "Seems like somebody cracked his head for him."

"Do you know him?" 'Nita asked.

"Dallas Redmile."

The name meant nothing to her, and Penmark didn't trouble to enlighten her. He began walking back and forth over the damp ground, his face set like iron. From the tension of his body 'Nita sensed the frustration and rage he felt. Where had the people he was looking for gone from here? The question would be tearing at him. She wished he might call it quits now, give up his mad quest, but she had no real hope that he would. He was a man driven; if he had to continue his search on blind guess-work, he'd do so.

He halted by a shallow mound that more or less blend-ed into the rain-pounded texture of the surrounding earth. "Now," he murmured, "what's this here look like to you?" Not waiting for an answer, he heeled the butt of his rifle deeply into the mound. "Pretty loose. I lay odds someone's been planted here, and inside the last day or so."

"Maybe," 'Nita said uneasily, "it is only sand piled up by the wind."

"Now that might be, sis. It just might."

Penmark knelt down and started digging with his hands. Shock held 'Nita silent for a moment, and then she said softly, "But you will not desecrate the dead—if it is a grave."

"If it's a grave, somebody's in it," he grunted, pitching out handfuls of dirt. "I aim to see if that somebody's Jack Heath."

'Nita stepped to the ground and led her paint off a little way, keeping her back to Penmark. She did not want to see what he found. No good could come of disturbing the dead. The grave wasn't very deep; presently she heard him cease to dig, but she did not look around. If there was a body, she hoped it was not that of the young gringo Jason Drum. After a minute she heard a sound of earth being thrown back in the hole. She came slowly to Pen-mark's side as he carelessly finished mounding up the dirt again and stood up.

"Well, it ain't Heath. 'Pears to be one of the Ermine brothers. Never met none of 'em, so can't be sure. . . ."

"But two are dead. Why did they bury the one and not the other?"

Penmark rasped a hand across his gray-stubbled jaw. "Can't be sure of nothing, 'cept there was a fight here. This boy now, he got shot to death. Could be him and Redmile was on different sides. Or they had a falling out of some kind and done for each other, though that don't seem likely." He shrugged. "Your guess is good as mine."

"How will you find the people now?"

The bitter stubbornness etched harder into his face. "They left here before the rain or sometime after it started. Wherever they was when it stopped, they begin making sign again."

"But you do not know which way they went."

"They was going south to the border. I hazard they went on that way—straight south."

"The rain lasted a long time. If they rode on while it rained, they went a long way before it stopped."

He gave her that iron look. "Wasn't much daylight left when the rain started. Night was pitch dark. I don't reckon they traveled much last night. My guess, we're closer to 'em than we been yet. All right, be easy to miss their track where it picks up, even so. But south's a good guess, and that's where we're going."

As he spoke, his gaze swung north across the glittering flats they had crossed. The Apaches he believed were on their trail would be coming south too. Yesterday the two of them had sought shelter soon after the storm had begun. Though the Apaches ignored physical discomfort, they wouldn't stir while darkness held. They weren't likely to decamp till shortly before sunrise. So she and the gringo had a good lead on the Indians, 'Nita thought. But it would not help them that the sandstorm and later the rain had broken their trail in a couple of places, for the Apaches too would know of Arrowhead Tanks; and coming south to that favorite camp, they would find the trail once more if they had not picked it up again earlier.

Perhaps it was premonition, perhaps only her own terror of Apaches; whatever, a sinking dread gnawed at 'Nita. For her and the gringo, for others too, this bright day might be *Día de los Muertos*. It was a custom in old Mexico to hold a festival of the dead in order to mock Death, to show a human scorn of Death. But behind such mockery lay the shape of fear, a fear she could strongly taste.

The Day of the Dead. So it might prove to be.

Without more words they mounted and rode away from the lava field, holding the rising disc of sun to their direct left. 'Nita rode behind the gringo, watching the high set of his shoulders. What is the good of this? she thought despairingly. It would be such an easy thing to miss the track he sought. Yet find it or not, he would never stop. She had a vision of them riding a hot wasteland forever. . . .

Penmark pulled up. He had been scanning the land and the sky unceasingly, and now he was looking east, into the sun.

'Nita blinked several times against its blinding rays before she made out a smudge of smoke mounting against the sky. Penmark swung his horse that way now, and she reined alongside him.

"You were looking for smoke?" she asked.

"For smoke, for any likely thing. Wonder if a fire got laid just now or if I missed it before on account of the sun in my eyes."

"But would they go that way . . . east?"

"Sis, I don't know a damn thing. But it's worth following up."

The smoke was thinning away, and then its wispy banner showed no more. Penmark kept on, never turning his eyes from the distant hill that had marked its source.

They rode perhaps an hour while the sun climbed higher. It was out of their eyes by the time they reached the sharp rise of land. Halting at its summit, they looked down into a steep draw whose sides were covered with heavy brush and boulders. A trickle of smoke still rose from the remains of a fire, but nobody was in sight. Penmark dismounted and led the way to the pebbly bottom of the draw. Someone had thrown sand on the fire, but it must have smoldered a long time before it died.

Penmark began sorting out sign. Three men had been here, he said, two of them booted, one wearing moccasins. They had sheltered here during last night's storm, had dried out by the fire after the rain let up, and had gone on maybe a couple or three hours ago. This much he was able to read from the well-trampled ground around the fire, but it took him several minutes to find where, among the flanking rocks, the men had left the draw and resumed their trek.

The trail pointed eastward. But the surprise was all three men had been afoot.

"Are they the ones you look for?" the girl asked.

Penmark cuffed back his hat and scratched his head. "Maybe. Three of 'em anyway. But that don't spell out right. Less Redmile and the Ermine kid, it still leaves four people unaccounted for. Heath, his woman, a Mex, a half-breed, two Ermines, the Drum kid. That's seven. None of these three was a woman, that's all I'm sure of. And what the hell happened to their horses? They had extra saddle mounts, packhorses too. Nary a horse with this bunch."

He stood a moment staring bleakly at the ground, his jaw clamped.

"Maybe," 'Nita ventured, "these are not any of them, *viejo.*"

"Dammit, how many white men you going to find in this country at any time? It's got to be them, three of 'em. Something happened back at the Tanks. There was a fight, we know that part. I aim to find out the rest of it."

He climbed back to his saddle and took up the track of the three men, going eastward. But it was slow going; the way led over flinty and boulder-strewn terrain. Penmark sweated and cursed under the climbing sun. The hours were trickling away, and so was the precious time he had gained.

The land ahead sloped gradually up to a black cliff that seemed to run for miles north and south. They followed the trail through a tight gorge that cut upward through the cliff, petering out on its other side in a gentle slant. The country beyond continued rugged and broken up, but now the track showed plainer.

As they proceeded down the long slant, Penmark halted with a sharp oath. Stepping to the ground, he examined the ground closely.

The track of the three men had crossed another trail. Ahead of them, two other people had come off this long height and had proceeded east. A man and a woman. The woman had been wearing moccasins, and Penmark identified her as Heath's woman, the girl called Christy. Who the man was, he couldn't be sure. A good-sized fellow; might be Heath himself.

Anyway, the track of the three men had crossed onto theirs and was now following it. Penmark, wearing a fresh spur on his anger, pushed along hard and fast. The trail was the whole focus of his attention, and it was 'Nita who kept her eyes open on every side. Her sense of apprehension was deepening, and nothing that happened now would surprise her very much.

The land rose and fell in irregular patterns so that she couldn't see very far ahead or behind. It wasn't till they came atop a ridge that she was able to see a long way to their rear. Now she saw at once some moving dots that were riders, a number of them coming down the now-distant grade where the trails had crossed. Here they were clustering and then stopping, as if to inspect the new sign.

"Look, *viejo* . . ."

Penmark quartered his horse around and looked. Then he swore quietly and shook his head.

"I had a hope of sorts," he muttered. "Hoped if them 'Paches was behind us and found our trail again, they might give up once we turned east. No such luck, though, once they seen how fresh it was. We're skylined, girl. Let's get off of here."

They rode down the far side of the ridge; Penmark urged a quicker pace. Trying to hold alongside him, 'Nita cried, "What will we do?"

"Like I said I'd do if trouble found us. Hide you. Don't

know if that can be managed, but I'll try."

Some minutes later they rode into a crooked valley, which must have been carved out long ago by a stream that twisted down its center like a sparkling snake. Last night's rain had raised the water so that the creek roiled briskly and widely overflowed the valley floor in many places. Ages of weathering had worn most of the valley to bare shale, which was rotted and crumbling, studded with huge outcrops. Here and there where loose soil had blown into gaps and crevices, scrubby vegetation had taken root.

Penmark hauled up and looked around, studying the whole landscape. "This here's as good a place as any. You keep right behind me, hear?"

He reined into the shallow creek and turned upstream. Its bed was crumbled shale that would leave no sign at all. But it could not go on so forever, and then they would have to leave the water. Knowing they had gone upstream or down, all the Apaches would have to do was split their force.

As the valley rode toward its upper end, deltas of sand sloped in broad slashes to the water's edge. Penmark, leading the packhorse, abruptly swung out of the stream and up one such sandy bank. 'Nita followed him till they climbed their horses onto a naked shale ledge, and there Penmark halted. She looked back in dismay at the plain tracks their three animals had left in the sand. Then Penmark stepped down and broke off a branch of scrub next to the ground.

He crossed the sand to where they'd left the water, then began walking backward, carefully brushing the hoofprints smooth. Every couple feet he stopped, gathered up handfuls of the fine sand, and sifted it lightly over the brush marks. Now she understood. Leaving the water on solid rock, they would have left wet traces and fresh shale nicks that the Apaches could not miss. A sifting of dry sand would cover every particle of sign clear to the ledge.

When Penmark was done, a five-yard belt of unmarked sand lay between them and the stream.

'Nita said, "You think that will fool them?"

Penmark shook his head tiredly. "Sis, I don't know. They'll look for us to leave the water on a rock stretch. All we can gamble is they won't figure on no trick like this. On account of they look close, they'll see things you and me would never spot. From here on, even if we stick on rock, we'll leave sign. What we got to hope, they won't look too far off the bank. Let's move on. We got to find a place for you to lay up."

Afoot and leading their horses, the two moved northerly across the hot shale beds, trying now to avoid treading on sand. They worked slowly up the valley's boulder-littered north slope, and Penmark didn't pause till they reached the rim. Here he stopped, pulling the horses around back of a massive outcrop. Crouching behind it, he sighted down a crack between two jags of rock.

"This'll do. Now listen." He looked at her, talking slowly and spacing his words. "Keep your head down and watch through this slot. You can make out the whole valley. When they come, no matter what they do, you stay put less'n you see 'em come up that bank where we left the stream and then start up this way. Then you'll know they cut our sign, so you fork that nag of yours and run for it. Otherwise, you stay set till they are gone. I can't tell you where to go then. Maybe—"

Stiff-backed at being spoken to as a child, she snapped, "That does not have to be your concern."

"Suit yourself." He started to turn away.

"But you . . . you will not stay?"

"Told you I was looking to hide you, that's all. This here's as safe as I can make it for you. Me, I'm hustling on that trail I was on before it goes cold. Come this close, I don't aim to lose those birds now."

'Nita caught hold of his hand. "Wait, *por favor!* If the Apaches find nothing here, they will go on. They will follow the other trail, yes? The one left by the *ladrones* you seek?"

"Sure they will. Only I'll be well ahead of 'em. Heath's bunch, they're on foot. I'll catch up fast now."

"And then the Apaches will come."

"Then," he said impatiently, "it won't matter. Time

they catch up, I'll be a dead man or Jack Heath will be. After that it don't matter a whit."

She held tight to his hand. "Not to you. But I will care. I will care very much."

Penmark stared at her for a long moment, then said softly, "Ah, Jesus." But he didn't try to pull his hand away. "Look, it won't do. I held on this far for just one thing. You know that."

"Yes, but it is wrong. It is wrong to think of nothing but to kill a man. It is wrong to throw away your life." She hesitated. "It is wrong for you to leave me here."

"Sure, that's the most of it. You're scared."

"For you," she said simply.

Penmark growled wearily, "Ah, for Christ's sake," and pulled his hand away from hers, then tramped to his horse.

"*Viejo*, wait," she said desperately. "Suppose that you wait here with me till the Apaches have gone. Where will they go?"

He gave her an impatient glance. "You said it. They'll go on that trail those fellows left, they'll . . ." He broke off; understanding flickered in his face. "What you're saying, they will hit Heath and his men."

"Won't that be a better thing than for you to fight so many *ladrones* alone? Let them fight the Apaches first. Then, I think, there won't be so many *ladrones*."

"Then you 'n me follow the 'Paches, huh?" Penmark took off his hat and sleeved his sweaty face. " 'Paches might even get Heath. Leastways they'll make it easier for me to get him. Well, by God now. I think we'll just do it your way, sis."

"Ah, but I have forgotten. The young gringo, your friend. If he is with them—"

Penmark shook his head grimly. "Drum'll just have to take his chances. Like enough they done for him already and dumped his body in a canyon some'eres. Anyways there's more'n him to think about."

'Nita wondered if he meant her; she hoped so.

"You got any of that petticoat o' yours left?"

"*Sí.*"

"All right, you tear that up and blindfold the horses. Horse with his eyes covered won't let a whicker out of him. I don't want 'em making no signals to them Apaches' ponies."

Penmark tramped back to the outcrop and, sitting on his heels, watched the valley through the eyeslot he'd chosen. 'Nita wriggled out of her petticoat. It was a filthy remnant of the garment it had been, but enough of it remained for her to tear it into three strips with the aid of her claspknife. She tied the pieces around each horse's head.

Afterward she sat down in the warm shade of the outcrop, her back against it, and shut her eyes. A trembling ran through her; she felt as spent as one who had run a hard race. Or was it a battle she had won? She had made this tough gringo listen. Perhaps she had even brought him to an awareness of something other than his own mad purpose.

Yes. A battle won.

"Listen, girl. . . ."

She opened her eyes.

Penmark wasn't looking at her; his gaunt profile showed nothing. "Tell you what . . . if we come out of this alive." He cleared his throat harshly. "I got a place outside New Hope. You want to come and stay there, you're welcome."

It was hard to believe what he was saying, harder to steady her voice. "If you are sure—"

"Well, Jesus, yes. I wouldn't a offered otherwise."

He sounded very cranky. A half minute went by before she ventured to say more. "I am a good worker. I can keep a good house for you and I can cook—"

"Hell, I'll spoil my own grub 'fore I fry my guts with Mex cooking." After a stiff silence, he said as if in grudging half-apology, "I got a Mex cook at the ranch. Pepe. He cooks pretty fair American for my crew. Lay odds you never had no schooling."

"No, *Señor*." Whispering it.

"Well, there's a good enough school in New Hope. You'll want some clothes and fixings like a girl should have. Dolores, that's Pepe's wife, she'll lend you a hand with all that fooferaw. I don't know a shuck about it."

'Nita closed her eyes again. She didn't dare to say anything. He would be roughly sardonic, she was sure, to any word of thanks; therefore she would say nothing. At least not yet.

"They're coming," Penmark muttered.

Standing up, she peered around the edge of the outcrop. The Apaches were riding swiftly down the west slope of the valley, clattering across the sun-blasted shale to the edge of the flashing stream. Here they stopped; there was discussion. Then one of them, a big man, pointed up and down the creek. Promptly the band split apart, half of the men riding upstream, the rest following the creek toward the valley's south end.

"Damn it, pull your head back," Penmark growled. "Better yet, get over by the horses, hold 'em ready. Might have to light out of here fast. We will know damn shortly. . . ."

XV

JASON AND CHRISTY had been hiking since early dawn with no idea of whether they were on the right track. For all purposes, they were good and lost. They couldn't find their way to any habitation unless they stumbled on it by accident. The rain had wiped out Heath's and Miguel's tail. The sun had come up bold and brassy, and they held a roughly south-easterly direction by it; but there was little chance of their being on an exact line with the route that Heath and Miguel had taken.

Jason's side began to pain him, and he worried about the wound tearing open again. But he said nothing.

It was Christy who finally said it, "Look, this is no good. Let's stop and figure what we'll do."

Jason was glad to stop; his legs felt wobbly. He plunked himself on the ground and eased his meager pack off his shoulders. Christy sat down beside him and said, "I'd say we've pretty well had it, wouldn't you?"

"I'm all right."

"Bull. We're both of us just about used up. We can keep on going till we drop, and there's no sense to that. When they catch up, we'll be in no shape to stand 'em off."

Jason took a small drink from his canteen; he nodded morosely. "I guess that makes sense."

"Sure it does. Say we find us some good cover. Something we can put our backs to. Then we can just rest and wait. They'll find us, but we can make a fight of it anyway."

Jason took in the terrain they were crossing. It was as rugged a stretch as he had seen, broken up by redrock mesas and lesser formations of all kinds, and he thought it unlikely that Heath and Miguel had crossed here. Miguel, knowing the country, might choose a better route. They could be going farther off-trail all the time, getting themselves more and more lost. It made sense to stop, and there was always a chance, however slight, that they'd lost the Ermines and Cherokee.

If they hadn't, they might as well wait for them.

"Let's get up higher," he said. "We'll want to see 'em coming."

They worked on an upward incline toward a high tilt of sandstone cliff. Much of its rimrock had crumbled away, forming a rough breastwork of splintered blocks along its base. The cliff rose in a concave arch so that the rim projected far out and a deep pocket lay between the fallaway rock and the cliff base. Snugged in that pocket, they had plenty of shade, a solid wall at their backs, and a solid overhang above their heads. From behind the breastwork they had a clear view of the rough but rolling terrain to the west.

No matter how anyone came at them, he could be seen a good ways off; he'd have no cross under their guns. Yet he might manage it by dodging from rock to rock, for the open stretch was littered with outcrops and loose chunks. He could work in damned close if he were willing to take his chances, then settle down to wait them out.

Christy echoed Jason's dismal thought. "We got water

enough for two days," she observed. "Three at the most. That sun works around this side, it's going to fry us."

"At least we got water. They ain't."

"Don't bet on it, Jason. It'll only take one man to pin us here. The others'll be free to forage . . . and that damn breed, I believe, could turn up water in hell."

Jason checked over his Winchester and Christy's; he counted their supply of shells. They had fifty rounds of .45-.70 ammunition apiece. It was enough to last them for maybe as long as their water did, depending how hard they were pressed. After that it wouldn't matter.

There was one hope, and he voiced it.

"We maybe gone off-trail from where Heath and the Mexican will come back," he said. "But not too far, I reckon. If they happen along anywhere close to here, we got a chance. Say we fire off a shot every half-hour. If they ain't too far off, that'll fetch 'em here."

"I'd say we might be firing off a lot more than that," Christy said tonelessly. "Look."

Three figures on foot were coming across an undulating rise. They were still distant enough that the heat shimmer made their forms quivering and indistinct . . . but they were coming straight on the track. Christy sighted in her rifle, nestling her jaw along the stock.

Looking at her, Jason thought of how it had been with them a few hours ago. Love's demand flaring in the face of danger; she guiding and patient with his awkwardness, bringing them both to the jet and joining of fulfillment; life's hunger reaching for the white-hot flowering that was life's essence, counterpointing death; these were precious things to have close in memory when the hot muzzles of death were seconds away. She's beautiful, he thought, the most beautiful thing I ever knew. Maybe I'm in love with her. Maybe I ought to say it.

But he didn't. Together they'd touched a moment of being that was isolated from past and present and future, shining and inviolable. Some vague intuition he couldn't begin to define told him that to speak of it, even at such a time as this, would destroy it.

Now the three men were coming into the long boulder field that faced the cliff, moving with the plodding tread of exhausted men. It took a lot of hate to flail men on like this, the kind of hate Val Penmark had felt. There would be no quarter given in this fight. And now they were moving faster, their gait lifting to a slow trot as they sized up the situation ahead of them. The tracks they followed led toward a natural fortress: even if they couldn't see their quarry yet, nothing could be plainer.

Jason settled his sights along the Winchester. "Hold your fire till I let go," he said quietly.

The men were coming into range, but taking advantage of the rock cover now, slipping along from one boulder to the next. Jason could get only glimpses of them, but the approach would be harder for them to manage as they got closer. His hands began to sweat, and he dried them carefully on his shirt, one at a time. He shut down coldly on a grain of panic.

You got your own rifle, he thought; you know what it can do. Don't worry about that. Just worry about what happens if they get to you and her.

Trask Ermine was ahead of the others, picking out their way as he loped in a bent-over run from one rock to another. His gangling movements had a kind of deadly rhythm so that Jason began to gauge when each short run would come. As he got nearer, he would get careful, Jason thought. Why wait?

As Trask ducked from sight once more, Jason sighted quickly along the edge of that rock. When the outlaw lifted up to run again, Jason led him just a trifle, then pulled trigger. Trask went spinning under the slug's impact and dropped in a cluster of low rocks.

Both Pete and Cherokee came scrambling out of shelter to reach Trask's side. Christy's rifle opened up with Jason's, echoes of gun-roar clapping across the rock field. But in seconds the two were out of sight, unhit, down beside Trask on the ground.

"Anyhow," Christy exulted, "that fixes the big one. You fixed him, Buster!"

Jason shook his head. "Winged him. Not much of a hit either."

"How could you tell?"

"You know, that's all. You get the feel of a shot and you know."

"Oh Lord—Jason! Look at that! Look—"

A band of riders were streaming darkly across the brow of the heat-shimmered rise. They were coming at a furious run, so that in matter of seconds Jason could make them out as Apaches.

The Ermines and the half-breed had seen them too. They came piling out of the rocks now, Pete supporting his brother, stumbling up along the incline toward Jason's and Christy's position. Making a desperate scramble for safety that was heedless of the guns before them—of everything but the danger pouring up on their rear.

Christy looked wildly at Jason. "What do we do?"

"Let 'em come," he muttered. "It's their only chance. And maybe ours . . ."

From behind these rock breastworks, he was thinking, five guns could stand off the Apaches. And maybe they could come to terms with the Ermines after. But even as the thought came, he knew with a chill certainty it wasn't going to happen that way.

Savagely and recklessly quirting their ponies through the rocks, the hostiles were already overtaking the three men. The Ermines had fallen well behind Cherokee; they were still a hundred yards from the cliff. Forced to turn at bay now, they began shooting. The Apaches had opened fire too, but they couldn't pull much of an aim from running horses.

Jason opened up at them, and so did Christy. Caught by their fire or the Ermines', two of three hostiles in the lead went spilling from their ponies. Then Pete Ermine was hit; his great bulk folded to the ground.

The third Apache came thundering down on Trask Ermine, his lance set. Trask had pulled himself erect to meet the charge, but apparently his rifle had jammed. He flung it aside now, palming up his pistol. His left hand

fanned the hammer in a racketing roar of shots as the
lance left the Apache's hand.

The hostile was crumpling sideways as he raced past,
then fell headlong from his pony. And Trask Ermine was
toppling backward, the lance projecting from his chest.

Cherokee kept coming in a weaving low-bent run toward the breastwork of rocks. Jason tried to give him a
covering fire, levering and shooting as fast as he could.
Pulled up short by the fates of their comrades, the other
Apaches were already off their ponies and scrambling for
cover. They weren't slow in returning fire.

Cherokee was two hundred feet from the breastworks
when a bullet broke his ankle. He plunged down. Floundering to his hands and one knee, he started to crawl, his
useless leg dragging. He hadn't gotten three yards when a
second bullet slammed into the back of his head.

"Oh God," whispered Christy.

"Hold 'em," Jason said hoarsely. "Space your shots.
Got to reload. . . ."

Hurriedly he refilled his magazine, swearing as the
Winchester's hot barrel singed his hands. He tore the
bandanna from his neck and wrapped it around his left
hand. Christy levered and fired steadily.

"Hold your fire," he said. "They've quit—hold it!
Don't waste any shots!"

Silence settled across the baking scape. Jason's heart
thundered against his ribs. The shocking toll of these few
savage minutes left him shaken—but not shaking. He was
steady, Christ, he was steady in spite of everything—or
because of it.

The Apaches opened fire again in a desultory way.
Some of the slugs came close, whining off the rocks.
Twice bullets came so near that Jason felt the sting of
flying chips. Yet he judged that by keeping low and using
ammunition sparingly, they could hold this position in-
definitely against the dozen or so braves.

Some of the Apaches now undertook to work in a little,
rock to rock, but they'd gotten nearly as far as they might
without becoming the open targets Cherokee had been.

That last hundred yards was the crucial distance. Even if they made a concerted rush, two repeating rifles would cut them down like wheat stalks.

It was another stand-off. Only worse.

He wondered what had pulled this band onto them in such a fury, swarming to the attack like wolves dogging a bleeding deer. From all he'd heard of Apaches, that wasn't their fighting style. It didn't make much difference, except that the odds against survival had taken an abrupt hike, like moving from a frying pan to hell's hottest fire. The hostiles wouldn't give up, not after losing a couple men. Jason did not hope anymore, except to see that neither Christy nor he were taken alive.

Several of the Apaches appeared to be holding a caucus of some kind. Afterward a pair of them went fading back through the rocks. Having an uneasy inkling of what they might be about, Jason shifted part of his attention to a tall promontory off to his and Christy's right. If a couple of men were to circle and get up on that, they'd have a far better angle of fire. And once that happened, it could all be over very suddenly.

"What're they up to?" Christy asked.

"I reckon they mean to get up on that side place yonder. I'll tend to that. You watch in front of us."

Minutes later he caught a hint of movement at the top of the promontory. A man had crawled on his belly to its rim. Jason flattened down against the shielding rocks as the shot came. It made a screaming ricochet that was way to his left, but the brave wouldn't be long in correcting his aim.

Jason shot back as another rifle opened up beside the first, shrouding the rim with powder smoke.

One of the Apaches below began to sneak nearer under the covering fire. He was a giant of a man Jason had sized as the leader, and he made a quick weaving run just as Christy fired. His body jerked to the slug's impact just as he reached another rock, plunging down behind it.

The two on the rim laid down a blistering fire at the breastworks now. Jason and Christy hugged the rocks.

Then Jason felt a numbing slam in his leg. He twisted his head till he could see the spreading darkness on his pants. No pain yet.

The rifle fire slacked off briefly. Christy saw he was hit; she began to crawl to him, and Jason waved her furiously back.

"That one in front you nicked," he said. "We got to get him. Him first of all. You got that?"

She nodded.

He'd remembered one of Pa's hands, an old Mexican, telling him that if a war chief was killed, it turned an Indian's medicine bad and spoiled his belly for fighting. It was something to fix on anyhow. Right now, what else did they have?

Another burst of cover fire from above. As Jason had hoped, the big brave made another reckless move, maybe to pull his men into a charge. He sprang up to sprint for another rock. But he was lurching with his wound; it slowed him fatally.

Jason's bullet twisted him in mid-stride. And then Christy's shot drove him back into the rocks.

A yell went up from the Apaches.

One of the braves on the rim leaped to his feet, taking aim. Before Jason could swing to cover him, another rifle spoke. The shot's brittle echoes still pounded as the Apache pitched outward, his body crashing down the face of the promontory, tearing loose an avalanche of rubble before it came to a stop.

Hope surged in Jason the same moment that a hot flare of pain hit his leg. "Someone," he said between his teeth. "Someone . . ."

Someone. A sudden ally, No—more than one. Now two rifles were banging away from a hidden position. In a moment Jason placed it as being somewhere on the cliff above Christy and him, but well to their left, two guns sweeping the rock field with steady fire.

Their positions almost entirely exposed to that fire, the Apaches broke into swift retreat, pausing long enough to gather up the bodies of their dead. A pair of them ran a risky gamut to race out and snatch up their fallen leader.

Then they were gone, fading like brown ghosts among the rocks. So had the remaining Apache on the rim.

The clatter of their ponies' hoofs sounded briefly and then dwindled away in a maze of canyons to the south.

XVI

THEIR SAVIOURS WERE Heath and Miguel. Returning
from the ranch of Miguel's cousin with the horses they
had purchased, the two had been some distance away
when the shooting began. They'd lost no time in getting to
this place and seeking a vantage point from which they
could determine what was going on. That vantage was the
sandstone rise at whose base Jason and Christy were fort-
ed up. Coming up on its other side, Heath and Miguel
had been too late to help the Ermines and Cherokee,
whose bodies they could see among the rocks. But it had
been clear from the way the Apaches were directing their
fire beneath the overhang that they had an additional
quarry cornered.

Nonplussed as they'd been by the situation, it had
seemed a time to shoot first and ask questions later. After
driving the Apaches off, Heath and Miguel circled down
to the base of the rise, where they found Christy looking
to Jason's wounded leg. Trask Ermine was dead, but his

brother Pete was alive, shot in the side but not seriously. He'd played possum after the Apache bullet had brought him down. It hadn't even penetrated his ribs, having lodged in the hard fat that sheathed his thick body.

After sending Miguel to bring the horses up, Heath listened to Christy tell what had happened. While she talked, she tended Jason's leg. It was a clean wound; the bullet had passed through the outer flesh of his thigh, and both openings had bled freely. After washing it, she put on a tight bandage.

"Well, well," Heath said idly. "Seems you folks have been up the mountain and down again since we saw you last. But you fell into a piece of luck after all."

Jason sat with his back against a rock, his leg straight out before him. Watching Heath's face as he casually lighted a cheroot, he had an uneasy feeling that his own luck hadn't taken much of a turn for the better. Christy was on her knees beside him tying the bandage, and now she looked up at Heath.

" 'Luck,' " she said bitterly. "I don't know what you call lucky, Jack. Dallas is dead. He died helping me. Or doesn't that part of it ring any kind of bell with you?"

Heath flipped the match away. "Of course it does. Dallas was a friend and comrade. We'll treasure his memory and all that, eh? But this is no time to be holding postmortems, my dear. . . ."

Pete Ermine glowered at them all. He was sitting in the overhang shade a few yards away, his shirt off, holding it wadded over his side. "One o' you might lend me a hand," he growled, " 'less'n you aim to leave me bleed to death."

"Well now, Pete," Heath said easily, pleasantly, "can you think of a good reason we just shouldn't?"

"Look, I didn't mean your woman no harm. It was Trask was all hellfire to run these two down. We just went along, Cherokee 'n me. Wasn't nothing else we could do."

"Is that right?"

"Sure. Way I figured, Clayt ast for it. Why, he—"

"Shut your lying mouth, you fat bastard. I've a mind to finish the job on you myself."

"Jack—" Christy got to her feet, and her voice held a quiet plea. "Hasn't there been enough killing? Look, let me plug that hole in his side, and we'll send him on his way."

Heath eyed her with a cold irony. "You seem to relish playing the devil's advocate, Christine. Funny, but I've the feeling we've been through all this before. That damned forgiving nature of yours has a way of slipping us into jackpots."

"Oh?" she said acidly. "You mean like talking you into keeping Jason here alive and well? Listen, mister, if he hadn't been alive and well back at Arrowhead Tanks, *I* might not be now. Or doesn't that ring much of a bell either?"

"Steady down, angel."

"Look, what's to be served by more bloodshed? There's all the money if you want it—his and Trask's and Cherokee's—and I'd imagine they took Dallas's share off his body; you'll likely find it on one of 'em. Give Pete a horse, some grub and water, and let him go. He's lost two brothers, and nothing to show for it but empty pockets and a chunk of lead in him he'll have to ride a long way to find someone to dig out. That ought to satisfy even your twenty-carat sense of justice."

Heath showed a dry and unpleasant smile. "Well, our little rustic Portia. You do argue your cases admirably, my sweet."

Miguel came up, leading the string of a dozen horses. They were tied together in pairs to a long rope with three-inch rings secured to it at eight-foot intervals; the horses' six-foot halters were attached to the rings. The Mexican said wryly, "I don't think we need so many horses, huh?"

"Seems not," Heath said. "We'll take the lot of 'em along and get rid of 'em in Sonora. We'll be moving without delay . . . those damned Apaches might be back."

"Ha, I don' think so, *jefe*. I see this one big Apach' is kill, they take his body away. I see him once before. That was Cayetano himself. With him kill', they don' fight no more for long time, I'm think."

"Well, now that's fine. The way is open to the border and we're all but home."

"Ha. W'at about these?" Miguel motioned at Jason, then at Pete Ermine. "W'at we do with 'em?"

"Leave 'em a horse apiece and let 'em go their ways." Heath glanced at Christy, adding dryly, "That satisfy you, angel?"

"Drum's been shot in the leg, Jack. He's in no shape to ride."

"That's too bad. I'm keeping my word to let him go. I can't heal his leg for him. And we're not waiting."

"Nobody's asking you to."

"Now," Heath said gently, "just what the hell does that mean?"

"It means I'm not going to just leave him like this."

"I can make out all right," Jason said. "Ain't all that much of a hurt."

Heath ignored him, eyeing the girl steadily. "Been through a lot together, you and this lad, eh?"

"He saved my life. That ought to mean something to you."

"Why yes. Naturally it does. I'm just wondering how much it means to you."

Christy's jaw hardened. "You can think whatever you damn please. I told you how it is."

Heath flicked ash from his cheroot. "Did you?" he murmured. "Everything, eh? Now I wonder. It might not be significant, but I noticed when you mentioned the different shares of money, you neglected to take note of Clayt Ermine's share. An oversight?"

"No," Christy said quietly. "Jason has Clayt's share. He took it off his body."

"And you weren't going to mention it. But I'd find out, wouldn't I, when I searched the bodies and found a share missing?"

"Just what are you trying to say, Jack?"

"What I'm saying, my sweet," Heath said harshly, "is that you're with me or you're not with me. Which is it?"

"Jack, listen . . . don't make it hard for me. You and

Miguel can go on, I can meet you later, just say where. Can't we let it go at that?"

Not taking his eyes off her, Heath dropped his cheroot, grinding it under his heel with a controlled violence. "Why no. A few things need to be settled first."

Jason's rifle was resting on his good leg, and he had his hands flexed around it, tensed for anything. No matter what, he thought with dismal stubbornness, he wasn't giving up that money. Heath would have to kill him to get it.

"I'll tell you what we're going to do," Heath said.

"*Jefe—*"

Miguel spoke in a quick, sharply warning tone, and he was looking off toward the west rise of land. Two riders were coming into sight across it, moving briskly and coming straight on toward them. All of them waited, just watching now.

Jason felt the heavy slugging of his own pulse. Were these allies or enemies? Just be ready, he thought, for anything.

The high shape of one rider was familiar even before Jason recognized him. Val Penmark. *Alive*. And right beside him rode the Mexican girl they had left at Corazon.

"*Sangre de Cristo!*" Miguel whispered.

"Well," Heath said gently. "Well."

He lifted his Colt from its holster and gave the cylinder a turn. Then he held the gun at his side, waiting. Nobody else said anything, nor did anyone move.

A swarm of questions mingled with Jason's bewildered amazement, but the answers would have to wait. The next few minutes would write an answer of their own, deadly and final.

Penmark reined up, handling his horse left-handed as he quartered the animal slowly around to face them. Holding the Sharps rifle in his right hand, he stepped to the ground, not changing from a direct front to Jack Heath. He walked slowly forward and halted some yards away. His stubble-bearded face had a battered and drawn look, but it was as grimly indomitable as ever. His raw-rimmed eyes took in all of them, and then he looked only at Heath.

"Well, old pot. Came a long way for it, didn't you?"

"A blamed long way, sonny. I'll give you the move. Don't keep me waiting."

The Mexican girl slipped to the ground now. Still holding her own horse, she picked up the halter rein that Penmark had dropped and pulled both animals and the packhorse off to the side. Miguel too was shifting carefully sideways, hauling his string of horses out of line.

"I think we're in a stand-off right here, old fellow," Heath said idly. "Hadn't we better—"

Penmark was holding the Sharps across his body; he cocked it in one swift, savage motion. "Here and now. Make your move. Or I'll kill you where you stand."

Jason had his rifle up, and now, in plain warning, he let its muzzle follow Miguel's movements. The Mexican looked at him and shook his head. "I don' wan' in this. Not unless you say, *jefe*."

"No." A strained smile twitched the corners of Heath's mouth. "No, stay out of it—"

His hand cocked the pistol as he whipped it up, a steely blur of motion that ended in the flat crash of the shot.

Penmark was rocked backward, but then his legs braced hard; the heavy boom of his Sharps mingled with the blast of Heath's second shot. Heath was smashed clear off his feet, his body hurled backward. He landed loose as a flung and broken doll, and then he was motionless.

Penmark was folding down on his knees, the light dying from his eyes even before he slid over on his side. Just that suddenly, it was done with.

Christy dropped down beside Heath. "Jack. Oh God, Jack. . . ."

Miguel moved to Heath's other side and bent down by him. "*Santa Maria*," he said, shaking his head. Then he tramped over to Penmark, thrust a foot against his shoulder, and turned him on his back. Heath's two shots had taken him in the chest in a space a man could cover with his hand.

Miguel looked at Jason. "Me, I'm think that's all. She's finish now. You think so?"

Jason nodded. The tension loosened from his belly and left him with a scoured and hollow feeling.

The Mexican girl walked slowly to Penmark's body, looking down at it. Her face was empty, showing nothing at all; and just as slowly then, she turned away.

Jason stared up at the black speck of a buzzard riding the white-blue sky. Even as he watched, a second bird coasted into sight. They always know, he thought dully. It was incredible how quickly they always knew.

The shadows of a waning afternoon stretched like gaunt fingers across the rock field when the burying was done. The broad common grave was packed with rock and marked by a rough cairn of more rocks. Yet anyone not knowing that it marked the last resting place of five men might pass it by without a second look. It was like part of the raw and tumbled landscape of its setting.

Jason stood with the others by the grave, holding his weight off his wounded leg. Miguel had done him the favor of searing both openings of the wound with hot iron. It had been excruciating as hell, and now the leg felt pretty stiff. But the pain was bearable, and he didn't figure to let it keep him down. He thought of Penmark's iron-bottomed toughness, and somehow it seemed a tribute to the man's memory not to let a knife scratch or a fleshing by a bullet put him down—leastways not yet.

The girl 'Nita Cortinas knelt by the grave and prayed silently. After a minute she rose and, still looking downward, spoke quietly in her own language.

Migel glanced at Jason; he lifted one shoulder in a fractional shrug. "She say the old gringo, he would of take her to his home. She would of live' there and go to school, she say. You think this old man, he do that for her?"

Jason shook his head. "I don't know. Maybe he would of. I didn't know him all that well."

Maybe, he thought, just maybe Penmark had found a reason to live before he died. It seemed better to think he had.

"Well, it don' matter no more." Miguel shuffled a palm across his black-whiskered jaw. "Goddom, she's fonny how things go som'time, huh? The *jefe,* now he's gone it's like the whole game she's gone bad. I dunno, maybe it's jus' Miguel is getting old. But I'm think I give up the trail now. Eduardo my cousin, he's tell me that's what I'm should do."

Christy gave a slight, dull nod. "I know what you mean. I feel kind of that way. Who knows . . . it might even last."

"Huh. Look, you and the kid here, the girl and Pete too, maybe you like come to my cousin's with me. She's not far away and we got plent' horses, huh?" Miguel rasped out a dry chuckle. "You all be welcome there, you want to rest up awhile."

"I guess that's not a bad idea."

Jason nodded; Pete Ermine grunted a surly assent.

"*Bueno.* Then we get going while the light is good. Maybe we get there after dark som'time. You think you sit a horse all right, Drum?"

"I'll manage," said Jason. "Just one thing."

"Huh?"

"That money you people took. It's going back to New Hope. All of it."

"You wan' to fight me on that, huh?"

"No," Jason said flatly. "But I will." He glanced at the last of the Ermines, but Pete didn't even meet his eyes.

"Ahhh!" Miguel made a wry face; he swung his arm in a chopping gesture. "She ain' worth the fight. Som' money though, she's go to pay for these horse. I don' think you get that back. But you argue that with Eduardo. Me, I don' fight no more."

They all started toward the horses. Jason and Christy moved slowly behind the others, she giving him the support of her shoulder and arm. There was something he wanted to tell her, had to tell her, and it had to be soon. But how to say it?

He made a lame beginning, "There's something I want to say. I dunno just how."

Christy halted and looked at him quizzically. Then she stepped away, turning a little to face him. "Maybe you just better say it, Jason.

"Well, you know, I was thinking we done pretty good together, you and me."

"Were you?" His face got warm under her clear-eyed look. "Or should I say, did we?"

"Uh, well, you know what I mean. Fighting the Apaches and all."

"Uh-uh. Well, I wouldn't call that the Lord's way of pointing to anything better."

"I don't just mean that," he said stubbornly. "There's more, Christy—"

"Don't," she broke in gently. "Don't even try to say it, Jason. It would never work with us."

"There ain't all that much difference as I see it. What it comes down to is maybe you're five or six years older than me, but—"

"Five or six years?" A curious little smile touched her mouth. "Oh honey, I'm a hundred years older. Older than you'll ever be. Don't you know that?"

He turned his face down, a hard tightness in his throat. "I guess not. I don't know much. That's all right, you wouldn't want no green kid anyway."

"Jason. . . ."

Looking up now, he saw a tenderness in her face. "You're every bit as much man as I ever met. Sometime you'll meet a woman, your own kind of woman, and then you'll think back on today and of me, and you'll know I was right. But I'll remember you asked, honey. I'll always remember and be grateful."

He jerked a nod, swallowing with difficulty. "I won't never forget you. Only . . . where will you go now?"

"Don't you fret about me. I'll make out. I always have." She hesitated. "There's a thing you might do for someone, though—I mean that Cortinas girl. Your friend Penmark made her a promise. It would be kind of nice if you kept it for him. I don't know how your people would feel, but she's a good girl, a decent girl. That way, any-how, she'd be their kind. It would be a fine thing for you and them to do for her. If you could see your way to it."

"Maybe," he said. "I don't know. Maybe we could do that."

"Hey," Miguel called. "Hey you two, come along. We got a ways to ride before she's get dark. . . ."

As they rode away and the sound of the horses faded, the wind stirred up a furl of dust. It sifted across the rock cairn and over the tracks, effacing the other signs of man's short stay. Soon their last traces would be gone, taken into the desert's workings. As it had for ages, only the timeless face of the desert would endure.

THERE WAS A SEASON
T. V. OLSEN

Winner Of The Golden Spur Award

A sprawling and magnificent novel, full of the sweeping grandeur and unforgettable beauty of the unconquered American continent—a remarkable story of glorious victories and tragic defeats, of perilous adventures and bloody battles to win the land.

Lt. Jefferson Davis has visions of greatness, but between him and a brilliant future lies the brutal Black Hawk War. In an incredible journey across the frontier, the young officer faces off against enemies known and unknown…tracking a cunning war chief who is making a merciless grab for power…fighting vicious diseases that decimate his troops before Indian arrows can cut them down…and struggling against incredible odds to return to the valiant woman he left behind. Guts, sweat, and grit are all Davis and his soldiers have in their favor. If that isn't enough, they'll wind up little more than dead legends.

_3652-5 $4.99 US/$5.99 CAN

Dorchester Publishing Co., Inc.
65 Commerce Road
Stamford, CT 06902